A PRINCE OF AUTUMN

A Prince

of

Autumn

A.L. KNORR

Books by A.L. Knorr
Elemental Origins Series
Born of Water
Born of Fire
Born of Earth
Born of Æther
Born of Air
The Elementals

The Siren's Curse
Salt & Stone
Salt & the Sovereign
Salt & the Sisters

Earth Magic Rises
Bones of the Witch
Ashes of the Wise
Heart of the Fae

Arcturus Academy
Firecracker
Fire Trap
Fire Games
Legends of Fire

Source Fire

Rings of the Inconquo
Born of Metal
Metal Guardian
Metal Angel

Mermaid's Return
Returning
Falling
Surfacing

Elemental Novellas
Pyro, A Fire Novella
Heat, A Fire Novella

The Kacy Chronicles
Descendant
Ascendant
Combatant
Transcendent

The Scented Court
A Blossom at Midnight
A Memory of Nightshade
A Daughter of Winter
A Prince of Autumn

To learn more visit www.alknorrbooks.com.

v

ISBN 5x8 paperback: 978-1-989338-66-7

ISBN 5.5x8.5 hardback: 978-1-989338-67-4

ISBN 6x9 large print hardback: 978-1-989338-68-1

There is no footprint too small to leave an imprint on this world. -Unknown.

JESSAMINE

GRAVES HAD BEEN freshly dug that morning by an army of volunteers. Now the time had come to fill them.

Jess walked slowly ahead of the four male Calyx carrying the wrapped body of Heath on a wooden stretcher. The stretchers supporting the dead were so enveloped by flowering vines that the wooden bars couldn't be seen. Shoulder to shoulder, Jess and Rose followed the female Calyx two-by-two to where Heath and his butterfly familiar would be laid to rest. Leading the Calyx in the long procession of one hundred and thirty-eight dead were ranks of Solanan soldiers carrying their fallen to their final resting places. Behind the Calyx were the Fahyli, doing the same for their lost comrades. Solanan citizens lined the way leading to the burial ground, swathed head-to-foot in dark colors. Palace staff wore black livery with the lion's head crest embroidered on the back and the chest. Noblewomen wore bonnets or wide-brimmed hats, with high-necked, long-sleeved gowns in grays, blacks and dark purples. Noblemen wore stiff jackets, over-the-shoulder sashes embroidered with their house crests, tailored trousers and white gloves. Though they passed thousands on the long march to the interment garden, the silence of the crowd was thick and heavy. The occasional bird twittered from the shrubs, and a gentle breeze swayed the treetops, but other than the shush of leather soles on dirt and grass, there was no sound.

When the dead had been settled into their graves and those interring the bodies had stepped back, the voice of King Agir carried over the burial ground, enhanced by an ether-powered bell that Hob had erected on a podium for the king to speak into. Jess couldn't see the king from where she stood behind Peony and Lotus, but she could see Çifta's elbow where she stood on the king's left on the wooden dais.

"My people," King Agir boomed, "it is a sad day for all Solanans. We come together today to memorialize our friends, our family members, our comrades."

Jess let her mind wander as the king, Queen Esha, the crofter, and Bradburn each took their turn speaking into the bell. The soft sound of weeping reached her ears from somewhere down the line of Calyx. She stared down at the grave where Heath's wrapped body had been laid. The Fahyli handled their losses with a stoicism that was typical of soldiers, though the grief and pain was no less sharp, but the Calyx were not accustomed to losing their friends in war and didn't know how to handle Heath's death. His and his familiar's absence were a constant reminder that the unthinkable had happened; they'd lost one of their own and for no other reason than that they'd been in the wrong place at the wrong time. The Calyx closest to him were often seen weeping near the heather, or sitting quietly by themselves, drowning in sadness and oblivious to the goings on around them.

Since the conflict with the Silverfae, the palace had been full of quiet mourning. Everyone had lost someone they'd loved. Many had lost several someones, and the soldiers had been hit hardest of all, including the Fahyli, who had lost three from their ranks of twenty-seven. Two fauna fae had been killed, which meant their familiars had died instantly as well. One familiar, a mastiff named Allan, had been frozen to death. His fae, Gitana, was left bereft. She'd resigned and was already on her way home to Tryske, carrying Allan's remains to bury in the earth of the farm where they grew up. Jess hoped that Gitana would acquire another familiar, but fauna fae magic was not flora fae magic. Cases of mammal familiars being replaced were rare and recorded instances had only happened to fauna fae who were still in their teens. It was a trade-off, Jess supposed. Flora fae lost their magic eventually, while even older fauna fae, like Ian with his bear, Kashmir, would never lose their magic entirely.

When the only remaining royal left to speak was Queen Çifta, King Agir gave his permission for the graves to be filled. The Calyx took their cue, spreading out across the garden so that every grave being filled in by soldiers or Fahyli was soon lush with flowers and greenery.

Çifta's enhanced voice was soft and sweet and full of sadness. "I am not of your land, but when I needed rescue, Solanans saved me. When I needed sanctuary, Solana welcomed me with open arms. Your kingdom became my home, and Solanans have become my friends. It is with a broken heart that I address you today, as the new sovereign of the kingdom that so recently harmed you. I will always carry with me sadness and regret about the fallen who we memorialize this day. Those lost will not be forgotten, in this kingdom, or in the North.

In memory of each of the fallen, I will place one hundred and thirty-eight pillars of ice, each topped with a unique snowflake. These are symbolic of my promise that future conflict between our kingdoms will never result in fatalities, so long as I am queen. I believe that peaceful solutions are always possible, and this will be a core tenet of my rule. An exact replica of the pillar we Silverfae conjure today will be erected in the North, so that those in Silverfall will also never forget this promise. The snowflakes will be renewed every year by a representative of Silverfall, upon the anniversary of battle, so long as I reign, and hopefully, beyond."

Çifta and the Silverfae who had winter magic made their way across the burial ground, stopping at each grave to conjure the snowflake pillars. Jess caught a glimpse of Sasha as he helped with this part, Rialta strolling along at his heels. He came nearer, working his way toward Heath's grave. When he arrived, he caught Jess's eye. They exchanged a sober look as Sasha's white hands moved, and the sound of crackling filled the air as a sparkling white column of ice formed at Heath's head. The snowflake came together last and more slowly than the rest, needing deft magical skill on Sasha's part. Jess felt her nose tingle with unshed tears when she saw that Sasha had made a snowflake suggestive of a butterfly.

When the pillars were erected and each grave covered over with a glorious profusion of flowers, the Solanan conductor led the orchestra in a requiem that plucked at heartstrings. By the time the king brought the ceremony to a close, there wasn't a dry eye on any fae or any human. Slowly, the crowd broke into smaller groups. People hugged, talked quietly, or stood over the graves of lost loved ones, comforting each other in silence. Jess stood with Rose, Aster and Snap by Heath's pillar. She held

Beazle in her palm and looked up at the group of Fahyli clustered around their fallen graves. Beyond them, the soldiers—so many soldiers, and soldier's families—gathered around burial mounds. The Calyx had only lost one; Solanan families had lost so many more, and most of them were young men. She stroked Beazle's back with her thumb as a tear streaked down her cheek.

Remember what Ilishec said this morning, Beazle reminded her. *The Calyx are lucky.*

Jess wiped her face. Heath's loss didn't feel lucky, but it truly was a miracle that they'd only lost one. Not only that, it marked a milestone in Solana's history: Heath was the first member of the Calyx ever lost in battle.

PART ONE

CHAPTER ONE

LAEC

FROSTBITE TOOK A long time to heal—Laec was learning this firsthand—even with access to healing botanicals. He shifted in his seat, pulling his jacket away from his shoulder where skin and muscle still ached. In the two-and-a-half weeks that had passed since the Silverfae invasion, the injury had gone from reddish-white to the deep blue of a bruise, and the skin had a tight and shiny appearance. It ached all the time and was painful to touch. Even the cuts he'd sustained from blades hurt less than the injuries from cold exposure, and they were healing faster. He hoped never to find himself in an altercation with high-powered Silverfae ever again.

Laec sat in an alcove outside the Koi Library, a half-full glass of apricot wine at his elbow as he penned a letter to Queen Elphame. The library itself was quiet but the alcoves lining the hall just outside the entrance were busy; the alcoves had not been damaged in the battle and Laec guessed that was the reason for their resurgence in popularity: a place to escape the ongoing renovations.

Mistik waited, sitting on the thick golden rope keeping the curtain drawn to one side. She cocked her head, watching him through an eye encircled by a patch of bright green feathers.

"I'm going, I'm going," he muttered, feeling judged. "Writing these letters has gotten complicated. Not that I'd expect you to understand."

Picking up his quill, Laec bent to his letter. He'd written to Elphame the day after the battle, a rushed and bluntly worded message that was sorely lacking in detail. There'd been so much to do, and Laec was in such shock at the time, that he hardly knew what words to use. He'd promised to write again soon, but that promise was only being fulfilled now. He felt guilty that it had taken so long, but only with the passage of time did Laec now feel competent to compile the information Elphame was waiting for.

> Princess Isabey and her lover—who recently reappeared after having been feared dead—have sequestered themselves in her suite. Shade arrived injured and malnourished, but has recovered almost completely.

The majority in the palace seemed to credit it to the reunification with his soul mate, more than the nutritious food and warm bed Solana had provided. He'd discarded his crutch for a cane and the only remaining evidence that he'd suffered a broken leg was a slight limp. The secretive couple had helped put the palace back to rights, but since most of what they'd been capable of helping with was now completed, they'd been out of the public eye. While it was easy to guess what they might be spending their time doing, it was much less easy to guess at what Isabey was thinking about the state of her kingdom.

> Solana still waits to see if the princess will hold true to her threat to go south, or— now that Shade has returned to her—if he might fortify her with the courage to challenge her brother. If she does not soon make her intentions known, King Agir and Queen Esha will command an audience with her. They've been faithful to provide her with shelter, security, and—most importantly—secrecy. As far as anyone knows, Prince Faraçek still believes Isabey to be dead.

Laec glanced up at Mistik, tapping the end of his quill against his lips as the Rahamlarin prince came to mind. He bent to the page again.

> As for Faraçek himself, we await the announcement of the date of his self-coronation. As you know, our spies have discovered the existence of a son. Faraçek plans to hand the entirety of the ancient kingdom of Rahamlar over to his boy one day, as whole as it was before Solana's existence.
>
> Solana's losses in the battle with Silverfall were not insubstantial. We buried 138 citizens and soldiers.
> Lady Çifta...

Laec's hand stilled, his gaze returning to her name. He put a single stroke through Lady and wrote above it: Queen. He stared at the title combined with her name, feeling too paralyzed to continue.

The woman he loved above all else was now a queen. Like a wound that was continuously reopened, the realization was as painful now as it had been the morning after Sylifke's execution. Prior to that morning, he'd been too relieved and euphoric that Çifta had survived the ice to think about what her new position really meant: that she belonged to the northern kingdom more completely than she had ever belonged to Kazery.

Kazery could no longer dictate who Çifta married, but what might the hundreds of thousands of Silverfall citizens—eager to receive their benevolent queen in place of a long-endured malevolent one—have to say about who their queen chose for a mate?

The morning after Sylifke's death, Laec had woken with a start, alone in his room, as the new thoughts rushed in with bared teeth. The exhilarating recollection that Çifta was alive and safe in her quarters was suddenly crushed by the realization that he might yet lose her… again, and so quickly after having regained her. It was too painful to contemplate.

While he and Çifta did their parts in returning Solana to rights they'd had no time to themselves to discuss anything. Now that she was a queen, he no longer had the right to approach her for spontaneous conversation, not only because she was truly a royal but also because she was constantly surrounded by Silverfae guards. It was apparent they were eager to get her away to their own land. Laec had come to resent their presence with an intensity he'd not realized he was capable of.

Worse than all that, Çifta had not made any attempt to reach out to him, which left him feeling confused (an emotion he disliked) and insecure (an emotion he despised with every fiber of his being). What was she thinking? What did she want? Did she even know anymore? Had she been given advice by someone from Silverfall? Rayven Sabran, perhaps, before the former prosecutor took the majority of the Silverfae home to prepare Silverfall for the new queen's arrival? Did Çifta feel as paralyzed as he did?

Laec put none of this into his letter to Elphame, it was too personal, and even if it wasn't, he wouldn't dare include it without Çifta's permission. Çifta and Elphame were now contemporaries, as close to equals as any sovereign could be with Elphame. The sensation of being socially lower than his love interest was new for Laec, and he had no clue how to handle it, so he had told himself to wait. Çifta was sensitive and intelligent; he knew that she loved him because love poured from her whenever they were close. But she was entangled in a new and complicated situation, and the next step was up to her. He would just have to be patient.

Laec concluded the letter to Elphame by outlining the battle with more specifics, ending with the remarkable events that had taken place in the foyer.

He wrote the final lines with mixed feelings:

The problem with Rahamlar is for Isabey, Agir, and Esha to resolve. The darkness you foresaw is most likely now fulfilled. With your permission, may I journey home?

If Çifta was no longer in Solana, Laec did not wish to be there either, he'd be closer to her if he returned to Stavarjak. He cared for his friends here, but with the darkness presumably now over, surely his commission was complete. He stared at the word "home" for a long time. The shadows had grown short by the time he roused himself to sign the letter.

Laec sealed the scroll, slipped it inside the tiny cylinder and strapped it to Mistik's twig-thin ankle. Opening the window, he watched the fae-Terran hybrid flutter into the evening sky. The air was fresh and moist with a promise of spring. She gave a single caw as she swooped over the gardens, then disappeared from sight.

Where was home? He didn't know anymore. He would have said it was by Çifta's side, had she come out of the ice without any change of station, and they could have dealt with Kazery's wrath together. But she had come out a queen, with the memories of the fearsome queen before her. Not just Karinya's memories, but her magic as well. Çifta was not simply a merchant's daughter anymore but Laec was still just a courtier of the spring court, still Elphame's eyes and ears, and—he drained his goblet and set it down with a clack—still a drunkard.

CHAPTER TWO

ÇIFTA

Ç IFTA GLANCED IN the mirror as she moved to answer the knock on her door. She'd invited Sasha to a private audience with her shortly after the battle's end, but he'd only now found the time for it. Everyone had prioritized Solana's needs before their own in the past several weeks.

The face in her mirror had changed a little. Was it Karinya's memories that had brought a look of slyness into her eyes? Would those recollections remain, or would she one day lose them altogether? If that were to be, she owed Sasha information and she meant to deliver it before she could no longer bring the details to mind.

Sasha stood outside her door, waiting. Çifta was delighted to see that he'd brought Rialta with him. He looked handsome in dark leggings, tall boots, and the typical jacket of Silverfall, a deep blue, double-breasted velvet coat with a stand-up collar. Rialta stood at Sasha's side, her fur so white it almost glowed. She looked up at Çifta with a cocked head, one ear half-flopped over. The two of them looked achingly beautiful together.

Çifta swung the door wide to make room. "Come in, come in. Well come."

"Well found, Your Grace." Sasha bowed deeply.

"If you call me Your Grace, or Ma'am, or anything other than Çifta, I shall boot you back into the hallway."

Not for the first time did she wish that nothing had changed between herself and those with whom she'd had friendships before 'the execution.' But her relationships had changed irrevocably. It made her sad, nostalgic for the days when she'd just been a merchant's daughter.

"Thank you for making time for me," Sasha told her as they followed her into the room.

"Don't be silly. I invited you, I'm grateful that you've made time for me."

Çifta invited them to sit in her parlor, a ridiculously large room upholstered with yellow silk wallpaper and burgundy overstuffed furniture with gold trim and a pattern of glittery yellow bows. Overbearing portraits of nobility and elaborately-framed, hand-painted maps cluttered the walls. Çifta found the decorating some of the ghastliest she'd ever seen, but she'd die before she complained about it. She'd been given one of the most luxurious apartments in the palace. She found it strange that her citizens had wreaked such havoc on Solana, yet she—and her Silverfae, too, those who'd remained behind—were being treated like guests of honor. Agir and Esha were grateful to be rid of Sylifke's threat, and their gratefulness could land nowhere else but upon Çifta herself.

Rialta made a few circles around on the rug in front of the crackling fireplace before curling up. Her tail lay over her paws and her chin lay on the floor, but she watched them with an interested expression. Çifta had learned that most mammal familiars understood every word, so she'd be addressing the dire wolf just as much as Sasha.

"I've wanted us to be able to talk privately ever since I came out of the ice, Mr. Drazek." She sank into the seat across from him.

"Me too, Ma'am... La—Queen Çifta," he replied, then cleared his throat. "And call me Sasha."

She nodded. "Alright, Sasha. First of all, I thank you for your quick thinking in the courtyard. I'll be forever indebted to you, as we both know that you saved my life."

Sasha's cheeks pinked. "No thanks necessary. I'm just happy that you survived. I don't know what you endured inside the ice, but the ritual is always difficult. For a queen, I'm guessing it's the most difficult of all."

She crossed her legs at the ankles, the way she'd been taught to sit by her older sisters while in polite company. "Frankly, knowing what I know now, I think you've had a more difficult time over the past several years than I had inside the ice. Karinya showed me things, historic events and important conversations, involving both my family and yours. There are things you need to know."

He waited, his pale eyes shadowed but interested.

"Most importantly—and forgive me if I am being presumptuous—I want to tell you that your father, Elvio, while he did many things he shouldn't have done, loved you as deeply as a father can love a son."

His neck rolled in a slow swallow just above the edge of his collar. "I hope..." he hesitated for a moment, "that he loves me still."

Çifta sucked in a breath. "So, Elvio Drazek is still alive? That was something Karinya did not know, or if she did, she did not convey it to me."

Sasha's bright, intelligent gaze clouded with sadness. "He is, though I've not seen him since I was very young. My memories of him are fuzzy. I'm not even sure where he lives, only that he's an outcast, and not permitted to set foot in Silverfall City."

"Is that something you'd like to see changed?" Çifta asked.

Sasha stared at her, his eyes wide. His voice came out a little froggy. "You don't… do you not still consider him a traitor?"

"Oh, I do," she returned fervently. "Most definitely, though not for the same reasons Sylifke considered him a traitor. Elvio betrayed Queen Karinya when he helped Sylifke use blood magic to usurp her throne. What he did was unforgivable, Sasha. I do not offer clemency for his sake, but for yours. Like I said, I owe you my life. If you wish me to repay this debt by clearing your father's name, then that's what I will do."

Sasha's gaze left her for the first time since they'd begun to talk. He looked down at the floor, struggling with private thoughts before looking at her again.

"If you're willing, my lady, I would like to know all that you know. I've pieced together a little over the years, but much of it was from palace gossip and can't be trusted. You're in a position to offer me the truth. Will you tell me everything?"

Çifta nodded. It was what she'd been hoping for. "It began before you were born, and I have wondered whether—had Elvio had you when Sylifke approached him for a partner-ship—he would have done what he did. I suppose it doesn't matter. He set off a chain of events that caused great suffering in the North."

Çifta left nothing out; not the crime that he committed

with Sylifke, not the hateful relationship that he'd built with her afterward, nor the torture of Salme, the attempted murder of herself as a child, and the successful—if accidental—murder of Evelin, her mother. She openly shared that Elvio seemed not to want to murder baby Çifta, but felt, if he would not, he risked losing his son, the only being he appeared to love more deeply than himself. She could tell Sasha nothing about his mother that he didn't already know, but she could at least give him some clarity about his past. As she talked, Sasha and Rialta listened quietly, letting her get it all out. He asked a few questions and she did her best to give him thorough answers. By the time she'd told them everything, Çifta's stomach was growling and the fire had burned low behind the grate.

Çifta got up to add logs, letting Sasha absorb everything she had told him. He was overcome, that was obvious when he didn't leap to his feet the moment she stood up. Çifta smiled to herself, appreciating that Sasha allowed her do something so domestic as stoke the fire. As she came close to the wolf, Rialta lifted the hem of her skirt with her nose and licked her ankle. Çifta crouched to stroke the wolf's enormous head before returning to the couch.

"If I may," Sasha asked after a long moment of silence, "I would appreciate an opportunity to see my father face-to-face, and my mother too, but separately, before I tell you what I think. Would that be acceptable?"

"More than acceptable, Sasha," Çifta told him with relief. "I wasn't expecting you to have an answer today. I wanted to give you your say, in case you had strong feelings about him one way or the other. Take as long as you need."

"You've given me a lot to think about." He rose to his feet and Rialta padded to his side as they made their way to the door.

Sasha faced her and bowed, but when he straightened, Çifta reached up and pulled Sasha in for a hug. It took him a second to respond—after all she was now his queen, and queens did not hug their subjects—but a moment later he melted against her, holding her with all the warmth of a friend. When they parted, his eyes were glassy.

"I've heard a rumor that you've been offered a place among the Fahyli," Çifta said. "Is it true?"

"It's true."

"Selfishly, I hope you come home, because I would like very much the opportunity to give you the life at Silverfall that you deserve. But whatever you decide, I know it'll be what's best for you. You'll always have a friend in me."

"Thank you, Queen Çifta." He smiled at her, his face as full of emotion as she'd ever seen it. "That means more to me than I can say."

They left, and Çifta closed the door. She leaned her forehead against the wood as a wave of loneliness washed over her.

Who would her friends be when she arrived in Silverfall? If Sasha did not come, and Laec... She closed her eyes against thoughts of Laec and the uncertainty that cramped her stomach whenever she thought of him.

Since she'd arrived back in Silverfall, Rayven Sabran sent letters to Çifta three times a week, updating her with news of Silverfall since the death of Sylifke. The urgency of her tone had increased letter by letter. Çifta was dismayed that Rayven had taken it upon herself to make lists of eligible Silverfall nobility, notes about their character, their historical allegiances, their occupations and any advice pertaining to future relations Çifta might want to build with them, including warnings about who she might want to avoid. Miss Sabran layered into her communications just how feverish the citizens were to welcome her home, and how the weather had improved since Sylifke's death—though it was still unsettled, and would remain so until Çifta was crowned. She never sent a letter without some hint about wanting to introduce Çifta to potential matches, every one of them a pureblood Silverfae with winter magic.

The expectations were too obvious to be missed; Çifta was presumed to select an appropriate partner, someone who would not become king, but who would be given a role referred to as the queen's consort, whatever that meant. It was not a position as elevated as a king's, of course, but it was a highly respected station—beyond that Rayven did not embellish. There were many aristocrats who would be honored to take the role, it remained only for Queen Çifta to meet them and make her choice.

These dissertations always left Çifta feeling queasy and heartsick. If she'd thought herself unfortunate when she was at the mercy of her father's choice of husband for her, her situation had only degraded. Now it wasn't simply her father who expected her to put duty above all else, it was an entire nation.

Çifta took a deep breath and straightened, pushing away from the door. Definitely not the posture of a queen, she thought, rubbing the indentations in the skin of her forehead. She glanced at the clock, realizing she had less than thirty minutes before her meeting with some of the palace staff about her sisters' and father's arrival tomorrow. She would host a dinner in her suite to reunite her family, and would be required to repeat much of what she'd told Sasha; her sisters would needle her for every last detail. It would help that Kazery could contribute a little, but the bulk of the job would fall on Çifta and she felt tired just thinking about it. She wished she could run down the hall to Laec's room and throw herself into his arms, cry for a while, then complain about how being a queen was so much harder than being a merchant's daughter.

Instead, she'd wash her face, change for dinner, then direct the small army of servants who would shortly arrive as to how she wanted her family's visit to go. She'd appear calm and in control, and rein in her emotions as she explained everything to her inquisitive sisters. She hadn't seen Una and Fetre in what felt like a lifetime. She should feel more excited, but instead Çifta felt deeply sad. How could she be proud of the heights she'd reached if she had to stand upon this clifftop without Laec beside her? Worse, how was she going to tell him that he had to forget her without pulverizing both their hearts into dust?

CHAPTER THREE

JESSAMINE

BEAZLE SAT IN Jessamine's gloved palm as they were jostled side to side in the carriage, heading back to Solana City. They were traveling from the nearby town of Aldwater where a small group of Calyx had given a requiem performance for families who had lost soldiers in the Silver-fae battle.

Beazle yawned wide and long, baring pin-sharp teeth. *Grief is tiring.*

Sandwiched between Rose and Snap, Jessamine fought to keep her head from drooping. She couldn't have agreed more. Grief was exhausting.

Snap nudged her shoulder, rousing Jessamine. "There's Sasha."

She looked out the carriage window in time to see a small group of riders pass them on the road, among them her pale, white-haired sweetheart. Rialta loped in the distance, with Tully on her heels. The two were hardly seen without each other these days, though today, they kept the frolicking antics to a minimum. The day was serious.

"Is he going to join the Fahyli?" Rose lay her head on Aster's shoulder and hid a yawn with a gloved hand. "He was offered a place, right? Or did I imagine that?"

"He hasn't answered the crofter yet." Jess's gaze remained glued to Sasha's back until he was lost from view. She kept her trepidation about this unanswered invitation under a veneer of confident calm. Yes, Sasha and Rialta had been invited to join the Fahyli—less than a full week after the battle with the Silverfae, yet Sasha had still not brought it up. Jess hadn't pried, but not because she didn't want to. She was trying to respect his privacy.

The two of them, along with every other able-bodied person in the city, had been kept busy from sunup until sundown working to restore Solana to rights. The gardens were a disaster, but gardens were easier to sort out than the foundations, streets, and walls. King Agir and Queen Esha had brought in what seemed like an army of craftsman to fix the broken stained glass, damaged sculptures and paintings, and the decorative railings and other architectural features of the continent's most beautiful palace. Time could not be wasted in returning Solana to its former beauty, for spring was well and truly here. Tourists would soon swell the population, nobility would fill the ballrooms, and shoppers would fill the markets, stores and streets, especially the fragrance shop on the high street.

Some of the inventory sitting in storage near the perfumery had been destroyed and had to be replaced. So, along with helping with repairs and recovering the gardens, the Calyx were required to fit in sweat sessions.

All the Calyx were tired, and what Jess really craved was

time alone with Sasha. To be quiet, or not be quiet, she didn't care, she just wanted more than a hurried embrace. Nothing had felt normal since the battle, and everyone wondered how long it would be until it was.

"So no answer from Sasha." Aster sighed. "Any news from the property offices? Surely there must be some progress from that corner?"

Jess shook her head, too tired to talk about it.

There'd been six apartments in the tower, all owned by different people. But when she'd gone to the land registry, she'd been told that the information was protected by privacy laws. One bright spot had appeared in the form of a young lawyer named Seth Harkin. Mr. Harkin had worked under Sasha's defense lawyer, Mr. Bedar, and when he understood who Jessamine was, he took over her request. Jessamine had hugged the man, who had laughed and told her that he would send a messenger for her the moment he had a result. That was eight days ago, and Jess was still waiting.

The carriage pulled up in front of the palace, and the flora fae got out, groaning. Jess looked around to see if Sasha was in sight, and instead spied a familiar head of red hair. Laec stood at the top of the stairs, talking quietly with Shade. Jess lifted Beazle to her shoulder as she climbed the steps. Laec and Shade saw her coming and greeted her as Beazle crawled under the hair at the nape of her neck.

"You're looking better," Jess told Shade, who'd discarded his cane and moved about under his own steam. He'd thickened since he'd arrived, losing some of the haunted look.

"Thank you, Jess. I'm sorry I don't have time to stay and chat. I'm expected upstairs." Shade gave them a polite nod and disappeared inside.

By "expected upstairs" he meant that Isabey needed him. The princess was Shade's reason for breathing, a fact that had been reinforced by every action the Rahamlarin soldier took.

"Commiserating, were you?" Jess asked Laec with a sly look. When Laec looked confused, she added: "You know... over the things you have in common?"

"What do you mean?" Laec looked bewildered.

Jess sighed. It seemed like Laec had lost the streak of irreverence that had been such a part of his brand. "You're both in love with royals. I don't usually have to explain jokes to you, poor as they are."

His lips tightened. "If only that were something to crack jokes about."

Jess resisted the urge to testily retort that she was just making conversation, as she could see that something was really bothering Laec. She put a hand on his forearm.

"You aren't yourself these days."

"Çifta," he said, simply.

Of course, Çifta. The girl they'd rescued what seemed like a lifetime ago from the clutches of Prince Faraçek had become the mighty sovereign of the North. She was always surrounded by Silverfae guards. Jess had heard she was planning to leave soon, all the aid she could give had been exhausted and her kingdom was waiting. So where did that leave Laec? Would Jess have to say goodbye to her Stavarjakian friend soon? The thought sent a fresh wave of loss over her.

She kept her voice low as people moved by them and into the palace. "Should I assume you'll be going with her?"

To her surprise, Laec's face cramped with pain. He looked away. "I don't know anything, Jess. She won't... hasn't talked to me. I don't know why. I don't know if I've done something wrong, or if she's trying—in a cowardly way, I might add—to send a message that we can't be together. I'm just waiting. I feel like my whole life these past eight months has been spent waiting. Waiting for an axe to fall over this kingdom, waiting to learn if I've completed my commission, waiting for Çifta to thaw, waiting to see if the woman I love loves me back, waiting for replies from Elphame. I know I'm just a courtier, a nobody, but—"

"You're not nobody, Laec. Far from it."

How could she convey what she saw when she looked at her Stavarjakian friend? She struggled for words. "You're... the trusted emissary of the most feared and respected monarch of our world. You're brave, impetuous, funny, one hell of a swordsman... how can you think you're—"

"Laec Fairijak?!"

A bright female voice interrupted their exchange. Jess turned to see a voluptuous strawberry-blond climbing the steps, her face flushed, her hands lifting her skirts. Pretty pink shoes flashed from beneath her hem as she rushed up to them. Her ample bosom was on display, highlighted by a deep sweetheart neckline lined with a pink ruffle. Her dress was of high quality, but a white cap—like those the farmer's wives back in Dagevli wore—sat on top of her curls. Jess could only stare as the woman bounced up the steps.

"As I live and breathe. I wondered when I might see you again." She stopped at the top of the stairs, one hand on her cleavage as she caught her breath. Her brown eyes raked Laec appreciatively from head to foot and back again.

Jess peered at Laec, waiting for an introduction. He looked dumbstruck, then recognition cleared his gaze.

"Lady Hashe, what a pleasant surprise." He tilted his chin.

"Jessamine, this is Çifta's sister. She and her husband housed me in a storm. Lady Hashe, this is Jessamine Fontana, a member of the Calyx and a friend of mine."

"Pleased to meet you, Lady Hashe." Jessamine gave a shallow curtsy, as was the custom for Calyx when greeting a new courtier. This woman looked part farmer's wife, part aristocrat, so Jessamine played it safe.

She smells like a newborn lamb, Beazle thought. *I like her.*

It took effort for Jess to keep her expression neutral.

Lady Hashe whipped a white kerchief out and dabbed her forehead. "I'm far from a lady, much to my husband's chagrin. Lovely to meet you, Jessamine. Just call me Gemma, please." She looked at Laec. "Thrilling times, aren't these? What secrets my father has kept from us!" Gemma threw back her head and laughed, then dabbed the kerchief to her lips again. "I haven't had this much excitement since I was a little girl, hiding in the walls of our manor and spying on all the boys. Well, I would love to stay and gossip, but—"

Gemma turned and lifted her kerchief, waving it wildly around. "Yoohoo!" She drew attention to herself. "Over here, ladies!"

Laec and Jess exchanged an amused look.

Turning back to them, Gemma winked conspiratorially. "They don't know what they're in for, poor dears."

Two more strawberry-blond ladies, one even more voluptuous than Gemma and the other willowy, more like Çifta, if not quite so tall, came up the stairs. Their eyes were lit up like children at a fair.

Gemma made introductions and Jessamine learned that Çifta, though she looked nothing like these larger-than-life human women, had a total of three sisters: Gemma, Una and

Fetre. Somehow the three sisters had the energy and impact of twice as many women. Una and Fetre—not quite so forward as Gemma—looked at Laec with such frank curiosity that Jessamine wondered what had been told to them about the Stavarjakian fae and their sister.

Laec looked like he wanted to run and hide, but to his credit, greeted the sisters politely, taking each hand in turn.

"We're here for a family meeting." Gemma winked at them. "I have a feeling the Unya family has never had a get-together like this one. There's a lot of explaining to be done, before Çifta is spirited away by those handsome ghosts of hers to a kingdom far away."

Una and Fetre seemed just as tickled by the situation as Gemma was, all of them giggled.

Gemma's words seemed to impact Laec like an earthquake, though Jess could see that she was oblivious to the effect her news had had on him.

"And when might that be?" Jess asked casually. "The spiriting away by handsome ghosts, I mean."

"In mere days, I'm told." Fetre's voice was soft and soothing next to her sister's loud, brassy one.

Laec's cheeks had lost their color.

All at once the sisters acquired a communal understanding that this was news to him. Unwelcome, jarring news.

Una frowned. "Oh dear, we've spilled the lentils."

Gemma put a hand on his arm. "Has she not said anything to you?"

Laec recovered and offered them a smile that did not reach his eyes. "It's nothing, Lady Hashe, but I will have to beg your pardon. I've remembered that I'm expected somewhere. Forgive me."

With a jerk of a bow, Laec took the stairs down to the courtyard and disappeared in the direction of the West Keep.

Una looked at Jessamine curiously. "What did we miss, my dear?"

Gemma put a hand to the side of her mouth, as if to shelter her words from eavesdroppers. "Something tells me our little sister hasn't been completely forthright with her lover."

Fetre's eyes popped. "He is her lover?"

Una clapped a hand over her mouth, then transferred it quickly to Gemma's mouth. "Hush you. A rumor like that is a spark in dry brush. Before you know it, it'll have burned its way to the borders of a certain northern kingdom."

Jess was too weary for this, and now she felt cornered. "I'm sure Lady—er, Queen Çifta will be very happy to fill you in. She's in the Freesia apartments, on the third floor."

The sisters thanked her and bustled inside. Jess followed at a distance, hoping Çifta was ready for the strawberry-blond storm that was about to hit her.

CHAPTER FOUR

LAEC

TONIGHT WAS THE first night Laec had not walked Çifta to her suite since she became queen, the Unya family reunion taking precedence. Though it wasn't as if they'd had much privacy during those walks.

It had started the very first night: Çifta had been recognized as the new queen of Silverfall for less than twelve hours when the Silverfae guards mobilized around her like a pack of sheepdogs vying for the privilege of guarding a single very precious ewe. The initial chaos of eager protectiveness was pruned into something more organized by Rayven Sabran. Laec wished she'd taken every last one of them with her when she'd left, but eight strong males and four impressive females were left to watch over their freshly minted royal.

Çifta had left the choice of who remained to Rayven, since Çifta did not know her people. Much to Laec's annoyance, those who stayed were fit, young, handsome and extremely protective of their new queen. It might only be jealousy, but he wondered if they might be jockeying for a romance with her.

At helping out around the palace and the city, Çifta was a natural, but smoothing foreign relations was outside of her experience. Çifta had asked Laec for advice while they worked side by side. Çifta had it easy, Laec believed, and told her so— Agir and Esha were the most rational and affable monarchs he'd ever worked with. Now, the best thing she could do to strengthen the kingdoms' bond would be show solidarity: help put things to right, bury the dead, minimize the number of Silverfae in the city—they were still seen as a threat by many—but ensure those who stayed did a lot of heavy lifting. They were the ones who'd made the mess, after all.

Every night, Laec walked Çifta to the door of her suite, both of them exhausted from the day's labors. Every night, Silverfae guards trailed behind, keeping back several paces but near enough to make Laec's eye twitch, although Çifta seemed too tired to notice that they were becoming increasingly overbearing.

Worse than the guards' presence was the way they altered her behavior. Laec and Çifta had always been able to converse with ease: sharing their thoughts, trading advice, laughing together. But the new queen now censored herself. At first Laec was sure it was because she believed the guards were eavesdropping, but now he wasn't so sure that it wasn't because of him. Had Çifta's feelings changed? She had cooled, grown distant.

When he managed to catch her in private and asked why, she denied that it was the case, apologized, and blamed exhaustion and uncertainty—valid complaints. She told him that she hadn't slept well since Sylifke had been killed. She was worried about wearing the mantle of a queen. She explained that her sisters were coming, that she would have to host them and explain everything. On top of all that, she felt that Kazery was upset, though he wasn't showing it. He told her he was proud of her, said he couldn't ask for anything better than for a daughter to reach the station of queen. But deep down Çifta suspected that he was grieving the loss of an important piece on his chessboard.

Laec sympathized but doubted Kazery was angry and so tried to reassure her on that at the very least. Yes, Kazery was ambitious, and yes, he'd made mistakes when it came to Çifta, but he loved his daughter deeply. Laec hadn't seen a drop of evidence suggesting that the merchant was anything other than thrilled. His daughter had been returned to him alive and she would shortly command an entire kingdom—one with many northern ports.

But as always, before Laec had a chance to mine Çifta for more of her true fears and feelings, the guards would move into listening range. Their icy, judgmental eyes and overlarge fae ears would clam her up. Laec was more tired of this than he was of doing manual labor.

Last night Laec had whispered: "Can we speak privately?"

He'd spoken with his back to the guards but he could still feel them—hovering, listening, judging.

She gave an expression he hadn't been able to read as they stopped outside her door. "I'm not ready."

"For what?"

"I just need a little more time. Just a little more. I'm sorry."

Laec gave away nothing of how deeply this cut him. She wasn't ready to speak with him privately? She needed more time? It struck him like a lash across the lower back: she was going to reject him. She had to sit on a throne and rule a nation… be its queen. He was just a courtier from Stavarjak.

He was beneath her, and not just a little. Now all that remained was to clue him in, but she was lovely and kind and terrified of hurting his feelings, of breaking his heart. A stroke of anger followed the sting.

"Coward," he said under his breath, meaning himself as much as her.

"Sorry?" Çifta's black brows crashed together. "What was that?"

He clenched his teeth, hating how much power she had to hurt him. Worst of all, hadn't he known this might happen? Hadn't this been why he'd fallen into a drunken stupor after Georjie? Self-loathing filled his mouth with an acrid taste. He'd left his home to get away from these kinds of feelings. Çifta was a coward for having made him wait this long to tell him the truth—and she still had yet to do it—but he was even more a coward for letting this happen. He'd knowingly put himself in a position to be rejected, again, have his heart torn out, again, by a lovely individual who simply had better things than Laec on her horizons, again.

"Let me make it easy for you, Çifta."

Confusion muddled her gaze as he took one of her hands between his palms.

"I can't pretend that I understand what you're going through," he said. "The adjustment to your new position, the discovery of your true heritage, whatever happened to you inside the ice. I haven't a clue. I would like to know, but you haven't seen fit to tell me. Your life has gotten a lot more complicated; finding room for me in that life must feel like a burden for you."

Çifta's eyes widened, she shook her head. "That's not it at all, Laec. What you did for me, trying to protect me, I'll never forget it. It's just... well, you're partially right. I'm *not* sure how to fit you into my life, but… I want to… but…" She looked away, swallowing audibly.

Two buts in a single sentence. He released her hand and kissed her cheek, ignoring the rustle of clothing as her guards fidgeted. Their dislike radiated like heat from a stone oven.

"It's fine, Çifta. You don't owe me anything. Not a thing." He stepped back. "I'm happy for you."

She took a short, sharp breath, but said nothing.

Here I go again. He turned away, heading down the hall, albeit slowly, in case she called him back. His ears burned, begging to hear her cry out that she loved him, wanted him. But silence followed him. He'd passed through her guards and they watched him go with looks of cruel pity. He had felt their disdain all the way down the corridor to the door of his own room.

Meeting Çifta's sisters today just confirmed that he had been right. After a supper he didn't taste, he went into his room and closed the door, leaning his back against it. He let his head tilt back until he was looking up at the aubergine-colored ceiling as a tear traced its way to his ear. He brushed it away in a sharp, annoyed motion. His chest felt hollow, but he knew it was only the beginning. Soon that hollow place would fill with pain, an ache that would take a very long time to go away. Maybe this time it wouldn't go away at all. When it had truly sunk in, he would descend into a cycle of depression and self-hatred that would go on and on. This heartbreak would make his former loss seem like a superficial scrape, something that should have been below his notice.

It would have hurt less if Çifta had died inside the ice, he realized with horror, and an ache so deep that it seemed he was made of it. He would have had to let her go, but he'd have done it believing that she loved him, believing that she'd been lost not out of choice but out of chance.

Now, he knew that she knew he wasn't worthy of her, and she could no longer make excuses for him. She'd previously been willing to overlook that she was far too good for him because she was just a merchant's daughter. A rich and successful one, sure, but still, the daughter of a trader, and one who'd once resorted to piracy at that. But now, she couldn't afford to overlook anything. She would have to marry for station, like all royals. She would have to make a strategic match, one that would benefit her people. Laec wouldn't cut it. He would never have enough to offer. Not ever.

He went through the motions of getting ready for bed, not really aware of what he was doing. How ironic that she had been trying to break free from her father's control so that she could choose her own husband, someone who made her happy. She had broken free of her father's control so spectacularly that she was like a comet streaking across the sky in her might and beauty. She was a celestial body now, a star in the heavens... and more restricted than she'd ever been. No wonder she was confused. No wonder she needed time. No wonder.

Laec crawled into bed and lay curled up on his side, feeling tired and wounded. He lay there with his eyes open, staring at nothing, seeing nothing, wondering if Elphame might let him come home.

He'd left a mess, and he would return a mess. How disappointed his queen would be in him. How disappointed he was in himself.

CHAPTER FIVE

ÇIFTA

I T WAS A sumptuous meal, and one native to Kirkik, the Unya's home city. Crispy potato wedges double-cooked and dusted with a salty blend of herbs and spices. Braised whitefish that melted on the tongue. Baked cherry tomatoes and caramelized sweet red onion drizzled with balsamic vinegar, and a salad made with Çifta's favorite peppery greens. Throughout their leisurely meal, including a dessert of pastry soaked in honey and cream then dusted with crushed nuts, Çifta told her sisters and her father about her experience in the ice.

Kazery added the occasional fact as he remembered it, and Çifta appreciated his loving comments about her mother, Evelin—because to Çifta, Evelin was a true hero. Yes, she'd run away from the ice ritual and her potential destiny, but she'd been young and frightened. In the end she'd stepped in front of her baby when it really counted, preserving Çifta's life so she could accomplish what Evelin had been unable to fulfill.

It brought tears to

Çifta's sister's eyes, and the three of them hardly said a word until the family moved into the parlor, where a fire was roaring and hot sweet tea was waiting in an urn. Before Çifta joined her family in the sitting room she made sure to thank the Solanan servants cleaning away the remains of the meal. It was not the kind of feast the Solanan kitchens typically made, and the meal had been selected with a consideration that surprised Çifta. Rather than a queen's fare, they delivered a meal from her childhood: simple, delicious and nostalgic. It put her sisters at ease—Fetre was especially intolerant of foreign dishes—so that they could concentrate on Çifta's story without being distracted by strange smells and tastes. Someone in the kitchen was astute and Çifta made a note to go down and thank the chef herself.

The women and Kazery settled in the sitting room, each with a steaming glass of tea.

"So what are your plans as queen?" Una asked as she tucked one leg under her, a posture she'd taken since she was a girl.

"She doesn't have a plan yet." Fetre dragged a yellow pouf close enough to the fire to singe eyelashes, then plopped down on top of it. She'd always loved being excessively warm. When they were girls, Fetre refused to sleep alone in the winter, and would crawl into Çifta's bed, putting her freezing feet on Çifta's calves and making her shriek.

"Her Majesty can answer for herself," chided Gemma.

"Please don't call me that." Çifta sank onto the small sofa beside her father, who threw an arm over the back of the couch, making her feel small and protected, the way he'd done when she was little. "And no, I don't have a plan, exactly, but Karinya did, so that gives me somewhere to start."

Una's forehead wrinkled like a puppy's. "There was time

for Karinya to tell you of her plans for Silverfall in the middle of all that?"

"It wasn't like that." Çifta stared into the fire. She took a sip of her sage tea, enjoying the way it soothed her overstuffed stomach. "For most of my time in the ice, I didn't realize that my host was Karinya. I thought I was dealing with some nebulous entity, but after it was all over, I discovered that she left some of her memories with me. I wasn't there when she executed Sylifke, I didn't experience it while it was happening, but I have the memory of it, and lots of other things that happened, as well as her character. I understand what Silverfall was like when she ruled it, how the kingdom functioned, and how she functioned as its queen. That's what I have to do, put it back the way it was."

"But you're not Karinya." Gemma got up and poured herself a fresh cup from the urn. "Surely you'll have your own ideas about the kind of queen you want to be?"

Çifta rubbed her right temple where a headache lurked. It had been a long day, and she felt drained. "Believe it or not, I never dreamed of becoming a ruler of any kind—even though my betrothal was to a prince, he wasn't supposed to inherit the crown. So, no. I don't have ideas."

For the next hour, the family discussed the various ways that kings and queens governed throughout Ivryndi. Çifta's sisters had no firsthand knowledge of the day-to-day realities of life in other kingdoms, but Kazery's experience had given him plenty of exposure. He was happy to go on about social systems, tax structures, treaties and other kinds of agreements that would boost international trade or security, penal codes and military structures. It was almost enough to put Çifta to sleep. She had to stifle a yawn three times before Una, Fetre and

Kazery took a hint and kissed her goodnight before retreating to their own quarters.

Gemma took the opportunity to move in on her like a predatory fish. Çifta watched her sister settle into the sofa, throwing an elbow over the back of the seat to face her, like she was planning a long, intimate chat. She studied Çifta's face intensely, expectantly.

Çifta yawned again, and didn't bother to stifle it. She was not just tired, she was emotionally and physically exhausted, not to mention sad.

"I'm not leaving until we talk about you-know-who." Gemma tapped Çifta on the chin as if to scold her for yawning. "We ran into him on our way into the palace, you know." She smirked with appreciation. "He looked amazing. Depressed as hell, but amazing. I forgot how gorgeous he is. I thought you said he'd been wounded?"

"He was." Çifta tried to straighten but immediately sank back into the depths of the couch. Thoughts of Laec seeped into her mind the way they always did. Filling her with warmth, followed by dread. "He's better now. He says the frostbite was the worst of it, worse even than his cuts, and some of them were pretty bad. He lost a lot of blood. Even so, he did a lot of heavy lifting during the clean up."

Çifta heard herself, heard the adoration in her tone, the pride. Laec was a prize. Yes, he was mischievous, an instigator, and irreverent, especially to authority that he should have respect for, like Ian Peneçek. But he was also brave, selfless, self-deprecating and noble.

"Çifta,"—Gemma let her hand fall on Çifta's shoulder—"what are you doing?"

Çifta snapped out of her private thoughts. "What do you mean?"

Gemma rolled her eyes. "Laec loves you. You love him. You haven't mentioned him once tonight, not a single time. But I can practically see his shape inside your pupils every time I look at you. Have you not told him how you feel?"

How did Gemma always know exactly where to press? She was like a surgeon, putting her finger precisely where it hurt the most.

Çifta sighed. "How can I?"

Gemma blinked at her, astonished. "Easy! You pull him aside and tell him that you're in love with him and you want to have his babies! Ideally, starting tonight."

Çifta barked laughter in spite of herself. "I've missed you, Gemma."

Gemma wagged a finger. "Oh no, you are not changing the subject, missy. It was not so long ago that we were having a conversation about happiness in my room back home. You were all doe-eyed for the fire-haired fae stallion back then, when you hardly even knew him. It's painfully obvious that you're even more in love with him now, and it's not just a matter of wanting to get beneath him naked, it's deeper than that. Much deeper. Tell me I'm wrong."

"But things are so much more complicated now."

"No, they're not. You only think they are. Have you even talked to Laec about your relationship?"

"No."

"Why not?"

Çifta couldn't give the reason a voice, but Gemma knew her well enough that she didn't have to.

"You're afraid."

Çifta nodded and Gemma laughed. "Good grief, woman. You decapitate your enemy in the middle of the palace foyer and you're afraid of having an honest conversation with the man you love?"

"I'm not afraid of Laec, Gemma. I'm afraid of the situation. Besides," she added, rubbing her hands over her face, "that wasn't me, that was Karinya. I get letters almost every day from Miss Sabran. She is very clear about what is expected of me. It's not like she's worried that I won't do my duty, she's not bossing me around, she never takes that kind of tone. She's eager, excited, and I think the woman actually really adores me for what Karinya did. It's more like... it hasn't even crossed her mind that I'll do anything other than what Karinya herself would have done, which is marry a Silverfae noble, ideally one who is extremely rich and influential. I'm supposed to gain as much benefit for my people out of the alliance as possible. She's already planning balls and parties and all kinds of soirees during which I'll be powdered and perfumed and presented like a brood mare at a spring fair. I can choose whoever I like, whoever pleases me, as long as they're Silver."

Gemma's response was swift and passionate. "Hang Rayven Sabran, even if she loves you. She doesn't own you. She doesn't know you, and Fetre is right: you might have her memories, but you're not Karinya. You're your own woman, with your own past and your own heart, and that heart clearly belongs to Laec. So why are you torturing yourself, and him, by pushing him away?"

Çifta wished with all her heart that it was as simple as Gemma was making it sound, but the conversation she'd had with the ice in the early part of her trial had never left her. The words echoed exactly as they'd been said. As time had passed, she remembered them as having even more impact than they'd had when she'd first heard them.

"When I first came to consciousness in the ice, before I knew who I was dealing with…" Çifta faced Gemma more fully, wanting Gemma to understand her inner strife. "She asked me what I wanted most. When I told her I wanted love, she rebuked me."

Gemma rolled her eyes.

"You weren't there. And I'm trying to explain why it's so complicated. Can you just let me get through this?"

Gemma pursed her lips and crossed her arms but said nothing.

"Thank you. She chided me like I was some naive little thing who knew nothing of the world. She told me that I should want power above all else. I told her that I disdained a hunger for power, that I believed it would only lead to loneliness. She told me my feelings about it don't matter, that I had to do my duty."

Gemma's eyes drifted shut with annoyance, and she shook her head.

"I know, I know," Çifta rushed on. "She sounded just like Father. I'm not going to lie, she was brutal. She told me that if I do not wish to serve others by giving up my own selfish desires, then perhaps I didn't deserve to survive the trial. I was angry, because it sounded like she wanted me to be power-mad and greedy, but then she told me that for someone like me, having power means carrying a heavy burden. Someone like me would be driven to wield it for the good of those around me. There is only so much power in the world. I should want more than my fair share so I can change the world for the better."

Gemma listened, and Çifta could see the gears turning in

her mind as she swung around the problem, viewing it from another angle.

"I realized then," Çifta went on, her arms prickling up with gooseflesh as even the tone of Karinya's voice in the moment came back to her, "that even though she was being hard on me, it was because she believed that I was capable of greatness, and more worthy than others to be powerful. She told me that power in the hands of someone lesser than me, or worse, in the hands of someone evil, would only lead to destruction. And she was right, because that's what happened to Silverfall while Sylifke was queen."

The parlor fell silent while Çifta let Gemma absorb this. Her sister gazed at the fire for a time, before facing Çifta again. She put a hand on Çifta's knee.

"I understand better than you think I do, my darling baby sister. I don't think Karinya's perspective on power is wrong, and I do think that there will be certain advantages if you match with a rich Silverfae. But I think you're discounting the advantages that you would gain if you give your heart to Laec, let him be your mate."

Çifta let her head tilt back and rest on the couch. Gemma was not helping—it was hard enough to hold onto her resolve. Explaining what she'd experienced inside the ice was supposed to convince Gemma that Çifta was doing the right thing, just as had been outlined by Karinya. Çifta had survived the ice, which meant Karinya had found her worthy. How could she betray that?

"Don't be frustrated," Gemma protested. "I listened to you, now you can listen to me. This is probably the last opportunity I'll ever have to counsel you. Soon you'll be surrounded by ministers and advisers and people who don't know you and don't love you, and they'll all think they know better than you. None of them will care about your heart, even Miss Sabran."

"Alright, alright." Çifta lifted her head, steeling herself. There was no stopping Gemma from having her say, even if Çifta already knew what that say was. "Go on, then."

"Were you aware that Laec was physically torturing himself every day, multiple times per day, while you were frozen, because he hoped—he didn't know, mind you—that it would help you?"

"What are you talking about?"

It was Çifta's turn to listen in silence, to let her sister's words punch into her heart and through her mind, poking holes in her resolve. Gemma relayed how the ice enclosing her had hurt others when they touched it. Not just hurt, but burned so badly that no one besides Laec would lay a hand on it for longer than a second, not even Kazery. Believing it might help her get out of the trial sooner, Laec stripped to the waist to roll himself against the ice…

"Like a hot corn-on-the-cob against butter," Gemma said. "If he wasn't eating or sleeping, he was there with you. Letting razors slice into his body, letting frost wound his skin. Then he'd cover up and go about palace life thinking hardly anyone knew about it."

Çifta moaned and leaned forward, putting her head in her hands as the images Gemma described slotted themselves into her imagination. "I thought he'd gotten those burns during the battle! How do you know this?"

"Kazery told me, but it's no secret. You can talk to anyone about it because everyone knows. Laec thought no one knew. He thought that, except for a few servants and one member of the Fahyli whom he swore to secrecy, his activities were beneath others' notice. Besides, the surest way to guarantee that everyone in a palace knows something is by swearing the servants to secrecy."

"Why didn't Father tell me? It's not like there hasn't been time." Çifta straightened, brushing at her eyes. Her heart was swollen from this realization.

Gemma waved a hand. "You know Father, he's always been conflicted about what he wants for himself versus what he wants for his daughters, especially you. A beautiful daughter is a great asset for Kazery Unya, of course he would want to use us for his advantage. He married me and Una and Fetre off to great benefit, but when your turn came, he softened. In a good way, realizing that perhaps love and happiness should rank a little higher than duty. If not a little higher, then at least neck and neck."

"Okay, then why didn't he tell me himself?"

"Well he is still the most successful merchant of the continent, Çifta. He is accustomed to delegating. He told *me* because he knew that *I* would tell *you*. It was his way of getting it done without abdicating his reputation and established character."

Glassy-eyed, Çifta stared at her sister. "I swear, I should have been the one to marry into a farm. You're the one who should be given a crown."

Gemma laughed. "Yes, well, I don't necessarily disagree with you, but this is how the chits have fallen. The question is, what are you going to do with this information? What Laec showed you—and the whole world—is that he values you above himself. He truly, madly, deeply loves you. He would never tell you what he did because he is far too noble. My dear, if you let that kind of love walk away from you without even making a try for it, then you don't deserve him, no matter how far above him you find yourself in station."

Çifta sucked in a breath. She felt lightheaded.

"If you still feel you need further justification that the man you love is in fact the right and best choice for you," Gemma said, patting Çifta's hand as she got to her feet and stretched her back, "then just ask yourself, will I be a better queen for my people with Laec at my side, loving me and supporting me? Or will I be better off with a rich Silver I don't know, who will bring an agenda of his own into my marriage?"

Gemma kissed her cheek and said goodnight, leaving Çifta caught in a thicket of emotions.

Chapter Six

Laec

L AEC WAS JOLTED awake by a knock. He looked around, body tense, unmoving—uncertain as to whether he had dreamed it. His fire had dwindled to coals and the room was swathed in shadows. When the sound came a second time, he threw his quilt back. Rubbing sleep from his eyes, he nearly tripped over one of the throw pillows he'd kicked off the foot of the emperor sized four-poster bed. The monstrosity was even outfitted with translucent lavender colored drapes, tied to each post with a silver rope.

After the battle, Laec had been moved back to the violet suite. Hob seemed to think that Laec was trying to be a gentleman when Laec suggested the steward give the purple-choked apartment to some other guest and that a more humble abode would suit him just fine. His objections fell on deaf ears.

It was too dark to make out the time on the clock over the fireplace, and a glance at the sky through one of the many windows didn't help either. It was a cloudy night, every star and the half-moon veiled with feathery layers.

Pausing only to strike a match and light a candle on his bedside table, Laec went to the door, opening it just wide enough to peek out. His heart leapt into his throat. There was a ghost in the hallway, peering up at him from huge hollow eyes. He bit off a startled cry, blinked and shook his head.

"Çifta?" he whispered, voice faltering.

Her long black hair lay over her shoulders, nearly reaching her waist. She wore a sleeveless white nightshift, voluminous and shapeless, with a bit of spidery lace at the neckline and a ribbon lacing the bodice closed. The fabric was so pale that it seemed to glow in the muted light of the etherlamps, giving her that ghostly appearance. She clutched a pale woolen shawl around herself with slender hands, her collarbones and cheekbones were sharp in the gloom.

"Your feet are bare," he said, feeling stupid. Was this real? All this time he'd been craving time alone with her, and now she was here? In the middle of the night? Without any warning at all? This had to be unplanned. Worry cramped his stomach.

"What's wrong?"

"Come with me." Her fingers tightened on the shawl, her eyes seeming to expand even wider.

He opened the door fully, still not convinced this wasn't a dream. But his room was warmer than the hall, and cool air swept into his suite, making him shiver. His toes curled against the freezing wooden planks where the hallway runner didn't quite cover. He wore only a pair of soft sleeping breeches, and his skin marbled against the nip in the air.

No, this was real.

"Okay." He drew the word out, still groggy with sleep. The

night air was silent, save for the howl of a distant dog and the ripple of wind through the gardens below his windows. "Where are we going? Should I bring a jacket? At least let me get a shirt." He looked down pointedly. "You definitely need slippers."

She moved forward, into his space, and was suddenly so close that his breath caught. A hint of her scent reached his nose, of lavender soap and vanilla, the sleep-warmed smell of her hair. She put a hand on his bare chest. Her palm was warm and her touch so lovely that he fought the urge to roll his eyes with pleasure. He'd never been self-conscious about being half-naked, he was a fae from Stavarjak, many of them walked around half-naked as a matter of course. But with Çifta's hand on his skin, his every nerve pulsed like a live wire, his body tensed and alive. All of his grogginess vanished the moment her physical being connected to his.

"No, I mean come with me to Silverfall."

He was so stunned that he couldn't move, couldn't think. He looked at her face, searching her soul, devouring her features like a starving man. Then he pulled her inside his room and closed the door, locking out the cold. Taking her by the hand, he led her to stand on the plush rug in front of the fireplace. He still couldn't find words.

"I realize what I'm asking," she said in a rush, fiddling with her shawl and speaking before he could rally himself. "Really, I do. It's probably not what you pictured for yourself, being a queen's consort. My life has changed in ways that are making my head spin. There are days that I feel calm and confident, in control. Those are the days Karinya's memories are standing close to my own, as if they were part of the same life, the same history. But there are other days, days when I wonder if I imagined her, because I can't recall anything from her life at all.

It's like I'm cut off, like she's left me to fend for myself, figure out on my own what kind of queen I'm supposed to be. I can't tell if that's what I want, or if I actually need her with me, to guide me, show me how to rule a nation, how to use her magic to benefit my people."

Laec's heart was flip-flopping behind his sternum like a freshly caught fish on a deck. What was she talking about? He still hadn't got past the first part, the part where she asked him to come with her to Silverfall, to be her consort. Had she really used that word? Consort? She had. He couldn't remember what it meant, not exactly, or if he'd ever known what it was. Elphame didn't keep one, at least not that he was aware of. But Çifta was still talking, words were pouring out of her like they would never stop. She was pacing now, floating a short distance across the floor in one direction, then back the other way, her nightdress catching on her knees, the ties at her bodice swaying. Her hands moved as she talked, giving away how anxious she was. Her shawl fell from one shoulder and lay hooked over her elbow. She looked so young and vulnerable like this, in her nightdress, with her hair down, her features full of hope and longing. She looked like the girl he'd met in the unnamed forest, the girl he'd fallen in love with in a sheep barn on the Hashe estate. A girl he'd thought was surely gone.

"You must think… well," she scoffed, pushing out a fretful exhale, "I can only guess at what you think." She put a hand to her brow, brushing back a long lock of that raven black Unya hair. "That I'm not the girl you fell in love with. That I'm a queen now, with a queen's responsibility. Not even the queen of somewhere warm and full of flowers, like here or your home kingdom. I'm queen of a cold place, a winter kingdom, and my people want me with a Silverfae. I'm told it's my duty, it's what's expected, but it's *my* life, and I'm tired of people telling me who I should and shouldn't be with. I'll be damned if I'm to be freed from the responsibility to wed a man of my father's choosing only to be beholden to a whole nation of fae—whom I do not even know. I'm not ashamed of"—she stopped in front of him, face full of passion—"needing you so badly. Love is all I've ever wanted, in fact. I've been given things that other people crave: power, magic, riches, authority. The ice—Karinya, I mean—even told me that all of that is what I *should* want, but honestly I would give it all up if it meant—"

"Çifta." He put his hands on her arms, touching her lightly. "Stop, darling. Stop."

She took a deep inhale, looking at him with fear in her eyes. It pierced him, that expression of foreboding. She was terrified of what he was about to say. If only she knew.

Her voice trembled. "What?"

"Are you asking me to be with you? To join you in Silverfall, as your... lover? Your partner in life?" He stopped short of saying husband, since she'd used the word consort, though he longed to include it in the list.

On her exhale, and immediately after he finished speaking, she said, "Yes."

"Yes," he parroted.

In an instant she seemed to grow taller, her eyes widening. "Yes?"

"Yes." He couldn't stop a smile from creeping across his face. This was all real, after all. "A thousand times yes. Do you think I care about any of those things? Your position, and what it might make of me, if I'm yours? Because I don't. I don't care about your status, your responsibilities, or the judgment of a hundred thousand of your citizens. I certainly don't care about the weather, not as it pertains to my being with you. None of that matters, only you matter. I thought you knew that. But now that I can see you didn't, I'm realizing just how daft I've been, not to have said it before. Loud and clear."

She shook her head and lifted her hands until her palms were resting on either side of his jaw, caressing the sides of his neck. "No, *I've* been daft. I've been so afraid of going after what I want. I'm still afraid that I will disappoint my people, that they'll judge me as selfish, as a poor ruler."

He lay his hands over top of hers. "After Sylifke? I think not."

She smiled, her gaze dropping to his mouth. "Gemma helped me see that being happy is not a crime, and would help me to be a better leader."

"And I'm what will make you happy?" Laec felt like his feet might leave the floor. Silently, he swore to be a better fae for her, the best fae he was capable of being.

She nodded. "And you? Am I what you want, Laec? Burdened though I am with a crown, will you give me the chance to make you happy?"

He touched her face, stroking her cheek before bending to kiss her.

When her mouth opened to his like a rose to a sunbeam, he wrapped his arms around her, picking her up off the ground. Their bodies fit together like puzzle pieces. They kissed until they were out of breath, finally savoring the passion they shared in the privacy of a closed room. Laec gave her everything he had in his kiss, hoping she understood what it meant, that he wanted her to have all of him.

He kept expecting her to touch the reins, to raise that wall of modesty, the wall she'd always kept between them. But the wall never came, and when his kisses grew deeper and more passionate, she gave it all back to him. She raked her fingers through his hair, kissed him roughly, generously. No wall. No restraint. No more barriers. She'd taken them down, and was showing him that the way was open for him.

When he broke the kiss and looked into her eyes, his gaze held a question. In answer, she held tightly to his neck and lifted her legs to wrap them around his waist. Her nightdress fell back, baring her thighs to the touch of his hands. It was all the reply he needed. He carried her to the bed and lay her among his rumpled silken bedsheets and violet-scented pillows. He stretched out to tug on a silver rope and the gauzy curtains drifted partially closed, then returned to kiss her again. The coals in the fireplace and the candle on the bedside table cast a warm flicker of illumination through the bed's drapes, lining the curve of Çifta's cheek. Kissing her with his eyes open, he smiled against her mouth, making her pause.

"What is it?" she whispered, her fingertips tracing the skin at the waistband of his trousers. "What's making you smile?"

"It's nothing, just... I've really hated this room." He brushed her hair away from her neck, fanning her locks out against the pale pillow-cover in a beautiful spray of dark against light. "But now, I can finally appreciate this suite for what it is."

She echoed his smile. "And what's that?"

He kissed her again, moving his body more fully over hers. "A worthy place to adore a queen."

Their laughter tangled together in the secret cocoon of Laec's bed, and their bodies swiftly followed.

As the light of dawn whispered in through the windows and crept across the floor, Laec smiled before he even opened his eyes, remembering what had taken place only hours before. Çifta was breathing peacefully and he savored the feeling of waking up for the first time beside her. Laec was a restless sleeper, always had been, but at no point throughout their shared slumber did they lose contact with each other. Çifta made sure they were always connected. Whenever Laec shifted positions, flipped over, curled up or spread-eagled, she recovered any gap between them. Touching his calf with her foot, pressing her back up against his, or placing her hand on his shoulder. Now, emerging from the deepest part of sleep, Çifta turned toward him, throwing a bare leg over his thighs.

He looked over at her. She was awake and watching him with the happiest expression he'd ever seen. There was only the ghost of a smile touching her lips, but joy radiated from those incandescent eyes.

He rolled toward her, holding his hair back from her face as he dropped a kiss on her lips. "Good morning, Your Majesty. Did you sleep well?"

"Good morning... beloved."

Ooh, Laec thought. *Beloved. I like that.*

"You know I didn't," she continued. "You kept me up most of the night."

"Excuse me!" His mouth crooked and he raised his eyebrows. "Who came to wake whom in the middle of the night? I was merely continuing what you started. Carrying on the torch, so to speak."

She smiled and ran her fingers through his hair. Laec fought the desire to purr. Instead, he said, "I owe that woman a debt of gratitude I can never repay."

She blinked. "Who? Karinya?"

He snorted. "No, your sister Gemma. What did she say

A.L. Knorr

to you to give you the nerve to materialize at my door like a phantom?"

She sighed and rubbed one eye, looking sheepish. "And after making you wait for weeks, too. I'm so sorry Laec. I was confused. Still am, honestly, but if you're with me, at least I'm not frightened of what is ahead. Ruling a nation strikes me as the most intimidating thing a person could ever attempt."

He couldn't disagree with that.

Her look softened as she scooted her face forward, resting her cheek on the pillow, their noses mere inches apart. She touched the still tender skin of his chest. "I know what you did for me, while I was inside the ice."

He froze. Laec had assumed that she was completely unaware of his rash-inducing activities, and would never admit such a thing to her voluntarily. How would that go? *Hey, could you tell while you were enduring your life-threatening trial that I was rubbing my half-naked body all over your ice cube in a vain attempt to melt you faster?* Um. No. Besides, it'd had no effect, as far as he could tell, and had turned out rather to be an activity he'd done more for his own benefit.

His face heated. "You know about that?"

She nodded, touching his cheek, soft as a butterfly.

"Have you always known?"

"Karinya told me that you really loved me, but I never understood how she could have known that. I didn't know the details until Gemma told me last night. Thank you, my love."

"It was an act of desperation. I didn't know what else to do, and I wasn't being much good to anyone else, not with you locked inside that thing. So…"

"You endured hours of agony for me. It doesn't matter that I couldn't tell while I was inside, Karinya could tell, so it did

56

make some kind of difference. No one has done anything like that for me before. It's amazing. You're amazing."

He took her hand and kissed it, tucking it into his chest. "Well, if it gets you to look at me like this every morning hereafter until we die, then I'd do it all again."

They enjoyed staring at one another for several long moments, until they heard footsteps pass in the hall. Servants were beginning to move about. Soon the smell of breakfast would drift through the palace, and the daily enterprise of Solana City would turn the castle into a beehive of activity.

Laec said: "What will your ice-guards do when they discover you're not in your room this morning? Howl at the sky? Beat their chests? Freeze the servants and throw them over the balconies?"

Çifta laughed. "They're a touch overprotective, I'll admit. I'm learning that they suffocate me as much as I allow them to. I have to set some boundaries. When they see us together and learn that you're coming with me, I'm hoping they'll back off."

He scowled. "They'd better. But I'm not convinced that a consort will hold much weight with your people. I have to admit, it's not a station I'm familiar with."

He'd brought it up in the hopes that she might enlighten him on what his new position would mean in the context of life in Silverfall, but Çifta looked as uncertain as he was.

"I'll write to Rayven about it. Or maybe it would be better to wait until we are there in person and I've met the aristocracy and previous advisers of Karinya, if they're available to me. I certainly don't want any of Sylifke's former people working for me."

"Rayven Sabran was a former person for Sylifke," Laec told her. "I hate to remind you."

"Yes but I've had no choice but to rely on her. She was here when it all happened, and the most senior person I could turn to for help. Also, I think she was terrified of Sylifke, and really wanted her reign to end."

Thinking of all the damage and deaths that had been wrought at the hands of the Silverfae that horrible night, Sabran's included, Laec believed that no one could be sure of her true allegiance, but it didn't matter. She'd sworn loyalty to Çifta, and that would have to be upheld upon pain of exile. But another matter crept into Laec's thoughts.

"Citizens of Stavarjak haven't been allowed to cross the border into Silverfall since Queen Sylifke's reign began. Not without written consent from Queen Elphame. I will have to get her permission to go to Silverfall with you." At Çifta's fraught expression, he added, "Her responses are usually swift, and I'm sure she will lift the decree now that Sylifke's rule has ended."

Çifta's expression eased. "Don't delay. I've pushed my departure for as long as I've been able, but I'm getting letters almost daily now, not just from Rayven, but from other ministers in Silverfall. They're eager for my return."

Laec was certain that eager was an understatement, if the behavior of the Silverfae guards was anything to go by. Çifta's nation was foaming at the mouth to have their benevolent new queen crowned and enthroned, especially considering that, by now, the entire kingdom would know that Karinya had inhabited Çifta's body for long enough to execute judgment on her usurper. Çifta would become famous throughout Ivryndi as word of her epic triumph spread, but she'd yet to set foot inside her own kingdom. No wonder Çifta was apprehensive. She was famous, but her fame had been Karinya's doing. It was no wonder she was feeling inadequate for the job. When he thought of it that way, he was glad she'd asked him to come with her, for more than personal reasons. She would need a friend at her side, someone who knew her before she'd become a living legend.

"I won't delay." Getting out of bed, he cast about for his clothing. "I'll write today, and I'll request a speedy response."

Çifta sat on the edge of the bed and reached for her night-dress, then pulled it over her head and stood, shaking out the fabric. "Have you told her anything about me?"

"Of course." Laec tied his breeches and slipped into the bathroom to warm up the water for a shower. When he returned, Çifta had her hand on the door.

"And what about us?" she asked.

He raked his hair back. "I've never included anything of a personal nature, so it'll be the first she's heard of it from me."

His words made Çifta nervous. "Great, so on top of being seen running down the hall from your room like a strumpet, I'm going to be on tenterhooks until Elphame writes back to you with permission." She groaned. "This queen business is overrated."

"A strumpet?" Laec was confused. "Why a strumpet?"

"I was raised not to do such things."

He smiled. "You're not in Boskaya any longer, no one here will judge you, and you're looking at things all wrong."

"Am I?"

"Obviously! You're the queen of an ancient monarchy," he reminded her. "A kingdom that still honors the old ways. Silverfall even allows challenges to the throne, a fight to the death to establish supremacy."

"You're not making me feel better."

"You should. As queen of such a kingdom, you can do

what you want. You're beholden to no one. Your word is the highest in the land."

She blew out a breath, her hand tightening on the handle of his door. "I'll remember that as I scamper down the corridor in a nightdress."

As soon as Çifta was gone, Laec hurried through his morning routine. He braided his hair into a queue and snipped several inches off the ends. Somehow, he felt that being presentable while he wrote this letter to Elphame might give him courage. It was the most important letter he'd ever write.

As the scent of toast and butter and eggs reached his room from the main dining hall, Laec's mouth began to water. But he wouldn't go for breakfast yet. He pulled a piece of parchment from the desk drawer and sat. Picking up his quill and dipping it, he began.

My Queen,

I write not from my position as emissary, but as a humble citizen. I've reported developments as they've happened, leaving out extraneous details that are below your attention. But now I must bother you with such, for a development in my personal situation requires that I ask your permission to end my commission here, and beg authorization to cross the border into Silverfall.

You are aware of the outcome for the merchant Kazery's daughter, Çifta Unya, who has inherited the position of queen in the winter kingdom. A development I am certain you are celebrating with great fervor, given how relations were between you and the prior queen. I too, celebrate, and all the more so because I have fallen in love with

Gifta. I fell in love with her before I ever arrived in Solana. I never reported it to you as Gifta was betrothed. Even after her betrothal was broken, she remained out of reach to me. But she is no longer out of reach, and has asked me to come to Silverfall in the position of consort, which I accept, and for which I beg your leave.

We eagerly await your reply, as Queen Gifta has delayed her journey for too long already.

Your humble servant,

Laec Fairijak

Laec read it and reread it. It was good. Perfect. Simple, yet sufficiently expressive of his need for a prompt reply, ideally accompanied by the paperwork he needed to cross the border without being struck down by some indelible magic.

Rolling up the message, he sealed it and tucked it into a cylinder. He threw open his bedroom windows, letting fresh air into the room and bringing with it the smell of new growth and tender blooms. Smells of spring. An open window being Mistik's signal, she appeared on the windowsill by the time Laec had finished pulling on his boots. Fastening the message to her leg, he wished her the speed of magic, and tossed her into the air.

CHAPTER SEVEN

JESSAMINE

"AND BACK, ONE, two, and turn. Turn. Keep your eyes up, Violet, don't stare at the floor. You'll deprive the court of those amethyst eyes, and we can't have that." Ilishec tapped the bottom of the slender stick he always carried during choreography classes on the parquet, keeping time with the music. He called instructions over the room as the Calyx swirled around in pairs in their practice clothes, their hair in ponytails or messy buns, their skin glowing with sweat. The room smelled like a field of flowers.

Three senior Calyx had put in notice that this spring season would be their last. Ilishec didn't have to host another Discovery to fill their spots, though, as he had several marked for an invitation when spaces came up. They would say goodbye to Clematis, who Ilishec was especially sad to lose since flowering climbers were needed to cover the bare walls which had so recently been repaired. Not only would Wisteria and Jessamine be overworked—as the only other two with flowering vines—Ilishec wanted diversity. So he had written to an older flora fae male who had been at Discovery six years earlier who was connected with *bougainvillea*. Bougain—as he was now known—had arrived only a few days later, as eager as a puppy. He was twenty-two and carried himself with the bearing of a soldier, because soldiering was what he'd been doing. Thick-chested and with rounded muscles, Bougain had already become a court favorite, but he was a menace on the dance floor and the other Calyx had to be aware of his position as they practiced. Ilishec made him attend every choreography class and he even took private lessons in the evenings.

Dancing with Proteas, Jessamine whirled by the open ballroom doors and noticed Hob approaching the entrance. She kept catching glimpses of the steward over Proteas's shoulder as their slippered feet bounced and tapped, pointed and kicked.

Proteas followed her line of sight. "Hob. Does that mean...?"

Jessamine's stomach gave a sickening lurch of anticipation. "I hope so."

Every Calyx knew that Jess was waiting for a list of names from the property registry, and that it had to do with the identity of her twin. She'd gotten so tired of telling them that she was still waiting that she'd snapped at Marigold two days ago. No one had dared ask her about it since, but they were almost as deeply invested in the mystery as she was.

Hob stood at the door craning his neck until he spotted Jess and Proteas. His brows went up and he lifted an envelope. She acknowledged the steward so he knew she'd seen him. Proteas's grip tightened as he gave her a smile of encouragement. They executed the remainder of the dance before she made her way over to Hob, snatching up her towel and water, heart thrumming in her chest. She could feel eyes on her, and heard whispers as the news passed around the room that her list had come.

Hob held the envelope out. "It just arrived from the land office, Miss Fontana. I wasted no time in delivering it personally. I know how important this is to you."

Jess took the letter, touched. "Thank you, Hob. You didn't have to do that. I know how busy you are."

"It was my pleasure. I hope it leads you to the knowledge that you seek." He turned on his heel and floated off down the hall.

Jess looked down at the letter in her hand. Her name had been stamped on its front—including her title as Calyx and a small line of italicized text which listed her botanicals. Only messages from official royal sources were labeled so thoroughly. The address of the land office was in the top left corner, and when she flipped the envelope over, she saw the generous dollop of blue wax imprinted with Solana's wreathed lion's head crest. For a long moment it seemed all she could do was stare at it.

Turning, she almost ran into the crowd of Calyx who had closed in around her. Even Ilishec was lingering not far away, pretending to make notes at the table near the doorway.

"Go on, Jess." Snap draped an arm over Rose's shoulders, wiping at his face with a towel. "Don't be scared. We're here for you."

"Yeah, we love you," said Asclepias.

"You're never alone," added Aster as she toed off her slippers and picked them up.

Her heart filled with warmth. "Thanks, everyone, but I promised Sasha and Beazle I'd open it with them."

The flora fae's disappointment was so thick that it soured the smell of the room. They moved away.

In their bedroom, Beazle blinked awake and yawned. *I'm coming.*

"We'll come with you to find Sasha," said Rose, grabbing Aster by the hand and pulling her through the crowd. "Come on, Snap."

Jess found herself escorted across the palace to the West Keep and down the steps to the exit that would take them to the Fahyli training yards. Sasha and Rialta spent much of their daylight hours there.

Beazle landed on her chest as they pushed through the side door to the doubletrack that ran along the inner bailey. Rose almost had a heart attack as Rialta came barreling around the bend, rushing up to Jess in a flurry of fur, teeth and flashing blue eyes. She put her nose under Jess's elbow, sniffing and licking, sensing her nerves.

"You've either got impeccable timing or amazing intuition, Rialta," she told the dire wolf, stroking her soft ears.

Sasha rounded the bend next, walking fast. He pulled up short when he saw them, a look of relief washing over his face. "Rialta told me something was wrong. You're worried."

"Not worried, exactly. Look what came." She showed him the envelope.

"What do we do if it's someone we know?" Aster asked, clutching at Rose's arm like it was a lifeline.

"We don't automatically assume foul play." Snap looked at Jess. "Right, Jess?"

"Right."

Aster was dancing in place. "Open it already. I need the

bathroom but I'm not leaving your side until I know who is on that list."

Jess tucked a lock of hair behind her ear. Beazle crawled to her shoulder as everyone watched her break the seal and slide the document out. She exhaled as she unfolded the single page, then read aloud: "Dear Miss Fontana, Your request for private information has been approved. Please find enclosed the list of owners of the six apartments at the address listed in your inquiry."

Her gaze dropped to the list, skimming over the names. Beside each was another address, presumably the locations of their permanent homes.

"Lord Nomahar Afof of Tryske, Sir Thomas Diamwen of Solana, Lady Gwedria of Solana, Lord Etobian of Stavarjak, Lady Aewin Brelicia of Boskaya, and Lord Artemon Gillner of Archelia." She looked up at Rose in surprise, her heart skipping a beat. "Lord Gillner?"

Rose looked just as shocked as she felt. "Are you sure?" She took the page from Jess to read it for herself.

Aster, Sasha and Snap shared a look of concern, Rialta released a whine and Sasha stroked her shoulder.

"Artie," Rose whispered. "I never knew he owned property in that tower, Jess. I swear. I would have said otherwise."

"I know that, Rose. Don't look so frightened. It doesn't mean he had anything to do with the bonnet. He's only one name in six."

"But the only one we recognize," said Snap.

"What will you do now?" Sasha cradled her elbow.

Jess considered the list, then looked at Rose. "Will you come with me to talk to him? He's the only name we have any connection with, and he might know something about his neighbors."

Rose nodded. "Of course. Do you want to go now? He'll be in the Koi Library this morning, probably playing chess with his friends."

Jess began to move, but when all of them moved at once like a clump of barnacles, she stopped again, looking at Snap and Aster.

"Do you mind if it's just Sasha and Rose who come with me? I don't want him to feel attacked."

"Oh." Aster's face fell.

"Sure, Jess. No problem." Snap hooked Aster's elbow and pulled her away. "We'll catch up with you later."

Sasha, Rose and Jess made their way up to the Koi Library. The closer they got, the damper Jess's hands felt. She imagined herself inching closer to truth.

At the entrance, Rose paused.

"Why don't I ask him to come out and meet you here?" She gestured to an empty alcove. "I don't want to put him on the spot in front of his peers."

Jess agreed as she and Sasha ducked into the alcove and sat on the plush couch. Jess lay the letter on the table. Her knee bounced up and down under her skirt until Sasha put a hand over hers. Then she let out a long exhale, trying to relax.

When Rose appeared with Artemon, they stood and began to greet him formally but Artie waved the etiquette off, making them sit. He was a plain-faced man with short mousy hair and kind eyes. Jess recalled that he was blind in one eye, and noticed that his right pupil contained a pale flaw drifting like a tiny cloud.

"Rose tells me I might be of some assistance to you, Jessamine." Artie threaded his fingers together, laying them on the table. He looked at her curiously. But just as Jess was about to launch into the story of her lost twin and the bonnets, he spoke again.

"She explained that you're trying to discover what happened to your brother. That you have bonnets that he once wore, and you recently found one after the unfortunate incident with the Silverfae."

Only a well-bred courtier would ever refer to the violence that had taken place in Solana as an "incident."

"Yes," she told Artie. "Another bonnet with Julian's nametag was found on the ground outside the Mandevilla Towers…"

Artie's brows hiked up. "Outside Mandevilla? You don't say?"

"That's why I've come to you." She unfolded the letter and lay it flat, then slid it toward him. "I made an inquiry about who owns the apartments in Mandevilla. The only name on the list that we recognized was yours, so I thought we'd come to you first."

Artie took up the letter, meeting Jess's eyes. "My family has owned an apartment in that tower since before I was born. It was my parents' summer home for a while, until I inherited it. I always preferred to stay in the palace, so I've had it rented for many years." He looked down, taking a moment to skim the list. "I know all of these courtiers in some way or another."

Rose looked at him, hope written all over her face.

He smiled, touching her cheek affectionately. "My darling. You know I'll do all I can."

Jess's heart had grown wings. "You'll help me?"

He held up the letter. "Do you mind if I keep this for a while? None of these property owners are presently in Solana except for Lady Gwedria, who lives here full time. I'll write to the others, and I will ask Lady Gwedria if we may call on her for an important matter. How does that sound?"

"It's more than I even hoped for," Jessamine told him. "And your rental? May I ask who your tenant is?"

"Who my tenant *was*," he corrected. "They've had to find somewhere else to live while the tower is being repaired. I'm a little embarrassed to tell you that I don't know their names. I don't administer our tenancies myself. I'll ask Evran, my manager, and we'll go from there."

"Thank you, Lord Gillner." Jess hoped he could sense just how grateful she was.

Rose squealed with joy and pulled him close, kissing his face several times. The fragrance of roses filled the booth. Artie blushed and gave Sasha a sheepish look, patting Rose's hand. She lay her head on his shoulder, looking lovestruck.

"It's lovely being with a flora fae," he told Sasha in a companionable way. "Unlike human women—who can be so difficult to read—I can always tell when I've made Rose happy."

CHAPTER EIGHT

ÇIFTA

TWO DAYS AFTER she'd invited Laec to Silverfall and he'd accepted, Çifta stood in the middle of her suite surrounded by half-packed trunks and stacks of clothing and belongings. Kazery sat at the table by the window, discussing business with one of his captains over tea, while Fetre and Una had left that morning to go back to their families. Gemma remained to help Çifta pack. She would travel with Çifta and Kazery as far as her estate. Çifta had tried to convince her father that she was perfectly comfortable traveling to Silverfall with the Silverfae guards and Laec at her side, but she was touched that Kazery insisted that he and his men would escort her all the way to her new home. And he would stay for as long as it took for her to feel comfortable there. One of Kazery's ships, a barque called the *Swallow*, was already sailing up the northwestern coast of Ivryndi. It would meet Kazery at Silverfall's most northern port when he was ready to leave.

Çifta held up one of the tunics she used to wear while

working in the artists' tower. She shook it out and folded it before setting it with the others. Stacks of sketchbooks and piles of colored pencils and other artists' tools occupied the coffee table, while all three sofas were cluttered with dresses, shoes, and outdoor wear.

"You've only been here for a few months." Gemma carried a stack of underthings over to a trunk and deposited them. "I don't understand how you accumulated this many belongings."

"This isn't even the half of it. Queen Esha sent a bird to Rahamlar on my behalf, requesting that they ship my things here. Since Jess and Laec rescued me in the middle of the night, I couldn't carry much."

Gemma shook her head and tsked, shooting a frown at Kazery. "I still can't believe what you went through. You should never have been betrothed to that madman."

Çifta was glad Kazery was too occupied to notice Gemma's disapproval. Her father felt terrible about what had happened in Rahamlar. When he had insisted she tell him every detail, not sparing his feelings, he had gripped the arms of his chair so hard his knuckles bled white. But he had listened, and thankfully she extracted a promise that he would not take any violent actions against Rahamlar because of Faraçek's cruelty.

"I suppose the success of your marriage—and Una's and Fetre's as well—gave Father a false sense of security." Çifta kept her voice low. "Anyway, it doesn't matter anymore. I'm fine, I never have to see Faraçek again, and I have a wonderful new person in my life."

Laec was on her mind more than food or sleep or anything else that she needed for survival. Since he'd agreed to come with her, she felt lighter than feathers and had lost nearly all of her anxiety about moving to Silverfall. The only unease that remained was that Queen Elphame's reply to Laec's request for permission to cross the border had still not arrived. Çifta had run out of excuses, and out of time. Her guards had drawn the carriage that Sylifke had arrived in out of the stables and were having carpenters repair the axle.

When a knock came at the door, Çifta had to exert masterful self-control not to run, even though Gemma was closer. Her heart fluttered around like a butterfly somewhere in the region of her throat, but plummeted to her shoes when it wasn't Laec.

"Ma'am." Hob bowed and straightened, his brow shiny with sweat. "Your things have arrived."

She held the door open as a parade of her Silverfall guards and a handful of Solanan servants carried her trunks from Rahamlar into her room and deposited them wherever they could find space.

"In point of fact they arrived a day and a half ago, but I quarantined them and had them cleaned and disinfected before bringing them to you." Hob bounced on his toes a little, looking proud of himself as the last of the boxes, bags and trunks were stacked.

Çifta gave Hob a look of confusion. "Disinfected?"

"Royal Gardener's orders, Ma'am."

When she still looked confused, he added that Ilishec had warned him that anything coming in from Rahamlar had to be given the going over of its life. There was to be absolutely no trace of dust found on any of it, and with the doing away of the dust, away would go the things that couldn't be seen. The spores, the magic, the *cordyceps* residue that was a threat to any insect familiar.

The small army filed out of her suite and Hob closed the door, leaving Çifta and Gemma with triple the work.

Gemma was already rummaging through trunks when Çifta joined her. She lifted a summer frock out of a wooden box.

"I remember this dress! Gosh, I didn't realize it still fit you. But I suppose you haven't changed much since you were seventeen. Unlike me." Then she glowered at the material as it slipped between her fingers. "I suppose these kind of gauzy frocks will be completely useless to you in Silverfall, unless you line them all with flannel, and that can't be practical."

Çifta grabbed a box that she knew had her old sketchbooks inside. Stepping over a small tower of shoe bags, she set the box on a chair and opened it. It had indeed been cleaned. It smelled like sage and limes.

"You might be impressed to learn that when under the rule of a benevolent monarch, Silverfall actually has very lovely summers, or so I'm told by Jacen. They're short, of course, but the daylight seems to last forever and the northern flowers are just as beautiful as our southern ones."

"Right." Gemma looked doubtful as she folded the dress. "Who is Jacen?"

"One of my guards."

"You're on a first name basis with your guards?"

"Sure. I need to know what to call them—I'm not exactly comfortable shouting "guard!"—and their first names are what they gave me." She shrugged. Why did it matter?

"Be careful with that," Gemma warned.

"What do you mean?"

"In my experience, being on a first name basis with someone of a lesser station fosters a familiarity that can grow into something more." She wiggled her brows suggestively. "How do you think I coaxed Dworic into playing find the blueberry with me after the Devet harvest festival? It didn't happen overnight. These things have to be planted and tended."

"You're irredeemable, Gemma. And I thought his name was Percy."

"That was last year. Honestly, I put all this in my letters. Don't you read them? Keep up."

"I forget," Çifta told her. "Not to read them," she added hastily at the horrified look Gemma gave her. "Of course I read them, but you always ask me to burn them afterward so I only ever get to read them once. If you'd stop putting such personal information in them, I could keep them for posterity. You know I like to do that."

"The things that mean you should burn them are the only things that make them worth reading, sister."

Çifta couldn't disagree there. She began to look through her old sketchbooks, admiring images that she'd created a long time ago. She was so absorbed that when another knock came and Gemma went to answer it, she hardly noticed.

When she heard Laec's voice beside her, she jumped like a flea, throwing her arms around him. He returned her hug but withdrew too soon, looking down at her, and she immediately knew something was wrong.

"Gemma," she said, without taking her eyes from Laec's. "We're going to step into my room for a moment. Do you mind?"

Not picking up on the seriousness passing between them, Gemma gave an unladylike snort. "Do I mind? Darling, you forget whom you address."

Çifta took Laec's hand and led him into her bedroom. She closed the door, heart racing around in her chest. She gestured to the couple of seats in front of her fireplace. The hearth was cold, but the temperature of the room was the last thing on her mind.

Before he sat down, Laec withdrew a small scroll from a pocket and handed it to her. "This arrived."

The parchment was beautiful, with hand-drawn flowers, vines, and crows around the borders. The writing was sharp and angular. Çifta unrolled the scroll.

Dear Laec,

Congratulations on your relationship with the new Silverfall queen. I am beyond happy for you, not only personally, but that one of my subjects has managed to claim the heart of my neighboring sovereign, and that she is seelie and of good character. This is a wonderful development for Stavarjak and I ordered a banquet to be thrown in your and Queen Çifta's honor even before I responded to you. Sylifke's death gives us much to celebrate all on its own, but your partnership adds a sweetness I have not enjoyed in decades.

Çifta glanced up at Laec. "So far so good. Great, actually."
"Keep going," he murmured.

I write all that first so that you understand that I am in no way angry with you for your request to end your commission prematurely, and so that you do not think that what I am about to say is any kind of punishment.

I must deny your request to cross the border. You are within your rights to come home at any time, but regardless, I'll not grant you permission to cross into Silverfall before your purpose is fulfilled.

The short battle that raged between the old queen and Solana was not the darkness that I foresaw for Esha. That darkness still lurks upon the horizon, growing darker and *ever more imminent. You are still needed there.*

When my premonition has lifted and the darkness has fled or dissolved, then I will wholeheartedly give my blessing for you to cross the border. Not only that, I will lift the mandate entirely for any Stavarjakian who wishes to visit the northern kingdom. All this I promise, with one additional stipulation and request, which I am sure I do not need to voice. And that is that you bring your bride to Stavarjak and grace my court with her presence.

Your Queen,

Elphame

Çifta let the scroll lie in her lap. Laec looked dejected. His brow was pinched and his lips tight.

"I'm delighted," she said, ignoring the disappointment making a cold stone in her gut.

She would have to travel without him, after all. All the excitement she had allowed to build in her heart was snuffed out in a moment. But she had no desire to see Laec's misery grow, and overall, the letter was positive.

Laec's shoulders straightened. "You are?"

"Of course! Naturally, I would rather you were permitted to come with me now, but Elphame has only temporarily denied you access to Silverfall. We'll just have to wait a little longer before we can be together."

Laec glowered and threaded his fingers behind his neck, stretching his head back and looking at the ceiling. She waited until he looked at her again—with a little less wretchedness, but it was not gone.

"We don't know if this will take days, weeks, months,"—he

swallowed—"or years. Elphame seems to be incapable of seeing specifics, so I'm just to sit here, waiting for no one knows what, and for no one knows how long? You're set to leave tomorrow. How long will it be before we're together again?"

Çifta's voice was soft as she moved to her knees before him, taking his hands. "I've been waiting for you for as long as I can remember, since I knew what love was. What is a few more weeks, or even months? We have the rest of our lives to be together."

He stroked her hair and she lifted her face. He cupped her chin and leaned forward. She thought he was going to kiss her but he moved to the floor beside her. He sat with his back against the chair then-stretching out his legs-drew her onto his lap. He wrapped her in an embrace, inhaling her scent and pressing his face to the side of her neck. They sat like that, breathing as one, for a long time. When Çifta's hips began to ache, she moved off his lap and sat beside him, threading her fingers through his.

"What are you thinking?"

He pushed out a breath, fast and hard. It was the sound of someone feeling hen-pecked. He stroked the back of her hand with the pad of his thumb, making little circles.

"When I first arrived, I did my job as best as I could. I made inquiries, needled courtiers for gossip, and sent letters to Elphame whenever there was anything to report. After Jess and I rescued you, you became the dominant focus in my life, whether I liked it or not. The threat to Solana was vague, and everything in the kingdom seemed fine, so falling in love with you was easy. My job was easy. I hardly had anything to think about. While you were in the ice, I thought for sure your situation had to do with the darkness, so I became absorbed in trying to fix it. Although, truth be told, I couldn't be roused to care much about other goings on in Solana."

He went quiet. She waited for him to resume, but finding he remained lost in his own thoughts, she prompted him. "What are you trying to say?"

He looked at her. "That I suddenly find myself acutely and profoundly invested in Solana's emancipation from this darkness. If there was a pedal I could step on, or a lever I could pull to draw this darkness forward and force it to show its face, I would do it without hesitation, consequences be damned. I just want it to be finished."

Çifta lay her head on his shoulder because his eyes were burning so intensely that she could hardly bear to look at them. "Just promise me that you won't do anything rash? I need you to arrive in Silverfall whole and healthy, with all of your limbs"— she smiled—"and other appendages intact."

When he didn't respond, and hadn't so much as moved a muscle for several long seconds, she looked up. He was not smiling at her joke, he was staring at the cold hearth, like he hadn't heard.

"Laec?" she whispered, kneeling in front of him. She put one hand on each of his shoulders.

His gaze flicked to her face, but nothing else changed. Her heartbeat picked up a notch.

"Promise me you won't do anything reckless?"

For the first time since entering her suite, she saw a glimmer of the old Laec.

"Define reckless."

Çifta and Gemma did a final sweep of the suite, ensuring they'd not forgotten any belongings and tidying the parlor. Çifta felt unexpectedly calm as she walked through the space a final time. She would return one day, she just didn't know when that day would be. Certainly for the next decennial Midwinter, but sooner if she could manage it. She'd made life-long friends here, friends who were gathering to see her off in the courtyard. And when Silverfall's weather settled, after she was officially crowned, she knew many of them would visit. After more than forty years of being shut off from the rest of Ivryndi, people were curious about the northern kingdom.

Gemma hooked Çifta's elbow as they headed for the corridor. Stepping out into the hall, they caught a glimpse of Kazery and a woman further down the hall. They stood close to one another and were speaking quietly, not realizing that they were being observed.

"Who's that?" Gemma wondered as Çifta tugged the door closed behind them.

Çifta paused in the hall, absorbing what she was seeing. She squinted, recognizing the woman as one of the Calyx. "That's Lilac!"

"Are they…?" Gemma started, then stopped as Kazery kissed Lilac's mouth then pulled her in for a hug.

"I guess they are," said Çifta. "Why didn't he say?"

Gemma pulled her closer, whispering. "Why would he change his pattern? He never tells us about his affairs. I suspect he has a different lady in every port, and now he has one among the Calyx too. What a cad."

She said this without animosity but it still stunned Çifta

into silence. After a moment's consideration, she adjusted her thoughts. Why wouldn't Kazery have relationships? He was still strong and healthy, he would be attractive to a great many females of both the fae and human populations. She wanted Kazery to have someone, although she hoped it wasn't quite as extensive as a lady in every port.

When the couple parted and Lilac hurried away without having noticed them, they approached their father. The three of them made their way to the main staircase, arm in arm.

"You're lucky, Papa," Çifta told him. "Ilishec only recently lifted the rule that Calyx are not to associate with courtiers."

He winked at her. "I'm no courtier."

"You know what I mean. Guests and visitors."

They started down the stairs and crossed the wide foyer.

"This place is infamous now," Kazery told them as they stepped into the morning sunlight. "There's no other palace foyer in Ivryndi that can claim the beheading of a queen."

"Nor a courtyard that can claim the death of a prince by dire wolf," Gemma added.

"And both of the same family," said Çifta.

"We would prefer to be known for our perfumes," came a dry response as Ilishec stepped around a pillar. "But I suppose even bad publicity is better than none at all."

Çifta's pulse quickened when she saw the crowd that had gathered around her carriage and on the courtyard stairs. Her Silverfae guards were positioned for departure. Familiar Sola-nan faces were everywhere she looked. Fahyli, servants, and courtiers she'd grown friendly with. The crofter was there too, standing alongside Queen Esha and King Agir. Lining the way to her carriage were the Calyx, wearing pastel colors and looking like sculptures made of icing. Seeing Auvo, Hob, Hazel, and so many more filled her heart with an ache of homesickness.

Çifta smiled, but her heart fell as she searched the crowd in vain for that distinctive red hair.

"Where's Laec?" Gemma whispered.

"He'll be here." Çifta stepped forward to take Esha's hand. The queen's gracious farewell was only the first in a long line of warm goodbyes. Çifta went slowly, savoring every interaction while also giving Laec time to turn up. When she reached Sasha, she tried to get him to commit to a date for a return to Silverfall, but he only promised that he would write to her.

Jessamine stood at the front of the line of Calyx, and they exchanged a warm hug.

"Safe journey, Queen Çifta," Jess said as she stepped back. "Thank you for being strong for us. No one will ever know what you endured inside the ice, but I have a vague idea, and I'm grateful."

Çifta covered her emotions by touching a finger to Beazle's fur where he clung to Jess's dangling earring, looking like a chrysalis with shining black eyes and a set of tiny ears.

"Beazle says thank you, too," Jess said.

"Please come and visit me."

Jess dimpled. "Of course. Your kingdom is Sasha's homeland, and you'll always be our friend."

Çifta nodded and brushed at her eyes. She had to move on or she would shame herself. Queens did not cry in public. As she passed through the Calyx, they tossed their mystic blooms into the air, filling the courtyard with the smell of summer. By the time Çifta, Gemma and Kazery reached the carriage, they were redolent with perfume. Gemma climbed into the carriage first, followed by Kazery, whose weight made the conveyance squeak. Çifta waved to the crowd one last time, but found it difficult to hold her smile. Laec was still nowhere to be seen. She settled onto the seat beside Gemma, facing Kazery.

Just before the door was closed, Çifta bent toward the footman. "Can we wait for a few moments, please?"

"Of course, Ma'am. Thump when you're ready." He closed the door and moved to the rear of the carriage.

Çifta peered out the window, sliding it open and putting her kerchief outside to wave. Solanans waved back, and the Calyx moved away from the carriage.

Several moments passed and Çifta grew restless. She could no longer muster a smile. The crowd outside did not disperse, but still Laec had not appeared.

"They can't get on with their day while we sit here, darling," Gemma told her with kindness.

"I'm sorry, Çifta," Kazery said, threading his fingers over his stomach. "I know it hurts, but one can't blame the man. Take it as a sign of how deep his love is for you."

Çifta withdrew, sliding the window closed. She thumped the ceiling with the wooden dowel that hung over the door. The carriage moved forward immediately, out of the courtyard and down the main throughway toward the front gates. Citizens lined the walkways.

"Look at this crowd," Gemma said. "Unbelievable. You've been an unofficial queen for six weeks and you're already beloved. The whole city turned out to see you off."

"Not the whole city." Çifta mustered smiles and waves that she did not feel. None of the faces smiling at the carriage were the one she needed to see.

Once they passed through the main gates, Çifta couldn't

hold in her tears any longer. She put her kerchief over her eyes and wept silently. Gemma stroked her back.

"Çifta, my minnow," Kazery said in a voice that lifted her gaze, hope burgeoning in her chest. Her father was looking out the window.

Çifta almost lunged forward, sliding the pane back and clinging to the sill, her gaze on the horizon.

Laec and Grex stood upon the hilltop, looking small and distant, but unmistakably them. Laec's long hair blew sideways in the breeze, and Grex tossed his head and stamped one hoof.

"Come to me, please," Çifta whispered, willing him to hear her with his heart.

Laec lifted one arm and she thought he was going to wave, but instead, a bird took flight. Her heart rushed, pounding its rhythm against her eardrums. The crow winged its way toward the carriage, carrying something in its claws.

As it neared, Çifta reached out of the window to grasp the item as it dropped into her hand. Mistik gave a cry, wheeled away and was gone. When Çifta looked up at the hilltop, Laec and Grex were gone too. Her chest hitched and she looked down at the flower in her hand. Fresh, alive, fragrant.

"A camellia," said Gemma. "How beautiful."

Çifta searched for a note attached but there was nothing. "No message," she said, sliding back into her seat.

"On the contrary. Camellias are full of meaning; passionate love, desire, and sexual longing being among them," her sister told her with a sly look.

Kazery shook his head, but was smiling at his strawberry-headed daughter. "Trust Gemma to highlight the amorous side of camellias. They also mean unconditional love, and there is currently no camellia among the Calyx retinue. I'm told it's at the top of Ilishec's wish list."

"Then where did he get it?" Çifta inhaled the soft fragrance of the flower.

"Camellia blooms in the winter," he told her, his big shoulders rocking back and forth as the carriage rolled over a rough patch. "And fall, and early spring. He would have found it in one of the hothouses, I imagine."

"How would you know all that?" Gemma asked, looking at Kazery as she crossed her arms.

Kazery's smile turned secretive and he looked out the window at the city nestled in the valley, growing smaller by the second. "I've learned a thing or two about botany in the last month."

Gemma leapt at the opportunity to push the door their father had opened only a crack. She launched a tirade of questions about Lilac, and injected that if she'd been in Solana much longer, she would have ended up having a dalliance of her own. Specifically with a Calyx named Stephanotis who had deliciously dark eyes to contrast with his wheat-blond hair. Kazery looked immediately regretful that he'd ever said anything, and appropriately scandalized by his daughter's admission.

Though she was interested in the topic, Çifta found it difficult to focus on their conversation. She touched the tender bracts along the stem of the camellia, admiring its multilayered petals. Longing, indeed. Her heart ached, her stomach quivered, and her body warmed as memories of their nights together surged into her imagination. His body, his skin, his scent, his voice, his tenderness, his everything. She closed her eyes as a wave of desire washed over her, then looked out the window at the rolling hills, wondering how many flowers existed that represented patience.

CHAPTER NINE

JESSAMINE

J ESS SAT AT one of the long tables in the dining hall, chin in hand, staring at a pile of opened letters—five to be precise. The owners of the five other apartments in Mandevilla Tower had—after receiving letters from Lord Gillner—responded swiftly. The problem was that none of them claimed responsibility. Worse, they'd never seen such a bonnet and had never heard of Julian Fontana. Beside the letters was a package of brown paper that contained the other bonnets, the ones she'd kept in her wardrobe. She'd examined them again, along with the new one, but the story they told had not changed. They'd all been made by Marion's precise hand, tiny and sweet, to cover the twins' fae ears for reasons still unknown.

Beazle perched in the crook of Jess's elbow, hunched over like a curled-up cat. *We're getting closer, though.*

She smiled. *Ever the optimist.*

But Jess was not feeling optimistic. She picked up the

recently discovered bonnet, stroking her thumb over the soft brim. There was only one question mark remaining, one last chance for a breakthrough: the tenant who had occupied Lord Gillner's apartment. Frustratingly, since Lord Gillner didn't actually know who in Solana managed his property, the letter had to go all the way to Archelia—to Lord Gillner's overseer—who then had to forward the letter to his contact in Solana.

Rose came rushing up to Jess, a little out of breath, and plopped down beside her. "I've got it."

Jess perked up but tried not to let hope penetrate too far into her heart. This path had been littered with disappointment.

Rose handed her an opened letter. "Artie is busy so he asked me to rush this over to you."

Jess took the letter, sliding out the contents. "Do you recognize the tenant?"

Rose shook her head. "Neither did Artie, but that doesn't mean anything. The property manager also included the address that the tenant moved to while the repairs are being done. We can go talk to them."

Jess's pulse quickened as she read the formal language informing her of the identity of the tenant. "V. Irina Salisbury. Never heard of her."

"But look at where she's staying now, Jess." Rose jabbed her finger at the page.

Hope surged in spite of Jess trying to temper it. "The West Keep?"

Rose's blue eyes were bright and hopeful. She grasped Jess's forearm. "Right under our noses. Shall we see if she's home now?"

Jess grabbed the bonnets and headed for the arched exit as Beazle crawled up to sit on Jess's shoulder and Rose looped her hand through the crook of her elbow. They strode from the dining hall at a fast walk. Weaving their way through the flow of traffic that always clogged the corridors after a meal, they crossed to the West Keep and turned down the hallway where many of the Fahyli lived. They stopped at the last door and Rose let Jess prepare herself.

Jess knocked. Heavy footfalls approached the door. When it opened, she looked up into a face that she recognized, a face that she had not seen in a couple of months.

"Mr. Strolight?"

"Hello," the big man grunted, looking down at her.

Jess's mouth opened and closed a few times. She hadn't seen the poison manager's assistant in ages. Rose looked from Jess to Mr. Strolight curiously, squeezing Jess's arm to remind her she was there.

"I-I'm looking for V. Irina Salisbury. I was told she is staying in this suite while her apartment is being repaired. Do you... is she here?"

"Who is it Strolight?" A female voice that Jess knew asked. A moment later, Vivian appeared beside her guard. She looked taken aback by their presence. "Miss Fontana! And Rose. What an unexpected visit. How did you know where to find me?"

Jess's heart was bounding around behind her sternum like a jackrabbit. Her palms had grown clammy. She shoved the paper at Vivian. "Are you V. Irina Salisbury?"

Vivian gave her a curious look as she took the page and skimmed it over. "That was my maiden name. Vivian Irina Salisbury. Why? What is this?"

"Do you recognize this?" Jess held up Julian's baby bonnet.

Vivian's face lit up as she took the cap. "You found it!" She held it to her breast, her eyes shining gratefully. "I thought for sure it had been destroyed, along with so many other things. Thank you so much. This means everything to me."

Jess felt nailed to the floor. She stared at Vivian, her skin prickling, hardly believing her ears. "Vivian…"

Something in her tone brought a worried expression into Vivian's face. "You look like you've seen a phantom. What is it, dear?"

Jess's hands were shaking. Her mouth felt coated with chalk. How could this be?

"Jess?" Rose put a comforting hand on her lower back. "Do you want me to—"

Jess shook her head. Taking the brown package of bonnets out from under her elbow, she handed them to Vivian, who took it, looking mystified. She opened the paper and looked at the pile. She stared at them for a long time, then picked one up and slowly, carefully, turned up the brim. She let out a long exhale as she read the name inside. "Jessica Fontana." She looked up, her expression sharp. "What is this? Where did you get these?"

Jess's voice trembled. "May we come in?"

Vivian stepped to the side, her expression now wary. Rose and Jess entered her suite, a room with thick, blocky furniture and dark masculine accents. It was clear that Vivian was not living here alone; a man's clothing and boots were strewn about the place. A fire crackled in the hearth at the far wall, bracketed on both sides by disorganized bookshelves. Vivian invited them to take one of the wooden seats in front of the fire. Mr. Strolight stood behind Vivian as she sat on a small couch with clawed feet.

"Julian Fontana was my twin," Jess said when they'd settled. Her heart no longer felt like it was going to pound its way out of her chest, but nerves made her hands and knees quake.

Vivian stared at her. For a long time she was silent, unmoving, then she whispered one word, rich with disbelief: "What?"

She seems genuinely confused to me, Beazle told Jess, sniffing the air.

"Where did you get that bonnet?" It took all of Jess's self-control to keep accusation out of her voice.

"It came on the head of my adopted son," Vivian replied, looking like someone had punched her in the stomach.

Jessamine's body felt like it was crawling with ants. "*What?*"

"Mr. Strolight?" Vivian's voice low and serene, though her complexion was ashen.

"Ma'am?" The scarred man straightened.

She didn't look at her servant, but lifted her eyes to Jessamine's. "Would you fetch my husband, please? I don't care what he is in the middle of, tell him this is important."

"Right away." He was out of the suite in a couple of long strides.

"When I married," Vivian told them as the door snicked shut, "my husband was already a father. His son was barely a year old, whom I came to love and legally adopted shortly after our wedding. Lucas has always been like a son of my own womb right from the start."

Jess felt winded. She gripped the arms of her chair, knuckles turning white. "Lucas Peneçek? Digit? Digit is your son? You're married to the crofter?"

Beazle took flight, arrowing for the open window. *I'll be back.*

Vivian watched Beazle go, then drew her gaze back to Jess. "That's right."

"How did—" Jess rubbed her temples. "I don't understand. How did you come to possess my dead twin's bonnet?"

"I'm sure the bonnet is second-hand, my dear. I'm sorry it's gotten you so worked up, and it's remarkable that after all this time you've come across it. My husband always insisted on buying Lucas's baby clothing from second-hand shops. He never believed it was worth it to pay for new clothing because babies grow out of everything so quickly."

Jess could hardly process what she was being told. She was staring at Vivian in shock. Somewhere deep inside she knew she was being rude, but she couldn't rouse the will to care.

Vivian's voice softened, grew thick with compassion. "What happened to Julian?"

"He... he... he was kidnapped when he was nine months old, taken from our home one night. Our neighbors heard the commotion, glass breaking and my mother screaming, but they arrived too late to help."

Vivian's apparent horror convinced Jess that the faceless manager truly didn't know anything about Julian's fate. She went on, finding that the words came more easily now. "My brother was taken by two men who escaped on horseback. Some time later someone submitted a death certificate, claiming that Julian had died of accidental poisoning. My mother believed that I would have been taken as well, but I was hidden in a drawer, along with Beazle, and my brother's familiar, Greta."

Vivian's fingers pressed to her lips. "And, your mother? Who was she?"

"Marion Fontana, but as for who she was, I am honestly not sure. She kept so many secrets from me—including the existence of my twin—that I don't think I ever really knew her. When I joined the Calyx, I learned that flora fae never have two familiars. The only way I could have had two was if I'd had a twin and that twin died young. Often the familiar who is left behind is able to bond with the remaining twin. That's what happened with me and Greta."

The door burst open and Digit rushed into the room, Ania buzzing around him. Beazle entered through the open door and made a beeline for Jess, plopping onto her shoulder. Jess could hear him panting. Digit came over to them, pink spots blossoming on his cheeks. He looked bright-eyed with alarm.

"Ania told me that Beazle told her we were needed here right away, an emergency. Is everything ok?"

Jessamine looked at her friend, a warm feeling blossoming in her chest. "Either you ended up with some of my twin brother's baby clothes by chance, Digit, or you and I are siblings. If the latter is true, then your father has some serious explaining to do."

Digit's eyes grew wide. He looked at his mother, then at Jess, then Rose, then back to Vivian again. "Say what?"

Vivian handed Digit the mystery bonnet. "This was yours as a baby." She handed him the other bonnets. "And these belonged to Jessamine and to her twin, Julian, whom she believes died as a baby. The name tags match. I believe your bonnet came into your father's possession from a second-hand clothing store."

Digit inspected the bonnet that had been found on the grass outside the tower, then the rest. He sank onto the sofa beside Vivian.

"That bonnet has been buried in a trunk for years," she explained, "along with a bunch of other baby things and family heirlooms. The trunk was smashed in the battle and its contents strewn about. Jess found it."

"Snap and Aster did, actually," Jess said. "They brought it straight to me because they had seen the others. They had been with me when I visited the registrar and found my brother's death certificate."

Digit sent Jess a sympathetic look. "I'm so sorry, Jess. How did your brother die?"

"According to the paperwork, he was poisoned… accidentally." Jess's stomach fell flat every time she recalled the handwritten notation on the certificate.

"According to the paperwork?" Vivian raised a brow. "You sound skeptical."

At the same time, Digit spoke: "Accidental *poisoning*?"

Jess and Digit exchanged a look and she knew he was thinking the same thing that she always thought: she exuded deadly toxins through her skin.

The door opened again and the crofter and Mr. Strolight clomped into the room. Strolight shut the door as Ian approached the group, looking cranky and holding a pair of gloves in his hand. "I was in the middle of working with Panther on—" He picked up on the tension in the room and paused. "What is it?"

"We're hoping,"—Vivian took the bonnet from Digit and held it out for her husband—"that you can shed some light on the mystery of this bonnet."

Ian grew still as his gaze dropped to the hat, but he didn't take it. Jess couldn't read Ian's face, couldn't tell if the bonnet had unsettled him, or ruffled him. Finally, he took the article.

"This is Lucas's baby bonnet. I haven't seen it in years. What do you mean 'the mystery of this bonnet'?"

Jess got to her feet, unable to stay seated any longer. Her heart was pounding again. "It's a mystery because it first belonged to my twin, Julian Fontana. As the tag on the inside verifies."

The crofter looked at her, his face reminding her of water

with a huge, submerged creature beneath it. He seemed to struggle with something deep inside himself.

"Darling?" Vivian said softly, getting to her feet as well. "Where did you get this bonnet? Jessamine needs to know, for her peace of mind."

Jess was staring at Ian and he was staring back at her as though seeing her for the first time. It struck Jess with all the force of a battering ram. Digit was poisonous. She was poisonous. They had similar coloring, similar gray eyes. He was her twin. He was Julian, and the truth of it was emerging now on Ian's face.

"It was you." Jess's whisper tore through her throat. Her body warmed, her skin began to prickle. "*It was you*," she repeated, louder this time.

"Jess," Digit warned. "Be careful… your skin."

Jess hardly heard him. A high-pitched buzz had begun in the center of her brain, intensifying by the second.

Ian backed away from her, putting a hand up. "Let me explain, Jess. Give me a moment. Please."

Jess took a step toward him but Mr. Strolight appeared between them. He set a heavy hand on her shoulder and spoke just above a whisper. "Sit down, Miss Fontana."

"Take your hand off me," she told Vivian's henchman, shaking him off. Her voice was full of threat but her gaze was welded to Ian's face.

Digit moved in front of his father, standing protectively between them, his eyes watchful, anticipating her next move. "Don't do anything you'll regret, Jess."

Rose, frozen to her seat by the drama until now, got up and touched Jess lightly through the back of her tunic. "Control yourself. You could hurt all of us."

Rose was right. Jess closed her eyes and turned away from Ian, shutting out his features and trying to control her anger. She went around Rose to stand on the other side of the furniture, a safe distance from the crofter, then faced Ian and Digit again. Angry tears gathered in her eyes. Angry, and confused. There were other emotions, too. Julian was not dead after all. He was alive and here in this room with her. Her only remaining family.

"Are you Digit's biological father?" she asked.

Vivian had moved to stand beside Ian, her eyes huge; one hand was on her stomach, like she was feeling sick. She braced the other hand on the back of a chair, looking back and forth from Jessamine to her son and her husband. She was a woman who had been blindsided. It was abundantly clear to Jess that whatever Ian had done, Vivian was innocent.

"Yes." Ian's voice was husky, his gaze filling with pain. "And yours too. I never knew… I never knew she had two babies."

Jess gasped, lifting her hands to her ears to block out Ian's confession. She dropped to her knees, feeling ill, then lowered her face toward the floor. She'd resigned herself to Julian being dead, to being without family save for Beazle. That Julian was alive, and a friend, and that it was the crofter who was guilty… their father, it was all too much. She could feel Beazle crawling through her hair, he was in shock too, but his main concern was her.

Jess! Jess! Focus on me! Beazle urged. *I'm here. Focus on me.*

Rose rushed to Jess's side, putting an arm around her, uncaring of any risk, unknowing if Jess had accidentally leaked something poisonous. "Breathe, love. Breathe."

Her fingers knotted into her hair, Jess stayed crouched on the floor. It was all she could do to breathe without screaming on every exhale. Her body was shaking.

"Jess, please don't." She heard Ian's voice, he'd moved nearer to her, his tone was pleading. "Please listen. I'll tell you everything."

"You'd better," said Vivian.

Another body came to her other side, and at first she thought it was Vivian, but the hand that took hers, the fingers that wove through hers, were Digit's. He leaned in close, squeezing her hand. His arm slipped around her and he kissed the side of her head then put his forehead to her temple.

"Sister," he whispered.

The word went through her like a warm wind. She closed her eyes and leaned against him.

"Brother," she whispered back, feeling less cold, less fragile. It was like finding footing in rough, shallow seas.

He squeezed her against himself. After several long moments of embracing her, and no one speaking, Digit said so that only she, Beazle and Rose could hear: "He's not evil. I can promise you that. There is an explanation. Let's hear it together. We'll be hearing it for the first time, and I'm here with you. I'm your family."

Jess wiped the tears from her face and straightened, nodding. Digit helped her stand. She lifted her blurry gaze to Ian's face once more. He waited awkwardly behind the couch, his expression as soft and agonized as she'd ever seen.

"Daughter," he said, sounding broken.

"Don't call me that," she said, sounding calmer than she felt. "You have no right to call me that. Not until you tell the truth. All of it."

He swallowed and gave a single nod. "I certainly owe you that. Yes. I'm not saying I haven't made mistakes, but when you hear the whole story, you'll understand why I did what I did. I would have taken you as well as Julian if I had known she'd had twins."

Jess was about to remind him that the woman he had impregnated had a name, but what Hanna had told her that Marion had said while drunk one night came whispering malignantly into her mind: *"She said that if she ever told me the truth that I would hate her, that everyone would hate her. That she'd be run out of town."*

The memory kept Jessamine's rebuke behind her teeth, because whatever Ian was guilty of, Marion had also done something that she was ashamed of. Something so horrific that she believed she deserved to be hated and exiled. Jess was too upset to take a seat, so she wrapped her arms around herself, happy for the presence of Beazle, Digit and Rose. She stayed where she was.

"Start talking, Ian," she said to her father.

Ian pulled in a breath so deep he seemed to double in size, then raked a hand through his hair. "It's a long story, and parts of it are so tragic they are almost unbelievable. I would much rather show you, if you'll give me that chance."

"What do you mean, show us?" Digit asked.

The crofter looked from Jess's face to Digit's and back again. "Your mother's name wasn't Marion, at least not when I met her. It was Tansy Littlehale, and she was a flora fae from Nasyk. It would seem your desire to visit Nasyk was well founded."

Jess sucked in a sharp breath. All the moments where Marion had dubiously eyed Beazle and Greta came rushing in like a crowd of ghosts. She had once wondered if Marion had had a familiar and lost it. How else could her aversion to Jess's beloved creatures be explained? Marion hadn't shown the same subtle hostility toward wild creatures.

"What was her familiar?" Jess asked in a throaty voice.

"Please," Ian said quietly. "Let me take you to Nasyk. It's important that you see some things with your own eyes."

We should go, Jess. Beazle licking her neck, just under her ear. *It might make it easier to hear whatever he has to say.*

Jess closed her eyes and took a few moments to breathe. Then she looked at the faces staring back at her. Vivian, looking shocked and worried, wondering who her husband really was in his soul. Ian, pleading and sorry. Strolight, waiting patiently for the plan to unfold. Julian, who looked at her with amazement and curiosity all over his face. Marion hadn't just been Jess's mom, she'd been Digit's as well, and he was just as invested as she was in learning the truth. The full truth.

"Fine," she told Ian. "I'll let Ilishec know I need to go away for a couple of days. When do we leave?"

PART TWO

CHAPTER TEN

JESSAMINE

THEY RODE THROUGH pretty pastoral land of rolling green hills and pockets of trees. Vivian and Ian rode side by side at the front, Digit and Jess behind them, with Mr. Strolight bringing up the rear. While Jess observed the panorama, she felt at peace, seeing the signs of spring everywhere. Whenever her gaze fell on Ian's back, anger bubbled up inside of her.

Jess broke the silence with the first thing that came to mind. "Mother was forty-nine when we were born."

"You've said." He gave her a tentative, lopsided smile. "I see steam coming from your ears whenever you look at him. I understand, don't get me wrong, you're justified in your anger. But you don't know Ian like I know him."

She looked away. "I never got that chance, no."

Ania buzzed up to Digit, hovering in front of his face before buzzing off again to explore. Passing through a beam of light made her patch of purple feathers sparkle. Digit watched her go, his voice gentle. "I'm just saying, we don't yet know who's at fault for what. He's not perfect, but he is a good person. He's had a hard life."

Jess didn't doubt that. Marion had also had a hard life. People who were excessively secretive were like that for a reason—most hiding something shameful or traumatic from their past. This was clearly the case with her mother. This was why Marion never spoke of Jess's father, never uttered his name and hardly acknowledged his existence. Not Marion... Tansy. Tansy Littlehale, from Nasyk. She could hardly equate the name with the woman who had raised her. It sounded so bizarre that she shook her head. It was even more bizarre to think of her mother as flora fae, all evidence of her once magical nature wiped away by age.

Beazle stretched under her loose bun, coming out of her hair to ride on her shoulder.

You never suspected we were related to Digit? Jess asked him, without accusation. *His smell never triggered a memory, or anything?*

Babies smell a lot different than mature flora fae do. Going off milk changes a child's smell, but it's nothing compared to how much maturity changes a person's scent. Digit smells nothing like Julian did as an infant. Same with you. Sometimes I miss that smell, Beazle thought wistfully. *You smelled of milk and the chamomile that Marion washed your blankets with. Pure baby.*

And Greta never gave you any indication once we were at court?
You know Greta didn't communicate like that, Jess.

She did know that. She also knew that Greta and Digit had never been in the same room together. Even if they had, their bond had been broken long ago. Greta had re-bonded to Jess, and been replaced by Ania. There was no going back.

I know you're trying to find reasons why we couldn't figure it out on our own, Beazle whispered gently. *Some things can't be figured until their time has come.*

Her lips twitched. *How did you get so wise?*

I was born with bat wisdom. He yawned and snapped his jaws shut with a quiet snick. *It's a burden but someone has to bear it.*

She smiled, looking out at the fields. Shafts of sunlight pushed down through gray clouds, setting green spotlights on the hillsides and valleys.

"So what made Ian's life so hard?" Jess asked her brother.

Digit slowed his horse a fraction, giving them a little more distance between them and their father. "He had two wives before Vivian."

Jess shot him a sharp look.

"Not including Tansy, if they were married. I didn't know about her… obviously."

"You thought Vivian was your biological mother?"

"No." His nostrils flared as he exhaled.

Jess wondered if he was angrier than he was letting on. By keeping his own wrath under control, he encouraged Jess to do the same, and it was working. Jess had no desire to be the hysterical twin. Already she felt some sense of good-natured sibling rivalry with Digit. Maybe she'd always felt it with him.

His jaw flexed as he bit down, thinking before speaking again. "I thought my mother died of an illness after child-birth. Now I know that Ian's second wife, Honor—the woman I believed gave birth to me—actually died of a miscarriage well before you and I were conceived. And before her… long before her, his first wife—according to Vivian, the love of his life—was found floating in a deep millpond. She was returning home from market and the horse pulling her wagon spooked and went out of control. When she hit the bridge, a wheel hooked the railing and she was thrown. She couldn't swim, and she was wearing thick skirts. Help came too slowly to save her."

"What was her name?" Jess asked.

"I don't know." Digit rubbed his chin.

Ania zipped up to him, landing on his shoulder. She gave a cheep, and ruffled her feathers before squatting, her little claws disappearing under her. Jess wondered if she was talking to him.

"I asked Vivian," he continued, "but she doesn't know either because Father never talks about her. He was in Archelia when it happened. Came home to a buried wife."

Jess shrank away from the knowledge, shrank away from the inclination to soften with sympathy for the man who had kidnapped her twin, split them up shortly after birth, and broke Marion's heart. Whatever his story was, it had better be good, no matter how much pain was in his past. It had better plug all the holes and wash away every last vestige of anger, because what she and Digit had missed out on, and what Marion had endured… it was too much.

A sign pronounced that Nasyk was eight miles ahead.

Jess took a shaky breath and spoke harshly. "Okay, so Ian has had tragedy in his life. We've all had tragedy in our lives. It doesn't give anyone the right to go around violently breaking up families."

"Obviously."

Jess looked away, feeling sheepish. This wasn't Digit's fault.

"Why don't you tell me about Marion and Greta." Digit shifted in his saddle, rubbing the inside of his knee.

Jess was happy for this more pleasant distraction. Digit's justifications of his father's behavior, if that's what they were, got her back up. She couldn't think of Ian as *her* father, there was a huge gap of empty space between how she felt about him now and calling him Father.

Jess told Digit as many happy memories about Marion and Greta as she could. She told him about life in Dagevli, their root vegetable business, and their pony, Apple. She described the town, the people, Clair and Hanna and Tad. She emphasized how quiet and peaceful it was. How neighbors would happily lend a hand, share food from their gardens, and look after each other's children. She hoped that Digit could see just how horrible the night of his kidnapping would have been for Marion and their neighbors to endure. Such a burst of violence would have scarred the whole town. Ian had resorted to criminal activity. And why? Because he'd had tragedy in his family and couldn't handle not having custody of his child? Why couldn't he use the court system and go through the proper channels to get what he wanted?

Jess realized they'd arrived only when Ian and Vivian dismounted and began leading their horses on foot toward what looked like an old graveyard. Beyond the cemetery was Nasyk, a quaint farming village that looked poorer than Dagevli. No house had a second story, and all of the stone buildings looked perilously cobbled together.

Digit and Jessamine dismounted and followed Vivian and Ian, though Mr. Strolight remained on the road. A figure moved stiffly through the graveyard, picking up brush and brambles, and pulling up weeds. The headstones were only half visible in a sea of long grass; graceful stone arches emerging like breaching whales.

Ian raised a hand to the figure in greeting, stopping on the overgrown doubletrack that wound around the graveyard and snaked over the hills beyond. The figure paused to stare for a moment, as though trying to determine whether he knew the crofter or not. He decided that he did, and lifted a hand in greeting. The elderly human male had a newsboy cap perched on his head, with tufts of iron-gray hair flicking out from beneath it. He waded through the vegetation, pushing a stick out in front of him to clear a path. He had a thin navy scarf, heavily pilled, shrouding the bottom half of his face. A worn quilted shirt hugged his torso, and his baggy trousers were tucked into boots with old uppers but new soles. His look said that he made everything he owned last as long as it possibly could.

"Mr. Peneçek," the man said in a dry voice. He looked neither happy nor unhappy to see Ian. He shook hands with the crofter. "Never 'spected to see you round these parts again."

The man's name was Mr. Tender—fitting for someone whose job it was to tend the graveyard, and apparently all of the public spaces around Nasyk.

"What can I do for you, Ian?" Mr. Tender asked.

"These are my twins." Ian gestured to Jess and Digit. "Children I had with Tansy."

Mr. Tender's rheumy gaze flicked from the crofter to the flora fae twins, holding the reins of their horses and patiently waiting for the point of this visit to make itself known.

"That explains the bird." Mr. Tender stuffed a hand in a pocket, jerking his chin at Ania. "Never knew she had another family. Thing like that—" He shook his head, tsking. "Such a bad business. Very bad business."

"It's a difficult conversation, I know," Ian said, "but necessary. Jessamine and Lucas need to know their mother's history, and she took it to her grave. I thought it would be best coming from you, since you were there."

Mr. Tender produced a toothpick from his pocket, put it in his mouth and began to chew as he considered Ian's request. He leaned one elbow on the top of a rotting post that might once have been part of a gate. "What do they know?"

"Nothing." Ian switched his reins from one hand to another, stroking his animal's chin.

Jess didn't know how the crofter could be so calm. Her heart felt like it had journeyed down into the region of her belt and back up again since this conversation had started. This human had been there... for what?

For the thing that Marion said she'd be hated for. Beazle stayed hidden in her hair but was no longer asleep. He had no desire to show himself to this stranger, though his ears were perked for Mr. Tender's every word.

"You'd better come in for some tea 'n' biscuits, in that case." The old man turned toward the main road. He poked the grass in front of his feet with his stick. "'S'not the kind of story one should hear or tell on an empty stomach, or standing out here in the damp. The missus will have a pot on."

Jess and Digit exchanged a look as they followed the strange little man back to the road.

"Have care. The snakes like the long grasses," he said over his shoulder.

Right. This place is known for snakes. Beazle shrank against her skull at the thought of one of his most feared predators. He was doubly happy for his choice to stay inside her hair. *Tad told us that.*

I remember.

Keeping their eyes on the grass for movement, they made it back to the bare dirt road. Mr. Tender walked ahead, rather than beside Ian. Jess assumed they weren't friends. She suspected that Mr. Tender might not be that happy to see the crofter, though he was being perfectly polite. He led them to the second cottage in town, showing them a paddock at the rear of his property where the horses could be released to eat and drink.

He led them in through the back door of his home and they all had to duck so as not to hit their heads on the low beam. The cottage was cozy warm, impeccably kept and smelled of fresh baking. A little woman in a frilly cap and a patched skirt stood at the stove, pouring hot water from a bucket into a kettle.

"What's this now?" she said in a high-pitched, nasal voice as a parade of strangers followed her husband into their home. "Ye've found a long-lost soul, and brought fae in with yerself. Is it a good luck day, Mr. Tender? Well come, Mr. Peneçek."

"Well found, Mrs. Tender." Ian nodded to the woman.

Her husband doffed his cap and hung it on one of the pegs behind the door. "Not sure about the luck, Mrs. Tender."

The lady shot her husband an enigmatic look, which he ignored.

"Take a seat," he told them. "Anywhere as suits you."

The table was oval, hugged by a deep window-well full of herbs in flowerpots. A bench seat followed the wall, curving around the table and making a kind of booth. Jess and Digit slid onto the bench, followed by Vivian and Mr. Tender. Ian took one of the wooden chairs, pulling it up to the table to sit, placing his gloves on his knee. Mr. Strolight had stayed outside with the horses, which was just as well. His presence unsettled Jess, and this wasn't his business anyway.

"Sorry to disturb you," Ian said to Mrs. Tender as she delivered a stack of mismatched teacups to the table.

"Ye've disturbed nothing but the dead," she replied.

Jess couldn't tell if this response alarmed anyone else but herself and Beazle.

"These are my children," said Ian.

Mrs. Tender's gray brows jumped up. "Oh?"

"Had 'em with Tansy," Mr. Tender added, setting the teacups out for pouring.

"That's a bad business." Mrs. Tender tsked exactly the way her husband had earlier.

Jess and Digit exchanged a bewildered look. Jess began to feel like she was shrinking inside, like the anger she'd been so carefully nursing had lost some of its teeth in a fistfight. What was this business that was so bad?

Mrs. Tender went to the stove and brought the kettle over to the table to fill the teacups.

"Wants me to tell 'em," said Mr. Tender with a jerk of his chin toward the twins.

"You knew this day might come," his wife replied as she returned the kettle to the stove.

His bushy eyebrows twitched. "Did I?"

Mrs. Tender brought over a basket covered with a tea towel, setting it in the middle of the table. "You were the first one on the scene, dear." She looked at Vivian. "We were Tansy and Andrew's neighbors. Mr. Tender was the first to hear the screaming. Golly, what an awful thing." She shook her head.

"I'm sure," Vivian murmured, looking sure of nothing. She took a sip, burying her discomfort behind her teacup.

"You lived beside our mother?" Jess asked, unable to bear the what-a-tragedy talk any longer. "And who was Andrew?"

"Her husband, of course." Mrs. Tender spoke as though surprised Jess didn't know Andrew. "Those two were the lovebirds of town for a little while. Them and their two beautiful children."

Jess felt Digit take her hand, which was good because it stopped Jess from shrieking: children?!

Mrs. Tender seemed to hiccup or hitch a breath. She grabbed the edge of her apron and lifted it to her lips, whether overcome by emotion or gastro upset, Jess couldn't tell.

"Children?" Digit squeezed her hand. "We have two half-siblings?"

"If'n they were alive they'd be... what?" Mr. Tender looked at his wife inquisitively. She was no good to him, still hiding behind her apron.

But the missus soon rallied. "They'd be in their mid-forties by now. Can't remember their birth date."

"Twins?" Digit asked.

"'S'right. Twins." Mr. Tender nodded. "Called 'em Elwin and Elsie, so they did. Beautiful half-faelings. Never saw Andrew so delighted and proud in all his life as he was when he pulled those wee ones in their little green wagon on market day. Tansy beautiful at his side with them copper curls."

"Tansy and Andrew married when Tansy was only seventeen," Ian interjected, which prompted Mr. Tender to go back to the beginning.

"'S'right." Mr. Tender pulled back the towel over the basket to reveal a pile of fresh crumpets. "Bring the plates, would you, missus?"

Mrs. Tender bustled about, bringing a stack of plates and knives to the table. She lay a fabric napkin in front of each of them. No matter how nice the baking smelled, Jess couldn't possibly put food in her mouth, and disagreed heartily with Mr. Tender that his story was best told on a full stomach.

"Was our mother born here?" Digit asked.

"Born and raised," she said, topping up Vivian's tea. "The only flora fae we've had in more'n a hundred years, and most of us be thankful for that after what happened. Butter?"

Ian nodded, looking ill, and Mrs. Tender fetched butter from a small icebox under her sink.

"Tansy and Andrew were poor, same as all of us, but they were happy." Mr. Tender took a sip of tea. "They had their faelings and their tumbledown cottage. No one saw either of the Littlehales without a smile on their face. Nasyk is a simple, humble place, but we knew we had something unusual in our company: a flora fae with a butterfly for a pet."

She had a butterfly, Beazle murmured, as Greta came into both their minds.

The missus nodded as she slid into the booth beside her husband, causing them all to shuffle over. She pulled a plate toward herself and plopped a crumpet on it, dusting off her fingertips. "Papilio, that's what she called him when she got older. Afore that, he didn't have a name. I remember because she explained to me that the queen's fae, the fancy ones that dance at court and all that, they use some official way to name their bugs. Tansy looked it up in some book and chose Papilio's name the same way, like she was one of them. One of the courtly fae, I mean. I think she had designs on a position."

Jessamine's recall of botanical names was pretty sharp, but her memory for pollinator genus was patchy at best. The name Papilio did not bring any particular species to mind.

Mr. Tender picked at his teeth with his toothpick, though he hadn't touched the biscuits. "Thought her plant was parsnip, so she did. Her magic kicked in after the twins were born, and lands, she was proud. Thought she might attend Discovery one day and show them at the palace what she could do."

"That's what I meant by designs." Mrs. Tender tapped on the tabletop with a blunt, calloused finger.

Her husband nodded. "First she was sad because her plant wasn't a pretty flower. She cried, thinking the queen would never be interested in someone who could only bring up an ugly root vegetable."

Her expression turned impossibly sorrowful. "Wishes he'd a never said such a thing to her now, yes he does."

Mr. Tender patted his wife's hand absently and explained. "Neighbor on her other side at the time, Mr. Werther, told her, 'Cheer up. At least you'll always be able to feed your family.'"

A tear streaked down the missus's cheek and she brushed it away. "Shoulda never said such a thing."

Jess felt like she was dematerializing, dissipating like a punctured chromatype.

I have a very bad feeling about what he's about to say, Beazle thought.

Me too. I don't know if I can hear this. But she didn't move. She couldn't.

"She didn't know any better," Mr. Tender was saying, shaking his head. "'Course she didn't. She was just a peasant. If it looks like a parsnip and smells like a parsnip, it's a parsnip."

"But it wasn't parsnip," Jess whispered. Her botanical studies had given her everything she needed to recall the poisonous plant that shared many characteristics with the parsnip plant. "It was *cicuta*, commonly known as cowbane."

"'S'right, and aren't you a bright one." Mr. Tender nodded at her with approval. "Her entire family was dead within hours of eating the mash she prepared for them from her own magic. The twins weren't yet four."

"First they was sick." She sniffed and rubbed her nose. "Then they was dead, and she started screaming. Couldn't stop. And that's when Mr. Tender came upon them, all three of them looking like they'd died in agony, and Tansy beside herself and hysterical."

Jess closed her eyes and bowed her head. She felt Digit put his arm around her shoulders, squeezing her into his side, pressing his temple into hers. This was hard for both of them, but Digit never knew Marion. He couldn't picture her as a young woman, a young flora fae, accidentally killing her entire family when she only meant to feed them.

Jess covered her face as her eyes poured over. Puzzle pieces were clicking into place, the mystery of her family was coming together—things she'd been wanting to know for such a long time—she just hadn't expected the picture to be such an ugly one, even with Marion's shame.

"I'm sorry, dearie," Mrs. Tender said.

Jess wiped her face and looked up at the elderly couple, both of them looking at her with compassion. "Then what happened?"

Some unspoken communication passed between them, perhaps a decision about who would tell her what had come next. Apparently, Mr. Tender was chosen. "They arrested her, of course. Soldiers took her away, put her in a cell in the basement of the old gaol with only her monarch for company."

A monarch butterfly, Jess nodded as it clicked into place. *Papilio was a monarch.*

A monarch is perfect for Marion, added Beazle. *So regal.*

Jess agreed. The beautiful species suited Marion so well that it brought more tears to Jess's eyes. Only humans who had no idea just how much a familiar meant to a flora fae could toss out a familiar's species like it was as meaningless as a pair of socks.

"Course, the monarch never made it out of the cell," Mr. Tender continued. "I suspect she did it because she knew her magic would die with him."

"Maybe she even blamed him," Mrs. Tender added as an afterthought. "But I don't think so. I think she did it to punish herself. He represented her flora fae magic, and because of it, her whole family died. With him gone, she'd never be able to poison anyone again."

Jess clenched her hand over Digit's as they both stiffened. Digit sucked in a breath, and Ania crawled beneath the collar of his shirt with a sad whistle.

Beazle shook with terror under Jess's hair. *Are they telling us that Marion killed Papilio while they were in the gaol?*

Jess couldn't answer, she was so horrified. She tried to swallow down the lump blocking her throat. Her stomach began to quiver and she wondered if she might be sick.

"There was a trial," Mr. Tender went on, seemingly unaware of the twins' reaction. "The whole town came out for it. Tansy was found not guilty, because she wasn't guilty of murder; 'twas an accident. She looked so miserable, and the judge felt sorry for her. We all did. There was no way he'd throw her in prison on top of such a loss."

His wife injected: "Don't leave out that she'd also cooked her own vegetable and eaten it before she served it to her faelings. She thought she did enough." She spread her hands, repeating emphatically: "They looked just like parsnips! I saw them myself!"

"But a poisonous botanical is never poisonous to the fae

who can produce it," Digit said, looking heartsick. "Nor is it poisonous to their familiar."

"Right." Mr. Tender nodded, jabbing a finger at the table. "*Now* we know that, but back then, no one in Nasyk knew that. Tansy never had anyone to teach her about herself or her magic. She was orphaned at a young age. We don't even know if only one of her parents was fae, or both were. But we all knew that Tansy'd never have done such a thing on purpose. I don't think she cared what happened to her, they could have thrown her in prison for life, she wouldn't have fought it. She might have even preferred that, but she was given her freedom and returned home." He shook his head. "I buried her kin in that graveyard myself."

Jess felt like her heart was full of lead. Her own half-siblings, and Marion's first husband—supposedly the love of her life—rested near where her feet had stood an hour ago.

Poor Marion. Beazle wilted against the base of Jessamine's neck.

"She didn't stay in Nasyk long though. Not after that. Couldn't bear living here anymore," said Mrs. Tender, taking a sip of her tea and setting her cup down. She broke her crumpet into pieces and put a morsel in her mouth. "Also the townsfolk treated her different, frightened of her, they were. Came close to shunning her, they did."

"She disappeared for a while," Mr. Tender told them. "Long time. Years. No one knows where she went. No one thought she'd come back. But she did. She cleaned up her cottage what sat empty for s'long, and moved back in. She never tried to sell it. She knew no one would buy it, not with what had happened in there. So it just sat quiet-like till she came home."

"Told me she was homesick, but who knows what that

woman had been through." The missus ate another piece of biscuit. "Homesick was probably the least of her pains."

"Yuh." Mr. Tender nodded. "She kept herself to herself, worked hard, grew squash and potatoes. Her ears, what were so pointy at one time, went all soft. She looked just like one of us. You'd never know she had fae blood."

That makes you all fae, Jess, Beazle realized. *Not half.*

In answer, Jess put her hand back to the lump under her hair and gave him a loving stroke.

Mrs. Tender nodded at Ian. "Then Nasyk won a flower festival, and that's where you came into her life."

Ian folded his hands on the table. "I wasn't the crofter then."

"The two of you seemed so happy," Mr. Tender said.

The crofter looked down at his hands, expression drawn. "We were. For a while."

Mrs. Tender perked up. "It was nice seeing her fall in love again. After all, it was more'n twenty-five years since the tragedy and Tansy deserved a little happiness. Only the older townsfolk even remembered what had happened. Of course the story was passed down to the next generation, the way things like that are, and with embroidery, I'm sure. But Tansy was happy again, or at least it seemed so, even though she was viewed as an outsider in her own home village. She didn't mind, not after she had you, Ian."

"You know the rest." Mr. Tender pushed his back against the rear of the booth. "Is that all you wanted me to tell 'em?"

Ian nodded. "Thank you. We won't occupy any more of your time. I have my side to explain, but we don't need to do that in your home."

"We wouldn't mind—" Mrs. Tender stopped as everyone followed the crofter's lead and got up from the table.

Obviously Ian didn't want to tell his side of the story in front of his old acquaintances. And no wonder, it was nothing to be proud of.

Jess followed her party outside as Mr. Strolight gathered their horses. They thanked the Tenders and Ian mounted. When Ian began heading back toward Solana City like he couldn't get away from Nasyk soon enough, Jess urged Kitabee to catch up to him.

"I'd show you her cottage, if you wanted to see it," Ian told her, "but it's someone else's home now."

She wasn't sure she wanted to see the house where her mother's entire previous family had died such a tragic death. "So, now what?"

Ian glanced at the evening sky. "Before we left, I sent a request to book rooms at that country inn we passed on the way here. I'll tell you the rest after we get the horses settled for the night and have dinner."

Jess nodded, satisfied. The inn was less than an hour's ride toward Solana. She had waited a long time to know these things; she could endure one more hour.

CHAPTER ELEVEN

LAEC

SHOUTS CAME FROM the lion's den, Laec could hear them down the hall even with the den's doors shut. He paused, checking a clock to verify that it was in fact still before breakfast—too early for the monarchs to be having a meltdown, but that's exactly what it sounded like.

Laec had gotten up before the sun, scrubbed himself raw, and washed his hair with the specialty soap that came as part of the violet suite's collection of toiletries. The brand name Perfumery of Solana was emblazoned in a flowery script across the label. He'd never used it before, preferring the unscented soap he could get from Ilishec, but this morning he'd lathered his whole body with its contents, as though it might wash away any remaining lethargy and mark a change in his attitude. Today he would fervently re-commit to Solana, wholeheartedly and with all the passion of a zealot. In it to win it. If he wasn't going to see Çifta until whatever dark cloud hovering over this place was obliterated, then he'd obliterate it single-handedly if he had to. Part of his new strategy to liberate Solana was to present himself to the king and queen… again—and to the crofter, Laec thought with chagrin—as wholly at their service.

Trailing the smell of violets down the corridor, Laec had gone in search of Hob. The steward held control of the king and queen's schedule, and Laec would have a better chance of getting a few minutes of their time today if he registered his request before breakfast. Hob was rarely in his office—a small clerk's closet down the hall from the lion's den—but the earlier the hour, the higher the likelihood that that's where he'd be. That's where Laec was heading when he heard shouting: King Agir's tenor, stretched as tight as a cello string.

Laec nodded at the soldier standing guard outside the den. He was about to ask if Hob was inside when Ilishec came bustling up the hallway, running his fingers through his long hair, still wet from his own morning ritual.

"Morning, Uncle." He gestured to the den. "Sounds like a crisis."

Ilishec pulled a leather wrap from his pocket and tied his hair back, missing several strands. "Morning, Laec. Glad to see you're already here. Shall we?"

Laec was mystified that Ilishec was already aware of the king's displeasure, but before he could get any further information, the soldier opened the door and Laec was herded in.

A company of Solanans clustered around the table beneath the windows, the king at its head, the queen at its foot, but no one was seated. A piece of parchment lay on the table, curled up like a dead beetle. Laec was surprised to see Princess Isabey and Shade among the group. Captain Bradburn and even Sasha were there too, among a number of senior Fahyli. Laec greeted Regalis, Kite and Panther with a nod. If their familiars were present, they were nowhere in sight. Neither was the crofter. Everyone looked tense. The gardener squeezed into the only space left around the table, and Laec went to stand beside Sasha, who stood back from the group, his place as a foreigner reinforced.

"Stavarjak." Sasha nodded in greeting, his arms crossed over his chest. The Silverfae looked like he'd been up for hours, his pale gaze alert, his silvery-blond hair brushed and gleaming.

"Silverfall," Laec returned, in what had become their customary greeting. "Where is the crofter?"

"He's gone to Nasyk with Jess," Sasha told him under his breath. "She said they'll be back tomorrow. Digit's with them."

"What's in Nasyk?"

"I'm not sure. Jess left in a hurry, saying she'd tell me everything when they got back. Something to do with her family." The Silverfae's eyes clouded with worry at the mention of Jess, which made Laec worry.

"She okay?"

Sasha shrugged. "She seemed upset but she couldn't talk about it before she left. I hope so. Captain Bradburn sent a familiar with a message about this mess…" He jutted his chin at the table where conversation seemed to have stalled. Everyone looked uncomfortable except for the king, who looked furious.

"What do you want to do, Sire?" Captain Bradburn asked after a lengthy silence.

"You tell me, Bradburn," the king snapped, pacing along the windows, but turning back abruptly, throwing an arm out in frustration. "You're my counselors. Tell me, is there a precedent for this type of thing? No. It's never happened before, not in more than five hundred years of history. It's appalling, and cannot possibly be legal."

"I'm not sure Prince Faraçek is concerned with the legality

of it, at least not where Solanan law is concerned," injected Panther, leaning against a windowsill. He seemed to remember himself and shifted to stand upright. He had the beginnings of a dark beard forming along his jaw.

"Perhaps that is where we should start," suggested Esha. She wore a soft-looking long-sleeved gown the color of a new fawn, complete with random white speckles. With her large fey eyes, hugging her elbows to her ribs, she looked a little fawn-like herself.

Agir braced his hands on the back of a chair, his head sinking into his shoulders as he leaned forward. He gripped and twisted the tops of the chair's stiles like they were jar-caps he wished to pry off. "What do you mean, dearest?"

"I suggest we invite Prince Faraçek to meet us on neutral ground, somewhere in the common lands. We don't reply to this..." She gestured at the letter that lay on the table, "these... threats. We ask for a face-to-face, and we present our case calmly, rationally, from a legal perspective."

"That's the only recourse we have," muttered Bradburn with a nod. He yanked out a chair and plopped into it, though the monarchs hadn't yet sat. It was a testament to how ruffled he was that he forgot the usual decorum. Agir and Esha either didn't notice or didn't care.

Laec moved closer to the table to peer at the letter. The king saw him looking, picked it up and handed it to him. Laec took it and moved into the morning light to read the message. He didn't get very far before discovering that the king and queen's last name—which Laec hadn't even known because it wasn't the custom in most kingdoms in Ivryndi to use the family names of royalty—had been used in place of their official titles. It wasn't a good start, purposefully disrespectful. Like a thumbing of the nose.

Agir & Esha Aelham of Solana,

This is your formal invitation to the coronation of King Faraçek of Rahamlar. You are invited to join citizens and nobility as we celebrate the crowning of our new monarch. The event will take place on the 12th day of Šest at noon in the main courtyard of the Rahamlar Fortress. We require a response within the week.

Further to your invitation, and in light of your recent silence, the offer of a duchy including country lands located in a Solanan region of your choosing has been amended. King Faraçek now offers you a marquessates with an estate that will be chosen for you by HRHoR at a time to be determined post-coronation. The amended offer shall remain valid until Petri 12, at which time, if it has not been accepted, it will (without further notice) be reduced to an earldom on Petri 17, falling to viscountship five days later on Petri 22, then to a barony on Šest 5. After the coronation, the offer of a title will be withdrawn, and the amalgamation of Solana's lands will commence.

We humbly encourage you to accept the king's generous offer, which will prevent the suffering of Solanan citizens during the amalgamation process. Upon acceptance, and your official pledges of allegiance to Rahamlar, any Solanan citizen who follows suit and pledges allegiance to their new king will be permitted to remain on their property, and retain legal ownership of all their assets. Anyone who does not wish to pledge allegiance must leave the Solanan region or they will be arrested and tried for treason.

Your humble servant,

Dracwald Blueden,

Honorable Attorney at Law

Kingdom of Rahamlar

Laec had to read the letter twice before the depth of its threats sank in. He became aware that the room was watching him. He looked around at his cohorts, who seemed to be expecting him to say something.

"Ambitious, isn't he?"

King Agir glowered. "What would Queen Elphame do if her neighboring sovereign made such threats?"

Laec wouldn't say the response that came to mind: that no one would dare send such a letter to Elphame, not even Sylifke.

Queen Esha saved him from having to answer, hugging herself as though cold. "He already offered us the duchy, now he has downgraded us, and will continue to downgrade us every five days until the moment of his coronation, when we will become—in his eyes—traitors. And he's using the safety of our own citizens as leverage against us."

"Who outside of this room is aware of this?" Laec asked.

"No one," she replied.

King Agir covered his face with his hands for a long moment, before pulling them away, leaving white handprints in his flushed cheeks.

"This is a threat against the entire kingdom," Bradburn said unnecessarily. "I hope that it will not need a military answer, but from where I'm sitting, that's the only kind that comes to mind. Unless of course you plan to actually consider his mad offer?"

"Don't be absurd," the king snapped.

Queen Esha put a hand out. "Let's not discuss military involvement just yet." She looked at Princess Isabey. "My dear princess, you've been quiet so far in the face of this. Do you not have any suggestions regarding your brother's letter? You're in a far better position to shed light on this situation than anyone else present. You know him."

The princess looked at Shade, who gave a look in answer that seemed to say *go ahead*.

Isabey let out a long exhale. "Once Faraçek gets an idea, especially one to do with power or position, he isn't easily shaken of it. I can only tell you what I think his rationale is, now that I know he has a son. His actions make more sense in light of my nephew. Although unknown, there is power in Toryan's crown. Faraçek will have confidence that, once crowned, the lands that Toryan once ruled can be repossessed by her heir. He will want them for his own son, and to return the entirety of Rahamlar's former lands to unseelie rule. If he is successful, he will have done something that no unseelie heir before him was able to manage since Toryan. If I were you,"—she looked around at the group—"I would take Queen Esha's suggestion to heart, try the legal route first. These lands were officially bequeathed to Erasmus by Iskandar. The story is well known. If you have kept the original documents…"

"Of course we have." But then the king threw an uncertain look at his wife. "We have, right?"

Esha nodded.

"Then I think you've presented a wise and logical first step," Isabey told Esha. "Ask to meet my brother in person. Take your most competent lawyers. Try to find out what has changed to make Faraçek think he has the right to reverse the original agreement. Re-commit to the stewardship that has been passed down to you by blood. Something like this…" She indicated the letter Laec had returned to the tabletop. "Even neighboring kingdoms may take exception to this type of… interference."

"And what about you, personally?" Esha pushed, her steady

gaze still on the princess. "You are the rightful heir. Have you come to any decisions about your inheritance? I cannot believe you honestly intend to reject your birthright."

Isabey swallowed. "The problem, Ma'am, is that Rahamlar's military forces are loyal to Faraçek. If I present myself to make my claim, and with accusations of murder on my lips, I could be shot where I stand. He ordered his captain to put a javelin through my sister, and dropped me off the bridge. What would prevent him from finishing the job?"

"That's not going to happen," murmured Shade, so quietly Laec almost missed it.

"In front of everyone?" Esha paled, not appearing to have heard Shade's remark. "He would commit sororicide a second time, and publicly? Would his own officers not remove him?"

"That's just it. I don't know." Isabey hugged her elbows, her brow furrowed. "I would be taking a dangerous risk while having no forces to back me up."

Everyone looked to the king, the unspoken question hanging in the air. Would the king volunteer Solana's forces to back up the princess, should she wish to make a stand?

"Are you prepared to make your claim?" Agir asked her.

"Are you prepared to back me up?" Isabey replied, lifting her chin.

"Against ten thousand strong unseelie warriors?" said Regalis, speaking for the first time from the corner of the table. "They outnumber us two to one. It's a big ask, Princess."

"I'm not asking only for myself," Isabey pointed out. "You have a dog in this fight, too. I could argue you have much more to lose than I do. Rahamlar is my home, and though I'd be sad to do it, I can walk away and make a new life elsewhere. Can you?"

Shade shot her a stricken look but she seemed not to notice, or she was ignoring him. Laec was willing to bet they'd been talking about little else but this matter since Shade's return.

Isabey finished with: "You could lose your entire kingdom, and your lives too, if you don't bend to him."

Esha gripped the back of the chair in front of her. "I do not approve of hasty actions, nor do I think it is wise to make assumptions. There is too much at stake." She looked at Isabey again, her expression earnest and grave. "Princess, before we commit to anything like that, you have a responsibility to get a true reading on the position of the captains of the Rahamlarin military."

"I agree," said Shade.

"How do you propose I do that?" Isabey spread her hands in a gesture of helplessness.

Shade took one of her hands and sent her a look Laec couldn't read.

"It's too dangerous," Isabey whispered, her voice hoarse and her huge eyes full of fear.

"These are dangerous times, yes," he told her softly. Unspoken in his gaze seemed to be a plea to be brave anyway.

"Yes, dangerous times," King Agir growled, putting his fingertips to his temples. "I need time to think."

"Indeed." Bradburn tapped the table. "This is not a decision we can come to lightly."

The king appeared to fight off an eye roll and didn't quite succeed, annoyed by Bradburn's proclivity to state the obvious. He moved away from the table and toward the door.

"We take this one step at a time. Follow me, please. All of you."

It took a second for everyone to move, the king's exit had

happened so abruptly. The party followed him out of the den and down the hall. Passing Hob's office, the king turned into a small door that led onto a narrow wooden staircase. At the top of the stairs was a library, small but well-furnished and snug, with many leatherbound books. Dusty rolls of parchment lay in open shelves, stacked like bottles of wine. Several oversized bookstands held large parchments stored flat under clear coverings, so their text could be flipped through and read. It had the look of a king's private study, but when the king got to the top of the steps, he cast about the room as though lost.

"Here, darling." Esha went around him, arrowing for one of the bookstands.

Everyone crowded around her as she flipped through parchments that hadn't been disturbed in years. Dust gusted into the air. She stopped at what looked like a diploma of graduation and pulled a lever beneath the bookstand. The book was lifted up so the pages lay flat, then clicked into place, the document became illuminated by a dusty beam of sunlight coming in from a skylight in the steep roof.

A hand-painted parchment sat beneath the clear barrier. Two signatures were scrawled across the bottom half, and more sat beneath those. Aside from the neatly printed names of Erasmus and Iskandar beside their messy autographs, Laec could read nothing of the ancient text.

Esha pointed to the words as she translated, dragging her fingertip across the page. "Official certificate of endowment, issued by the house of lords at Rahamlar. The region indicated by the accompanying map, yet to be named, is thus permanently and irrevocably gifted to Prince Erasmus of Rahamlar—by King Iskandar of Rahamlar, son of Alkim and Seamie, husband of Toryan—to develop as he sees fit."

"And the map?" King Agir said from her elbow.

"It's here." Esha flipped over two more pages.

Another hand-painted page was revealed, a map rendered beautifully with many colors. The territory of Rahamlar was outlined in gold flake. The gifted but as yet unnamed territory that became Solana was outlined in reflective silver ink. The neighboring regions belonging to Archelia, Tryske, Stavarjak, Boskaya and Silverfall were indicated by other, non-metallic colors. Silvery blue paint marked the Valdivian and Ivryndian seas.

"It's exactly as it is today," she said. "Nothing has changed, and here,"—Esha flipped back one more page—"is the certificate that came two months after the gift was given, christening the territory the Kingdom of Solana. This one is recognized by all of the reigning monarchs of the time. Aside from its legal value, this certificate is priceless."

Laec moved closer. His breath caught as he recognized Elphame's five-hundred-year-old signature at the bottom of the page, scrawled between the signatures of other sovereigns he did not recognize. His throat closed unexpectedly with a wave of homesickness, followed by a warm flush of affection for his unpredictable and temperamental queen.

Queen Esha looked up at Laec with a little smile. "Incredible, isn't it? Elphame was alive when Solana was carved away from Rahamlar, and she's alive today while Faraçek is making a play to get it back."

He nodded. Pride swelled in his heart. Sometimes the irritation he felt toward his queen clouded the reality: Stavarjak was the kingdom of the eldest and most powerful monarch of this age and so many that came before, and he was one of the few fae that she allowed in her company.

"Queen Elphame signed this?" King Agir sounded shocked. He leaned closer to the page to squint at her autograph, which—unlike the others—was truly regal, with flowing curves and elegantly placed accents that were part of the ancient version of her name: Ẻłphåmé.

Laec nodded. "I'd recognize her signature anywhere."

Agir looked up at Laec, his expression wide and enlightened. "Would she come and stand with us?"

Laec blinked at him, wondering how it was that Agir didn't know that Elphame never left home.

"If we set up this meeting with Faraçek, would she come?" the king pressed, his features alive with hope for the first time this morning.

Laec stomach tightened, wishing he didn't have to disappoint them, but he already knew the answer. He needed to put a stop to this line of expectation before the sovereigns warmed further to the idea.

"Imagine." Agir turned to Esha, his voice full of energy. "Imagine the look on Faraçek's unholy face when the most powerful queen of Ivryndi, the oldest queen alive, who was present when these documents were signed, stands with us at our meeting! Shows him that she's allied with us." He looked at Laec. "She keeps wanting to help. This is how!"

Laec and Ilishec exchanged a look and Laec could see that his uncle knew precisely what he was thinking.

"What is it?" asked Esha, noticing their exchange.

"She won't come," Laec told them, feeling hollow. "I'm sorry to disappoint you, but Elphame doesn't leave home. She hasn't done so for... I don't know how long. Centuries."

Ilishec was nodding, his expression regretful. "It's true. There have been many dire conflicts in Ivryndi where Elphame might have helped someone she cared for, but she's only ever sent representatives."

"But why?" Agir's voice was breathy, uncomprehending in his distress. "She used to, didn't she?"

Ilishec nodded. "In her early life, Elphame traveled a lot. Her exploits were famous. Not only within Ivryndi, but she often crossed over to the Terran lands." The gardener stopped talking at a look from Laec. Explaining Elphame's history to them wouldn't help right now.

"It's complicated," Laec said simply, "and very personal to her."

"But, would you ask her for us?" Esha put her hand over Laec's, her eyes wide and pleading. "She can only say no, but if we don't ask, then we haven't even given her the opportunity to consider it. I will also write a letter of my own, to send with yours."

Laec found it impossible to deny the queen. He sighed. "Of course, Ma'am. I'll ask. Just… please don't get your hopes up."

Esha sunned him with a smile and Agir grinned, galvanized.

"Don't waste a moment, young Mr. Fairijak. Do it now! In the meantime I will have our lawyer draft a request that Faraçek meet us in the commons." Agir rubbed his palms together. "I hope that strange crow you have is a fast one, the one with the green eye."

"Mistik," said Esha.

"She is, Sire."

She'll return with a rejection letter sooner than you'd like, Laec added silently.

CHAPTER TWELVE

JESSAMINE

THE LIGHTHAVEN INN sat a half-mile from the main road at the end of a winding track that meandered through copses of evergreens. A two story, gray-brick building with white scalloped trim, it looked like it was once a family manor that had been renovated into the perfect place for weary travelers to rest and have their horses cared for. They were greeted by an eager stablehand, who took their horses toward the back of the property and told them to go inside.

Beazle had gone hunting while they'd eaten dinner, and now sat on Jess's shoulder. Ania had sipped from the *helle-bore* and *mahonia* growing in the ditches along the way to the inn, so she'd perched on the top of Digit's head during dinner until she realized she was drawing attention. Then she dropped inside his open collar, where she could peek out. After dinner, Strolight went about some other business while Ian gathered Jess, Vivian and Digit in front of one of the wood stoves positioned in a corner. The crofter ordered a pot of tea for them to share. At odds with the cozy interior, tension was thick within the group. Jess felt grief about everything she'd learned about Marion, which was overwhelmed by a rush of angry heat whenever she thought about what Ian had done. She might have been imagining it, but she thought Vivian was behaving distantly toward Ian. She had never observed them together before so it could be how Vivian always was with her husband, but somehow Jess doubted it.

A cluster of high-backed furniture gave them some measure of privacy. Jess sat beside Digit, with Ian across from them, looking anxious and restless, like he couldn't get comfortable.

When the tea arrived, Ian finally stopped fidgeting to pour, and cleared his throat to begin. "I met your mother while I was a Fahyli escort for the Calyx. They performed at Nasyk's flower festival two years before you were conceived. Your mother and I became friends…" He set down the teapot and raised his gaze to his children. "I think because we had a lot in common."

Jess picked up her tea, thinking that the commonality he must be referring to was the tragedy in their lives.

"We were single, without offspring or living parents, though we didn't talk about that at first." Ian threaded his fingers together. A blush rose in his cheeks, but he spoke without self-pity. "Perhaps those who experience loss reach silently for others who have also endured hardship. I don't know. I only know that Tansy and I bonded. I hadn't loved anyone so much since my first wife.

"She returned my love, and we began to see one another seriously. I wanted to ask for her hand, but I had to take my time. She was… damaged, and even more reluctant to love again than I was. She told me that she wanted a partner but that she would never have a family again, not only because she was on the cusp of being too old, but because she was afraid of something tragic happening again. I did want children, and I knew that while we were a good match in all other ways, that was one important thing that didn't fit."

"Why didn't you let her go then?" Digit asked, lifting his tea to blow the steam away.

Ian shrugged. "I was powerless to deny the love I felt for her, incapable of depriving myself of her company. I had believed I'd never love again, and she taught me that I was wrong. I certainly didn't think I would get so lucky twice, so it was better to be with this person I adored who didn't want children, than alone for the rest of my life."

He paused, reaching for his cup. Jess saw his hand tremor. Vivian touched his thigh encouragingly. It was the first gesture of comfort Jess had seen Vivian offer him. Jess looked at the poisons manager, wondering what this was like for her. What was it like to finally know this huge secret that Ian had been keeping from her for their entire relationship? Was she angry? She didn't look angry—shocked and sad, but not angry. Jess also wondered what it was like to have had as many loved ones as Ian had: three wives, and a fourth who hadn't quite made it to the vows. Jess couldn't imagine ever loving anyone but Sasha. If she lost Sasha... she gulped her tea, burning her tongue as she pushed thoughts of losing her sweetheart away.

Ian went on. "I visited Nasyk faithfully with all the free time I had, and she visited me in Solana City as her life permitted. We found contentment and happiness in one another. I felt she understood me, my pain and the scars that I liked to pretend weren't there. We were good for one another, and everything was as perfect as it could be. She and Kashmir loved each other too. It mattered a lot to me that Kashmir and Tansy were friends. Having familiars, you'll both understand that. Most people are frightened of Kashmir."

Jess nodded. This resonated at her deepest core. If Beazle and Sasha hated each other, she didn't know what she'd do. It would put her in the most difficult position she could imagine. Beazle shifted closer to her neck, sensing the direction of her thoughts.

"I'll never forget the day that I meant to propose." Ian's voice turned gravelly. "Because that was the day she vanished."

Jess blinked. "Vanished?"

Digit's cup paused halfway to his lips. "What do you mean?"

Ian put the cup down, rubbing his knee self-consciously. "I turned up at her cottage in Nasyk, the way I always did before a two-day break from work. She knew I was coming because we exchanged letters constantly. We even used the palace birds to do it, though it was against the rules. She'd written me back with the usual message, that she was excited to see me, and that she was planning something special. But when I knocked on her door, there was no answer. I thought it had something to do with the surprise, but no one was home. I looked everywhere. It struck me as odd that things were missing from her house: clothes and shoes, and other belongings. I looked under her bed where she kept her traveling bag. It was gone too. I searched her yard, the town, the shops. I asked her neighbors if they knew where she went. No one knew anything. I searched her house again, and that's when I found the note. I don't know how I missed it the first time. It must have fallen under the table when I opened the door."

Jess felt Digit go tense. "What did it say?"

"It told me she was sorry but not to come after her," Ian said, spreading his hands.

Jess felt her jaw sag. "That's it?"

Ian nodded, his eyes red. It was difficult to equate the tough, stalwart crofter who was always in command, with this heartbroken fae. He was notoriously private about his personal life, especially with his Fahyli. Jess knew this was difficult for him, but he obviously knew he had to be vulnerable with her, lay his heart bare, or they would never have a relationship.

"That was it," he said once he'd got himself under control. "I was wild with worry. Every situation imaginable came into my mind, but foremost was that she'd been taken by someone and forced to write the note. Otherwise, why would it be so abrupt and impersonal? After everything we'd shared, the deep love that we'd grown to have, such a cold message made no sense."

Vivian slid forward to perch on the edge of the couch, her hands in her lap. "What did you do?"

"Being Fahyli, I had resources, and I used them all. I utilized any winged familiar that my colleagues would allow me to send. They went all over the countryside looking for her. It took a couple of months, but I did find her." His voice went flat with pain. "She was pregnant."

"Oh, Ian," Vivian murmured.

"She had run away and was hiding from me, the man who loved her more than anything, who had never done anything to harm her. Pregnant with my child."

Children, Beazle corrected.

Ian's eyes were glassy and he looked at the floor. When he looked up, it was with such naked pain that it made Jess's heart ache.

"Obviously I was upset, but I was more confused than angry, and I was worried about her. I knew she didn't want children after what she'd been through. It might sound dramatic, but I was also worried for the babe." He took a deep breath, held it for a moment, then let it out slowly through his nose. "So I confronted her. I'd learned that she visited a healer for help with the pregnancy. I approached her as she was walking home from the healer's cottage, on a trail through the woods where a flowery meadow opened up."

Jess tried to picture which trail and meadow he was talking about, but she couldn't recall one between the healer's house and their cottage in Dagevli.

"She was, of course, shocked to see me, but she didn't run away. I was as gentle and calm as I could manage. She seemed resigned to the fact that she'd been caught. I learned that she found out about her pregnancy after she'd written her last letter to me but before I arrived in Nasyk to visit her. She told me she panicked. When she discovered she was pregnant, she was shocked. She didn't think it was possible for a woman of her age."

"Marion called me her miracle baby," said Jess.

Ian nodded. "But the pregnancy made her realize that she actually wanted a child, very much. She didn't know how much until it happened, but now, she was all in. She said, 'I won't let anything jeopardize my child's life.' I asked her to explain, because it sounded like she meant me." He ran a hand over his face, looking drawn. "That was even more shocking to me than Tansy disappearing the way she did."

"She was worried that you would hurt her child?" Jess thought that this belief was extreme but not surprising. She knew Marion better than anyone else around the fire, and putting distance between herself and someone she thought had the potential to be dangerous did fit with Marion's overprotective nature, no matter that it swung too far over the line.

Ian's face expressed shock, even now, years later. "Yes! I couldn't believe it. I told her I would never, ever do anything to hurt our baby, and asked her where she got that idea. She said one name: Kashmir."

Jess's eyes stretched wide. She'd been around Kashmir on several occasions. The bear was big, yes, but she slept a lot and mainly ate a ton of berries and tubers. She was one of the least feared familiars at court.

Ian lifted a hand to salute her expression. "Thank you! It's ridiculous, I know. But Tansy had gotten it into her mind that she couldn't fully trust a bear, even if the bear was her husband's familiar. I argued and pleaded with her until I was exhausted. I reminded her that she'd once had a familiar. Didn't she remember what it was like to be that connected to another creature? Hadn't she fully trusted Papilio?"

Jess closed her eyes against the knowledge of Papilio's end. Marion's distancing herself from Jess's familiars made more sense in light of Papilio; she'd been deeply traumatized by what had happened to her first family, and her reaction had been extreme. Jess could only guess that Marion held regrets over what she had done to her familiar, and was hesitant to allow herself a relationship with Jess's pollinators. Perhaps she wanted to love them, but not allowing herself to was a kind of self-imposed penance. Jess would never know for sure.

Ian went on. "She argued that, in fact she hadn't trusted Papilio, and that's why she…did what she did. I tried to make her see that what had happened in the gaol was an extreme grief response and completely unlike Marion. She'd been in an altered state after her family died. She conceded that, but next she argued that Papilio was an insect, Kashmir was an apex predator. That wasn't anywhere near the point and she knew it, but she just kept coming back at me with the same thing, over and over. She would take zero risks. Without flora fae magic she was no risk to the child. That only left me... and my bear." Ian stopped, a little out of breath.

He gathered himself and went on, calmer.

"She made me promise to stay away from her. She was sorry about us, but a switch had flipped in her heart. Nothing was more important than her child, not even the child's father. So, I did the only thing I could think to do, because being in that child's life mattered to me as much as anything could."

He paused and Jess braced herself for his confession of kidnapping.

"I got a court order."

Jess forgot to breathe for a moment. "A... court order?"

Ian nodded. "I submitted my case and had an agent serve her with a summons so we could resolve the issue in front of a third party, one qualified to deal with such things."

Vivian's brow furrowed. "And... how did she take that?"

"Not well," Ian replied. "She didn't show up on the court date, not realizing that being a no-show would count against her. I had my lawyer write her a letter—because at that point I was forbidden to have any contact with her until the case was settled—to warn her that her behavior could be used against her. In fact, all of her behavior from the moment she learned of her pregnancy could be used against her. My lawyer's intent was not to threaten her, but to provoke her to show up and face the court. She had put us there, as far as I was concerned. I'd be damned if I would let her run away from me as well as the legal system.

"But, of course, she took it as a threat. Can't blame her for that, I guess. By this time, the situation was on the edge of hostile. She just failed to realize that it was she who had put us in that position, not me. So when agents of the court went to find out why she missed her court date, they discovered she had flown a second time. I didn't know it at the time, but she had already begun the process of changing her legal name. It was completed just before she moved to Dagevli."

Jess canted her head. "Wait, where was she the first time you found her? I thought she was in Dagevli."

He shook his head. "No, she had first hidden in a southern town called Wellwood."

Jess did a quick calculation. "Then she wasn't very far along when you found her."

Ian nodded. "She wasn't even showing yet."

"How did you even know she was pregnant?" Digit asked as Ania dropped from his collar into the palm of his hand. She began to preen her feathers.

"Mr. Strolight?" guessed Vivian, her voice quiet.

Ian nodded.

"Strolight?" Jess straightened. "He was around then?"

Shoulda guessed, thought Beazle. *I get intense feelings from that guy.*

"He was my man before he was Vivian's," Ian told them. "We've known each other since we were boys. No one has ever been more committed to me. He learned of Tansy's pregnancy when he discovered the nature of the herbs she was getting every week from the healer in Wellwood. Their only purpose is to help with nausea in the early stages of pregnancy."

"Ok, so you found her in Wellwood. Confronted her, but when she wouldn't include you in the child's life, you got a court order..." Jess reviewed.

Digit finished: "And she dodged it."

"Exactly." Ian nodded. "Her name change also kicked in

at that time, and in Solana, you can't easily learn what some-one changed their name to without going through a laborious bureaucratic procedure."

Having recently gone through something similar to learn the identities of the apartment owners in the tower, Jess could appreciate this.

"I started the lengthy process anyway," the crofter said. "I was not at all confident that her new identity would be revealed to me—thinking that she could have even identified me as an abuser of some kind to prevent the authorities from releasing her name. Meanwhile, time passed, and her due date came and went. I was beside myself. Now we were looking for a mature fae female who looked human and was mothering a newborn faeling. While my lawyer's request was still being processed, Strolight located her again. This time in Dagevli. He witnessed her with a baby in a basket." Ian gave Jess a meaningful look. "One baby. He never saw two."

"Uncommonly resourceful, that man," Vivian muttered with respect.

Beazle gave a soft sneeze. *Uncommonly dodgy, she means.*

"The baby was less than one month old at that point, and I was livid. I told the authorities that my man had located Tansy, but because of the name change there were long delays. They couldn't approach her without the proper warrants because she had altered her identity and put layers of legal fences between her old identity and her new one." He paused and made a face Jess couldn't decode, bracing himself perhaps. "But that didn't stop Strolight. He's never had patience for the legal system."

Jess felt cold. "It was Strolight who took Julian that night?"

Oh boy, thought Beazle. *See? Dodgy! Dodgy baby snatcher. If*

I hadn't been stuffed in a drawer that smelled like bay leaves and nappies, maybe I'd have recognized him.

You were just a baby yourself, Beeze, Jess returned. *The size of a button.*

"I didn't ask him to do it, Jess," Ian was saying, his expression pleading. "I hope you can believe that."

Her heart felt like a caged bird. "But Tad, our neighbor, said there were two men that night. They saw two riders gallop down the road afterward."

"Yes. Strolight recruited someone to help him. To this day, I don't know who it was and he won't tell. Not only that, he made sure that I couldn't just return the baby to Tansy. Not that I would have."

"How?" Digit asked.

"By registering that he'd died," Jess said, her voice hollow.

Ian nodded. "He submitted a death certificate. Knowing what I know now, he couldn't have done it without aggression, because the clerks need a blood relation to register a death certificate. He signed the document with an X, and he thought there was some kind of poetic justice in documenting that the babe had been accidentally poisoned."

Jess covered her mouth, finding it difficult to process just how cruel it was of Strolight to make that small, simple notation on Julian's death certificate. Poor Marion.

"How could he do that?" she choked out.

Ian's voice was hushed. "He was angry, Jess. Furious on my behalf. He'd had enough of Tansy's antics by that point. He was fed up and decided to put an end to it. We were a boys' club since our youth. I don't expect you to agree with it but that's how it was. Strolight never blinked twice at flouting the law, and he's cleverer than he looks."

Vivian crossed her arms. "Which is why I keep him on. Not every problem has a legal solution."

"So he kidnapped Julian and brought him to you." Jess took a shuddery breath. "And you felt you couldn't return the baby to Marion, but that seems like an excuse to me. The death certificate could have been recanted as a mistake, and Julian given back to us."

Ian looked at her for a long moment. "This is where I make my full confession. I just... decided not to. I fell in love with my son the moment I met him, and once he was in my care, I knew there was no way I would voluntarily return him to his mother. By that time, I had serious doubts about her—"

"Please don't say sanity," Jess ground out through clenched teeth.

"I was going to say rationality," said Ian, putting a hand out.

"Marion was a wonderful mother." Jessamine was seething inside. "You should have given him back. You almost destroyed her."

"*She* almost destroyed *me*," Ian replied with thinly veiled passion, his eyes flashing hurt and anger. "I knew she would stop at nothing to get the baby back, that it would be only a matter of time before she tracked me down. Then we would be forced back into the courts, which was where I had taken the mess in the first place. But while I had Lucas, I had leverage. She couldn't just not show up to court, because I had the babe."

"His name was Julian," Jess whispered, angry tears lining her lower lids.

Digit took her hand and she grabbed it like it was a lifeline. It was strange that her twin was sitting beside her, alive and well, and yet she still felt the pain of his loss.

Ian looked sad. "I am sure she was a good mother to you,

Jessamine. I can see evidence of that in the adult that you've become, but I wanted my child. Desperately. I felt I might die if I lost him, and it was the easiest thing in the world to justify my decision by believing she was unfit."

"She never did come after him, Jess," Vivian told her, looking more comfortable now that she was part of the picture. "Of course, I didn't know about any of this, I thought Lucas's mother died in childbirth, so I never expected anyone to approach us."

"We didn't hear a peep from her," Ian said. "A few months later, Ania showed up, giving us further proof for the court that he was ours."

"How was Ania proof, exactly?" Digit asked, still holding Jess's hand. Ania stopped preening and looked at the crofter.

"If Marion had been asked by a judge what species your familiar was, she wouldn't have known it," Ian told him, matter-of-factly.

"But how could you get away with just claiming him as yours?" Jess asked. "He was ten months old by then. Didn't you have to go through an official adoption procedure? Explain to authorities where he'd come from?"

Ian threaded his fingers over the low table between them. "No. I was the biological father. A simple test, a forged death certificate for the mother—"

Those were popular back then, Beazle commented, thinking of Julian's.

"—And Strolight's help to make sure no one asked questions we didn't want to answer, and that was that."

Jess closed her eyes and shook her head, then she looked at Digit, who was looking back at her with eyes that were so similar to hers.

"She didn't come after you because of me, Digit. She loved you so much."

Digit nodded. "I know that, Jess. She was afraid that she'd lose you too."

"And she might have," Ian said softly. "By that point I had a strong case against her. If I'd known there were two babies, I would have used every resource I had to get you as well."

Jess gaped at him.

His gaze was soft. "When Tansy didn't make any attempt to get Lucas back, I was relieved. I didn't know the reason why, and honestly, I no longer cared. I had my son, and he was legally mine. I informed the court that I wished to drop the case and it all went away."

"And the bonnet?" Jess asked. "It never crossed your mind that the last name inside the bonnet matched one of the Fahyli under your leadership?"

"He never handled the bonnet, Jessamine," Vivian answered.

"I didn't even *want* to know what Tansy had named him," Ian admitted. "It was immature and selfish of me, I know, but I had been so raked over the coals that I had no compassion or love left in my heart for her. Knowing him only as Lucas Peneçek helped me to move on."

Jess felt weighed down by sadness. Most of her anger had deflated, to be replaced by weariness and sorrow. There had been errors on both sides, big ones. Ian hadn't deserved to be treated the way Marion had treated him, but just as equally, Marion hadn't deserved what Strolight had done that night. Jess was glad the man wasn't there. She needed to absorb the story before she'd trust herself to be in his company without slapping him. Maybe she would slap him regardless.

If you don't, I will, and with all the fury of a thousand of me, Beazle said grumpily.

Jess bit off a smile. The rest of the world really did miss out because they couldn't hear her bat.

"When Strolight delivered the baby to me," Ian said, "Lucas was wearing the bonnet. I passed him into Vivian's care without removing it."

Vivian agreed, adoration on her face. "I don't believe the tag was ever seen by Ian. He told me the wet nurse who had been caring for Lucas had become ill, so I bathed and changed the baby. We immediately acquired everything an infant could need from the second-hand shops in the city, and it got mixed in with everything else. I'm the only one who read the name inside, and thought it without consequence—the name of the bonnet's first owner, by then possibly an adult. Years later, when I met you, I never thought twice about your last name. Never put you and the bonnet together. Even if I had remembered that Fontana was the last name inside the bonnet, it would never have occurred to me to connect the two, Fontana is not an uncommon name."

"Which is why Tansy chose it, I believe," said Ian. "And I believed Tansy to have only had one baby. The possibility of twins never entered my mind."

"It should have," Jess snapped. "Elsie and Elwin were twins, and twins are more common in older mothers."

Not very bright.

Jess didn't agree. There was nothing wrong with Ian's mind. Making a connection between her and Digit would have required an enormous mental leap, which a busy person just wouldn't have made without help. Without the Silverfae destruction, the mystery might have remained locked away forever. Jess collapsed against the back of her seat and looked up at the ceiling, feeling drained. Everyone was quiet for a long time. A servant stoked the fire inside the stove, feeding new logs into it, then went away.

"How do you feel?" Digit asked Jess.

She rolled her head to look at him, knowing Ian was listening for her answer with great interest. "Tired. Sad. Angry, but not as angry as I was. You?"

"I feel sad, too. It was an ugly thing that happened, but the worst part is that I missed out on seventeen years of you, of us." His mouth quirked with an almost-smile. "I always wanted a sibling."

"You're not sad about not knowing your real mother?"

Digit squeezed her forearm. "Sure I am, but I was raised by two loving parents. I don't feel deprived. I'm sorry that I never knew Marion, and that you never got to know Ian as a father." He stage-whispered: "He's a better father than he is a crofter."

"I heard that," Ian said, but without any ire.

Digit tugged on a lock of her hair. "I have a twin. In spite of the crazy story we just heard, I'm excited about that. Aren't you?"

Ania fluttered her wings and hopped to the back of Jessamine's hand. The beautiful little hummingbird cocked her head and looked up at Jess with shining black eyes. Beazle crawled down Jess's sleeve, stopping beside the bird. Then he too looked up at Jess.

Jess allowed a smile. Together they made a team that, along with Sasha and Rialta, made her heart full. They were family. She wasn't sure yet how she felt about Ian. She wasn't about to call him Father or thank him for any of what he'd done, but, in some small way, she could understand what had driven his actions. Digit she already loved, and now that she knew he was her brother, the doors to her heart swung wide open for him and Ania.

"We're family," she told Digit, keeping her gaze on his.

She could feel Ian and Vivian watching them, and sensed some level of relief in them, even though Jess hadn't included them in that statement.

Digit touched the top of Beazle's head, stroking the bat gently with a fingertip. Her brother looked from her bat to her, eyes shining.

"The poison twins," he whispered.

Gooseflesh rippled across her arms. She repeated it quietly, trying out their new identity and feeling how well it fit.

"Yes. The poison twins."

CHAPTER THIRTEEN

JESSAMINE

JESS WAS STILL processing all she had learned in Nasyk as the Solanan contingent rode out to meet with the Rahamalarins two days later. Even after repeating the story to Rose, Snap, Aster, Sasha, Ilishec, and an abbreviated version to the rest of the Calyx and Fahyli, she still hadn't fully forgiven Ian—and had concluded she was unlikely to ever forgive Strolight. Though she wished Marion had made different choices when she'd learned of her pregnancy, forgiving her departed mother was easier. She didn't have the heart to include Papilio's fate in the story, it was too awful, and she had no wish to traumatize her Calyx friends.

The party—a group of fifty which included several Fahyli and many of Bradburn's soldiers, along with Esha and Agir—rode in military formation, Jess on Kitabee. Sasha looked striking atop a white mare named Swanmoor, borrowed from Solana's stables, their white hair gusting sideways in the wind together.

The common land

chosen for the meeting was a wide plateau nestled in the foothills of the far side of the Vargilath range, near the border. The Vargon itself was considered common land, but it was too inhospitable for such a meeting—and afforded too much sheltered forest for comfort. Jess didn't think there was any serious suspicion that Faraçek would ambush them, but neither was anyone at ease.

When Jess and Sasha saw that Bertrand Bedar had joined the group as Solana's lawyer, they were pleased. They waved to him from their place with the Fahyli. When Regalis and Panther saw who they were greeting, they also waved hello to Bertrand. The lawyer had nodded back politely, but seemed not to register that he was lauded as a hero in the eyes of many for his work on Sasha's case. Jess was sure the bumbling was an act, part of his strategy to be underestimated; an attempt to catch his opponent on the back foot. However, he wasn't a horseman, and his bumping around in his saddle the way Jess had herself at one time rang of truth.

Bradburn and the crofter stopped, and each held up a fist as the party reached the edge of the plateau. Jess and Sasha nudged their mounts out from behind a cluster of horses for a better view. Her stomach dropped when she saw the Raham-lar group, a large party of unseelie soldiers spread across the opposite side of the plateau. Faraçek had been told to bring no more than fifty, the same number Solana would bring. He'd clearly ignored that.

In the center of the grassy expanse, Solanan soldiers had erected a white and blue canvas tent and placed a table and chairs beneath it. A soldier from the monarchs' party rode forward with a pennant and thrust it into the ground to one side of the tent. Solana's wreathed lion's head flag began to flutter in the breeze. An unseelie soldier carried forward the brown and orange flag of Rahamlar, with the cowbird sigil in the center, and set it up on the opposite side. Both soldiers signaled for the parties to approach. Bradburn and the crofter moved forward. The rest of the Solanans stayed several feet behind them.

Rialta and Tully moved through the horses' legs, weaving in and out of the group. Ferrugin, Erasmus and Ratchet could be glimpsed in the sky, gliding smoothly overhead, sending reports to their fae. All must be well in their eyes, as Regalis, Kite and Kestrel sat relaxed in their saddles, though they were bristling with weapons.

Beazle fluttered away and came back to Jess's hair. Summer was approaching, but it was still too cool a morning for the bat's liking. He crawled up the back of her head to perch on top.

Stop fidgeting and sit still. Jess scratched at her scalp. *You're tickling me.*

I wish Isabey and Shade had come.

Think of them like a hidden weapon. She's our best card in this crazy game, better not to reveal her yet. At least, that's what Jess had gathered.

The Solanan party dismounted. Jess and Sasha drew their horses near to where Laec was standing. They watched as King Agir and Queen Esha dismounted and were escorted to the table by Bradburn and the crofter. The monarchs stood beside the negotiating table, waiting for Faraçek to join them before they sat down—a gesture of respect that Faraçek did not deserve.

Faraçek dismounted as Captain Yorin held the bridle of the prince's big red charger, a horse Jess couldn't have mounted without a step stool. An unseelie soldier took Faraçek's horse. The prince—Jess refused to think of him as a king—and his captain approached the table as another joined them from the Rahamlar party, a human male dressed in a black suit and a black felt hat. His hair was long and threaded with gray, his cheeks were networked with lines, and his eyes were dark and flinty.

"That'll be their lawyer," Laec whispered to Jess and Sasha. "Dracwald Blueden, who has been signing the threats from Faraçek."

Dracwald looked as though he'd been carved out of oak, thick, broad and stocky, with a rounded belly. He wasn't nearly as big as Kazery, but he took up a lot of space in his own way, and had none of the air of kindness that Çifta's father exuded.

Formal introductions were made, which the wind carried away from Jess's ears. Once the monarchs were seated, Ian gave a signal to the Fahyli that they should move in. They were to stand behind Esha and Agir, while the soldiers were to place themselves around the tent in formations. Weapons had been worn by all, but those were to remain untouched at all times.

The Fahyli left their horses in soldiers' care and moved into the space behind Agir and Esha. Jess didn't look at Faraçek until she was standing in position, at ease, with her hands behind her back. Then she lifted her gaze to her enemy. His eyes were flicking over the party and the animals who accompanied them. He passed over her, pausing only briefly with a frown, before carrying on. Tully and Rialta drew the most looks from the Rahamlarin group, though they were now lying on their bellies in unthreatening postures. Rialta's tongue flopped out and she looked like she was grinning hungrily at the prince, incisors gleaming.

Bertrand Bedar approached the table carrying the legal documents that were the crux of Esha and Agir's arguments. He lay one in front of Faraçek.

"Prince Faraçek, may I present the original certificate of

endowment of Solana's lands, given by Iskandar to Erasmus, more than five hundred years ago." Bertrand gestured to the parchment. "If you'll take a moment to view it, sir."

After a lengthy stare at the page, Faraçek's only response was a look of boredom. Dracwald looked more interested as he peered over Faraçek's shoulder.

Bertrand followed the certificate with the ratification document, signed by the monarchs of the day. He explained that item to Faraçek as well, in flowery terms. The lawyer then produced a map, outlining the ratified territory, explaining it all to Faraçek calmly and patiently. Then he stood back, waiting.

Dracwald looked up with contempt. "These documents hold no legal power." He dismissed them with a wave.

Bertrand seemed frozen with shock for a second. "I beg your pardon, Mr. Blueden, but that is precisely what they hold. They were authorized by Rahamlar's ministers and king himself, as well as every involved party of the day. They were certified by all the monarchs of Ivryndi. You cannot dismiss them as meaningless simply because you wish to."

"I defer to my sovereign," replied Dracwald.

Faraçek ignored the lawyers and addressed Agir and Esha directly, jabbing at the paperwork disrespectfully. "Is this why you brought me out here? To view a bunch of old documents signed by fools who thought they had the right to divide land that existed long before them?"

"Solana has been a kingdom for more than half a millennium," King Agir said, his voice loud enough to carry beyond the tent, laced with disgust. "You cannot just dissolve an entire nation to feed your ego. Lives and economies are at stake. You can't just mash things back to the way they were. Even if it were legal, it would never work. It will cause chaos and sow division. Not only is what you want to do incomprehensively destructive, it's an act of war!"

"Your point?" Faraçek fired back.

King Agir, flustered, thumped his fist on the table. "You must desist with this madness!"

Dracwald seemed unbothered by Agir's display of temper. "It only seems like madness to you, Agir. We are simply returning our kingdom to its rightful state, a state it should never have left in the first place. Iskandar did not have the authority to divide the kingdom in this way. Those documents"—he pointed at the parchments—"never had the weight of law in the first place."

Bedar looked indignant. "Say what you wish about their standing in Rahamlarin law, in the rest of Ivryndi they most certainly did, and still do."

"How have they stood for five hundred years then?" Queen Esha asked, never taking her eyes from the prince.

"Because no one bothered to challenge them... until now." The prince threaded long fingers together. His nails had become sharp black talons. Jess wondered if he had control over the unseelie feature, or if the raptor-like nails came out of their own accord when the prince was angry.

"Then challenge them in a court of law." Bedard was looking directly at Dracwald, probably knowing that the lawyers were now superfluous to the discussion.

The prince's black gaze stayed on Agir. "I am challenging them, yes, but I'm also doing everything in my power to make this painless for you."

Solanans exchanged looks of disbelief that the Rahamlarin ignored.

"The king is being more than generous," Dracwald sniffed.

"Even offering you a position. Not a single person has to suffer violence or lose a possession."

Faraçek opened his palms out in a gesture of generosity. "All they need do is renounce you and swear allegiance to me. It's very simple. Life won't change for them. And for you it need not change much. I tire of the fortress, it will become our military headquarters. The palace will become my home, Solana City the new Rahamlar City. Your life in the countryside will be pleasant and luxurious, without any of the strain of ruling. Even your businesses—the perfumery and all products associated with it—need not cease. I don't intend to disrupt Solana's economy."

Esha gave a ladylike noise of vexation. "Why would you? Solana has become the wealthiest kingdom in Ivryndi under our care. You intend to purloin our lives' work!"

Faraçek shot her a look that said she was being dramatic, but that he would be generous enough to explain it to her. He spoke slowly and softly, so patronizingly that it set Jess's teeth on edge. "My dear, anyone involved can stay involved, anyone invested can stay invested. Only the head of the body will change, not the body itself. Why risk your necks to resist me?"

"Switch heads and the body dies, *my dear*," said Esha, baring her teeth. "It will not work out the way you think."

"Yes it will." Faraçek spread his arms wide. "Rulers change all the time. Nations go on. The citizens will barely notice."

King Agir touched a finger to the ratification document. "Do you not realize that the undersigned have sworn to protect Solana should she come under attack? There are five other kingdoms that you would have to face, not us alone. Why risk *your* neck? Why not be happy with what you have already accomplished? You'll be the first unseelie to rule Rahamlar in centuries."

Faraçek laughed, a throaty sound. The faint smell of mulch drifted by Jess's nose. She had to resist taking a step back, and sent a silent thank you to Bradburn for ensuring that the Solana party had been positioned upwind of the prince.

"You think any of today's monarchs care one whit about a document their predecessors signed half a millennia ago? Why would they get involved? War is a nasty and expensive business. Are you sure that your allies will come to your aid? No. Even if they wanted to, there's no time to mobilize. The commitment to that document expired when those who signed it died."

"There is one still living," said Esha, her tone simmering with rage. "My cousin, Queen Elphame of Stavarjak."

Faraçek waved his hand. "Elphame is a relic and a hermit. The most she'll do is send a few seelie soldiers like him." Faraçek jutted his chin toward Laec, his lip curling to show what he thought of Elphame's man. "And we all know that Stavarjakians would rather drink and rut than fight."

Jess couldn't see Laec's face but he must have reacted, because the prince added: "Yes, I know where you're from, and I remember you from the gorge. You were impotent then and you're impotent now." He looked at Agir. "My fae outnumber your Fahyli and human soldiers twofold. Even if Boskaya sent a thousand men and Archelia sent two thousand to tramp over the Esigoth dunes and come to your aid, they'd arrive too late and be a force too small."

"You're a madman," the king uttered, his face pale.

"Queen Elphame sees Solana as a sister kingdom," said Esha, regulating her wrath better than her husband. "She foresaw your threat, even before your brother died. Make no mistake, she is highly interested in what transpires here, and will not remain neutral if you proceed."

"If she chooses to involve herself, that is her decision," the prince said dismissively. "It matters not to me. Outside of Stavarjak, her magic is no threat to us."

Agir fisted his hands and put them on the tabletop. "And you also assume that the new queen of Silverfall, whom we also count a friend, will do nothing to aid us?"

"She is a child." Faraçek smiled and it turned his face into something terrifying. "She doesn't know her hair from her heels. You think the first thing she will do is take her soldiers to war? Soldiers she doesn't even know yet?" He shook his head. "Her kingdom is limping from the suffering they endured from Sylifke's rule. She'll need a decade to sort out her own nation. No, I don't think the novice winter queen will come anywhere near this. My plan proceeds. You have until the day of my coronation to make your intentions clear, after that, the window of kindness will close and the amalgamation will begin."

"You'll regret this, Faraçek." The king's neck and face were red with anger.

"I don't think so, Agir," Faraçek said, matter-of-factly. "As I told my son, The Prince Regent, Toryan Ander, I can sleep well knowing that I gave you every opportunity to avoid hostilities. If I must resort to violence, it will be your doing, not mine. Your people will also know that, Agir. Do not ask them to bleed so that you can cling to power. They won't appreciate having to make such a sacrifice."

Prince Faraçek stood and waited a moment as though hoping to hear Agir and Esha swear allegiance right then. He gave a quick and shallow bow. Dracwald and Yorin made equally shallow bows before following Faraçek away from the table. The Rahamlarin soldiers meandered away from the tent, leaving the Solanan party in stunned silence.

CHAPTER FOURTEEN

JESSAMINE

MUSIC FILLED THE ballroom as courtiers and Calyx swirled across the floor. In celebration and anticipation of summer, their outfits were bright and vibrant. The result was a rainbow of candy-colored couples filling the ballroom.

Held in the embrace of an elderly courtier, Jessamine swept by the dais and caught a glimpse of Queen Esha and King Agir, lost in deep discussion. Their brows were puckered with worry. Why they had made the decision to resume the normal schedule of balls after what had happened in the common land two days ago, Jess couldn't understand. Pretending like nothing was wrong wasn't going to make the problem go away. No formal announcement had been made about the meeting, but citizens were becoming aware of the looming threat anyway as word spread unofficially. She understood that Agir wanted to present his people with a solution, but the longer he left things, the more that court gossip gained credence and fomented anxiety.

The dance ended and she curtsied to her partner. There were three dances left before the orchestra would take a break and Jess could too. She put on a serene smile and headed toward the edge of the ballroom, sending out signals that she was open for a partner.

When Sasha appeared, her heart lifted and she added a flourish to her curtsy. Moving into his arms, she let out a sigh of pleasure. Next to Sasha, the world seemed a lot less scary. He braced his hand against her lower back, sweeping her into the crowd as a waltz began. She felt his lips brush her forehead as he inhaled her scent.

"When do you think they'll address it?" he murmured against her temple.

"I don't know," she replied. "They need to take control of the situation to avoid panic."

"And you?" He held her closer.

"Me?"

"Are you alright?"

She took a minute to consider how she felt. "I'm not sure. I feel... concerned, but not frantic. I'm also still reeling about everything I learned about Marion and Ian. I'm reconsidering everything I know about my childhood, and so too about myself. Which means I'm also rethinking how I can be the most help in these scary times." She paused and then smiled up at him. "Somehow though, as long as I have you, Beazle, Rialta, Digit, and Ania, I believe everything will be okay. Even if it's not okay. Does that make sense?"

He almost smiled. "Oddly, it does."

Her gaze dropped to his lips, as it inevitably did when they were close. She wanted him to kiss her so badly that her mouth tingled. She looked away. Ilishec's rules had eased but Calyx were still expected to behave professionally in public. Ilishec would have a fit if he saw her smooching with Sasha, and he was in the room, somewhere.

There was a commotion at the dais, angry shouts, and the sound of something metal hitting the floor then rolling. The dancing ceased abruptly as the orchestra went quiet.

"Was that the king's voice?" Sasha pulled Jess closer, brows pinching. He craned his neck to look above the crowd.

Jess couldn't see anything over the sea of bodies. There was muttering as dancers slid sideways for a better view. The room filled with whispers, people asking taller partners what was happening. She looked up at Sasha, watching as his gaze followed someone across the floor and out the door.

"Was it?" she whispered.

Sasha nodded, watching more people leave the ballroom. "Agir's gone. He might have thrown a platter of... fruit?"

Jess's hands felt cold. "He's so stressed. I don't know why he's here tonight. I don't know why any of us are."

Hob's voice lifted over the rustlings of concern. "Ladies and gentlemen, excuse the interruption. King Agir and Queen Esha have retired for the evening. They beg me to pass on their regrets. Conductor? Please, carry on."

After a few false starts, the orchestra resumed the waltz and the dancers went back to dancing. Everyone looked worried, performing the steps like marionettes. Couples stopped and began to drift away, talking in hushed voices.

Ilishec rushed from the front of the room to the rear, keeping close to the wall and looking upset. He was trailed by Snap, then Iris, Nympha and Asclepias. More Calyx disengaged to follow the gardener out of the room.

"Something has happened." Jess was barely executing the steps anymore.

"Do you want to go?" Sasha asked.

"I'm not supposed to. I'm on shift for another two songs, but..."

Rose, Dianthus, Peony and Proteas followed Ilishec and the others out the rear doors.

"So are they."

"Go on."

She grabbed Sasha's hand and squeezed it in thanks, then wove her way through the remaining couples to the back of the room. She entered the corridor, following the sound of voices to one of the larger Calyx lounges. The tension in the room was as thick as jelly. Flora fae perched on furniture or stood in small groups, looking uncertain. A few had teary eyes. Ilishec stood near the windows, his back to the room, his face in his hands.

"Gardener?" Jess asked, trying not to wring her hands.

Ilishec turned, his face a mask of heartbreak. "I never thought the day would come when the Calyx were incapable of cheering up the scented court. We've always been able to lift spirits and comfort the downtrodden. Turns out there is a scenario where we are viewed more as a nuisance than a blessing."

"A nuisance?" Jess's stomach tightened. She hadn't expected this. Agir was upset, yes, but the Calyx hadn't done anything wrong. If anything, they'd honored the king's request to make things feel as normal as possible. "What do you mean?"

Ilishec rubbed his temple then dropped his hand, looking weary. "The king has, apparently, tired of us."

Shocked looks ricocheted around the lounge. Dianthus and Peony both gasped in horror.

"I heard him," Proteas told the room. "He wanted to send us away. Esha stopped him."

"Send us away?" Jess blinked at Ilishec, stung and confused. "Why? He ordered us to perform. That makes no sense."

"It's because of Faraçek." Ilishec sank onto the chair behind him. "The ultimatum has stressed King Agir more than he—or anyone—realized. He didn't mean it. I'm sure he was just lashing out."

"What did he say, exactly?" asked Rose, addressing Proteas as she moved to Jess's side.

Proteas crossed his arms and set his narrow bottom against the arm of a chair. "That the Calyx are useless, a waste of time and energy."

There were gasps throughout the room, peppered by unhappy mutterings.

"He said to Esha, and I quote: 'Can they defend us? Can they advise us? They can do none of those things. Away with them. I never believed I would tire of them, but I have. The kingdom is in grave danger. Balls and perfumes and costumes are not going to help.'"

"He *wanted* the ball." Jess clenched her fists, her cheeks heating with anger. "He ordered everyone to continue as normal. No one feels like dancing, least of all us."

"I know, Jess." Ilishec sighed.

Aster put an arm around Dahlia, who was wiping away tears. "We're useless? How can he say that? We are the wealth of this place."

"Because, this is one instance where wealth won't help." Snap was standing in front of the fireplace, looking mutinous and red-faced. He yanked at the top buttons of his dress shirt, opening it to his chest. "Solana's income will just become Faraçek's income, to do with as he sees fit."

Ilishec rose again, rubbing his arms as though cold. "I need some time to think. I apologize for my reaction. It was emotional. Try not to worry. I'm sure King Agir already regrets his words. If you have the will, go back to the ball, but I'll not force any of you."

Jess said. "The ball is over. I was the last of us to leave and everything was breaking up."

Ilishec nodded. "We will talk about this further tomorrow. I'm going to find Hazel."

The gardener left the room, leaving the Calyx in morose silence.

"He's right, though," said Snap, turning his back more solidly to the fireplace.

Aster lay her temple against Dahlia's and shushed her, rubbing her shoulder as Dahlia wiped her face. "Yes, I'm sure Agir already regrets it too."

Snap shook his head. "No, I mean Agir. He's right."

The Calyx stared at him, confused.

"What can you possibly mean by *that*?" Jess moved further into the room, sitting on one of the chaise lounges.

Snap grew insistent. "Well, we *can't* help, can we? Our kingdom is under the biggest threat we've ever seen, and we're useless. If an attack comes, we'll even be a liability, like we were when the Silverfae attacked."

"Don't say that, Snap." Proteas moved to stand with Asclepias, both of them pictures of masculine beauty, with wide shoulders, tapered waists and long, lean muscles. The flora fae had dancer physiques, even Snap, though he was more muscular than the others. They didn't *look* useless, but… Jess understood Snap's point. These beautiful fae were trained for entertainment, fit only because they worked out regularly.

Snap gestured at the room. "Why not? It's true. We have to be protected. We're weak and fragile. I hate that."

"There are always groups who are not meant to fight, Snap," Asclepias told him, looking less angry than Proteas. "How are the kitchen staff or the cleaning staff any different?"

"They're human, for one thing," Snap replied. "And most of them are either very young or past their prime. I'm not saying that every individual in the palace should fight, but we're fae, we have magic. Some of us might even have deadly magic that we don't know we possess."

"What do you expect us to do, Snap?" Peony retorted, hands on her hips. "Start learning swordplay? It's a little late for that."

"I'm not sure I could even lift a sword," said Rose.

Jess almost laughed. Rose was lithe and powerful from lots of daily exercise, she'd just never touched a sword. She had no idea how heavy they were.

"You're plenty capable, Rose."

"Exactly." Snap's eyes flashed. "Look at Jessamine. She's a force to be reckoned with even though she's flora fae. She found the defensive aspects of her magic in Rahamlar. Later, she perfected them."

Jess felt uncomfortable as the Calyx looked at her. Everyone knew she made poison and trained with weapons. The Calyx didn't ask about it or even seem interested. It was well outside the scope of things they were supposed to care about.

Jess put her hands up. "I didn't really *find* my defensive aspects, Snap. I was in danger, and my body reacted to protect me the best way it knew how."

But he was nodding. "Exactly, and why can't we do that?"

"Jess controls *belladonna* and *datura*, Snap," Aster said, her patience thinning. "Two of the deadliest plants there are. There's nothing poisonous about my flowers."

"Maybe not all of us can do it," Snap admitted, but he hadn't lost his passion, and he looked around the room trying to rally them to his vision. "But some of us have components that are toxic, and who says our defensive abilities have to come from our raw materials? We're fit and coordinated, every one of us. Why can't we learn to use bows or daggers? Why can't we train like Jess has? She faced unseelie soldiers by herself in Rahamlar, and she won."

"This is crazy talk, Snap," said Nympha, the feathers in her hair waving back and forth, emphasizing her irritation. "First of all, there's no time. It takes years to master those kinds of skills, just ask Kite or any of the Fahyli. Second, Jess isn't just Calyx, she's Fahyli too. She has a mammal familiar. She's in a different category, with a different level of magic." Nympha looked to Jessamine for back up.

Jess hesitated. She disliked being categorized as different. She already struggled with the gap between herself and the flora fae, she didn't want to bring attention to it. "Well, you're right about it taking time to gain skills, but I'm not sure I would say that I'm that different..."

Nympha's eyes widened. "You're not seriously siding with him, are you? You expect the rest of us to try to be soldiers or spies? We'll end up killed if we go down that path!"

"No, no." Jess stood, because now all the Calyx in the room were looking at her. "I'm not saying that at all, but I do think Snap has a point. Wouldn't you feel a little better knowing how to at least defend yourself?"

"That's what the Fahyli and the soldiers are for," Peony said with a shrug. Sphex lay along her forearm, a gleaming black predator with twitching antennae.

"That's just the attitude I mean." Snap gestured toward Peony. "If we just expect the soldiers to defend us, then we're exactly what Agir thinks we are: a liability."

"Snap, you need to let this go." Aster moved to her friend and put her hands on his arms, leaning in to kiss his cheek. "I love you for your bravery but we can't be something we're not. Don't push us toward danger. You'll only end up with regrets."

She moved out of the room, and most Calyx looked like they agreed with her. Several of them said goodnight and followed Aster, signaling the end of the conversation.

"Jessamine is rare, Snap," said Proteas. "I know what you're trying to do, and I get it, but we're not like her and neither are you."

He too left the lounge, and was followed by the rest of the Calyx. Jessamine, Snap, and Rose were left alone, looking at one another.

"I wouldn't mind being able to draw some unseelie blood," said Rose, collapsing on the nearest divan. "But it's just a fantasy, Snap."

"I don't see why anyone who wants to learn defensive skills shouldn't do it though," said Jess. "There's no downside."

Snap moved to a chair, finally looking defeated. "Easy for you to say, I guess. You already have skills. I have some too. I miss training. I wish they knew how good it feels to know how to handle yourself in combat."

Rose and Jess exchanged a look, suppressing smiles. Snap had never seen combat. A few training rounds in his backyard with neighbor boys was a far cry from battle experience. Still, he had a point.

Rose said: "Try not to hold it against them, Snap. It doesn't come naturally to flora fae. You and Jess are the odd ones out when it comes to this."

"*I* don't hold it against them," said Snap. "But obviously the king might."

"That's not fair and he knows it," said Jess. "You can't expect fae who spend all their time learning how to dance and make perfumes to be suddenly useful in war. Agir knows that. He's just upset. He didn't mean anything he said."

"Precisely," said Rose, looking like she felt a little better.

"Still," said Snap, getting up from his chair. "If I don't at least *try* to be helpful, I won't be able to look at myself in the mirror when the dust settles. Good night you two."

His words hung in the air.

Jess went to find Sasha to update him. His room was one level above the Fahyli rooms, a small apartment with a bedroom, a sitting room and a bathing room. He opened the door in bare feet, with his shirt untucked and half unbuttoned. His hair was damp and the room was humid and scented with soap that smelled of cedar trees.

As always when there was more of his skin on display than usual, Jessamine's face flushed. "Are you going to bed? I can say goodnight."

He reached out and pulled her inside, shutting the door as he hugged her. His body was warm and fragrant. "How did it go with Ilishec? What happened?"

They sank onto the couch. She pulled one foot up beneath herself as she faced him. Jess explained why Ilishec was upset, and the difference of opinions among the Calyx. Sasha listened quietly.

"What do *you* think?" he asked.

She lay her arm across the back of the sofa, touching the velvety trim with her fingers. "I think the Calyx should explore their defensive side, if they want to."

He nodded. "But you're different. You're Fahyli, with deadly magic. I don't think it's fair to put expectations on flora fae to become warriors. Not everyone is cut out for confrontation, especially the violent kind."

"Not expectations," Jess said quickly. "No one wants them to be on the front lines or anything, I think Snap just wants them not to be so helpless."

"I understand that." Sasha shifted sideways and drew up a leg so his knee was touching hers. He lay his arm across the back of the sofa, behind hers, and let his fingertips touch her collarbone. He looked at her steadily and without speaking.

She swallowed, then asked him something that she'd been afraid to ask since Sylifke's death. They couldn't avoid the topic forever. "Are you missing home?"

He took a deep, slow breath, chest expanding. "I wouldn't say I miss it, but I'm curious to see it again now that it has a new queen. Elders told stories of a beautiful Silverfall all through my childhood. I always wondered if they were true, if the queen's magic could really change an entire kingdom so much. I don't exchange letters with anyone there, so I have no way of knowing how things are changing."

"Queen Çifta said she'd write to you."

"Yes but she's new to Silverfall herself, and incredibly busy. I can't expect her to describe my homeland in detail, what it looks like under a clear sky and sun. How the city looks when it's not swathed in shadows."

Jess's tummy felt like a dry leaf drifting on the wind, hearing Sasha talk like this. They'd often tiptoed up to the subject of Sasha's life and future, but always ended up shying away from it. Jess shied because she was afraid that his homesickness was growing. She understood the desire to go home—it was what might follow that she was frightened of.

As Jess was trying to screw up the courage to ask him about his future, Sasha went to the basket of logs sitting at the fireside, propping a large one on top of the half-burned remains. He shifted things a little with the poker before returning to the couch.

Jess braced herself, deciding that they couldn't keep delaying this conversation. "You still haven't given the crofter an answer, have you?"

His pale gaze snagged hers. "You know I haven't. You'd be the first to know."

"What's... holding you back?"

He sat forward on the couch, both feet planted and elbows resting on his knees, looking into the fire. His hair hung in wavy damp strands, his profile cutting a strong shape against the backdrop of stone walls. He turned his head to peer at her from over his own arm. "Would you like that? If I joined the Fahyli?"

Jess's eyes widened in disbelief. "How can you even ask me that? I would love it! We'd get to be together even more. Maybe we'd even get to do missions together."

He smiled and his gaze returned to the fire. "It's a great opportunity for me: a formerly rejected fae of the northern kingdom given a place at the scented court. Rialta and I would finally feel accepted. We'd never have to walk these halls in fear, looking over our shoulders for enemies pretending to be friends."

She moved closer to him, looping her hand under his bicep. "So why do I get the feeling that... that you're not going to accept?"

He lifted his arm and put it around her, drawing her close as he sat back. She settled against his chest, soaking in the warmth of his body. Kissing the top of her head, he lay his cheek on her hair.

"My mother tried to visit me at court once. Did I ever tell you that?"

Jess pulled back so she could look at him. "No. When?"

"Years ago. Ruskin told me. It was before he came to hate me, before he knew what my father had done. Her name is Halyn, and she lived in a little village not far from Silverfall. I don't know which one."

"Ruskin didn't tell you that?"

He shook his head, tucking a stray lock behind Jess's ear. "He knew I would have gone to look for her. He'd have already been in trouble if his mother had found out he'd told me that much."

"So, you don't know her... at all?"

"I don't know anything about her other than her name and that she has a hare familiar named Walloon. I'm not even sure she's still alive, although she'd be young enough to have had more children after me. Ruskin told me she looked young. He said she looked poor, too, dressed in skins and worn-out boots, but that she was tall and beautiful."

"She must be, to have made you."

Sasha looked at her for a long moment, and she wished she knew what he was thinking. There was such a yearning in his eyes. What was it for? His mother? His kingdom? Ruskin, the brother from his past who had turned against him? Her?

"There must be some satisfaction," Sasha said, "in having finally uncovered the identities of your father and your twin— even if it was difficult or disappointing—and to know what it was that your mother did that she was so ashamed of."

Jess thought she knew where this was headed and dreaded it, but she could only be truthful with Sasha. "I'm not sure I would say it's been satisfying, but yes I do know what you mean. There is no big scary mystery hanging over my head anymore, no more barriers to moving forward in my life. I'm obviously sad about my mother, and not happy with what Mr. Strolight did. I still have a lot to make sense of... but even though a lot of what I learned was unsettling, overall I feel more steady now that I know the truth. And like you said, now I have a family."

"Does it include your father?"

Jess looked at the fire. "That... will take a while." She stared into the flames, gathering her nerve before looking up at him and taking his hand. "You want to meet her, your mother. I get that, Sasha... and you should. I want you to."

He watched her, gauging her reaction. "Yes... but not just her."

Jess took a moment to process his meaning. "You want to see Elvio? Even after everything he did?"

"He's my father, Jess. You only get one."

"Some of us don't even get that many." She immediately regretted the statement. "Sorry," she added. She did have a father, he just hadn't been there to raise her— but he would have been if he'd known about her. She didn't have any right to self-pity. Sasha's life had been harder than hers, he'd been a pawn used to punish his father.

"Everyone makes mistakes, and some people do really bad things," Sasha said simply. "Things they often regret."

Jess thought about Ian. She knew he had regrets; she also knew his actions didn't make him a bad person. Same with her mother. But Elvio had been bad on a whole other scale. "How do you know Elvio has regrets?"

"I don't, but I'd like the chance to ask him." Sasha's expression was soft and sad in the flickering firelight. He looked at her expectantly, like he was still dancing around something else he wanted to say.

"Face-to-face," she said, unable to imagine how that might go.

He nodded, tracing her cheekbone with a fingertip, down to the corner of her mouth. "Would you like to come with me?"

Jess started, finally realizing why he had been skirting this conversation. It wasn't because he was afraid to tell her that he needed to go home, it was because he hoped she'd come with him.

He registered her surprise and added, "You don't have to meet my father, Jess. I just thought it would be nice to show you my home kingdom, hopefully in a much better state than when I left it. I want to see it myself, and I would love for you to see it too."

"I'm... flattered, Sasha." She put her hand on his knee, leaning her cheek into his palm.

"Flattered?" He looked surprised, then he laughed. "Jess, how is it that you still underestimate how I feel about you?"

He touched her bottom lip with the pad of his thumb, his gaze dropping to her mouth then climbing back to her eyes. Her heart stuttered for a second, before surging into a riotous gallop. How could he do this to her with just a few words and the softest touch? She felt beautiful in a ballroom, and powerful in conflict. She and Beazle were a force to be reckoned with on a dark night when the moon was veiled. But under Sasha's icy-hot gaze, she melted into a quivering pile of nerves. She was keenly aware of her virginal state, her lack of experience. Yet desire heated her blood, made her breath come faster. Crazy things were going on inside of her. Sasha's hands were steady, his heartbeat inaudible, though her own blood rushed past her ears. If feelings were crashing around inside his body the same way they were inside of her, it was not apparent.

"I don't believe in love at first sight, Jess. But from the moment I saw you, I wanted to be the one to dance with you, make you smile, steal all your time for myself. At first, I put it down to lust, but then I got to know you and Beazle. I learned about your past, your family mystery, your extraordinary talents, the way you walk the line between Calyx and Fahyli with grace and ease. It was so easy to fall in love with you."

"Sasha…"

"Now? I don't just want your smile, your time, and your scent always around me. I want your tomorrow, and your next year." He threaded his fingers into her hair, curling them around the back of her neck. "I want your forever."

How was it that he could say such things to her so easily? Were his knees not weak and shaky? His confessions were close to a proposal yet he was so calm and confident. He'd been like that from the moment they met, shamelessly dropping bold flatteries that made her heart stop, but always patient and self-possessed, even while he was tried for murder. How could he be impressed with her? Sasha was the amazing one, not her. She had all the big feelings he inspired in her but none of the words.

She was still searching for what to say when he added: "Even though I have nothing to offer you."

"Nothing to... what do you mean, you have nothing to offer me?"

"I'm a pariah."

"You're not a pariah anymore. Queen Çifta wants you at court, and you're wanted here, too."

"That's not what I mean. I mean that I've been a pariah for most of my life. I had a bed to sleep on and people knew me at court, but I don't have a family, at least not a stable one. I don't own anything aside from the clothes on my back. I have no land, no wealth."

"I don't care about any of that, and anyway, if you became Fahyli, they get a decent wage. If you went back to live in Silverfall, you'd be a courtier. Queen Çifta would give you whatever you need."

"But would you come with me?"

"To live in Silverfall?"

The realization suddenly hit her. He wasn't just asking her to visit the North, he was thinking about them living there together. She'd spoken theoretically about him being a courtier in Silverfall—it was nowhere near a reality in her mind—and her home was Solana. Leaving it had never entered her imagination except when she thought Ilishec was going to sack her, and the thought of it back then had shredded her. How could she choose between her home and Sasha? On the other hand, if he really wanted to go back, how could she make him choose between his home and her? She tried to stay as calm as he looked, but her heart was punching around in her chest like a prize fighter.

"Is that what you're hoping for, Sasha?" she managed. "You want me to live in Silverfall with you? Leave Solana for good?"

He frowned. "I didn't say that."

Some of the tightness in her chest loosened, but not entirely.

"I only know that I need to go home," he continued. "I can't give the crofter an answer until I've done what I need to do, and I would love it if you came with me."

She put her hands on his shoulders, turning him toward her. It was important that he understood how sincere she felt. "I do want to, Sasha. I would love to see where you came from, especially now that your kingdom has Çifta as queen. I want to see where you and Rialta grew up, where you studied and learned to fight and to dance…"

"But?"

"But Solana is in trouble right now, and I'm involved up to my neck. I swore an oath to my king and queen, but beyond oaths, I love Digit and Ilishec, and my Fahyli and Calyx friends. I can't leave them right now, even for a few days. When the danger has passed and my duties allow me to leave, yes, but not right now."

He nodded, his hands going to her. "I understand that."

Relief washed over her. Of course he understood. He was Sasha. Calm, in control, reasonable Sasha. Beautiful, cold-eyed, hot-blooded Sasha, who was gripping her by the waist and telling her everything was ok, even if they had to separate for a while. Her ribs expanded under his hands as she inhaled, heart still pinging around like a hummingbird.

"When will you leave?"

"The hardest part was telling you," he said. "Now that that's over, there's no reason to delay. I should leave tomorrow."

She felt a prick of shock and something inside her felt like it had begun to bleed. Her fingers on his shoulders tightened. "And… when will you come back?"

He pulled back a little, expression grave. "I don't know, Jess. It depends on what I find there."

He meant his parents, and the way he said it, so hesitant to be specific, made Jess feel like whatever had started to bleed was now gushing. But what could she say? She couldn't ask him to stay, and she couldn't demand he come back right away either. She had to let him go without knowing when she'd see him again. She put her forehead to his, emotion closing her throat. Moisture lined her eyes, spilling over. She hugged Sasha tight so he couldn't see her tears, but he only drew her back so he could kiss her. When his thumbs brushed her cheeks and he felt the damp on her skin, he kissed her more deeply. Her heart was bleeding, her body craving his.

She put one leg on either side of his hips as he wrapped his arms around her, burying his nose against her neck. Now she could feel his heart against her own, beating steadily. She had a powerful yearning to see if she could make his heart behave the way hers did.

He inhaled her scent and groaned. "You smell so good."

She moved back enough to put her hands on either side of his neck, her fingers threading up into his hair. His hands flattened out against the ribbons of her corset, one hand going up toward the nape of her neck, the other to her lower back. He straightened his spine, shifting closer. Their noses touched. She heard the sound of a tie coming undone, felt a tug followed by the sensation of her corset loosening a fraction. Desire crashed through her. How could she bear for them to be apart?

He nuzzled along her jaw as he loosened her stays one rivet at a time. When his hand slipped beneath her corset to find the skin of her lower back, she melted. It took all of her willpower not to let her mind go blank.

"Jess," he whispered, looking into her eyes, "I've told you that I want your forever—if you don't feel the same, tell me to stop, because if you give yourself to me, my soul will be yours. There will be no going back, not for me."

She understood perfectly. It would not be fair of her to take his soul without giving him hers in return. What she hadn't been able to tell him because she was not nearly so good with words as he was, was that he already had her in the palm of his hand, heart and soul.

"Don't stop."

He pressed his lips to hers and she could feel his smile. "I love you, Jessamine Fontana."

"I love you too, Sasha Drazek."

He stroked away another tear with the pad of his thumb. "I don't know when I'll be back, but I will come back to you. Nothing can keep me away."

She took a shaky breath, nodding, and surrendered herself. She couldn't control any part of their situation, and she couldn't know the future, but they could at least have tonight.

Jess started awake, thinking she'd heard someone say her name. She lifted her head, listening. The fire in Sasha's bedroom had burned low and was a dim glow in the hearth. Sasha's breathing beside her was deep and even. His calf was warm against her foot.

Jess?

Her bat's call blossomed in her mind. He was nearby. She drew herself up to sitting, pulling the blanket up and holding it to her chest. Sasha stirred.

Beazle? Where are you?

The sound of dirt spattering on the floor drew Sasha to full wakefulness. He pushed himself onto his elbows. "Jess?"

Beazle plopped onto the bed.

"What time is it?" Sasha asked as he sat up.

It's past three, Beazle replied, crawling up Jess's shin and into her lap.

"Beazle says it's past three," she relayed to Sasha.

"Hello Beazle," said Sasha. "Were you wondering where your fae was? I'm sorry, I stole her for the night."

I knew what was happening. Beazle looked at her, then Sasha. He bared his teeth and licked his lips. *Why do you think I stayed away? But you two lovebirds have missed an important meeting.*

"He says we missed a meeting," Jess told Sasha.

"At this hour?" Sasha set a pillow against the headboard and leaned against it. "No one told us."

You were invited, Jess, but when they couldn't find you the meeting went on without you. I could have led Graf to you, but I didn't want to embarrass you, so I stayed hidden.

Jess put her face in her hands, her cheeks flushed with heat. This would be embarrassing regardless. She hadn't been in her room at three in the morning, she'd missed an important middle-of-the-night meeting, and she would be required to explain why. She felt Sasha's hand on her back.

"What is it, Jess?"

She passed on what Beazle had said.

"Should we go now?" Sasha asked, body tensing to get out of bed.

Beazle blinked at Sasha. Jess sensed that her bat wasn't quite sure how he felt about what they'd done. He wrestled with the desire to nip the end of Sasha's nose, but Jess couldn't tell if the desire was playful or punishing.

It's over now. They've all gone to bed.

"He says it's over now," Jess said.

Sasha relaxed. "Do you know what it was about?"

Oh yes. Beazle scratched behind his ear with a claw, enjoying keeping them in suspense. *I was there for the whole thing.*

Jess scooped him up in her palm and held him at eye level. *Tell us then.*

Agir and Esha have come to a decision.

Jess gasped. *What decision?*

They called everyone to an emergency meeting, all the usual talking heads were there, except for you and Sasha of course.

We're not talking heads.

You're silly if you don't think so.

"Jess?" Sasha touched her hip with his knuckles. "What's he saying?"

"He says the king and queen have made some decision, but he's being a little slow with the details."

The royals told everyone that the situation with Faraçek needed to be responded to democratically, not monarchically. Beazle blinked and cocked his head. *Is that a word?*

"They took a vote?" Jess's skin felt cold. King Agir and Queen Esha had held a vote about Faraçek and she'd missed it? *Why didn't you come get me?*

They haven't held the vote yet.

Relief flooded her as she relayed Beazle's words to Sasha.

Esha asked for messages to be sent to every Solanan village, Beazle went on. *They're each to choose a representative and send them to the city as soon as possible. Agir wants every town to have a say, but the vote is two days after tomorrow, in the evening. If they miss it, they miss it.*

"Wow." Jess, mulled this over. As she caught Sasha up, his silver brows lifted.

"Is that even enough time for the delegates from the furthest villages to get here?"

"Just, if the message arrives tonight and they leave immediately from the border towns." Jess looked at Beazle. "Did they send birds?"

Only to the farthest places, Beazle replied, *there aren't enough birds in the aviary for all the villages, so some messengers have been sent on horseback.*

Jess wondered who Dagevli would send, probably their local knight.

"How much information was put in these letters? Do you know?" Sasha asked Beazle.

All of it.

"He says all of it." Jess did a double take. "All of it? Really?"

The king and queen want everyone to know why they're coming before they arrive so they can go straight to the vote.

"So… they'll all know that Agir and Esha have been offered a place in the country if they'll swear allegiance to Faraçek? And what will happen if they don't?"

Yes.

Jess nodded to Sasha. He looked as amazed by this development as she felt.

"In a way, it's brilliant," Sasha said, tapping a finger on the coverlet. "They're letting Solana decide where their allegiance lies, rather than making a decision for everyone about whether or not to resist."

"You mean whether or not they're willing to go to war for the monarchy. That's what it'll come down to if Faraçek won't stand down, and he shows no sign of that."

That's why it has to happen fast, thought Beazle. *Agir and Esha need the decision made before the coronation.*

"You're from a small village." Sasha brushed Jess's hair back from one shoulder. "What do you think the people there will say? What would they choose?"

Jess thought for a long time before speaking. She deposited Beazle on her lap and he curled up there, wrapping himself with his wings. "Dagevlians love the king and queen. They don't have the wealth of the city, but they don't lack either. They feel well rewarded when they work hard, and life is good. Every town has at least one healer, one teacher, and one knight. Those positions are all paid for by Solana City. Every town has at least one mill, one forge, and a market square. Everyone is free to buy and sell, and their rents fluctuate according to the value of crops. Overall, I think the people are happy. They won't want to swear allegiance to Rahamlar."

"But under threat of losing everything?" Sasha asked softly.

Jess thought about Hanna and Tad, Clair and Finn, and so many other faces from what felt like her past life. How would they feel about becoming Rahamlarins? She believed instinctively that Tad would hate it. Being Solanan was his identity, he was patriotic and fearless. But Hanna would want to keep their home. Maybe it wouldn't matter so much to her if Solana got amalgamated, as long as her children were safe and fed.

"I don't know," Jess said on an exhale. "The delegates won't have much time to gather the sentiment of the people, and the people will hardly have time to absorb what it all means before the meeting happens. This could go either way."

"Well one thing is for certain," said Sasha. "If King Agir

and Queen Esha really want their citizens to make this decision, they'd better not be bluffing."

"Yes, you're right." Jess sank against her pillow, cradling Beazle toward her chest. Fear and uncertainty swirled in her gut. "They have to be ready to step down, if that's what the people choose."

Chapter Fifteen

Laec

L AEC ENTERED THE main ballroom and immediately came to a halt, almost running into the broad back of a man in armor. The grand space was as full as it was during Solana's most anticipated balls, but rather than glittering courtiers, the room buzzed with citizens of all classes. Courtiers and nobles filled the balconies, looking down at the hubbub below. On the floor, peasants in plain, homespun clothing talked with knights wearing tunics, their house sigils emblazoned across their chests or tactfully embroidered over their hearts. Greenby of Aelbank, Lightash of Oubel, Freymead of Moorborough, Highsnow of Newoak… the names of families and villages seemed never to end. The room smelled of sweat, dirt, metal, and farm animals, and every face was hardened with determination and wrinkled with worry. Some people were holding small objects in their hands, fiddling with them nervously. Laec spied Jessamine, wearing Fahyli leathers and standing in front of the dais, chatting with Regalis as they observed the crowd. He wove through the citizens to join them, studying Jessamine's face. Sasha had left yesterday morning, seen off by many of the Fahyli. He'd been gifted the white horse, Swanmoor, by the crofter. Sasha had promised to send a letter when he and Rialta reached Kittrell. Jess had watched him go with her heart in her eyes, but she looked calm and self-possessed now. Beazle was perched on her braid, dangling upside down.

"Not a single village failed to send someone," Regalis said proudly as Laec joined them and turned to observe the room. "Even Kittrell, my home village, though much of our town is in Silverfall territory." He gestured to a broad-chested knight with iron-gray hair talking with a noblewoman in trousers and a surcoat. "That's Fintauk Alexander, a distant relative of mine. He's excellent with a sword, though his best fighting days are behind him."

The noblewoman wore a dagger belted at her waist. Blades and bows weren't usually allowed in the ballrooms, but now was not the time to ask Solanans to be without them. It was a show of trust on the monarchs' part that their people had been allowed to keep their weapons.

"Are the best fighting days ahead of any of them?" Laec muttered as his gaze skipped from gray head to white head.

"Don't underestimate them," Jess reproached. "These are delegates, of course they'll be more mature. Every village has a knight and a small contingent of fighters."

But Regalis differed. "It's dangerous to *over*estimate them, Jess. You've experienced Faraçek's unseelie soldiers in action firsthand. They're ruthless. You got the better of them thanks to your magic, but the majority of Solanans would be outmatched by the average Rahamlarin soldier."

"If you don't stop talking like that," Jess replied, "I'm going to find somewhere else to stand."

Jess folded her arms and grimaced, but as she looked toward the floor, a smile turned up the corners of her mouth. Laec felt certain that Beazle had whispered something clever to cheer her up.

"Are they planning to feed this lot?" Laec asked as more knights and civilians entered the room, greeting those they knew and introducing themselves to those they didn't. The room was growing warm and very crowded.

"Of course," Regalis said. "There are tables at the back of the room loaded with food. A few have helped themselves, but overall, I don't think they're hungry. They just want to—"

A trumpet blast drew attention to the dais where Hob stood, waiting for the conversation to dim. When the ballroom was quiet, he announced the king and queen, then stepped aside as Agir and Esha walked along the dais. Esha took a seat on the queen's bench, but Agir remained on his feet. Moving to the front of the platform, he looked out at everyone. He wore a simple dark blue surcoat, belted at the waist and with the wreathed lion's head on the chest. His beard and hair had recently been trimmed, highlighting his angular jaw and high forehead. He looked much less fraught than he'd been. Jess wondered if he'd apologized to Ilishec for his outburst the other evening.

"Thank you all for coming." King Agir templed his fingers in front of his belly. "I see many familiar faces, many loyal friends, and many whom I look forward to meeting. I'm sorry this reunion is not under happier circumstances. We—in this room—have many things in common, but most importantly, we are respected leaders of our communities. In many cases we are official protectors, and we all call the Kingdom of Solana our home. Queen Esha and I have sworn fealty to Solana, as you have sworn fealty to us. We have lived in peace and prosperity for many centuries, but now our homeland has come under threat from our neighbor. We have managed until now to maintain peace with Rahamlar, with nothing more serious than a few skirmishes at the borders."

There were grumblings throughout the room, sounds of disapproval. It was easy to tell who lived near Rahamlar's borders, as opposed to the silent listeners who came from further away and had never personally known trouble with them.

King Agir waited for calm to return. "Through our letter, I hope you're all aware of the situation, but I'll recap it briefly for those of you who've had less time to absorb it. I know many of you traveled all night and all day to get here in time. Prince Faraçek plans to crown himself Rahamlar's king in less than a month. Subsequent to his illegal coronation—illegal because there are witnesses to the murder of his sister, which Faraçek commanded—he plans to amalgamate Solana and Rahamlar."

Further grumblings, angrier this time. Heads were shaking, arms were crossed, brows were furrowed.

Someone yelled from a balcony: "What of the princess? Will Isabey not step up to challenge her brother? She's the rightful ruler, is she not? She can't hide here forever!"

Laec held his breath and exchanged a tense look with Regalis and Jess. Isabey's presence in Solana had not been general knowledge beyond the city. A murmur swept through the crowd like wind over a barley field.

The king paused before answering, taken off guard. "I regret that we've been unable to motivate the princess to make a stand for her birthright." King Agir put his hands behind his back and began to pace. "We had many conversations with the princess, to no avail."

"This is unacceptable!" called an angry female.

"She can't just run away!" yelled another.

"It is her duty to stop him," barked a knight near the front.

"I agree." King Agir glowered. "But are any of you willing to back her as she marches upon her own fortress? Step in front of her brother's soldiers when he sees her coming?"

The room went quiet.

"I thought not," Agir murmured, "and I don't blame you. It's not your responsibility, just as it isn't mine. Yet, we are the ones who have everything to lose."

"You mean you, Sire," someone called from the middle of the crowd. "You have everything to lose."

Laec heard Jess gasp at the boldness, and Regalis growled. They weren't alone in their shock: the statement sparked an uproar. Citizens yelled their disagreement and condemned the speaker for his disrespect. Others looked as though they agreed but were reluctant to say so.

King Agir put up a hand and the room quietened. "You are not wrong. The prince has offered me and my queen a peaceful life in the countryside. All we need do is step aside and swear allegiance—let him take our thrones without protest."

More yelling ensued, but not everyone looked upset by this proposal.

"You see them?" Regalis leaned closer to Laec. "Those who are loyal to the throne, and those who are loyal to themselves have never been easier to spot. I mark them, mind you. I mark them well."

Laec felt anger baking off the Fahyli, but he couldn't feel vitriol against those who thought Agir and Esha stepping aside might be the better option. They were frightened, and didn't want war.

"What will you do, Sire?" someone else called, with a little too much taunt in his tone for Regalis's pleasure. Laec could practically hear the fae's fists tightening.

"We have lost much sleep since we met the prince on the common lands," said Agir. "Faced with an impossible choice: step aside in exchange for a peaceful life or fight to maintain control over our kingdom. If we fight, then you must fight too, for though the prince pretends to be generous and reasonable, he knows that our unwillingness to step aside will put many thousands of Solana's citizens straight in the path of danger. This is why I called you here, because, though I am the king and my wife the queen, we feel that this is not our decision to make."

Stillness broke over the hall. Not a boot-heel squeaked on the parquet. Not a single person sniffed or coughed.

King Agir raised his voice, getting stronger as he sensed the consideration of the crowd. "You are the ones who are most vulnerable. Many of you live in villages that do not even have walls. So, what is your choice, my people? Do Esha and I step aside and allow a new ruler to lead you? Or do we risk everything, and fight until a victor is determined, by fate or by sword?"

"I say we fight," bellowed Fintauk Alexander. "Those of us from faraway lands can join those near the border, fortify their numbers. The unseelie should not be allowed a single inch onto our land!"

"They have ten thousand unseelie soldiers," cried a fearful voice. "We don't have those numbers, and we don't have more than a handful of fighters in every village. How are we supposed to defeat them? We're farmers!"

"I'll not swear fealty to an unseelie murderer," another yelled. "I'd rather die!"

"And die you shall, you idiot," said his neighbor in disgust. "We can't defeat them in face-to-face combat. Do you think Agir will send our military away from the city? He'll sit behind his high walls and let the unseelie run over us!"

The neighbor hissed and shoved the other man. "You coward! You would take to your knee so easily and subject your family to Toryan's heir?"

"You dullards have forgotten the old stories," called the woman in the trousers, her voice deep, loud and strong. "Toryan slaughtered our ancestors. Women and children included. Faraçek is of her blood. You're human, most of you, and the fae among you are seelie. You're the descendants of the survivors of that massacre. You want to roll over and show your belly to Toryan's evil spawn? What's to say he won't run us off our land like she did?"

"He says he'll let anyone who swears fealty keep their homes and possessions. We don't have to lose anything," replied a red-faced man in a hood. "Only King Agir and Queen Esha will lose, and not even their lives, only their station."

"And you believe him?" The woman wheeled on him, incredulous. "He's unseelie. They lie as easily as they breathe! There's not a kind bone among them, not a single drop of pure goodness."

"Princess Isabey is not evil," called Jessamine, surprising Laec.

"Cowardice is worse, in my opinion." The woman sent a hard look at Jess. "Faraçek cannot be trusted, Fahyli female, and you're too young to throw out opinions on this matter."

King Agir put up a hand and the argument stopped. "We have no further time for debate, as we must plan swiftly, depending on our course. You've each been given two stones, one of red marble, and another of green. Servants will come around with pots. Those who are in favor of me and Esha abdicating without protest, drop in the red stone. Those who wish us to remain as your sovereigns and lead the kingdom against the prince, drop in the green stone. We will tally them for a final decision. Choose where your hearts lie."

As he spoke, servants in blue and green livery threaded their way through the crowd, and the sound of stones plinking into jars echoed through the ballroom. Some held up their stones for others to see which way they'd chosen to vote, while others dropped them discretely, hiding their decision from the rest. When everyone had deposited their stones, the jars were carried to a rear corner of the dais where Hob received them. The pots were emptied into a large trough and sorted. Servants shoved the red stones to one side of the vessel, the green to the other. Once they were separated, Hob counted them twice, then Bradburn stepped forward and counted them twice. The two agreed, and Hob called to the monarchs, looking relieved. Esha moved to stand next to Agir.

"Sixty-seven representatives for your abdication, eighty-nine representatives for preservation, Your Majesties. The result is for you to remain."

The ballroom exploded with a cacophony: yells of victory and bellows of frustration and anger. Citizens began to argue with one another, gesturing and yelling at those who had not voted in alignment with their own views.

"Silence!" King Agir barked, taking away Hob's job. "We have a result, and we shall honor it."

Queen Esha stepped forward and spoke more softly. "You must return to your villages and prepare to defend your lands and homes. You may decide among yourselves how you do this, but know that all are welcome to take shelter behind Solana City's walls until a resolution with Rahamlar has been reached. Knight Alexander's suggestion of sending forces from outlying villages who are further from Rahamlar to bolster the numbers at border towns is a good one. Captain Bradburn and Ian Peneçek will sit down with all delegates to discuss strategies tomorrow morning before you depart. Please help yourselves to the food provided."

Laec noted looks of disappointment on faces in the crowd. This might be the only visit to Solana City that many of them would make. He felt certain that they were hoping to experience the Calyx for themselves; after all it's what made the kingdom famous. He exchanged a look with Regalis, but he was a closed book.

Some citizens stormed out in a huff, not staying to break bread with their fellows. Others moved into excited little circles, already discussing defensive strategies and sharing stories. While the mood wasn't exactly light, there was hope on many faces, and Laec was glad to see it.

He noticed Jess was pale and glowering. As Regalis moved toward his relative from Kittrell, Laec stepped closer to Jess.

"Not happy with the outcome?"

"I love their courage and loyalty, but…" She looked at a loss for words. "Look at them."

"I have looked at them, Jess." Laec kept his voice low. "I see brave souls who want to defend their families and lands. They should not have to swear allegiance to a ruler they don't trust. They may even believe, as that lady said, that they'll eventually be run off their lands or killed at some future date, the way their ancestors were. They'll have to live with that hanging over their heads. They won't be able to sleep well, not for a moment, with Faraçek as king. Better to fight it now with everything they have. Don't you think?"

"I understand that." Jess turned toward him, tugging on her braid and making Beazle swing. He squeaked once and fluttered away. "But, surely there is a better way than abandoning them to defend themselves when he comes?"

"What do you suggest?"

She huffed. "I don't know, Laec. I only know that most of these people will die if they're left to themselves. I can't live with that. I don't know how any of us could live with that."

"Laec?" The crofter called from the ballroom doorway. When they made eye contact, he beckoned.

Laec went out into the hall, surprised to find that King Agir was there with Captain Bradburn, several other captains and Regalis. Agir caught Laec's eye and the king's gaze speared him.

"Has Queen Elphame responded to our request?"

Laec swallowed, feeling heat rush into his face. All he could do was say: "No, Sire."

"That's what I thought," the king growled, his gaze narrowing. His tone turned acidic, sarcastic. "For someone who wanted to help us avoid trouble, Elphame seems conveniently reluctant to help us now that it's finally here. Is she or is she not our ally? What good does all her supposed magic do if she cowers at home when she is needed?"

Laec had no satisfactory answer. "I'm sorry, Sire."

"Some powerful sovereign Stavarjak has," Agir muttered as he turned away. "I can't stand a coward. Princess Isabey and Queen Elphame are cut from the same cloth, as far as I'm concerned."

Agir's captains turned to follow their king, but not before shooting their own hostile looks in Laec's direction.

CHAPTER SIXTEEN

JESSAMINE

J ESS SAT IN the dining hall by herself, eating a late dinner of rice and vegetables, but barely tasting it as she played back every word that had been spoken in Nasyk, and later, in the Lighthaven Inn. Beazle was out hunting. Digit had gone to bed.

She wished Sasha was there to talk to about all she was feeling. She was amazed and happy that she had been reunited with her twin, that was expected. But new and unexpected feelings had begun to surface over the past few days, unwelcome feelings. She was starting to have a reluctant understanding of the choices that Ian had made, and, dismayingly, feeling angry with Marion for having run away from Ian in the first place. Marion had said that if people had known what she had done, they would hate her, but Jess couldn't blame Marion for what had happened in Nasyk, that had been an accident. Horrific, yes, but still unintentional. What Marion had done to Papilio in the gaol, now that was another matter. That was something Jessamine would never understand. The only sentiment Jess had to temper her wrath with was that Jess herself had never accidentally killed anyone she loved with her magic. No matter how hard she tried, she couldn't imagine the emotional fallout from that. Even so, she would never, ever harm Beazle. That much, she knew. She felt alternately infuriated by and sorry for Marion. The only conclusion she could come back to was: trauma made people do strange things.

But about Julian, the more Jess thought about it, the more she had to admit that Marion might actually be more to blame for what had happened to Julian than anyone else. Jess did not want to feel this way. She wanted to hold her anger with Ian between them like a righteous torch, burning brightly and keeping him away from her heart. She might be angry with her mother, but she loved Marion deeply, and felt she should be loyal. Marion had raised her, protected her, loved her. Ian was not a stranger, but he was nowhere near family. He was her superior officer, her commander. She felt that she must choose a side, and it was only right that she choose her mother.

She looked up from her musings when she heard her name. A servant stood over her, a letter in her hand. She held it out, looking tired. "Came for you quite a while ago. I'm so sorry I wasn't able to get it to you sooner, Miss Fontana. Everything is out of sorts right now."

"That's alright. Thank you." Jess took the letter, holding it to her heart for a moment. The scrawl on the outside was distinctly Sasha's. She'd known that his letters might be delayed; still, it had been difficult not to worry. She opened the letter, reading it while she chewed. The servant had said it was delayed, but according to the date Sasha had penned it, the letter was four days old.

Dear Jess,

We've reached Kittrell. Aside from a short-lived skirmish with a very muddy section of road, we've made it to the border without incident. Already I am amazed by the difference in this northern landscape viewed under sunlight. We still have three or four days of travel and I'm curious to see if this huge open sky will accompany us the rest of the way.

I've sent a letter to Queen Gifta, letting her know we are coming. She replied by bird. We are to expect a couple of Silverfae guards to meet us halfway between here and there. I suppose she wants an escort as a way of showing the court that I'm to be forgiven, but I can't shake the feeling of being in trouble. Residual fears of a lad who was continually in trouble, I suppose.

I'll write again when I reach Silverfall City. I'm not often nervous, but the closer I get, the more edgy I feel. You already know why.

I love you, Jess.

We love you.

Sasha & Rialta

Jess read the letter three times, wishing it was longer and gave more detail, but it was better than nothing. He was safe. By now he was in Silverfall City. Another letter was surely on its way to her. This one too, would be delayed. Folding the letter, she lay it against her aching heart and closed her eyes. *Come back to me soon, my love. Everything seems so much harder without you.*

CHAPTER SEVENTEEN

LAEC

"IT IS DONE." Regalis said the words so quietly that Laec almost missed them, but for those soldiers along the wall who had heard, the reaction was dramatic and instantaneous.

"It's done!" a soldier bellowed, sparking echoes along Solana's walls and beyond. The message spread across the city, along the streets. It was shouted from every rooftop and window.

"Faraçek has made himself king of Rahamlar!"

"The prince has crowned himself!"

"Ready yourselves for the morrow!"

Before nightfall, the whole kingdom would know.

"Ferrugin had a front row seat, I presume?" Laec asked Regalis, who was still staring out over the pastureland.

The landscape was pastoral and peaceful. Sun lit the colored heads of flowers, warming the earth and making the air smell of damp soil. Regalis had been here since dawn, as Ferrugin winged her way over Rahamlar, Erasmus and Ratchet

A.L. Knorr

at her side. The three raptors sent constant streams of information to their Fahyli as the neighboring capital city buzzed with activity.

Kite was in the king's tower, giving Agir and Esha frequent reports. Three court scribes were also present, making lists of the Solanan nobility who attended the coronation. What the monarchs intended to do with these lists, Laec wasn't sure, but he doubted it would be friendly, not after the vote had been taken and a decision made. The royals' commitment to honoring the citizens' desires ran deep. They wouldn't be pleased with those who went against the rest.

Kestrel was with Captain Bradburn and the crofter in the maproom, giving them the movements of Faraçek's soldiers and captains. Laec had visited the maproom several times already, watching as Bradburn and Ian moved small playing pieces across a map of Rahamlar and Solana, getting a visual idea of how many soldiers were stationed where.

"Ferrugin sits on the top of a flagpole in their main courtyard right now," Regalis replied. "Following the prince and his entourage as they go from the courtyard back into the fortress."

"Is she under threat?"

Regalis shook his head. "Faraçek has seen all three raptors. I think he's pleased that we sent spies. He wants us to know what's happening." The Fahyli's eyes were focused on the Vargon. "He wasn't crowned with his father's iron crown."

Laec absorbed this with unease. "Of course. He chose Toryan's crown. Wish we knew if the rumors about that crown are true."

"Oh, they're true," replied Regalis grimly.

Laec looked over at his friend, brows up. "How do you know? Did something happen during the coronation?"

196

He pictured some mysterious wave of power rippling outward from Faraçek's skull as the delicate circlet with the ominous cowbird was set on the prince's devious head, but Regalis shook his head.

"Nothing that Ferrugin could see, but she sensed something. A... cold, damp feeling, she said. I suspect the circlet didn't bestow any new magic on the prince, just enhanced his own."

Laec shivered hard this time, feeling his gorge rise. He took his waterskin from his belt and took long swallows. Wiping his mouth with the back of his hand, he returned the pouch to its place. "That's... really bad. The prince has mind-control abilities."

"Aye, from the *cordyceps*." Regalis let out a long sigh and sent Laec a sideways glance. "The gardener says *cordyceps* isn't fatal to creatures larger than insects."

"But mind-control could be, Regalis. Don't you remember Jess's story?"

"Yes, she almost died. Faith saved her." The Fahyli tucked his hands under his armpits. "Most of us don't have much of that."

"Faith?" Laec canted his head. "Faith in what?"

Regalis opened his mouth to respond but he was interrupted when a young man appeared at the top of the steps, his eyes bright and full of panic. "Laec Fairijak?"

Laec recognized the boy as the son of one of the chemists, a wiry little twelve-year-old who ran everywhere he went. "Lan? What's wrong?"

The lad bounced on the top step, one skinny long-fingered hand clutching the railing. "Your uncle requires you. It's an emergency. I'm to escort you back right away."

Laec looked back at Regalis.

"Go on," the Fahyli said. "This may very well be our last night of peace. Nothing will happen today, or even this evening. Go be with Ilishec."

Laec went with Lan as the boy wheeled and ran down the steps two at a time.

"Where is he?" Laec asked as they hit the cobblestones and began to jog.

"The perfumery, sir."

Laec saved his breath for the run. The boy was tireless and the way was entirely uphill. By the time they arrived at the gardens, Laec's heart was pounding and his throat felt raw. He slowed to a fast walk, letting Lan run ahead. Crossing the gardens, Laec turned toward the hothouses and followed the curving path toward the perfumery, mystified by what might be so urgent that Ilishec needed him without delay.

Laec followed Lan past the harvesting stations and through a wooden door leading down into a cellar-like laboratory. Down here the air was cool but fresh from the ether-powered ventilation system. The soapy scent of raw materials would taint this place forever but at least it was a pleasant smell. Tables full of distilling and emulsifying equipment, cooking kettles for body lotions and cosmetics sat along the floor and on shelves. Everything was neatly labeled and sparkling clean. A couple of chemists with serious expressions talked quietly by a row of bottles.

Lan gestured for Laec to enter another room then scampered away. Laec pushed through a metal door into a lab that was much colder than the first—kept at a constant low temperature by ether-powered refrigeration elements snaking along the ceiling—and filled with crates and boxes, neatly stacked on both sides of an aisle. Ilishec was at the rear of this storage room with another chemist. They both wore jackets, hats and fingerless gloves, and had bottles of product all around them, on the floor and on every nearby surface.

"Wish I'd known you were waiting for me in a fridge," Laec joked. "I'd have dressed—" he cut himself off when the gardener looked up. "What's wrong?"

Ilishec waved him over. "I need you. Come, come." He picked up a bottle containing a clear liquid just a little thicker than water. "Smell this. It's from Rose's last sweat session."

Laec took the bottle and sniffed. He made a face and recoiled. "Ugh!"

"It's gone off." Ilishec's tone was calm, but his eyes were feverish and his hands trembled. "They've all gone off, as far as we can tell. Teyvik will check every recent batch, but so far every one we have checked has gone bad." The gardener put both hands to his forehead in despair. "I don't understand. This has never happened before. We're very diligent. We have to be. The raw materials are worth a fortune by themselves, let alone what they're worth after we're done processing them. This"—he gestured to room—"entire space is full of raw material. If it's all bad... it represents more than a year's worth of revenues. Gone. Just... gone."

Laec looked around the large storage facility, the impact of what Ilishec was saying starting to sink in. "I thought you had a preservative that you added to the raw materials."

"We do, but there's a resting phase first. Every botanical has its own process, but they all require a resting phase because when they're first harvested the components are all jumbled up. They need time to separate, which makes the next step possible. They must be kept cool for a few weeks to a few months, depending on the species." Ilishec was talking fast now, panic setting in.

Teyvik was digging through boxes on the other end of the room, untwisting caps and sniffing. He raised bottle after bottle to his nose, recapping each one and setting it aside. "Good news, Gardener, the processed ones haven't gone off, only the raw ones."

"That's a small mercy," replied Ilishec, looking tired. "After the Midwinter celebrations we had a glut of orders. Months' worth of finished product waiting to be shipped. But we need to refresh our inventory as orders come in daily." He gestured to the rows and rows of boxed raw materials. "This is a disaster. An utter disaster."

"What preserves the finished product?" Laec asked, reluctantly sniffing at the contents of another bottle, and pulling back with a moue of distaste. It smelled of rot and decay; sharp and sickly sweet.

"Something called *phenoxyethanol,*" Teyvik replied from the other side of the room.

"Sounds toxic."

"It's just a fancy name for rose alcohol."

"It's another reason why Rose is so valuable to us." Ilishec put caps back on a cluster of open bottles. "She doesn't just provide the best-selling perfumes—along with Peony and a couple of others—she gives us the raw materials to make the alcohol that preserves the contribution of every other Calyx. She's going to be extremely upset with us, and with good reason."

"They all will." Teyvik came over, bringing an armful of potions with him, some watery and transparent, others creamy and opaque.

Finished product was beautiful, preserved in stunning, custom-made bottles with charming shapes. Each was crowned with a frosted glass stopper representing the scent and had a colorful label with embossed writing. Teyvik gave them to the gardener and Ilishec proceeded to break the seals and sniff each one. When he was done, he let out a long sigh and looked around.

"I'm grateful we can still ship what hasn't gone off, it buys us a little time." He looked around, despair and overwhelm etched into his features.

"What do you want me to do, Gardener?" Teyvik rubbed the back of his neck, looking around like a lost child. "I suppose I should throw out all the bad, to start with. But then what? And what will you tell the Calyx?"

"Don't throw it all out quite yet," Ilishec told him hastily. "We need to understand what went wrong, first. I can't go to them without some kind of explanation. They're going to be devastated. Months and months of hard work, gone." The gardener's eyes rimmed with moisture. "It's enough to make a fae weep."

Laec's heart ached for him. "How can I help, Uncle? Tell me what to do."

"I need you to report what's happened to Esha. Try and tell only her, if you can. The king is tense enough already but the queen will want to know." He let out a long shaky breath. "This is a blow we Solanans can't take right now. Next year's revenues… gone in a puff of smoke."

Laec chewed his lower lip. "If Faraçek gets his way, maybe it's a blessing in disguise? There'll be no revenues for him to steal."

Ilishec grabbed Laec's arm. "Don't say that, my boy. I cannot operate under the assumption that we would have lost all of this anyway. Now go. Tell the queen that I am sorry I cannot deliver the news myself. I must stay here and try to figure out what's gone wrong. I must have everything documented. Every step we take from here must be chronicled, in case it ever happens again, pride forbid."

"I'm on my way." Laec grabbed his distraught uncle, pulling him into a hug. "I'm sorry, Ilishec. So sorry."

Ilishec clung to him for a second, then released him and patted him on the shoulder. "If you see any Calyx, say nothing. The queen must know before anyone. She and I can meet later and discuss next steps. Thank you, Laec."

Laec headed toward the door, pulling up his collar to warm his neck. He paused and turned back. "Quite a coincidence that this happened the day Faraçek was crowned with Toryan's crown, don't you think?"

Ilishec and Teyvik froze, staring at Laec with open horror.

"It's done then?" the chemist gasped.

The gardener paled. "We've been listening for the announcement but we can't hear anything down here."

"Less than an hour ago," Laec said.

Teyvik touched Ilishec's arm, speaking quietly to the gardener, but Laec could hear him even from the exit. "I was down here all morning, Gardener, sorting and checking the dates. I didn't notice any bad smell until an hour ago. Can it really be a coincidence?"

Ilishec's shoulders fell. "I don't know, Teyvik." He looked toward the door as though getting an idea. "Laec. Wait."

Laec paused, one foot on the threshold.

The gardener skirted a pile of open boxes and stepped around bottles of rotten raw materials. "On second thought, I'd better come with you."

Ilishec and Laec found Esha in her main parlor, the doors propped wide open and the queen in the midst of a group of ladies, young and old, fae and human. Every forehead was pleated with worry. Siege mentality had set in.

"—and be with your families," Esha was saying, holding hands with two of the women. The petite queen was a picture of self-control and confidence. "Everything is going to be fine. Our walls are thick, and we're prepared for this. This isn't the first time Solana has defended itself against Rahamlar's ambitions." She let go of one hand to cup the chin of a younger woman. "Try not to worry."

"How will we know what's happening, Ma'am?" the girl asked, lower lip quivering.

"We have scouts flying over Rahamlar who convey information to our Fahyli without delay. I'm telling you, Rahamlar is celebrating right now. Nothing will happen today."

"He threatened to come the day after his coronation," said an older woman with a basket on her hip.

"Yes, and the moment he and his soldiers leave their city walls, we'll know about it," Esha told her. "Now go. All of you. You've done everything I've asked without complaint. I thank you for that. It's time to look to your children, your parents, and others you care about."

The women bobbed curtsies, some of them kissed the wreathed lion's head ring on Esha's narrow finger. The women bustled past, leaving Laec and Ilishec standing just inside the doors.

Esha waved them in. "Gardener. Laec. What is it?"

The gardener took the queen's hand. "My Queen, I bring terrible news."

Rather than shrinking back from Ilishec's words, the queen seemed to step into them, not wishing to be sheltered from anything. "Spare me nothing, Gardener. I implore you."

Ilishec didn't sugarcoat his news. "Earlier today, chemist Teyvik discovered that all of the resting batches of raw materials have gone rancid."

Esha's eyes widened. "All of it?"

The gardener nodded. "Every last bottle."

"And the finished product?"

"The *phenoxyethanol* has preserved it, so the Midwinter orders can be fulfilled. But we have no new inventory. Teyvik and I have been trying to diagnose the problem. I thought it might be the temperature control, or the ventilation, but our storage rooms are fully operational. He thought it might be a pest, or bottles that weren't thoroughly disinfected before filling, but there's no evidence of either. My chemists are good, Ma'am. It wasn't any mistake of theirs." He took a breath, then added, "It may be a coincidence, but it's also worthy of note that we noticed the problem in the same hour as the coronation."

"And take note, I shall." Esha enclosed both of his hands with her own. "I'm sorry my friend. I know this is upsetting. But we're not going to solve this dilemma today, and probably not tomorrow, nor possibly for quite some time. Not with invasion looming."

A flash of lightning outside briefly drew their attention to the windows. "Looks like we're in for a storm," Laec said. "It moved in fast."

The queen looked from the gardener to Laec and back again. "Both of you have places you need to be. I'm sure Hazel is waiting for you, Gardener. And you,"—she looked at Laec—"I was told you'd be on the wall."

"Yes, Ma'am." Laec was surprised Esha was so specifically informed. "I was there when my uncle sent for me, it's there I'll return to for the rest of my shift."

"Then go, please. We will meet about this problem as soon as we are able."

"But…" Ilishec let out a long sigh. "What will we tell our customers? If we cannot fix it, the vast majority of Solana's wealth for the coming year will be gone."

"I'm aware of that, Gardener." Esha put her hands on Ilishec's shoulders, lowering her voice so those passing in the hallway wouldn't hear. "Every worry you have is well founded and I have no wish to be dismissive, but you are not a youngster to be mollycoddled. We may be invaded tomorrow. If we are not able to keep Faraçek away, the fouled materials won't matter."

Ilishec bowed his head. "Yes, Ma'am."

Two messenger boys thundered into the parlor foyer, skidding to a stop as though they had raced. They sprang to attention when they saw the queen, then executed clumsy bows.

"I have news, Ma'am," one gasped.

"My Queen, I have a message for the gardener," panted the other.

Esha released Ilishec and took her skirts in her hand, lifting them to take a few steps toward the boys.

"You first," she told the one who had something for Ilishec.

"It's your wife, Gardener. She collapsed in Mrs. Tierney's kitchen. She's sent for a healer." He rushed to clarify: "Mrs. Tierney sent for a healer, not your wife. Hazel is unconscious."

"What?" Ilishec rushed forward, pale, and too distraught to even excuse himself from the queen's presence. He followed the boy out of the room and the two were gone before Laec and Esha could say anything.

"May I go with him?" Laec asked, turning to Esha.

Esha dismissed him with the wave of a hand. "As you wish, Laec. Return to your post when you can. I tire of issuing commands."

Laec bowed and headed for the door. He could still hear the queen as he turned into the corridor.

"And you?" Esha addressed the remaining messenger. "I hope you have better news, but I have a feeling you do not."

"It's about the princess."

Laec froze and held his breath, pulse ratcheting upward. A passing servant gave him a dirty look, knowing he was eavesdropping. He gave her an apologetic smile but didn't move. There was no way he could go until he heard what the boy had to say about Isabey.

"What's happened?" Esha's voice quivered, revealing the first drop of real fear.

The boy sounded frightened too. "Princess Isabey and her soldier, Shade. They can't be found. They're not in their suites and they didn't attend the most recent meeting. The king thought you should know right away."

There was a long silence while Esha absorbed this, then: "Who saw them last, my dear? Do you at least know that much?"

The boy sounded relieved that he could give her an answer. "Yes, Ma'am. The guards at the main gates believe they saw them leave the city before the order was given that no one could go out or come in without permission from the Royal Crofter or Captain Bradburn."

Esha gasped. "They've *left* the city? Why were they not stopped?"

"She was dressed like a peasant, Ma'am. The guard didn't realize it was the princess until it was too late."

"Oh for pride's sake," Esha cursed, sounding both impressed and irritated. "Dressing like a peasant. Honestly. It's the oldest trick in the book because it still works. You'd think it might occur to guards to look at a face now and again."

The boy sounded like a sad bird. "Yes, Ma'am."

"No others went with them? It was just the two of them?"

"Yes, Ma'am."

Another servant was coming, so Laec carried on down the corridor and out of earshot. Isabey and Shade had run; the princess had not been bluffing. So much for replacing Faraçek with the rightful heir.

CHAPTER EIGHTEEN

LAEC

LAEC SAT IN an alcove outside the Koi Library, rain pouring over the windowpanes and resulting in strange shadows being thrown over the open book lying on the table before him. Unread. His gaze was fixed on the carpet runner outside the alcove, frozen and unseeing. He'd visited Hazel and Ilishec's cottage yesterday after the news of her collapse, only to realize that there was nothing he could do to help. He'd gone back to the wall to finish out his shift, but the day had passed without anything more interesting than increasingly soggy weather.

"Mr. Fairijak?"

Laec looked up at Graf, who appeared like a genie. The boy had been nicknamed the mole, popping up here and there, with very little time to get from one place to the other.

"What is it, Graf?"

"There's someone looking for you."

Graf nodded at someone Laec couldn't see behind the alcove curtains. "Found him, Miss."

A tall, cloaked figure stepped into view as Graf bolted off in search of his next commission. Face swathed in shadows, the slender figure peered in at Laec. A graceful hand lifted back the hood of the cloak. Long blond hair lay over the shoulders of her tunic. Though her clothes were boyish and rough, made for traveling, Georjayna Sutherland could not look masculine if she donned a burlap tunic and slathered coffee grounds across her jaw. Her pale brown eyes—the color of a newborn fawn—found his, and she smiled.

"Hello, Laec."

Laec sucked in a breath, blinking hard. Somehow, he found the power to emerge from the alcove. He stood in front of her, taking in a face he hadn't been sure he'd ever see again. Then he opened his arms and she stepped into his embrace. Laec could hardly believe she was here, though he could feel her warm, vibrant body under his arms. When they parted, he drank in her features. She had not changed one whit, though she'd been living in Scotland, a place where her immortality could not reach her. She had chosen to live where she could be with Lachlan, the human she loved, and where she could be accessed by friends she'd known since childhood. A decision Laec would never fully grasp.

"What are you doing here, Georjie?"

"Not happy to see me?"

"'Course I am. Just... shocked to my boot-heels. You couldn't have sent a bird or a bee or one of the wee folk to let me know? My heart almost didn't restart."

Georjie laughed. "Elphame summoned me, and when Elphame summons"—she made a gesture that said *you know what happens*—"there's no ignoring her, not even from the other side of the veil."

"Did she send Fyfa?"

Georjie shook her head. "Byrne."

Of course Elphame would send Georjie's fae father. He was still so tickled to have a daughter, he'd do anything for her, and Fyfa had sworn never to return to Scotland.

"She told me that King Agir and Queen Esha of Solana—she showed me where Solana was on a map—practically begged her to come. She's spent the past weeks in an agony over how to respond."

Laec narrowed his eyes. "Ha. Elphame? In agony?"

"I know, right?" Georjie shook her head. "She hides behind a layer of crypticism so thick you couldn't cut it with a chainsaw. Anyway, she felt bad so she asked me if I'd come in her stead." Georjie shrugged. "Here I am. At your service, er... the king and queen's service."

Laec tsked. "You didn't have to come. Do you even know what you're getting yourself into?"

"It doesn't matter. I owed Elphame for helping me with Daracha. I don't like owing anyone, especially her. After this visit, I won't anymore."

Laec narrowed his eyes with suspicion. "That's it? You owe her, so you journeyed all this way just because Elphame asked you to?" He looked her up and down. She didn't look tired, or dirty, or even wet, though the rain had not ceased since last night. It was now the dinner hour. "When did you arrive?"

"Just now. You are the first person I've spoken to, aside from Graf." Georjie took off her cloak and lay it over an arm, looking around at the alcoves and the etherlamps. She gestured around her at the hallway, the rich curtains on the windows, the elaborate designs on the carpet runner, the paintings. She took in the palace while Laec examined her outfit skeptically. She wore plain leggings and a tunic that looked as though they'd been purchased at a period costume shop in Scotland.

"This place is really magical," she was saying. "I thought Stavarjak was magical, and it is, but... I don't know. Something about how it's so comfortable, while being medieval at the same time. These lights, for instance. I've not seen anything like them anywhere."

But something she'd said earlier finally clicked. "I don't understand. You *just* arrived? The whole city is locked down and secured. How did you get in? It's pouring rain and you're not even wet."

He lifted one edge of her cloak to emphasize. It was a style he recognized as Stavarjakian from its bias cut, a tailoring technique that the fae of the spring kingdom loved because it made their cloaks billow in an attractive way. So, she got her clothing from a shop in Blackmouth, but someone in Stavarjak had loaned her the cloak.

Georjie smiled. "You forget what I am. It took me minutes to get here from Stavarjak, and hardly a drop of rain has fallen on my head. I popped up in one of the palace gardens and walked straight in through a side door."

"Right..." Laec shook his head, feeling stupid. "Wise magic." He'd forgotten that Georjie couldn't just move tons of earth, she could also travel through it.

Georjie's brows tightened. "This place is beautiful. I've never seen anything like it. I'm glad to have an opportunity to see Solana, but Elphame didn't tell me why she wanted me to come."

"What *has* Elphame told you, exactly?" Laec asked while

steering her down the hall. He needed to make her presence known to Agir and Esha.

"Not much." Georjie craned her neck to stare at a mural on the wall as they passed. "She told me that Queen Esha is a distant cousin, and that she—Elphame, not Esha—had a dark premonition about Solana. She sent you to report back to her and she touched on some very old conflict with a neighboring kingdom, which I've already forgotten the name of—"

"Rahamlar."

"That's the one!" Georjie made claws with her long fingers and looked at the ceiling. "I *knew* it sounded like someone growling. Anyway, she mentioned them but she didn't give me any specifics. She said you'd do that."

Laec led Georjie toward the lion's den. "I'll explain everything, but first, I have to let them know you're here. There's no movement in or out of the city right now. An unexplained presence is going to raise hackles."

There was no one stationed outside the den, as guards had been reassigned. Usual palace protocol had fallen by the wayside too. Hob was too busy to make introductions, and schedules were upside down. They stopped and Laec knocked. Voices could be heard through the door, lots of voices. It almost sounded like a busy bar inside.

The door opened and Panther peeked out. His gaze cut to Georjie, whom he looked up and down again. "Who's this?"

"I'm—"

"Eyes back in your head, Pan." Laec pushed past Panther.

The den smelled of stale coffee and unwashed bodies, and was as loud as a Scottish pub after midnight. The king and the crofter were in discussion, debating the virtues of different defensive strategies. Around the room were fauna fae and many captains from Bradburn's military, all arguing over one another in loud voices. Familiars lay on the floor underfoot, sat on top of rafters, or, in the case of Erasmus, on top of Kite's head—wings half-splayed and beak half open—as she argued passionately with Bradburn. When she glanced over midsentence and stopped talking, the rest of them followed her gaze.

"Laec." King Agir straightened, his gaze flicking from Laec to Georjie and back again, revealing none of his earlier ire. Laec had Georjayna's presence to thank for that. Agir could always be relied upon to be a gentleman, especially to a stranger. "What is it?"

"I won't take much of your time, Sire." Laec bowed, feeling uncomfortable about the intense study the men in the room were making of Georjie. Even the females were too appraising for his comfort. He moved further into the room, and Georjie followed, staring at Tully dozing sprawl-legged and belly up on the floor.

"This is Georjayna, an emissary sent by Queen Elphame."

His recent criticism not yet cleared from the air, King Agir lifted an eyebrow. "What curious timing."

Laec managed a smile. "Isn't it? Since the queen cannot come herself, she has sent a representative. I just wanted to make you aware of her presence. With your permission, we'll be going."

"Wait."

As the king approached, Georjie sank into a curtsy, though she was wearing trousers and boots.

"Welcome, Georjayna of Stavarjak." Agir held out his hand. "Any friend of Queen Elphame's is a friend of Solana's."

Laec couldn't help but look at Agir with obvious annoyance. Agir ignored him.

Georjie put her hand in the king's. "I'm charmed by your palace. Solana City is beautiful."

The king studied her face intensely, just as his men were doing. Laec understood why. It wasn't Georjayna's beauty—Solanans were surrounded by beautiful fae all the time—it was her other-ness. She was fae, that much was clear from the points of her ears, but she was as strange to them as a modern taxi driver from Glasgow. Her accent, her choice of words, her casual way of walking and talking, her earnest curiosity and open expression. On top of being a modern teenager from Earth, she carried immense supernatural power within her reedy figure. All told, Georjie was a mystifying being to stand in the presence of. She seemed young, yet old. Familiar, yet strange.

"You must be exhausted after such a long journey," King Agir said, slowly and with obvious intrigue.

Georjie smiled with a trace of irony. "Not really, Your Majesty. I'm fine. A little hungry and thirsty, maybe."

Agir made a gentlemanly gesture toward the door. "By all means, my dear. We can talk again later. Laec, will you show her to the dining hall? Hob, please take note of Georjayna's presence and have her situated in a suite near Laec's."

Hob gestured for her cloak. "I'll take that, shall I? It'll be waiting for you in your room. Will that be suitable, Miss?"

"Oh, perfect." Georjie handed Hob her cloak. "Thanks a bunch."

There was a titter from a few of the females in the room.

"Wait." Bradburn barked. He moved toward Georjie, suspicion darkening his face. "Who let you in, Miss? The city is closed. I was not informed of your arrival. I demand to know which guards defied my orders. By which gate did you enter?"

"Hush, Bradburn," King Agir said to the rudeness of his captain.

Laec thought—under the circumstances—Bradburn's ire was justified. He was charged with the security of the city.

"I can explain, Mr. Bradburn," Georjie replied, calm as a summer day. "There wasn't time for Elphame to send a bird. She asked me to come to you about an hour ago. I travel quickly, through the ground, and came up through the soil of your garden." At the stunned silence that followed this statement, she added hastily: "Which I'm sure are very beautiful under normal circumstances."

"What is she talking about?" Bradburn growled at Laec.

Laec surrendered with a sigh. "Georjie is an earth elemental, a Wise. That's what we call them in Stavarjak."

The room froze, and Laec was surprised by the great pleasure he took in their befuddlement. Unable to stop himself from bragging a little more, rubbing it in a little further, he added: "No guard defied your orders, Bradburn. Georjie can travel underground faster than any bird can fly. She doesn't need to beg entry at a gate."

Panther—who up until this point had been observing with interest—brightened. "I think I've read about this, though I'm not familiar with the term "Wise." The texts I've read called you an "earth mother." You're related to the flora fae, and probably—though more distantly—also to fauna fae. Your kind is exceedingly rare."

"Thank you, Pan," Bradburn grumbled, annoyance written all over his features. "But I'm as yet unclear how she is going to help, other than to be another mouth to feed just when we're having to ration goods."

"I don't need to eat your food, Mr. Bradburn," Georjie said

with far more patience than the captain deserved. "I can leave the city and find grub elsewhere."

"Bradburn, you're outrageous and embarrassing." Agir took Georjie's elbow gently, steering her toward the door. "Don't listen to my captain. You are welcome to anything we have to offer. Laec will show you the way. I look forward to talking with you again after you've had a chance to refresh yourself. Especially concerning your... means of travel, and other... gifts."

"Thank you, Your Majesty," Georjie said as Hob opened the door for them.

Laec and Georjayna stood in the hallway as the door to the lion's den snicked shut. They exchanged a loaded look.

"Whoa," she breathed.

"You can call him, Sire, Georjie," Laec told her. "We don't say 'Your Majesty' like they do in the storybooks you only stopped reading like two years ago."

"Shut up." Georjie punched his arm, then gave him a deep side-eye. "That was so *weird*. I felt like I was on a medieval movie set." She lowered her voice. "Some of those guys were beautiful. Like b-e-a-utiful. That one guy had the energy of... like, I don't know... a big predatory cat."

Laec smothered a snort.

"What? He was oozing muscular stealth all over the room. What was his name? It can't possibly be Panther, not for real."

"It is, and you'll want to watch what you say." Smiling, Laec took her elbow and led her away from the den. "He has excellent hearing and I'm sure you just made his entire year. Though you'd best hope it doesn't get back to Peony."

Georjie covered her mouth, embarrassed. As they turned a corner she recovered, grabbing him and jerking him to a stop. "What was... Panther, huh what a name! What was he saying about me being related to flora and fauna fae? I could tell he wasn't talking about the wee folk."

"You've not met any flora or fauna fae in Stavarjak?"

She spread her hands wide. "There's been a distinct lack of fae in my life these days, unless you count the new waitress at the Blackmouth cafe with the pixie haircut."

"Solana is full of them." Laec led her toward the dining hall.

Georjie squealed like the teenager she was, then startled him by grabbing him again. "Are you kidding me? I've only read about them in Fyfa's history books. You have to introduce me!"

"Did you want to eat first?" Laec knocked his head toward the open double doors, through which people were entering hungry and leaving full. The smell of roasted meats and vegetables made his mouth water.

They stepped into the dining hall and Georjie halted in the doorway. "Wow."

"I forgot how easy it is to impress Earthlings," Laec muttered, pulling Georjayna to a table stacked with plates and cutlery. "This isn't even a real banquet where you get served and entertained. Those have been canceled. It's just a buffet. Grab a plate."

Georjie took a plate, gaping around the hall in a daze. "It's so pretty. The tapestries, the beams, the light fixtures. There's flowers everywhere, and"—she pointed, eyes wide—"that's a figure eight butterfly!"

Laec glanced at the table where pollinators drank colored nectar from bowls and from bouquets of fresh flowers brought to full bloom every morning by the Calyx, which were starting to wilt. He couldn't tell which butterfly Georjie was referring to and didn't care. He went to the main table and dished himself roasted beets and courgettes spiced with rosemary and slick with melted butter.

Georjie talked as she followed him down the table, putting bits of food on her plate, though not enough for a full meal. It appeared she had taken Bradburn's comment to heart. In spite of there being rations, there was plenty of food available; simple dishes of potatoes, roasted vegetables, tender braised meats, and fresh bread and biscuits.

"Some of those species' are crazy rare, Laec. I think some are even considered extinct on Earth." She blinked at all the food. "I thought this kingdom was in trouble. How is there so much to eat?"

"This is nothing compared to the usual," Laec replied, feeling his chest swell with pride. "Solana is famous for fae who can conjure the big showy flowers, but many of them can conjure plants that give food, too. Like my friend Jess. She's known for honeysuckle but she can also bring up sweet potatoes."

"Huh." Georjie looked down at the sweet potato mash with the caramelized onion glaze on her plate. "So, how long could Solana survive under siege?"

Laec speared a slice of venison onto his plate. "A lot longer than anywhere else. There are freshwater springs under the city, too. That's the main reason Erasmus chose this spot for his palace."

"Who?"

Laec took a deep breath. "I'll tell you everything while we eat."

They sat down and he told Georjayna as much as he had learned since he arrived, skimming over the conflict with Silverfall so he could focus on the threat from Rahamlar. Georjie took small, ladylike bites as she listened. When he'd downloaded all the necessary information, he finally got to dig into his own meal, which had grown cold.

Georjie asked him questions as he tried with only modest success to finish all the food on his plate. At the first sign of bare ceramic under his meal, Georjie asked him again to introduce her to some flora fae. Laec put down his fork with a sigh.

"Since you're not going to let me eat in peace, you might be interested to know that one of them just walked in. Why don't you go introduce yourself?"

Georjie looked toward the door. "The gorgeous one with the long hair?"

"They're all gorgeous," Laec said. "But yes, he—"

Georjayna was up and away before Laec could tell her anything else. She walked straight up to Proteas and introduced herself. Too far away to hear their exchange, Laec continued shoveling food into his mouth as he watched. Proteas took Georjie's hand, looking a little mystified, but the moment they touched his enormous fae eyes grew even wider. They both stopped speaking and just stared at one another in what could only be described as astonishment.

Laec stopped chewing as they hugged one another like old friends. When Proteas grabbed Georjie's hand and pulled her from the dining room, Laec cursed under his breath. Throwing down his fork, he took one big swig from his thus far untouched red wine, set it down, and went after them. By the time he reached the hall, they were out of sight.

CHAPTER NINETEEN

JESSAMINE

J ESS SAT CROSS-LEGGED in a patch of dirt. Rain pattered on the glass roof over her head. It was dark outside although it was nearing noon, so the hothouse was lit with etherlamps. The humid air was rich with a confused muddle of scents emanating from the beds of soil. Most of the Calyx were present, each working in their own plot of dirt. No one spoke, they hardly even looked at one another as they drew up botanicals and watched in dismay as they wilted.

After Ilishec had told them that all of their raw materials had gone bad, he'd assigned the Calyx to a hothouse to work in that was full of empty beds. After Rose had done a sweat session, what she produced had gone bad within an hour, so Ilishec had determined that sweat sessions were currently an exercise in futility. The Calyx were devastated but determined, and in an odd way, the problem provided a distraction from the much worse issue of looming invasion.

Jess put her hand out over the soil, watching as perfect

little sprouts of honeysuckle stretched upward, thickening and growing woody stems. Leaves and blossoms burst to life, filling the air with the warm, honeyed scent of her trademark perfume. It was perfect. It was beautiful. It was whole—the ideal specimen. But the moment Jessamine withdrew her magic to let the plant find its own natural rhythm of growth, the honeysuckle wilted and turned yellow, drooping and dropping its leaves until it was nothing but bare branches with a puddle of mulch beneath it. When a tear tracked down her cheek, it surprised her. She brushed it away, looking around with embarrassment.

You're not the only one who's upset, Jess. Beazle was watching from somewhere near the ceiling. *You don't have to feel ashamed.*

Indeed there were a few covert sniffles to be heard around the hothouse, as Jess's flora fae companions all experienced the same thing. Peony's bushy flowers dropped their heads, the limp petals scattering to the ground. Rose's shrubs went from full-foliaged with fat pink blossoms to a collection of thorny, naked sticks. Aster's tiny, delicate flowers turned to mush mere moments after she released her hold over them. The implications of this were too big to grasp, and the Calyx were in shock.

"Everyone!"

Proteas's voice made Jess jump as it echoed through the greenhouse, drawing every eye toward the door. He stepped inside leading a fae female by the hand.

"There's someone you need to meet," Proteas announced. His eyes were bright, his chest inflated. The Calyx stared at him with morose expressions; many were teary-eyed. The blond stranger in the boring clothes drew little interest.

Iris had her bare feet planted in a far corner of the hothouse, clusters of wilted stems littering the soil. "Your timing is appalling," she told Proteas. "We're in the middle of a crisis here." She had her hands on her hips in a posture of annoyance. "Which you seem to have forgotten."

"That's why you need to meet her." Proteas stepped aside so the Calyx could better view this person he held is such high regard. "This is Georjayna. She's a Wise."

Most of the Calyx just looked confused, but the term rang a bell for Jess.

"She's wise?" Snap was kneeling in the dirt and encircled by brown, slimy lumps of mulch that used to be snapdragon plants. "I don't get it."

"She's *a* Wise, Snap." Jess stepped out of her soil-bed onto the stone floor, then slipped her dirty feet into the slippers she kept in the hothouse. "She's an earth elemental."

"Hello. So nice to meet you all." The girl waved, her strange accent scraping oddly but not unpleasantly against Jessamine's eardrums.

The Calyx standing in the beds nearest to Georjayna were frozen and staring. Then Delphi dropped into a curtsy. Nympha followed, and so did the other females who stood closest to Georjayna. Asclepias, the nearest male to her, bent in a deep and graceful bow from the waist. Jess had never seen him bow that deeply, not even for the king and queen.

Peony, kneeling in the soil-bed beside Iris, tossed a limp peony stem onto the ground with disgust, shaking slime off her hand. "What are you doing, you morons?"

Jess approached Georjayna. As she neared, a strange sensation washed over her—power emanated from the girl. It bathed Jess, warming her, like walking into a beam of pure summer sunlight. All the hairs on her body lifted and she understood suddenly why the others had genuflected. This girl was bursting with earth magic, radiating nature's energy. She was their

queen, and majestic in a way that Esha never could be. Filled
with a potent desire to show respect, Jess dropped into a curtsy.

There were further murmurings of confusion from the
Calyx behind her, but one by one, as they approached Georjayna, each had similar reactions as they felt the power oozing
from the strange young woman standing before them.

"Oh, please don't," Georjayna said, sounding uncomfortable. "You don't have to—"

But Asclepias stepped forward and hugged her, melting
against her. Georjayna looked surprised at first, but then hugged
him back and the two appeared to be fused for a moment. They
separated, and Asclepias beamed at her, eyes glistening.

Curious, others stepped forward to hug Georjayna, making
either a noise of surprise or pleasure. Looking into the girl's
eyes—the shade of new bark—Jess felt sunned by her beauty
and power. She took her turn stepping into Georjayna's arms.
Tears sprang to her eyes as a powerful feeling of protection
and care soaked into her. The intoxicating scent of rainwater
and spring growth emanated from Georjayna's body and hair.
Wishing she could stay in this young woman's embrace forever,
she withdrew to let others have their turn.

"Georjayna Sutherland." Someone tried out her name.
"What an odd name."

Georjie looked over Jess's shoulder. "Only my mom uses my
full name, makes me feel like I'm in trouble. Call me Georjie."

Asclepias asked: "Why does it feel like you're my..." He
trailed off, either not sure of the word he wanted, or too embarrassed to say it.

"Mother?" supplied Alstro.

"Queen?" suggested Marigold.

There were murmurs of agreement to both descriptors.

Jess caught a glimpse of Laec walking toward the green-house, looking cranky.

"You're Laec's friend?" Jess asked as Snap approached for his turn in Georjie's embrace. By now everyone wanted a turn, and Georjie seemed happy to oblige.

"Yes," Georjie said, as the broad male swallowed her willowy frame up in a close, warm hug. She laughed at his enthusiasm. "Easy there, *Antirrhinum*."

More startled looks as the Wise identified Snap's botanical. *Of course* she could feel their species, because she was linked with all of them.

"Call me Snap." He stepped back, grinning and blushing.

Laec stepped through the doorway, bewildered to see how the Calyx had clustered around Georjie like adoring puppies. "Making friends without me?" He frowned. "Sorry they're being so familiar with you. Bit odd. Step back, flora children. Give her some air."

No one listened, all their attention was on the Wise. Georjie threw him a dazzling smile but was too busy being hugged and venerated to talk to him. She greeted every member of the Calyx, returning their hugs with a fetching blush in her cheeks. Jess felt unable to take her eyes from the statuesque Wise. Aside from Georjayna's clothing, she fit right in with the flora fae: eyes that were a little too large, delicately pointed ears, long lustrous hair, long neck, long limbs, cheekbones and lips to make an artist sigh.

Look at her. She's only just met us and she's so comfortable. She knows every one of our botanicals, Jess commented to Beazle when he dropped to her shoulder.

Because, Beazle thought, *she's connected to all plants and the soil too.*

Imagine. At nine botanicals, I'm the Calyx with the widest magic, but Georjayna dwarfs me by orders of magnitude.

Beazle crawled over her shoulder toward her neck. His fur tickled her skin. *Remember what Laec said she could do?*

Jess did remember. *That she could make a passage through the earth with a wave of her hand. I thought he was joking.*

Jessamine stood beside Laec as Georjie talked with the Calyx. "Why did she come here? Did she know we were having trouble with our magic?"

"Elphame sent her." Laec leaned against the frame of a window. The dreary light and water running down the glass outside gave his hair a greenish cast.

Jess shot Laec a look of surprise. "Elphame knows?"

"Not about your trouble, at least, not yet. I'll tell her in my next report. King Agir and Queen Esha asked Elphame to come to the meeting with Faraçek on the common land."

"Right, but that was weeks ago."

"Elphame never answered. I tried to tell them she wouldn't come. Elphame never leaves Stavarjak, but she wanted to help so she asked Georjie to come instead."

Jess studied his profile. "You don't look happy about this development."

Laec scratched at his chin, bristling with several days' growth. "She's my friend and she has no idea what trouble she's walked into. What Elphame expects her to do is beyond me."

Jess looked at Georjayna, who was kneeling in one of the garden beds, listening to Marigold talk about her magic. The Calyx had drawn in close, partially blocking the Wise from view. Loath to miss anything, Jess left Laec to squeeze her way into the crowd.

"Can you fix us?" Peony's voice was soft and with an edge

of pleading. Her tune had completely changed after she'd exchanged a hug with Georjie.

Georjie looked up at all the worried faces. "I don't know, but I'll do whatever I can to help."

"Georjayna?" Something in Snap's tone made everyone fall silent. "Do you believe—like our king does—that we flora fae are defenseless in the face of a threat?"

"Snap," reproached Peony with a roll of her eyes. "Not that again."

But others were interested to hear the Wise's response. Georjie dimpled with a near-smile. "Not to answer your question with another question, Snap, but do you think Jessamine is defenseless in the face of a threat?"

"Ha!" Snap looked around in triumph.

Iris huffed, brushing off her hands. "How many times do we have to go over this? Jess is different. Her botanicals are poisonous."

"You don't have to be connected to a poisonous plant to be defensive," Georjayna said, scanning their bewildered faces. "I've never been up against an army but I've been in my share of life-threatening situations and managed to defend myself."

"You're a Wise, though," said Proteas. "You're more powerful than all of us put together."

Georjie cocked an eyebrow. "It might surprise you to learn that—in most instances—I used common nontoxic plants to help myself or friends out of trouble. Come." She put a hand out toward Snap in invitation. "Let's try."

Snap rubbed his hands together, eyes bright. "What do you want me to do?"

"You command snapdragons. Right?" Georjie moved toward an empty patch of soil. "Show me."

Snap stepped into the flowerbed and crouched. Georjie knelt beside him.

He held his hand out over the soil and tender young snapdragon stems emerged. He pulled his hand back but the plants continued to grow, stretching upward, filling out with green leaves then pushing out buds. Their tips turned from green to yellows, oranges, pinks and reds as the plants matured and the blossoms opened. Growth slowed to the point where it was difficult to detect the process by sight, then the snapdragons began to brown and wilt—Snap's expression along with them—until Georjie put her hand on his back, then they surged forward a second time, green and healthy.

The Calyx shifted, leaning over so they could see better, as Georjie moved her lips to his ear. "Now imagine an enemy army has laid siege to your city. Imagine the city walls breaking, fires consuming homes, and soldiers slaying the innocent."

Snap glowered, setting his shoulders. He glared at the plants with a determined expression. The blossoms opened further, then shivered with tension, as though trying to exceed maturity and reach some state beyond their maximum fullness. The blossoms became bright and juicy in color, even more vibrant than what nature would typically produce. The scent of snapdragons filled the air as the blossoms shook and stretched.

"Imagine soldiers threatening the person you love most," Georjie continued.

Snap growled and—with the faintest popping sound—one of the blossoms jumped off its stem. The Calyx gasped and recoiled in wonder and shock as a tiny pink dragon with a protruding brow and a ruffled beard beneath its chin fluttered into the air. Little petal-like wings beat at its side, and a short stubby tail of green protruded from the rear of its body. It snapped its tiny jaws and spiraled in circles. Over their initial shock, the Calyx made exclamations of surprise and delight as the dragon spiraled around in the air.

"Don't stop," Georjie told Snap. "Ignore your friends. Stay angry and protective. Feel your emotions, let them come and channel them with your magic."

The snapdragon scent filling the air turned astringent and sharp. A second blossom jumped its stem and a yellow dragon the size of Beazle flew into the air. Another followed, then another. Suddenly all the blossoms were spiraling in the sky, snapping their colorful jaws and buzzing around in a flurry of pretty, painted-looking reptiles made of petals and stems. A couple of fae reached out to touch the dragons but withdrew their fingers when they were snapped at. Alstro got bit and started laughing, shaking out his finger. The dragons brushed against cheeks and clothing, filling the air around them. Then they began to dissipate in tiny puffs of colored fog, like party favors bursting. Snap straightened, having released his magic to watch the results. He looked just as amazed as the rest of them.

Proteas reached a hand into the vapor left behind by a snapdragon. "They're like a cross between chromatypes and duplicates."

"Snap, that was amazing!" Jess's heart was pounding. "You duplicated your blossoms!"

"Sort of, I guess." Snap grinned at Georjie, looking a little sheepish.

"This must be the first time ever in the history of the Calyx that such a thing has happened," said Peony, holding Sphex in her palm and looking dubious.

Georjie straightened too, brushing off the knees of her leggings. "Snap is definitely not the first flora fae to do that."

"You just haven't been encouraged to try," said Jess, elated. "Fahyli's familiars are able to duplicate, why shouldn't flora fae have a similar ability?"

"We make chromatypes," said Marigold, looking dazed. "I always thought that *was* our version of duplication."

"But mystic blossoms are just raw materials congealed into a perfume," Jess pointed out. "Duplicates are replicas of real animals. Beazle's duplicates have actual teeth that can draw blood. So it's not quite the same. Those little dragons were real, for a time."

"So… how did you know I could do that?" Snap asked Georjie, red brows drawn together.

"I didn't." She shrugged. "Not for sure. I just guessed that you've never used anger as fuel to conjure before. I was right. Then, when I felt your botanical moving into a phase of decay, I pushed some of my power into you to bring it back."

"We're discouraged from letting negative emotions taint our botanicals," Peony told Georjie. "It makes for poor quality perfumes."

"That makes sense." Georjie nodded. "I almost killed my mother once when I didn't realize that my negative emotions could harm others. I had to learn to control my own feelings in order to direct aggression. I learned that wrath doesn't have to be your enemy. It can be righteous; fuel for doing something to correct what has gone wrong, or to defend yourself or others."

"That's so intense," said Asclepias, putting his palm to his forehead in a comic gesture.

Georjie smiled. "It's another skillset you can develop, if you choose."

Snap shrugged his meaty shoulders. "It's great, but what kind of damage can I inflict with those little guys?"

Georjie tucked a strand of hair behind her ear. "This was just an exercise. You always knew that there was no real danger. What do you think the result would be if your life was really threatened? Or your friend's lives? You'll never know unless you get a chance to test it."

"Ilishec won't like this," said Iris. "It's amazing to see what Snap can do, but the gardener will never allow us to put ourselves in harm's way, especially as an experiment."

Georjie put her palms out. "I'm not telling you to do that either, I just think it's important to understand that our magic is much deeper than we might think. I would personally want to know all the tools I had in my toolbox. I've never liked feeling helpless or… ornamental."

Uneasy looks were exchanged among the Calyx. This was precisely the kind of talk that Ilishec had never liked or allowed, but for many of them, Jess included, it struck a chord.

Snap ran with it, of course. "I agree. I would be ashamed not to know what I'm capable of. Maybe it's because snapdragons don't make great perfume, maybe it's because I'm male and it's ingrained in me to be protective. I don't know. But everything inside of me hates being a liability, someone that others have to risk their lives to protect. I just… can't live like that. It's not how I was raised."

Jess chewed her lip. "Panther believes that fauna magic has no limit. Our skills are contained only by our beliefs. If that's right, then it should apply to flora magic too."

Snap studied her, thinking. "You mean: if you don't believe your magic can accomplish something, then it won't, not because it can't but because you're standing in its way?"

Jess and Peony exchanged a look. It came close to some

things that Peony had once said to Jessamine when she'd tutored her.

"Something like that," said Jess. "Look what you just did because you believed yourself capable of more."

"Georjie helped me, though," Snap said. "When she touched me, my power surged."

"What's going on in here?"

Ilishec's voice made everyone turn. The Calyx exchanged guilty looks, though the gardener sounded more curious than disapproving. Ilishec's focus went to Georjie—the apparent center of attention and the only being in the hothouse whom he didn't know.

"Hello. Who're you?"

Laec touched the gardener's arm. "Uncle, this is my friend Georjayna Sutherland. She's here as a favor to Elphame. Georjie, this is the Royal Gardener and my Uncle Ilishec."

Georjie approached, holding out her hand. "Pleasure to meet you."

"And you." Ilishec shook hands with her, but looked nonplussed as he took in her appearance. Jess could practically see the gears turn in his mind as he tried to categorize her.

"How is Hazel, Gardener?" asked Rose.

Ilishec gave Rose an inscrutable look as he released Georjayna's hand. "Sleeping now, which is good. When she's awake she's... not herself. Thanks for asking." He looked at Georjie again. "Forgive me but are you... flora fae?"

Georjie grinned. "Sort of. Are you?"

"Sort of," Ilishec responded in kind. "Elphame seems to think you can help, does she?"

"I'm not sure what Elphame thinks, to be honest." Georjie

scratched the back of her neck in a self-conscious way. "She asked me to come, so here I am."

Snap stepped closer to Georjie, putting a hand on her lower back in a protective way, like he was worried that Ilishec would be dismissive of the Wise. "She says that she's used common botanicals to defend herself when she was in danger. She was about to explain—"

"Snap, you didn't." Ilishec sent Georjie a look of apology.

"Actually, I don't mind," Georjayna began. "I think—"

"Please tell me he hasn't been pestering you about developing defensive magic." Ilishec shook his head and tsked, looking around. "My Calyx know that I do not approve. It's far too dangerous, and it's not our place. Everyone in the palace has clearly defined responsibilities; that's what has made Solana so wealthy, and that's how it needs to stay."

"Yes, Gardener," murmured several of the Calyx.

Georjie gave a demure smile and looked down.

"Now, fill me in on your progress, then you can take a break." Ilishec ushered them back to their garden beds. Jess was sorry that the fun was over. She looked to see if Georjie was still there, but she and Laec were already gone.

CHAPTER TWENTY

ÇIFTA

ÇIFTA PACED OUTSIDE the closed door, chewing a thumbnail. With a glance at Rayven—standing beside the chair she'd vacated the moment that Çifta stood, because if the queen wasn't seated, no one else could sit—she covertly slipped a finger up underneath her crown to scratch her scalp.

Miss Sabran didn't look up from the documents in her hands. "Why don't you just take it off, My Queen?"

Çifta, letting out a pent-up breath, plucked the crown off and tossed it onto a nearby table with a clatter. She resumed pacing and Rayven resumed reading... or whatever she was doing. Honestly, she had more energy than a herd of kid goats, the woman never stopped from morning until night. Çifta got it. Rayven was excited. The whole of Silverfall was excited. Çifta was too. Good things were finally on the horizon for this kingdom, but did they have to happen all at once? Rayven wanted Çifta's coronation to take place as soon as possible. Çifta refused, not until Laec arrived. He had to be by her side. Rayven had no choice but to acquiesce, but had begged Çifta to wear a stand-in crown until the real one could be officially placed. She wanted the citizens to grow accustomed to seeing Çifta as their sovereign. Çifta felt unable to say no, since delaying the coronation appeared to cause Rayven physical pain. But wearing a crown for most of a day was uncomfortable. She was beginning to see it as a ploy to wear her down so she'd agree to the coronation without Laec. It had become a battle of wills.

Çifta eyed the grandfather clock—a monstrosity made of white marble that weighed about as much as one of Kazery's ships. Only a half-hour had passed since Sasha had gone inside the private parlor with his father.

"He may be in there for some time, Your Grace." Rayven looked up from under silver brows. "He hasn't seen Elvio since he was... what... five?"

"Four, I think."

The former sorcerer had been fetched by soldiers and brought to the palace on a litter. He couldn't bear to ride in a carriage, nor would he ever sit in a proper chair or on a bench. He lived in squalor, she'd learned, so she had requested her soldiers clean him up and make him presentable for his son.

She'd known that the backfiring spell had twisted him, but Elvio's appearance in person had still alarmed Çifta. Lying on the litter, his shoulders faced left, but his knees and feet pointed right. She dared not picture how his body looked beneath the quilts, it would be the stuff of nightmares. His physical being aside, his face had surprised her on a level she could not possibly have anticipated. There was pain in his eyes, yes, but there had been immense joy too.

Her soldiers had brought Elvio into the room—a little-used parlor with an adjacent private salon—and paused before the queen. He had been bathed and anointed with lavender oil. His hair was very long, and had been combed back away from his forehead, exposing a receding hairline, and tied into a queue. Swaddled in a blanket taken from the palace, he had been propped up with pillows. All of this fuss was for Sasha's sake. Çifta did not care to meet the sorcerer. She'd seen enough of him while trapped inside the ice—enough of him and of his dark deeds—to last several lifetimes. But she wanted to support Sasha, who had no other friends in Silverfall. So here she was, welcoming a traitor and murderer. She had been prepared to harden her heart, but Elvio had looked up at Çifta with all the humility and adoration of a zealot. He was not able to bow, but had lowered his chin to his chest in a gesture that she was sure had pained him. When he'd opened his eyes, his gaze swam with emotion: gratitude and no small amount of awe.

"I am not sure what I expected," she'd said—because she had to speak before Elvio had permission to say anything—"but you aren't it."

Words burst out like water through a brittle dam. "Your Grace! Thank you! I believed I would die without ever seeing my son again. I cannot express my gratitude, not only for what you have done for me, but for what you have done for Silverfall. You've done what I was not strong enough to do: removed a wicked sovereign. You are a paragon. A legend."

Çifta looked away, embarrassed. "It wasn't me. It was Queen Karinya."

"No," Elvio said on a hushed exhale. "She had a hand in it, yes, but it was your heart and your courage that made a way for us. You have given us an opportunity at redemption. Do not diminish yourself. You went into the ice a merchant's daughter and came out a queen. Only a selfless act could do this."

"You seem to know a lot about it. Who has talked?"

"No one. I know the ice, My Queen. That is all." He coughed into a fist made of twisted fingers, the nails pointing in unnatural directions. "I have many regrets. I was so weak. I do not deserve to be in your presence."

Çifta canted her head. "I witnessed the way you were back then. What has changed you, Elvio?"

He smiled and gestured to his ruined body. "Humility changes everyone. I was arrogant and selfish. I thought I was unconquerable. I knew spells and strategies but nothing of real value. In one moment, everything was taken from me: magic, health, family, self-respect, identity... all gone." He raised a warped finger; the nail was black. "When the world knocks you this low—by which I mean to the very bottom—you have to ask yourself 'who am I now'? Who am I without all the things that once defined me? The answer frightened me more than anything I have seen or endured; I was no one good. I was weak, shallow and wicked. Not until I was broken could I see what spilled out. I know it is difficult to believe, My Queen, but I am thankful for this." He swept a hand down his lumpy form. "It changed me into someone I'm not afraid to look at in the mirror... ironic, isn't it?"

Çifta cupped her elbows. Elvio's speech touched her, but she didn't wish to show her emotions. She hoped Sasha's father was sincere in his repentance. "Sasha is waiting for you."

The ex-sorcerer's eyes misted up. There was also a flash of fear. "How is he? How does he look?"

Çifta found a smile for the wrecked fae. "Your son is beautiful, inside and out. He is strong, noble, kind and courageous.

He saved my life. If he ever needs me, I will be there for him, no matter what."

A tear slipped down Elvio's cheek. He brushed it away with the back of his hand. "And Rialta? Is she also here?"

"She is."

Another tear escaped. Elvio let this one fall to his chest. "Bless you, My Queen. I do not deserve such kindness."

Çifta stood aside and let the litter-bearers carry Elvio to the room where he would be reunited with his son. When the door closed behind them, she found that she did not know what to do with herself. Rayven—who had observed their conversation silently from a corner—had rustled the papers in her hand as though wanting to remind Çifta she was still there. Çifta didn't know what Miss Sabran thought of Elvio. She didn't want to know. If the citizens didn't like her generosity, she didn't want to hear about it. Sasha was her only concern. She wanted to give him whatever he wanted where his father was concerned.

Her own feelings were less clear. This sorcerer had killed her mother in his attempt to kill her. He had tortured her grand-mother. In so doing he'd stolen Çifta's chance at a relationship with a loving mother and grandmother. He had also broken Kazery's heart—which was why Çifta had ensured that Kazery had left before she allowed Elvio anywhere near the palace. These were the facts, and they danced in the periphery of Çifta's mind. She should be angry and vengeful. She should want to execute Elvio, and she had the right to do it. A single command and he would be gone from this world forever. But how would that make anything better? It wouldn't bring Salme or Evelin back. It wouldn't return to Kazery the years he'd lost with the fae he'd loved. It wouldn't restore Çifta's family or even make her feel better. There had been enough killing.

That Elvio viewed his condition as a blessing left Çifta's mind whirling. She had to admit that she was impressed. Would she have responded in such a way? It was impossible to say, but she had learned today that drastic change was possible, even for those who seemed beyond redemption. It had cost him everything, but how could it have cost anything less, given what he'd done to others?

She surrendered to her aching feet and parked herself on a sofa, sending for tea. She tried to read and failed. She could focus on nothing but what was happening behind that closed door, so when the door finally opened again, Çifta leapt to her feet.

The litter-bearers came out first. They stopped so Elvio could pay homage to Queen Çifta one more time, then carried him from the room.

Çifta waited but Sasha did not emerge. She exchanged a questioning look with Rayven, who only shrugged and gestured that she should go in. The door had been left ajar, an invitation. She approached, her slippered feet quiet on the carpeted floor. Sasha sat on the divan, perched on its edge, elbows on his knees. He stared forward at nothing. Rialta lay at his feet, looking up at him, head tilted, ears perked.

The door creaked, and Sasha looked over, brightening. His glacial eyes—so like her own—were glassy with unshed tears.

"My Queen." Sasha got to his feet and melted into a bow.

She came into the room. "Are you alright? I've been beside myself with worry."

"You are too kind, Your Grace." Sasha smiled at her as he straightened. "I am fine. There was no need to worry."

"I'm glad." Çifta laced her fingers together; her palms were clammy. "I've no wish to intrude on your private affairs, but may I ask…"

"Anything."

"Will you see him again?"

Sasha's gaze clouded but she sensed it was not in a pained way. "I would, but my father does not wish it."

Çifta's jaw sagged for a moment. "He doesn't wish to see you again? But, he loves you."

Sasha nodded. "That is why he does not wish to see me again."

"I don't understand."

Sasha rubbed the back of his neck. "I told him about Jessamine. He wants me to be happy. He said he has everything he ever wanted: my forgiveness and to see me once before he dies. The only thing that could be better than those two things—he said—would be knowing that I've found love."

Çifta felt winded. It was real then. Elvio's love for his boy was genuine and selfless. Sasha was here, prepared to forgive, prepared to take care of his father—Çifta assumed—and care was something Elvio desperately needed. Yet he'd eschewed all that for his son's sake.

"He wants to atone," Sasha told her, seeing her conflicted expression. "And the best way he can think to do that is to prioritize my happiness."

"Even if it means he'll never see you again."

He nodded. "*Especially* if it means he'll never see me again. Atonement should hurt, he said."

Çifta found herself hugging her ribcage. "What would you like me to do with him, or... for him?"

Rialta moved closer to Sasha, leaning against his thigh. He put a hand on her neck, ruffling her fur. "My Queen, I cannot tell you. You've lost so much because of him. I can't ask for more than what you've already given."

"Say you did, for the sake of argument."

Sasha studied her, continuing to stroke Rialta. The wolf looked up, listening. "I suppose I wouldn't want to see him suffer any more than he already does. I understand that he lives outside the city in Thieves Thicket—a shantytown where the outcasts and pickpockets live."

"Sounds uncomfortable."

"He did not complain, but I know the cold pains him. Perhaps a small but warm hut inside the city walls, and regular visits from someone who knows herbs? Someone who might ease his pain until he passes?"

"Consider it done."

Sasha's expression was one of relief and amazement. "Thank you, and… I'm sorry."

"You've nothing to apologize for."

Sasha looked sheepish. "I just feel I should say it. Perhaps on his behalf."

"Regarding your mother, Halyn." Çifta cleared her throat. "I'm sorry but I have not had success in locating her. I'm told she left Silverfall, for Stavarjak oddly enough. I can keep looking for you, if you wish? Perhaps send Queen Elphame a letter?"

"Thank you, Your Grace. It is enough. With your permission, I'd like to return home."

Çifta's stomach filled with butterflies. The way he said "home" made her heart ache. He did not and nor would he ever feel that Silverfall was his home, though he'd been raised here. And it did not surprise her—he'd been reviled by this court. In Solana, he was loved. He had a place, a sweetheart, respect.

She swallowed her disappointment. "I am so sorry for how you were treated here. I'm sorry that you no longer think of Silverfall as your home."

He smiled, eyes crinkling at the corners. "I think of it as the land of my youth. For me, home is not a place but a person. I have a feeling you understand that."

She put her hands on his shoulders and pulled him down so she could kiss each of his cheeks. "Better than anyone. You go, Sasha Drazek. And you, Rialta Drazek." She bent to caress the wolf's head and Rialta licked her chin. "Go with my blessing. May your journey be safe."

"Thank you, My Queen. Is there anything I can do for you?"

She considered. There was only one thing she wanted. "When you get back," she said in a low voice, "if it is at all within your power to send my own *home* back to me, I would be forever grateful."

Sasha nodded, his handsome features serious. "I will do whatever I can."

CHAPTER TWENTY-ONE

JESSAMINE

STEPPING FROM HER bathing room, wet hair dripping, and with a towel wrapped around her body, Jess cast about for something clean to wear. Two days had passed, and still there was no invasion, but it was supposedly imminent. Normal palace routine had stuttered to a near halt. Aside from feeding everyone, servants had been reassigned to activities that had more to do with preparing the city for a siege. The majority of Jess's clean clothes were dresses. She resigned herself to wearing the same grubby tunic and leggings she'd worn all day, and pulled those on over damp skin. Braiding her wet hair, she pulled her woolen Fahyli-issued cap over her head to help keep warm. The weather had taken a bitter turn—even though the calendar said they were now into summer—and dry firewood was not being delivered. Jess shivered as she crossed her stone floor to her dresser to scrounge for a clean pair of socks. She looked at the paper and quill sitting on her desk, waiting for her to write a response to Sasha. She'd not found the time yet, but would do it today, no matter how tired she was.

At a knock, she hurriedly jammed her feet into a pair of knee-high hose that weren't made to pair with leggings, then shoved her feet into a pair of ankle-high boots. Anytime she was approached with news, her heart flew around behind her sternum like a panicked sparrow in anticipation of the announcement that Solana had been invaded. Truthfully, everyone thought that it would have happened by now, but scouts continued to report no aggressive movement of troops from Rahamlar's fortress.

She opened the door to find her brother shifting anxiously from one foot to the other, his hand resting on the dagger he rarely wore. Ania zipped around his head so fast she almost blurred into a halo.

"What's wrong, Digit?" Jess opened the door wider. The lights in the hall were low, as they always were after eleven. "Is it finally happening?"

"We still haven't been invaded, but I got a message from the gardener asking for help with Hazel. Do you want to come? I don't know the gardener's wife very well, but I know she likes you."

"Sure. What does he want with you?" Jess did up her belt and held the door open as Beazle dropped from the ceiling, landing on top of her hat.

"The message didn't say."

Casting a longing look back at her desk, Jess closed the door. She'd try to find the time to write to Sasha tomorrow. The halls were much busier than they would be at this time of night under normal circumstances. Servants rushed about carrying various supplies; some were even jogging. As Digit and Jess descended to the ground floor, they passed an increasing number of soldiers and Fahyli in hushed conversations.

They took the winding stone trail leading to the cottage where Ilishec and Hazel lived. As they approached, the round door swung open and a stooped man in a hood came out. He grumbled something, perhaps a greeting, then hurried away. Digit held the door for Jess and she ducked inside.

Ilishec's home was a clean, quaint three-room cottage with a loft. The cottage was much warmer than Jess's room, with a fire roaring in a woodstove adjacent to the kitchen. Comfortable, well-worn furniture clustered around the fire. Near a window across from the living area was a small dining table with three chairs. It reminded Jess a lot of her home back in Dagevli and she felt immediately at ease.

The gardener was in the kitchen, pouring water into the sink from the brass tap. A small cluster of dirty dishes sat at his elbow He looked over his shoulder as he heard the door close. "Thank you for coming, Digit. Hello, Jessamine."

"Hello, Gardener." Jess toed off her boots, leaving them on the rack beside the door. Digit copied her.

Ilishec turned off the water and slid the dirty dishes into the sink. "Can I get you anything?"

The twins shook their heads. Ilishec gestured to the furniture in front of the stove.

Not one to waste time, Digit got to the point before his weight had even settled on the cushions. "How is Hazel?"

Ilishec perched on the edge of his chair as Jess sat beside Digit. She could feel waves of worry coming off the gardener. He gave a response she didn't quite understand.

"When it rains, it pours, or so they say. Thing is, this episode is overdue. I call it an episode, but only because I refuse to think that she won't come out of it."

"Her dementia has worsened?" Jess guessed.

Ilishec raked his hair back with both fingers. It needed a wash, and stayed where he'd raked it, in rows. "She collapsed in Mrs. Tierney's kitchen the day before yesterday. Not long after I discovered the problem with the raw materials."

"What can I do to help?" Digit asked.

"Not much, I'm afraid," Ilishec told him. "But I believe you can calm her nerves with your *digitalis*. I'm told you're a master at regulating dosages. You know exactly how much to administer in order to put someone to sleep and no more."

Jess knew firsthand just how effective Digit could be at knocking someone out.

Digit looked relieved that he could, in fact, be helpful. "Sure. Would you like me to do it now?"

Ilishec gestured toward a closed door. "Please. I'll stay here. I don't wish to upset her further."

Digit opened the bedroom door slowly. He peered in, then slipped inside. Jess heard Hazel's voice immediately—laced with tension and asking questions. Digit answered in a calm, kind voice.

"How did you upset her?" Jess asked softly, and became alarmed when she saw tears gathering in the corners of the gardener's eyes. He looked away, embarrassed, and his face worked as he got himself under control. When he met her eyes again, he looked so fragile.

"Everyone upsets her, but no one more than me. She *knows* me, but she doesn't know me. And that distresses and confuses her even more than strangers do, like the healer who just left."

"Oh, Gardener." Jess put a hand over her heart. Ilishec's pain made her feel like crying.

"I can't reach her this time. Usually when she has these spells, I just wait patiently until she comes back. If it takes a while, I'll show her the drawings she loves. She's a great fan of watercolor paintings, so I have many books full of prints. They usually help her come back to me, but not this time. She's too upset to eat, and hasn't had a proper meal since she fainted." He wiped at his eyes.

"Is there anything I can do?"

"I'm hoping Digit can give her a restful sleep, and that will do the trick."

Jess nodded and tried to look encouraging.

Digit came out of the bedroom holding his elbows and looking sad. The sight of Hazel had struck him hard.

"Did she know you?" Ilishec asked, his expression lifting with hope. "Sometimes less familiar faces trigger her memory better than those she sees every day."

"No, Gardener. She didn't know me, and I barely recognized her. I didn't know dementia could… do that to someone. When she fell asleep, she looked like herself, but before that… she looked at me like I was her worst enemy."

Ilishec sighed. "I'm sorry for that, Digit. She's frightened. When she forgets people, she feels so alone." Ilishec got to his feet, perhaps feeling Digit's discomfort. "Thank you for coming. I'm hopeful that in the morning she'll be better."

Digit nodded. Jess took the hint and got up, following her twin to the door where they pulled on their shoes. She straightened and gave Ilishec a hug.

"Try and get some sleep yourself," Jess told him.

"Easier said than done." Ilishec sniffed and produced a kerchief from a rear pocket to wipe his nose.

"I can put you down too, if you'd like?" Digit offered.

The gardener smiled sadly. "Tempting, but no. Thank you. I'm going to read these books that Devlin left me. He's known Hazel for a long time and has helped us a lot in the past. He ordered these titles from a university in Archelia that does research on Hazel's condition. There might be something helpful in them."

The twins returned to the palace without speaking, other than to say goodnight. Jess was heading back up to her room when she halted on the stairs with a harsh whisper: "Georjie!"

Laec had told her that Georjie had healing powers that outmatched any flora fae because she could draw from all growing things simultaneously.

Jess scampered up the rest of the stairs two at a time, then jogged toward Laec's corridor. Passing the violet suite, she went to the next door—labeled *Hibiscus*—and knocked. Footsteps approached and Laec opened the door. His tunic was open at the neck and almost falling off one shoulder. His hair was mussed and lay on his shoulders in waves. Jess took a half step back, surprised to find him in Georjayna's suite, especially this late at night.

"Laec!"

"Jess!" Laec mimicked the scandal in her voice. "Don't be such a prude. She's healing the last of the frostbite damage."

Georjie appeared at Laec's shoulder, smiling. "Hello *belladonna*."

Jess blinked again, thinking what an appropriate name that would have been for her had she known which botanical she'd become most famous for.

"I'm sorry to disturb you, it's just that I've come from Ilishec's cottage—" The sad look they exchanged made her pause. "You know about Hazel?"

Laec leaned a hand on the doorjamb. "We were there earlier today."

Jess gave Georjie a pleading look. "And you can't help her?"

Georjie curled long fingers around the edge of the door, widening the gap so they could see one another better. The Wise looked regretful. "Unfortunately, what's wrong with Hazel is not something earth magic can fix. I did try, but all I could manage was to improve her circulation. Her mind is too far gone. I am sorry."

Disappointment made Jess's hands feel cold. She tucked them inside her armpits. "Thanks anyway."

She walked back to her room wondering how Hazel could be so far gone that even the healing power of the earth couldn't reach her.

CHAPTER TWENTY-TWO

JESSAMINE

IT WAS DAWN on the third morning following Faraçek's coronation and no Rahamlarin soldiers had crossed Solana's borders. Tensions were mounting. Jess stood on the rampart wall with Regalis and Kestrel, their exhales steaming into the air. The temperature had dropped, each day cooler and wetter than the last. The air felt clammy and smelled of damp earth mingled with the scent of the fresh bread emanating from the city's many bakeries.

The population of Solana City had swelled to triple its permanent residents. Women, children and the elderly from villages scattered along the Rahamlar border had been billeted with families who lived within the city walls. Every spare room in the palace was full, with the larger suites housing up to four families. Everyone was unhappy and taut with anxiety about those left behind. Fights had broken out among villagers—over who would be permitted to live inside the castle and who would have to billet in homes—but it had been quickly stomped out by Bradburn. Jess had never been fond of Bradburn—there were times when she wondered how he'd achieved the third-highest position in Solana's military beneath the crofter and the king himself—but now that push was coming to shove, she was grateful for his disciplinarian nature.

Bradburn had mandated a curfew: everyone had to be in their homes— temporary or permanent—by sundown, and no one was allowed out until dawn except stablehands, cooks, bakers, soldiers, and Fahyli. Shouting by soldiers was permitted, shouting by citizens was forbidden. Fighting over accommodation was rewarded with a downgrade. If you'd been given a room in a humble dwelling and you complained, you were moved to a hovel. If you complained about your hovel, you were given a canvas tent in a park or garden. With the weather unseasonably cold and wet, no one wanted to stay in a tent. Bradburn had successfully maintained three days of peace, barring the churn and chaos as villagers had first flooded the city.

Behind the Fahyli stretched a city still mostly slumbering, except for kitchens setting up for the day. Shops had been closed or temporarily turned into dining areas. Volunteer cooks were plenty, thankfully, as many of the village women were the chefs of their household. Food was flavorful but rationed. No one knew how long they'd have to live like this, but Jess had overheard Bradburn say to one of his captains that his goal was to find a quick resolution, otherwise there'd be domestic murders to deal with on top of the foreign invaders. Most people struggled to endure sharing their home with a bunch of strangers for an extended period of time.

The raptor familiars spent most of their time over Rahamlar spying, resting in Rahamlarin forests and hunting in Rahamlarin skies. They shared a constant stream of information with their fae, and the information had not changed; soldiers could remain somewhat at ease.

This morning, Jess had been assigned to a spying shift with Regalis. The raptors reported soldiers moving over Rahamlar territory, but never mounting any coordinated move toward Solana. After three days of nothing, the crofter wanted more specific information about what Rahamlar was up to, and that meant a smaller spy, one that could get inside the fortress undetected. When Ferrugin had winged out toward Rahamlar before the sun was a hint on the horizon, Beazle was on her back, saving his energy for their mission.

As the first of the sun's rays touched the tops of Solana's tallest turrets, Beazle sent Jess her first overhead view of Rahamlar. From the elevated height of Ferrugin's back it looked much as it always had: thick walls and the ugly fortress crouched between two wide rivers. Where the Tadylat and the Tamyrat snaked close together, Rahamlar's brooding castle squatted between its iron gates. Further along, the rivers wound away from one another, leaving an ever-widening tract of land where farms and villages sprouted.

Ferrugin swooped lower—skimming over the Tadylat before wheeling to perch on top of the flagpole of the aviary near the main courtyard—and Beazle took flight for himself.

There's a weird smell here. He landed on a mossy shingle above the dormer belonging to the room that had once been Çifta's prison.

As Beazle found a shadow to hide in, a commotion grew in the courtyard. Riders in hoods and boiled leather, eight of them, cantered through the gate, making a loud clatter on the stones. Stableboys came through a side gate to gather the horses as the unseelie soldiers dismounted and filed their way inside. A few pulled their hoods back, giving Beazle a good view of their grayish skin and wickedly pointed unseelie ears. Every one of them was well-muscled and taller than an average human soldier. None of them wore Rahamlarin livery. Instead, they each wore a unique outfit, dark and camouflaged, with many pockets and mysterious holsters.

You think they're mercenaries?

Jess never failed to be surprised by how much Beazle knew. Mercenaries were not something they'd ever discussed, or had even been present in any room where they were discussed. *How do you know what a mercenary is?*

I wasn't born yesterday, Beazle told her with a touch of annoyance. *Bats are intelligent, and wild ones don't live as long as I have. Why shouldn't I know about career soldiers?*

Jess shook her head in wonder. *Follow them, will you?*

Beazle closed his vision from her, but she sensed him crawling through a crack he'd invaded once before, which led into a stairwell connected to the doorway through which the soldiers had entered. He followed the sound of male voices down several torch-lined halls, around corners and down short flights of stairs. He hid outside the room the men had filed into and nosed around until he found a crack that took him through the wall.

When Beazle returned his sight to her, the first person Jess saw was Faraçek. She couldn't stop the hiss that escaped through her teeth. The prince—she would never think of him as king— stood in a dim, windowless room at the head of a table. Though she'd recognize him anywhere, he was in a state she'd never seen: a manic look filled his eyes, and he looked unwashed.

"What is it, Jess?" Regalis's mouth sounded close to her ear.

"The prince is about to have a meeting," she told him "Faraçek is pacing. He looks deranged. Something must have happened."

She could sense the fauna fae tense. "Maybe that's why they haven't invaded yet."

"Let me watch."

She focused on Faraçek. The prince had always taken pride in his appearance—his hair was typically brushed to a shine and tied back, beard impeccably groomed, and clothing beautiful and well-fitted. But now, Faraçek's hair was greasy and lay ragged against his neck. His beard was unkempt, even knotted from constant twisting. His clothing was dirty and one sleeve was torn. His boots were caked with dried mud. Beyond his harassed appearance, there was something else amiss about the prince, something Jess couldn't quite put her finger on.

The unseelie soldiers filled the room, an ugly square space lit with smoking torches. The ceiling was coated with soot. The tabletop before the prince was cluttered with things, mostly books and maps but also weapons and unfriendly-looking metal devices Jess couldn't identify. Twelve crude chairs surrounded the table, but no one sat. If Faraçek wasn't sitting, they couldn't either. Faraçek displayed signs of a ruler who feared he might never sit again.

"Well?" Faraçek barked as the door closed. Cocking both hands on his hips, he paced, head swiveling like an owl. His eyes were wide open but bloodshot.

"It's spreading, Sire," one of the soldiers stated. "As you suspected."

Faraçek bared his teeth. The expression was terrifying, more predator than fae. A maniacal laugh escaped his mouth, but a moment later he screamed with fury. He attacked the table, sweeping anything close enough to reach onto the floor. Jess felt adrenaline surge through her at this show of violence.

He turned away, tearing at his hair before whirling back to face the unseelie.

"Where is Yorin?" he screamed, spit flying. "Where is my captain?"

The soldier seemed unaffected by the prince's display of temper. "He was behind us."

Beazle was tickled to see the normally stoic prince so out of control. Jess sensed the bat version of a grin as he peered out from the soot-caked wall. *Something not gone your way, Faraçek old boy?*

What are they talking about? What is 'spreading?' Jess wondered.

She swayed a little, then felt Regalis put a hand on her back to steady her.

Yorin strode into the room, all business and industry. He looked identical to the last time Jess had seen him, even wearing the same boiled-leather vest with the orange cowbird stamped onto the chest.

His captain's entrance made Faraçek's eyes almost pop out of his head. "It's true then?"

The captain tugged off his gloves and reached for a pouch at his side. He was clearly unhappy about something, but he was not out of control the way the prince was. He placed the bag on the table then pulled out lumpy handkerchiefs, which he set in a line beside it.

"Yes Sire. Everywhere within a mile and a half radius from the fortress—and spreading at a rate I would never have thought possible. Many kinds, not just yours."

Jess counted fourteen of the lumpy, closed sacks—simple squares folded over and held with twine. Yorin undid the twine, fingers working deftly, then stepped back and put up his hands. "I learned my lesson, even with gloves. I still don't feel well. See for yourself, Sire."

Faraçek moved forward and removed the loosened twine from the first bundle, then unfolded the fabric. It contained a little pile of brown items that looked like tiny, misshapen brains. The prince studied them for a moment, like a man in a trance. Then he murmured something so quietly that even Beazle had to strain to hear.

"*Gyromitra esculenta.*"

"Regalis," Jess hissed, patting the air blindly in search of him. "Write this down. *Gyromitra esculenta.*"

Kestrel's voice sounded from near enough to make her jump. "Nomenclature?"

Jess heard the rustle of paper and the sound of pencil scratching. "Yes, I've got it, Jess," Regalis said. "I'm listening."

Faraçek moved to the next kerchief, unfolding it to expose a small heap of something Jess recognized without the prince's help.

"*Coprinopsis atramentaria,*" Jess said as a sense of dread stole over her. "They're mushrooms, Regalis."

The prince echoed Jess's identification of *atramentaria* correctly, before moving on to the next and the next. He identified them all on sight, and Jess repeated: "*Amanita phalloides, amanita bisporigera, chlorophyllum molybdites, omphalotus illudens, clitocybe dealbata...*"

Beazle gave Jess as good a look as he was able to with his fuzzy bat vision, and from a distance: mushrooms that looked like little white umbrellas, others that looked like melted orange plates, more that looked like mini black stems of broccoli. Some were as white as a feather and looked like a single bird's wing. One had bright pink stems beneath fat rounded tops.

"I recommend you don't open that one, Sire," Yorin told Faraçek as he reached for the last one. The kerchief stood out thanks to the white stripes running across it. "They're fragile, and they puff dust into the air. We're not sure how safe it is. I hadn't even begun to identify them yet, but I'm pleased to see that you can."

Faraçek glared at him. "This is not the kind of enhancement I was expecting. Having a thorough knowledge of fungi suddenly *appear* in my brain is not helpful to us right now. It's like a sick joke from my dead ancestor." He gestured angrily at the air, eyes blazing. "Is Toryan laughing at me from the grave, I wonder? Although I'm happy that you're pleased." His tone was laced with sarcasm.

"That's what it is," Jess murmured as she realized what hadn't looked right about the prince.

"What?" Regalis asked.

"He's not wearing the crown."

"But... they put it on his head during the coronation, Ferrugin saw it."

"So did Ratchet," Kestrel added.

"I guess he took it off again... but the enhancement remains," Jess said.

She studied the varieties Faraçek had not named aloud, noting their appearance. She had studied fungi only in passing since it was not applicable to her role, but she did know that one of them—*amanita phalloides*—was also known as death cap. It was deadly. Did that mean the rest of them were deadly too? She shivered at the thought. A whole nation covered in poisonous mushrooms? Was that what they meant by 'it was spreading'?

"Have the raptors take a closer look at the ground, but tell them to be careful not to touch anything," Jess told the Fahyli.

Regalis replied: "Ferrugin's already flying over the pasture-land behind the fortress. She says the earth and the lower trunks of all the trees are covered in mushrooms. They're even growing on the sides of houses."

Jess couldn't stop a sharp smile. "Serves him right, the tyrant."

"Don't smile, Jess. What if the fungi doesn't know where to stop?"

She lost her grin. The suggestion startled her into losing her connection to Beazle's vision. She looked up to see Regalis's solemn expression, her eyes wide. "That's... not possible."

"Isn't it? If Toryan's crown has enhanced the prince's powers, and the original owner of the crown believed that Solana's territory rightfully belonged to Rahamlar, what's to stop the infestation from crossing the border? We're already getting unseasonable weather."

"That's a coincidence, surely."

Regalis didn't look so sure.

Jess shook her head, not wanting to believe such a horrible thing might be true.

Jess! A mental screech from Beazle brought her bat vision snapping back with such violence that she winced. Vertigo followed, as what he was seeing was a lot of fast movement. Jess felt dizzy and was thankful Regalis was there to hold her up.

"I've got you," he said in her ear. "What's happening?"

Jess wished she knew. Two of the soldiers in the room had begun to fight. The other unseelie had moved to the corners of the room. Faraçek remained where he was, watching with the curiosity of a scientist, as the two soldiers, daggers in hand, fought with a kind of fury Jess had never seen. Jess quested toward Beazle's mind for understanding.

He breathed on them, he told her. *He breathed on them and told them to kill one another.*

These words rocked through her. *Why?!*

I don't know. Beazle's claws gripped the sooty mortar as he leaned out to watch.

The soldiers' movements were aggressive, skillful, and full of power. Neither bested the other. They were perfectly matched in size, strength and ability. When one thrust, the other parried. When one circled, the other mirrored his counterpart with perfect footwork. It was a deadly dance that Jess had never seen executed better by anyone.

Dust crumbled beneath Beazle's claws, falling down the wall to spatter on the floor. It was only a little, but it was enough.

"Stop!" yelled Faraçek, and the soldiers stopped. They stared at one another, chests heaving, daggers gripped, thighs flexed, waiting for the command to spring.

"You're friends again. All is well," the prince said, eyes narrowing at the wall.

The soldiers sheathed their daggers and wiped their brows. They looked as though waking from a dream. Those who'd been observing looked shifty and uncertain. But Faraçek's gaze was on the dust by the door. His dark eyes flicked upward, to the place where Beazle hid.

"Get out of there, Beeze!" Jess cried aloud, and felt Regalis grip her bicep.

Faraçek rushed forward, hands lifting, fingers forming claws.

Beazle scrabbled backward through the crack, popping out the other side and fluttering into the air in the corridor.

"I know you, you little rat!" Faraçek yelled. "You tell them I'm coming! I am coming!"

The prince's screams grew distant as Beazle flew away as fast as he could manage, his little heart pattering with fright. He zipped out the nearest open window.

I thought he was going to breathe on me. Beazle shook his head as though shaking off his fear. He flew over the main courtyard, casting about with his sonar, looking for Ferrugin.

"The prince saw Beazle," Jess explained as Beazle's vision faded to black. She put a hand over her eyes to stave off the dizziness of returning to her own sight.

"Is he alright?"

Jess bent over, posting her hands on her knees. Her heart was a sledgehammer, her palms slick with sweat. "He's looking for Ferrugin. Beazle's ok, he just had a scare."

After a beat, Regalis said: "She's got him. They're coming back."

Jess straightened, wishing the dizzy feeling would pass faster. Kestrel touched her shoulder. "You okay?"

She looked at her Fahyli companions. "Faraçek said to tell us that he's coming."

Jess wasn't ready to face the worry on the gardener's face. She stood outside Ilishec's cottage door, staring at the wood. Jess had completed her shift on the wall, then journeyed by the dining hall and Mrs. Tierney's kitchen, cramming a meal down her throat so quickly she hardly tasted it, and chasing it with an elixir. In her hand was a crumpled piece of paper upon which she'd scrawled a duplicate of the list Regalis had made, because he was presenting it for discussion with Agir and Esha.

Beazle sniffed the air and burrowed into her hair, curling up in a ball. Jess didn't need to ask him what was wrong: they weren't even inside yet, but the cottage smelled of death.

Before her blows could fall, the door opened. Out came Peony, Nympha, Marigold and Iris. The Calyx said nothing, keeping their eyes cast toward the ground. She didn't have the heart to question them, and was certain she didn't want to hear what they had to say. They moved down the path toward the hothouses.

"Jess?" Ilishec looked at her from just inside, holding the door open.

Jess stepped inside, suffocating under the weight of sorrow. "I'm so sorry to bother you." She knew how it would sound asking for his help. Terrible. Selfish.

Ilishec let out a long sigh and closed the door.

Jess folded and unfolded the paper in her hand. "How is she?"

"Not good." Ilishec moved toward the kitchen in a daze. He went to a cupboard, scanning the contents. He poked about the bottles before pulling one down, reading the label, then putting it back in favor of another.

"There's been no change?"

"She's only deteriorated, I'm afraid. What would you like to drink?" He retrieved a couple of glasses from another cupboard. "I could do with something potent myself."

"I'm so sorry, Gardener." Jess sank onto the nearest piece of furniture. "I don't understand…"

"It's easy to understand, Jessamine." Ilishec set two small clear glasses with delicate curved handles on the table, then twisted the cap off a bottle of purple liquid. "She's likely coming to the end of her life. Time gets us all in the end and we never know when that will be."

"But she's so young," Jess protested. Hazel's pleasant features swam into her mind, shadowed by confusion, but lively and vibrant. She didn't know how old Ilishec or Hazel were, it would be rude to ask, but surely, they couldn't even be in their sixties yet.

"Death can come at any age," Ilishec told her. "We are not guaranteed a long life, just like we are not guaranteed perfect health. We must be grateful for every day. Hazel is young in body, but old in mind." Ilishec poured an inch of liquid into each cup. His gaze went hazy and he stared at nothing for a long moment, then came back to himself with a shake. He carried both cups over to Jess, handing her one.

Numbly, she took it, registering how strange it was that the gardener was giving her alcohol to drink. "She could come back from this, though, right?"

"She could, but I have to prepare myself for her not to. She's never been this far gone, and nothing I've tried seems to help." Ilishec sat on the footrest in front of a hand-crafted rocking chair and took a sip of his drink. A dimple cratered deeply in his grizzled cheek as he swallowed.

"For the last three days she's either been unconscious or yelling about how everything is going backward."

"Backward?"

"Strange isn't it?" He gestured with the hand holding his cup, the violet liquid sloshing. "You're not drinking."

Jess took a sip, wincing as the alcohol burned its way down her throat and into her stomach, where it pooled like molten lava. She coughed a few times, but the initial heat soon softened, turning into a warm sensation that soothed her abused digestive system. As the intense heat faded from her mouth, a flavor blossomed on her tongue that reminded her of pansies.

"It's Hazel's favorite," the gardener told her with what was almost a smile. "It's an Archelian liquor. We took a vacation there after we were married. Brought back a dozen bottles."

"What is it?" Jess held up the glass so the light of the nearest etherlamp could shine through it. A thousand shades of purple swirled inside her glass, moving slowly. It was beautiful, and looked almost like a living thing.

Ilishec eyed the contents of her glass with obvious fondness. "It's called Caludia. It's made with a fae species of sand crocus mixed with Terran pansies and a fermented tuber I always forget the name of." He winked over his glass. "I know. Don't tell anyone."

Jess glanced toward the closed door of the bedroom, not sure if she wasn't supposed to tell anyone that the Royal Gardener forgot the name of a tuber, or that he'd given hard alcohol to one of his flora fae. Ilishec didn't have any rule against the Calyx drinking reasonable amounts of wine or champagne during banquets, but he frowned upon them drinking during their down time. This was the opposite of how the crofter felt about the Fahyli drinking—no alcohol while on duty, but they were permitted to drink otherwise, in moderation.

Ilishec noticed Jessamine's covert glance at the bedroom door.

"It's better we leave her be."

"Of course."

"My Hazel." The gardener sighed and he took another sip with trembling lips. "They tried to comfort her: Peony, Iris, Dahlia, and the others. To be honest I'm not certain their presence didn't push her over an edge." A tear streaked down one cheek and into his beard. He palmed it away. "Please don't tell them. It would crush them."

"I won't." Her own eyes were stinging with unshed tears. She hesitated to burden Ilishec with what she and Beazle had discovered, but he was the most likely person to have insight, and the situation was urgent. It was cruel, but Ilishec didn't have time just to grieve, not with Faraçek breathing down their necks.

"Gardener?"

"What is it, Jessamine? Come, you need not spare me. I have loved and lost before. Tell me what you came for. I know it wasn't for Hazel."

Jess felt her face go hot.

Ilishec saw her shame and put out a hand. "No, no. You misunderstand me. It's not a criticism, my dear. Solana is in crisis. I know you have been busy with the Fahyli. You must have come because you need something. What can I do for you?"

She set her cup on the little side table and handed the gardener the crumpled paper with her chicken-scratch writing on it. Ilishec squinted at the words as Jessamine described what Beazle had witnessed inside Rahamlar's fortress.

"There were more species', fourteen in all," Jess said. "But the prince didn't identify all of them out loud. I recognized a couple, but I didn't have a clear view of some."

The gardener looked like he was either barely listening, or he was listening so deeply that he'd fallen into a trance. His gaze on the page and his body still, Jess wondered whether he'd fallen asleep with his eyes open.

"Gardener?" She lowered her head, trying to catch his eye.

He took a deep breath and lifted huge eyes to her face. "Going backward!"

"Sorry?"

"Hazel has been trying to tell me... Oh!" Ilishec covered

his mouth with a hand, looking to the page again then back at Jess. He put his cup aside and stood, going to the nearest window to peer out—a useless exercise as it was too dark to see anything. He turned back.

"The weather." He seemed breathless with astonishment. "The seasons… they're going backward. Spring is always followed by summer, which we're supposed to be in now. But the day Hazel fell ill, the same day the raw materials in the storage facility went bad, the same day the weather turned cool and wet, was the same day the prince had himself crowned. That's why Hazel was going on about everything going backward. She understands what's happening, she just wasn't capable of expressing it in a way I could understand."

"The unseelie prince has triggered the old magic," Jess supplied. "We're getting autumn now, not summer."

"Right." Ilishec sagged against his counter. "In ancient times, Rahamlar was the kingdom of perpetual fall."

Jess sat taller, pulling one foot up beneath her. "But it's not just a matter of the weather sliding into a state of untimely autumn. Rahamlar is covered in fungi. It's spreading, and Regalis is worried that because Toryan never wanted Erasmus to emancipate Solana from Rahamlar, the magic won't respect our borders."

Ilishec's expression turned calculating. "So not only do we face the invasion of a foreign army—larger and stronger than ours—we face an infestation of the kind of fungi no one wants anywhere near their gardens." He raised the crumpled page. "Death Cap, Destroying Angel, Elfin Saddle, Deadly Webcap, these are just a few of the common names of the nomenclature you have listed here. If these take over Rahamlar, it will soon become uninhabitable. If they cross the border into Solana, we too are finished."

They stared at one another across the small cottage. Jess saw her own terror and dread reflected in Ilishec's eyes. He rubbed his forehead and came over to the living area to sit down.

"Do the king and queen know?"

"Regalis went to see them while I came here," Jess replied. "They'll surely know by now. What do we do, Gardener?"

Ilishec stroked his jaw, and Jess felt encouraged by the serenity that came over him. "I must visit our monarchs." He looked at her sharply. "Are you on duty right now?"

She shook her head. "Not till daybreak, I just came off the wall."

"Good. You need to get some sleep. You look exhausted." He tossed down the rest of his Caludia like a shot then took the empty glass to the kitchen and put it in the sink.

Jess sighed, wishing it were that easy. "How do you propose I do that?"

He nodded at her cup, with a bit of liquid still in the bottom. "I think you'll find it won't be too difficult. Caludia has soothing effects, which is why I chose it. Sorry, I should have told you that before I offered some to you." He blinked. "Come to think of it, I shouldn't have offered you any at all. You're still a teenager. I'm completely out of sorts, please forgive me."

He reached for her glass but she downed the remains before he could take it away, then handed it to him with a close-mouthed smile.

He shook his head fondly as he took the cup. "Go on, brat. To bed with you."

She walked with the gardener to the palace entrance, where their paths diverged, then went up to her room. As promised, by the time she'd closed her door and was toeing off her boots, her mind felt muzzy and her body felt warm and relaxed. She wormed out of her jacket and tunic, then lay on her quilts with her leggings and undershirt still on, letting her heavy eyelids drift closed.

CHAPTER TWENTY-THREE

LAEC

LAEC SKIDDED TO a halt outside the maproom, hooking the doorjamb to arrest his momentum. He pulled himself through the doorway and into a crush of bodies. Something warm and solid pressed against his leg and he looked down to see Tully standing inside the door; next to her sat a cat with beautiful markings, too big to be a domesticated cat but much smaller than Tulliana. There were other familiars sprinkled throughout the room, sitting in the rafters. King Agir and Captain Bradburn stood at the maproom table. The king looked ill-at-ease, his face waxen but his jaw set—thick with stubble though it was—with a thin circlet crowning his head. In a dark blue velvet vest, he looked regal and somber. The short sword at his waist, a ceremonial blade, inspired courage.

Panther stood against the wall, arms crossed and expression grim. He waved Laec over, shuffling sideways to make room. Laec squeezed through the crowd. The room was relatively quiet, so Laec leaned close to Panther and kept his voice low.

"Someone yelled down my corridor that the invasion had started. Just about gave me a heart attack."

Panther jerked his chin toward Regalis, standing at the end of the maproom table. "Ferrugin reported a contingent of soldiers leaving Rahamlar fortress before dawn. They followed the king's road but turned toward Stoneiron, a border town. They're approaching it now."

"How many?" Laec's pulse jumped and he shifted from foot to foot, flexing one thigh, then the other. The urge to move his muscles was strong.

"Ferrugin can only count to eighteen, after that she loses track," Pan said with a twitch of amusement. "She says she counted that number one and a half times, not including the prince."

Laec calculated. "Twenty-seven soldiers? That's not enough for an invasion. That's more like an armed escort."

Panther stroked his jaw, canting his head toward Laec. "If he thinks they can take Stoneiron with twenty-seven, he's in for a shock. It's a big village, with a defensive force of over one hundred. Forty are Bradburn's, twenty-five from Stoneiron and the rest are Sir Garen Deerdall's knights, from a big estate outside Stoneiron."

"Is the village walled?"

Panther made a seesaw motion with his free hand. "Sort of. Over the last week, they've erected a wooden wall and four watchtowers."

"Have they been warned?"

Someone shushed them, so Panther lowered his voice to a whisper. "Soon as we knew their heading, Bradburn sent a bird to Deerdall, warning him to prepare. They're as ready as they can be. Ferrugin is following and reporting."

"They've reached Stoneiron," Regalis said in a loud voice, and the room settled. "The prince's party has halted on the road. The gates are shut and locked from the inside."

"And the towers?" King Agir asked, making fists and leaning his knuckles on the table.

"There are between three and five archers in each tower, Sire," Regalis said.

Bodies shuffled, heads bowed as they listened. The experience reminded Laec of radio broadcasts he'd heard while visiting Scotland, only this was a real-time play-by-play of an actual invasion.

"The prince has dismounted." Regalis spoke slowly as he relayed everything his familiar showed him. "Captain Yorin is with him. They're approaching the gate on foot. Sir Deerdall and his men are inside the gate. Deerdall has demanded to know what the prince wants, and warned him that he's not welcome, that Stoneiron will not give its allegiance. Not now. Not ever."

A sense of pride filled the room and could be seen on King Agir's face. Silence stretched out and everyone present seemed to be holding their collective breaths.

"The prince hasn't answered yet." Regalis sounded bewildered. "He is approaching the gate. Four soldiers with shields are with him. Faraçek has reached the gate, and appears to be... studying it."

"As in, looking for a weakness?" the crofter asked.

"I'm not sure, Crofter," Regalis answered. "But now the prince has turned to look back at Captain Yorin, who has given a command. One of the unseelie has dismounted and is approaching the gate. He has a…"—Regalis's voice took on a tone of incredulity—"an axe."

Murmurs went through the room. Someone guffawed. "One soldier with an axe?! What, is he going to try to chop down the gate?"

Laec shook his head, mystified. Any soldier who attacked the gate would get shot with an arrow from the nearest watchtower.

"It looks that way." Regalis shook his head, but his expression shifted. "He has attacked the gate. He's been fired at, but they've missed."

There was a collective groan and the crofter held up a hand to stop the noise.

"He's backing away, protected by a shield. He's made a hole. The prince has now approached, sheltered by soldiers with shields. They're being fired on. As instructed, Deerdall's men have moved six feet back from the gate."

King Agir nodded with approval. All villages had been warned about the prince's mind-control powers. Letting him get closer than six feet had been forbidden.

But Regalis now looked stunned. Moments passed where no information was being shared, and the tension in the room mounted to a near unbearable peak.

"What's happening, Regalis?" one of the Fahyli finally cried out.

"I'm not sure." Regalis sounded dazed. "Nothing has been said, or at least not that Ferrugin could hear. They're… the Stoneiron men are moving forward. Now they're… opening the gate."

Gasps and groans echoed throughout the room.

"Why?" someone moaned as though in pain.

"Stoneiron resolved to fight," said another. "What are they doing?"

"They're... they're... the gate is open. Faraçek has walked right in, and Stoneiron... they're... kneeling," Regalis told the room. "They're swearing allegiance to the prince. People are coming out of the houses now, mostly peasants, men of the village who aren't fighters. A few women, not many. They're coming toward the gate. They look... they looked drugged."

Laec put a hand over his mouth. *Oh no.*

"They're kneeling. Every last one, even our own soldiers and Deerdall. All of them. The archers have come down from the watchtowers. They're throwing down their bows and arrows. Unseelie soldiers on the road are dismounting, they're entering through the open gate. They're... armed, they've got swords in their hands."

Laec closed his eyes, steeling himself.

Regalis went quiet. When nothing was said for a long time, Laec opened his eyes and looked at his Fahyli friend. Regalis had dropped his chin toward his chest, his eyes were closed. He had one hand over his mouth, as though absorbing disturbing news.

"Regalis?" The crofter prompted. "We're waiting. Do not spare us."

Regalis lifted glassy eyes to his commander. "They're killing the soldiers and the archers. No one is fighting back. They are being cut down where they kneel. They do not seem to recognize death is coming, or that it's happening all around them. It's a slaughter."

The room went as silent as a mausoleum. Minutes ticked by, achingly slow, painful minutes. The familiars let their heads droop. Wings hung low from shoulders. Tully's huge black head was down, her nose pointed to the floor. She and the smaller cat leaned against one another. For a long time, nothing was said. Those wearing hats or hoods took them off, bowing their heads in sorrow for the deceived and departed.

"It is finished," Regalis murmured. "All our men are dead, and all of Deerdall's knights."

"And the villagers?" The crofter prompted, his voice throaty.

Regalis braced his hands flat on the tabletop, leaning his weight on it, as though his legs couldn't hold up his bulk anymore. "They're alive. The prince has commanded them to clean up the bodies and burn them. He's told one of the elderly men to gather weapons and armor, to pile them onto a wagon for delivery to the fortress."

Shock settled over the room like a thick shroud. Precautions had been taken, scenarios discussed. The prince's breath had been deemed dangerous—everyone knew it—but to breathe upon an entire village and bend their minds to his will?

"Friends and soldiers." King Agir's expression was grave. "Stoneiron has fallen. We've underestimated our enemy. We must send messages to every village, commanding them to retreat to the safety of our walls as quickly as they can. We must do whatever is necessary to ensure that no other village shares the fate of Stoneiron."

Heads nodded in agreement, but Laec could read his own fears reflected in their faces. How did they fight an adversary that had the power to make all of them drop their swords simply by breathing? Laec closed his eyes and thought of Elphame and her premonition.

"Where is the prince now?" the crofter asked Regalis.

"They've mounted and appear to be cutting along the border…" The Fahyli looked down at the map and found the location he sought. "Toward Aelmoor."

"A bird to Aelmoor now!" Captain Bradburn barked at

someone near the doorway. "Sir Tomas Coterel. They must retreat to Solana City, immediately!"

"Run lad!" thundered King Agir, eyes flinty with fear and rage.

Laec caught the flash of a shirtsleeve before footsteps pounded away from the maproom.

"Captain. Crofter," King Agir said. "Meet me in the den in one hour."

The king sliced through the crowd, the prow of a ship parting water. Fahyli and soldiers filed out, headed to wherever they were assigned. Solana was in a kind of trouble they had never seen before. Silverfall had been bad, but this was something else entirely.

CHAPTER TWENTY-FOUR

JESSAMINE

THUNDER CRASHED OVER Solana palace. Rain hammered against every window, filling Jess's ears with the pattering shoosh of millions of droplets against glass, tile and stone. She sighed and pushed her book away as the etherlamps guttered and dimmed.

"I'm closing the doors soon, Miss Fontana." The librarian poked his head out of his office doors. "Did you find what you were looking for?"

"Not really." In this case, not really meant no. Jess got up and took the book on Rahamlar's history back to its place on the shelf. Nothing made finding something more difficult than not knowing what one was looking for in the first place. Jess had hoped to find some clue in the history books, some helpful hint that would enlighten her darkened mind and give her a sliver of hope. Perhaps a little-known weakness, or some secret that might be used to derail or slow the prince's progress. All she'd uncovered were boring genealogies and dry accounts of historic events, obviously written by scholars who were half asleep.

Jess helped the librarian check the windows in the library before saying goodnight as he shut down the etherlights and closed his office door. The lamps along the corridor dimmed a shade as the library clock struck ten. Jess passed the alcoves, her eye drawn into one with curtains drawn back. Peering into the darkness, she saw her twin sitting beside the window, legs propped up on cushions and crossed at the ankles. He gazed out at the darkness, watching rainwater run down the glass, his chin resting on his forearm.

"Digit?"

His face was swathed in shadows. "Jess. You alright?"

She nodded. "What are you doing here, sitting all alone in the dark?"

"I'm not alone." He jerked his chin toward the curtain and Jess saw Ania perched on the rope tying the drapes open. "I'm just thinking."

As she slid in beside him, he elaborated: "About our big problem."

She nodded.

He looked at her pensively. "There's something I've been wanting to ask you. I'm not sure I'm ready for the answer, but hey, since you're here..."

Jess canted her head, wondering what was particularly troubling her twin. "What is it?"

His hair looked almost black in the shade of the alcove, but his eyes reflected the etherlamp across the hall. "If there were a way we could stop Faraçek, even though it would come with a pretty big chance of... becoming unalive... would you want to do it?"

She opened her mouth, but he lifted his hand, stopping her.

"I'm for serious, Jess. Don't say yes unless you really mean it. If you need to think it through for a bit, that's ok too, but don't take too long. My idea has a time limit."

She closed her mouth but opened it again. "It's not only my decision, Digit. My death also means Beazle's death."

Digit nodded. "Of course. Ania and I agree. I wouldn't have asked you such a thing before asking her."

Jess eyed the pretty little hummingbird. Such a tiny creature sitting there so docilely, her bright black eyes on them. She was smaller than a walnut in the shell. How could such a wee thing contain so much courage? But Jess knew how. Magic. Digit's magic, which would only exist so long as he was young and healthy and had Ania with him.

I would do it, Beazle whispered into Jess's mind as he hunted for bugs behind a tapestry hanging further down along the corridor. *I'm coming.*

"Beazle's coming," she told Digit. "And we're already agreed. We would do it."

Digit sat back and crossed his arms, nodding. "I figured you might."

"Fahyli already risk their lives for Solana, it's part of the job."

"Risk is one thing, Jess," Digit replied, raking his hair back from his forehead. It had grown long and shaggy. "Near-certain death is another."

"What are we talking about, exactly?"

"That's why I wasn't quite ready to ask you yet. I don't have the details worked out. I've been thinking… Solana's soldiers— even with the Fahyli onside—don't have a good chance against Faraçek's army. He'll keep moving into our territory, taking over villages. They don't stand a chance either, even if Bradburn sent contingents to every town. They'd take a knee just like Stonei-ron did. Worse, Faraçek could turn Solana's soldiers back upon us. We can't play this game the way we might against a normal foe. We have to shake up the board, somehow."

"I don't disagree, but I'm not sure how. Pulling every-one back into the city seems like the only reasonable option right now."

Digit cracked his knuckles.

Beazle zipped into the alcove and landed on Jess's arm. He snuggled down into the folds of her sleeve, still chewing his snack.

"Hey, Beeze," Digit said.

Beazle blinked at him. *Solved all our problems yet, Julian?*

Jess dimpled.

"What?" Digit smiled at her expression.

"He'd like to know if you've come up with a solution yet. And by the way, he almost always calls you Julian now."

"I don't mind." Digit replied. "It was my name once." He blew a soft exhale. "My big idea starts with us. You and me, Beazle and Ania, are not a force to be sneezed at. Maybe there's something we can do pre-emptively. It's too late for Stoneiron, but it's not too late for the city."

"You mean go on the offense?"

Jess felt a warm current move past her face. Somewhere, someone closed a window or door, moving heated air through the corridors. On windy days, the halls of the palace whistled as air swept through the castle.

Digit lowered his voice, his jaw flexed. "I mean: go after Faraçek. Cut the head off the cowbird himself."

"The crofter would never even let us try."

Her twin's eyes glimmered. "That's why we move independently. If no one knows, no one will stop us, nor can they be in any danger."

"That's insane," she whispered, but her heart stirred at the idea. He was talking about going rogue, ignoring their oath to do as they were told. No wonder he was thinking they'd get killed—if they didn't die executing the mission, their own team would wring their necks when they got back.

Digit glanced covertly into the hall when footfalls approached. A servant passed carrying a load of folded towels. Digit waited for them to pass, then whispered: "We're the poison twins, Jess. If I can get close enough, I can give him a heart attack. Who better to try than us? If we're successful, no one else will die. But we have to do it before he reaches the city gates."

It wasn't the first time she had dreamed of killing Faraçek, but it was the first time she applied logistics to such an undertaking. They didn't know where, exactly, Faraçek was, but Beazle and Ania could find him. After he was located, it would be a matter of sneaking into the enemy camp, finding the prince without getting caught, killing him, and then getting out alive.

Would Rahamlar anticipate a move like this? Of course they would. Faraçek would be heavily guarded. If they miraculously managed to get past the guards, then they'd have Faraçek's magic to deal with, against which there seemed to be little defense. They'd have to take him by surprise, and Digit would have to act fast with his *digitalis*. It was a crazy plan, but if they managed to succeed...

She opened her mouth to share her thoughts with Digit, but Beazle said: *Something comes this way.*

Her bat's phrasing struck her as odd, but before she could ask him about it, a light drew their attention to the hallway. A pale illumination cast itself over the carpet outside the alcove, as though someone was carrying a big candle as they approached. But the light was too white to be from fire, so it had to be from an etherlamp.

A transparent, illuminated lion padded into view, facing forward and down the hall. He stopped just outside the alcove, as though he didn't know they were there. Jess grabbed Digit by the arm. A quick glance confirmed he could see the lion too—Digit's eyes were round and staring, the lion's light reflected in his pupils. It was the big male she'd been saved by in the unnamed forest, she was sure of it. The noble creature lowered his head then swung it to the side, looking straight at them. His eyes were pools of white light, his mane a corona of lit threads. The details of the wallpaper and skirting board could be seen through his body.

Jess and Digit sat completely still. Ania craned her neck to peer around the trim of the curtain, and Beazle craned his to look over the top of Jess's sleeve. Jess's heart thundered in her chest, and for a moment she wondered if she was going to cry from the joy of seeing him again.

"Hello," Jess whispered. "Old friend."

The lion lifted his head, keeping his gaze on them. He didn't send any thoughts, just looked at them, huge paws still but long tail twitching. Then he licked his upper lip with a long, bright tongue, swung his bulk to the left and continued down the hall.

Digit and Jess scrambled out of the booth. He nearly fell over her in his effort not to lose sight of the lion. Ania buzzed to Digit's hair. Beazle flapped around wildly as the twins untangled themselves, then flopped clumsily onto the top of Jess's head.

The lion walked calmly away from them, but paused where

a set of wide wooden steps descended. He looked back with a curious expression, cocking his head, round ears twitching, then carried on down the steps and out of view.

"He wants us to follow him," Digit whispered. He was so close Jess could feel his breath stir her hair. He sounded excited, but hesitated, nudging her. "Go on. I'm right behind you."

Jess ran to the top of the steps. A young female servant carrying a basket full of cleaning brushes, rags and polish was coming up the stairs. She walked right through the lion, seeming to have no idea she'd just shared space with the mascot on Solana's sigil. The maid looked up at them gaping down at her, probably looking deranged. There was uncertainty in her gaze.

"Good evening, Ms. Fontana, Mr. Peneçek. Is there anything I can do for you?"

"No. No thank you," Jess said in a strangled voice.

"We're good." Digit gave her an idiotic wave.

Her brows tightened. "Are you alright? You look like you've seen a ghost."

Digit let out a laugh but cut it off abruptly. "No, nothing like that. We were just, on our way down to the kitchens... for a drink."

"I can bring it to your rooms, if you'd like?" She reached the top of the stairs and stood with one hand on the newel post and the other around her basket.

The lion reached the landing below then disappeared to the right where the steps continued down to the next level.

"That's alright." Jess grinned, trying to cover her exhilaration with cheerfulness. Stupid. No wonder the maid thought there was something wrong with them. "Thank you, though."

Without waiting for an answer, Jess took off down the

stairs, afraid that when she turned the corner the lion would be gone.

"Goodnight," Digit called, pounding down after her.

From the landing, Jess saw the lion reach the first floor and take a corridor to the left. She bolted after him, relieved that he'd not evaporated, and uncaring of how crazy she might look to anyone still wandering the halls. Digit didn't care either, she could hear him breathing down her neck, keeping close.

They caught up to the lion, slowing their pace. He took them through a walking gallery—a long broad hallway lined with paintings and sculptures where courtiers could walk laps on rainy days. They passed a piano and a harp and many empty benches beneath windows. The lion turned down a narrower hallway, stopping at a set of closed double doors. A plaque beside the door announced that this was the Oleander Parlor. The lion's tail twitched as he looked at them before walking straight through the doors and disappearing.

Jess grabbed the handle and pulled, praying that the parlor wasn't locked. Relief washed over her when the door swung open with a rusty squeak. The room smelled stale and little-used. The lion moved through the dark space, a feline-shaped lamp casting a glow across furniture draped with dustcloths.

"This is one of the queen's parlors," Digit whispered.

"You've been here before?"

"Once. When I was really little. She doesn't like it because it has no windows."

Jess let the door close slowly. The only source of light was the lion himself, and he was taking that with him as he crossed a dusty but elaborate parquet floor meant for dancing. If it were mopped, it would reflect light like a mirror.

The lion stopped in front of the cold fireplace, sat on his haunches and watched them approach.

Jess asked in a hushed voice. "What do you want us to see?"

The huge cat lifted his nose, pointing to the large dark tapestry hanging over the mantel. Above the tapestry hung a series of etherlights, dark and probably covered in dust.

Beazle suggested from his place on the top of her head: *Turn on those lamps.*

Jess found a series of switches to the right of the fireplace and flicked them on. The lamps cast their glow down over the tapestry thanks to little brass hoods.

At the same moment the light flooded the tapestry, the lion vanished.

"He's gone!" Digit mourned. "Dammit Jess. I wish you hadn't done that."

"I didn't know it would chase him away." Jess pouted, but then she looked up and her breath caught in her throat.

Digit followed her gaze and gasped as he took in the scene.

They moved back to better view it. A gold plate set into the bottom of the frame pronounced that this was a representation of Toryan's Massacre by Heinin Gregorjak. A broad valley surrounded by trees and steep rocky terrain lay beneath an early-morning sky of tumultuous red and peach clouds, as though a fire blazed beneath them. Bodies were strewn throughout the scene: all over the valley floor but also amid the trees and rocks in the background. Women and children were numbered among the dead. Pools of blood glittered wetly under beams of sunlight. Unseelie, seelie and humans were caught in a raging battle, fighting with bows, swords, daggers. Many were mid-flight, some clinging to the backs of horses, but most were fleeing on foot. Terrifying-looking unseelie soldiers mounted on horses were poised with arms upraised, about to rain killing blows upon those they pursued.

Jess shuddered like an icy breeze had wrapped around her, not realizing until her shoulder brushed Digit's that he had stepped closer to her. Jess lay a hand over her throbbing heart, finding it difficult to look away from the art, as painful as it was to take in.

Digit's voice was hollow. "I didn't know it had been memorialized as a tapestry. It looks... so much worse than I ever imagined it."

"Laec told me about this when we were in the underground passage."

Digit shot her a look of surprise. "Laec's a foreigner. How does he know about Toryan's Massacre?"

"Queen Esha told him about it. The survivors used the passage we found to escape and were given sanctuary in Solana by Erasmus."

"I never really thought about it before, but the survivors are the ancestors of Solana's population today." Digit hugged himself as a shiver went through him. "My whole body is covered in goosebumps."

Jess nodded, swallowing. Her eyes tingled with unshed tears as she took in the brutal scene before them. A wisp of light glimmered inside the canvas. She thought it was a flicker from the etherlamp, but the thread of light came again, in another place.

"Jess." Digit pointed. "Look."

"I see it," she whispered.

More glimmers of light followed the first, increasing in number. Soon the tapestry was filled with little wisps, curls of illuminated smoke. They came faster now.

"They're over the dead bodies." Digit took her elbow gently. "Right? Tell me I'm not seeing things?"

He was right. Wherever a dead body lay in the scene, the light glimmered and danced. They expanded, forming shapes as they grew; finally the lights coalesced into the shapes of lions. Some were cubs, others were females, and fewer were males with big, majestic manes, but each stood over a body in a protective stance.

"They're watching us," Digit said in a strangled voice, squeezing her elbow harder.

He was right about that too. The lions looked out from the scene, breathing, ears twitching, licking their lips. Some sat on their haunches, others stood as if waiting, tails twitching. Looking at them made it difficult to breathe but it also filled Jess with a kind of pride.

"For pride's sake," Jessamine whispered the common Solanan saying, amazed. "A pride of lions."

"They're moving."

Every lion—the young cubs, the old grizzled elderly, females and males in their prime—padded toward the right side of the tapestry, moving together as a massive pride. Now Jess could see so many more of them. There were small glowing shapes back in the hills, far behind the foreground, moving behind trees and stones. There were hundreds of them, maybe as many as a thousand.

She thought they'd disappear behind the frame, but instead they stalked over the frame and out along the walls of the room. By fifties and more they exited the scene and crossed the wooden paneling of the parlor, a huge pride of silent felines. Graceful, they moved as one. When the last of them left the tapestry, they left it as it had been… inert threads woven into a scene.

Jess and Digit kept up with them, walking the perimeter of the room, their eyes glued to the pride. Every member turned the corner and continued to cross the wall to another darkened painting. This one was portrait-shaped, a dark rectangle that looked like a hole in the wall in the gloom of the parlor.

The lions leading the pack marched over the frame of this painting as well, stepping onto the canvas, where they stopped. Their light cast itself against the painted figure of a woman in a stately dress. Where the first of the pride stopped, the rest stopped too, all stepping into the same space and melting into one body.

Digit found the switch on the wall and threw it, illuminating the portrait as the pride continued to march forward. As the last of the shapes congealed, the big male that had rescued Jess in the forest was the only remaining lion. He stood beside the image of a beautiful, aging queen, her painted hand rested against his neck, hidden behind his mane.

Tears lined Jess's eyes as she read the plaque below the portrait: "Queen Nella & Jezaret, the Lion of Solana."

"Jezaret," she repeated as a tear slipped down her cheek.

"It's nice to know his name," murmured Digit.

They gazed up at the queen. Regal, with kind brown eyes and plenty of long gray hair half-piled on top of her head. Her Solana-blue dress was high-necked and long-sleeved, with a Solana-green satin sash over one shoulder. Jess recognized the style as the fashion often used in illustrated storybooks to teach children and faelings about history. Over the queen's left breast was the wreathed lion's head crest with the kingdom's motto: *Beauty is our Strength*.

Jessamine looked at Jezaret. His light had faded, leaving behind just a portrait rendered in bright oil paints. She would know that face, those kind and loving eyes, anywhere. Queen Nella's noble expression—a pleasant expression, not quite a smile—mirrored her feline familiar's.

Digit gestured at the painting. "Why do they hide this portrait in a room they hardly use, where no one gets to see it?"

Jessamine thought about Agir's reaction when she'd told him and Esha about the lion rescuing her in the forest. Esha had tempered her own excitement in response to the king's obvious unease. There had been something about her testimony that made Agir uncomfortable. It had to have been connected to his decision to keep this painting somewhere it would be forgotten over time.

"Esha told me that I'm not the only Solanan to see lions," Jess said. "But there are a lot of Solanans who believe they are figments of fancy. I think Agir may be one of them."

Digit made a thoughtful sound. "Maybe it makes them feel unworthy. Why should some Solanans see the lions, but not others? It's not like we're anything special, but that girl on the stairs definitely didn't see him."

"It's up to Jezaret, I guess, who he shows himself to."

"They don't teach much about Nella in school, either," Digit said, looking up at the likeness of the peacemaking queen of old. "They give the children the mechanics of what happened, but they don't go very deep."

"To avoid the topic of Jezaret?" Jess wondered.

Digit put an arm around her. They stared up at the painting, ruminating.

"Why appear to us both tonight?" asked Digit. "What's he trying to tell us?"

Jess chewed her bottom lip, thinking about the timing of

the lion's appearance. "He came to me when I was in trouble. I needed help and there was no one around to save me."

"But we weren't in trouble this time, at least... not imminent trouble."

"No." Jess thought about what they had been doing. "But we were talking about..."

"...doing something crazy that would likely get us killed."

Jess nodded. "I don't think his timing was an accident. I don't think he does anything by chance. He wanted us to see the massacre scene, all those Solanans who died. I don't know if he was trying to say that their spirits went into him, or..."

"Nella reigned one hundred and fifty years after the massacre. Well after Toryan's death."

Jess's gaze went to the face of the lion-hearted queen who risked her life to propose a treaty. "But remember that they'd had one hundred and fifty years of violence before she brought it to an end. She was the one who negotiated peace with Rahamlar."

"Maybe fate had been waiting for the right person to be born, the right fauna fae with the right animal."

"So, is this Jezaret's way of telling us that we should go ahead with our crazy plan? That he'll back us up? Or is he telling us to reconsider, trying to save our lives?"

"I don't know. He didn't say anything this time."

Digit looked at her, eyes big. "He spoke before?"

"Into my mind. He had to, or I would never have come down from the tree. He needed to wake me up, make me remember who I was, coax me down. Maybe he prefers not to speak if he doesn't have to."

Jezaret's shape lit up, but he didn't move like before. His

tail didn't twitch, his eyes didn't blink. Digit and Jess stepped closer, because there was something new in the painting.

"What's in his mouth?" Jess asked, squinting.

"A... ring... of some kind?"

There was something familiar about it. Then it came to her: the dark unidentified metal, the ominous bird with the onyx eyes and its wings outspread.

"It's Toryan's crown," she breathed. "What's it doing in this painting?"

This crown bequeaths Toryan's heir with power. Toryan's heir is not the true heir. The true heir has the power to destroy it.

Jess exchanged a look of astonishment with Digit. From the look on his face, he had heard Jezaret's voice too.

"Isabey," Digit whispered.

The door to the parlor opened.

Chapter Twenty-Five

Jessamine

J ESS AND DIGIT whirled, guilt etched on their faces. Several silhouettes were outlined against the light from the hallway, but one of them Jess would know anywhere. "Rose?"

Rose came into the parlor, stepping into the circle of light thrown by the etherlamp over Nella's portrait. She was followed by Snap, then Peony, Aster and Proteas. All but Rose and Aster looked serious and white-faced. Bougain came in behind them and closed the door. His broad shoulders were swaddled in a fuchsia-colored bathrobe that was tied at the waist and ended at mid-thigh. Matching fuzzy slippers hugged his huge feet.

"What are you—" Digit began, but stopped short when the door opened again.

More flora fae poured into the room. They kept coming until every last member of the Calyx was present. Marigold—in an orange babydoll pajama with ruffles at the hem—was the last, and she closed the door. All the flora fae crowded into the parlor, making the space seem a lot smaller. Their attention flicked around the room, taking in the shadowy furniture, the paintings on the walls.

When Georjie entered a few moments later, Jess gaped. She looked around in curiosity, but didn't look overly shocked by whatever was happening. "I followed a ghost here," she said, matter-of-factly. "The ghost of a lion."

She wasn't even Solanan, let alone Calyx, but she had been drawn by a lion too?

"Us as well," Rose said, gesturing to herself, Snap and Aster. "We were playing a card game before bed in Snap's room when a lioness walked through the wall. She made us follow her."

Proteas was nodding. "Mine was a cub. So cute." He looked at Digit. "You?"

"Big male," said Digit, and Jess nodded.

"How come I could see it, but none of the servants?" asked Georjie. She was wearing a nightshirt and a pair of slouchy socks that were too big.

"Asclepias was distracting them with his rippling abdominals," joked Rose, gesturing at the muscular fae who wore only a pair of soft shorts for sleeping in. Asclepias waved her off with a roll of his eyes, but couldn't quite stop a smile.

Aster's dark spirals were tied in a huge bun on top of her head and covered with a silky kerchief. She slept with her hair protected because it was agony to untangle. She and Rose didn't look quite as stunned as the rest, probably because they had been told about Jezaret by Jessamine, though Jess hadn't known his name then.

Others mumbled that they too had followed a lion to this parlor. The staleness of the room was overcome by the smell of night-blooming flowers as the Calyx looked at Jess and Digit for an explanation.

"So?" Nympha came out of the crowd in an ombre satin negligee and matching robe. Elegant slippers hugged her feet. "Why are we here?"

Jess looked up at Jezaret for help but the light had faded, leaving only the lifeless portrait. The crown was gone from Jezaret's closed jaws. "I don't know. I'm as confused as you."

"Not *quite* as confused," Digit amended. "Tell them what we saw, Jess. I'm the only one here that's not Calyx. You should share it."

Georjayna and the Calyx perched on furniture or sank to the floor, as Jess described what she and Digit had seen. Digit capped Jess's story with the final and most relevant piece of information.

"Jezaret told us that only the true heir can destroy Toryan's crown."

Their audience absorbed it all in silence.

Finally, Dahlia commented: "That's Princess Isabey."

"Big problem," Alstro added. "No one knows where she is."

"Jess can find her," said Snap. His normally sleek curls were bushy and frizzy. He must have been losing the card game. "With her *solidago* magic. Right Jess?"

"She can't locate people," said Rose. "Only things."

Jess scratched the back of her head. "But when I was searching for the princesses after Prince Ander died, we used her seal to find her. So long as Princess Isabey has it on her, then Beazle and I should be able to locate her again."

"But then what?" Peony asked, adjusting her white robe where the neckline was folded over. Sphex was a black slash against her abdomen.

"What do you mean, *then what?*" Digit replied. "We get her to come back."

"And what if she won't?" Wisteria asked, with her moth, Hemaris, clinging to her cheekbone. "She ran away because she isn't interested in fighting her brother. Why would she turn around and come back?"

"I don't think she knows what Jezaret just told us," said Jess. "That she, as the true heir, has the power to destroy the crown. If she'd known that, I'm sure she would have said. I was there when she and Serya first told us about the crown. She said there have been many attempts over the years to destroy it. It was even taken far out to sea and dropped overboard. By the time the sailors returned to Rahamlar, the crown was back in its usual place, waiting for its heir. She believes it can't be destroyed or even lost."

"Right, and at that time Serya was the rightful heir." Snap got up and moved closer to Rose, who was shivering. He put an arm around her and she smiled up at him, snuggling against his heat.

"If they'd known Serya could have destroyed it, they would have done it." Jess nodded in agreement. "So, we have to find Isabey, ask her to come back."

"Or make her," said Asclepias, crossing his arms over his naked chest. "The princess hasn't exactly inspired confidence, hiding out here, crying herself to sleep every night."

"Well, until her secret lover turned up." Wisteria put a finger under Hemaris and took him off her face. She wrinkled her nose and scratched where his little feet had tickled her skin.

"Right," nodded Asclepias.

Peony crossed her arms over Sphex, who buzzed his wings.

"And now that her brother has had the audacity to crown himself, she's vanished."

"If you ask me," said Marigold, "this is all her fault. I wouldn't be hanging any hopes on her. Just saying."

"Mark my words." Alstroemeria was shaking his head. "She's going to have to be dragged back here and forced to do the right thing."

"Harsh, Alstro," said Rose. "She's still just a faeling—younger than most of us. She lost her father, her brother, her sister, all in the span of a few months. She thought she lost her lover too. When he came out of the woodwork alive, we can hardly blame her for running away with him."

"Yeah," said Iris softly, her big eyes glistening with empathy. "At least she can enjoy being with the last person left alive that she ever cared about."

"She's a princess, not a peasant. She doesn't get the privilege of shirking her responsibilities." Aster put her hands on her hips. Trea sat on her bosom, his beautiful wings flat and wide, his antennae twitching like mad, signaling his fae's irritation.

"All of this is beside the point," said Digit, slicing a hand through the air. "The point is that Isabey has the power to destroy the crown, therefore she can stop the prince from mind-controlling whole villages with a single breath. The way forward is clear. We have to find the princess and bring her back here where she can be protected."

"Right," said Jess. "Then we have to figure out a way to get the crown into her hands. That'll be the hardest part."

"Why us, though?" Peony looked incredulous. "Why the Calyx?"

"And me," said Georjie. "I'm not Calyx."

"We're all flora fae," said Rose. "There must be something we're supposed to do."

"Finally," said Snap.

Georjie's brows knitted together. "I'm only half fae."

"Close enough." Aster shrugged a shoulder.

Digit was nodding. "Yes. You're in the same family. We can all feel that. The lions chose us for some reason."

"*All* of us." Jess looked pointedly at Georjayna, though the Wise had mostly just listened so far, having little to contribute.

Rose and several others were nodding—the Calyx seemed to have accepted this much.

Digit looked downright excited. "Exactly. And we have a whole pride of lions on our side. Solana's lions."

The Calyx agreed to loop the gardener and the crofter in immediately. Digit went to fetch Ian while Proteas went to get the gardener. The rest of them waited in the Oleander Parlor. The etherlamps were turned on, and the dustcloths were removed from the furniture so the Calyx could rest on clean surfaces while they waited. Those wearing skimpy pajamas returned to their rooms to dress more warmly, hurrying back as quickly as they could.

The Calyx and Georjie were calm and settled when the crofter and the gardener entered the parlor with Digit and Proteas. Proteas had a large pot in his arms.

Ian's dark eyes went to Jess as he and Ilishec crossed the floor, coming to stand at an opening in the circle of furniture where they could see all the fae. Jess gave Ian the smallest of smiles, needing him to listen to them, buy into their idea.

"What's going on here?" The gardener gestured at Digit, who now stood beside Jess, and Proteas, who took up a cross-legged position on the floor, setting the pot in front of him. Jess could smell the scent of fresh soil.

"They said something big has happened. What's the something big?" He found Georjie in the group and his eyes widened. "Does it have something to do with you?"

Georjie shook her head, putting her hands palm-up in defense. "I'm just another face in the crowd tonight, Gardener."

The Calyx looked to Digit and Jess to explain, so the twins went through it all again. They drew Ian and Ilishec's attention to the tapestry and the painting in turn, ending with what Jezaret had told them about the crown. Only when Toryan's crown was mentioned did the crofter express any emotion. A possible solution to the looming invasion sparked his interest in a way that the lions hadn't. When the twins stopped talking, the crofter and gardener exchanged a look that Jess couldn't read.

"You do believe them, right?" said Rose. She gestured to the group at large. "We're all witnesses that the lions are real. They came to each of us and brought us here to this room."

"I believe you," said the gardener.

The crofter nodded. "I've never seen a lion myself but I've read accounts. If you say you saw them, I believe you."

The room filled with palpable relief.

"And if you say that Nella's familiar told you that Isabey can destroy Toryan's crown," the crofter added, putting his hands behind his back. "I believe that too. Two problems present themselves: we don't know where Isabey is, and we don't know where the crown is either."

"Jess can locate both of them with *solidago* magic." Digit put a hand on Jess's shoulder, pulling her a little closer to his side. She felt his brotherly pride and smiled at the floor. "Once we know where they are, we can make a plan."

Proteas slid the pot of soil toward Jess and she looked at the crofter for permission. He nodded. She looked at Ilishec too.

He said: "Go on then, Jessamine."

Beazle crawled down Jess's arm as she knelt by the pot of soil. *Ready?*

He hopped onto the lip of the container. *Ready.*

She hovered a hand over the soil and closed her eyes, thinking of Isabey's seal. *Solidago* sprouted from the dirt, stretching upward. Beazle gave a squeak and dove headfirst into the soil, eliciting sounds of surprise from the Calyx who'd never witnessed Jess using her magic this way. Her bat wiggled himself into the pot until he was gone from sight as the goldenrod sent out yellow flowers. Jess received flashes of scenery that she recognized, and smiled when she understood that Isabey hadn't gone to Archelia or Tryske. Releasing her magic, she sat back with a sigh. Beazle popped his head out of the dirt, flicking his ears. The goldenrod immediately began to decay.

"The princess went back to the unnamed forest," she told Ian and Ilishec. "She and Shade are with Calvatia."

The crofter looked surprised and pleased. "She's not fully committed to abandoning us to her brother then?"

"I couldn't say, Crofter," Jess said. "Maybe they went there to prepare for a longer journey. I don't know. But that's where they are. Permission to leave first thing in the morning?"

Ilishec shot Ian a look of alarm.

Digit helped Jess get to her feet. "I'll go with her."

The gardener sounded worried. "Ian? Is it safe? Rahamlarins are out there."

"The swamp doesn't lie between us and the border, Gardener," Ian replied. "They're coming this way. Jess and Digit—if they leave at first light—should be able to sneak north without being seen. They both know the way." Ian considered his twins thoughtfully. "Be specific about your objective."

Jess and Digit shared a look of thinly veiled excitement. Digit answered: "Locate the princess and communicate what Jezaret told us. We'll return her to Solana for safekeeping before Rahamlar arrives." He narrowed his eyes. "Then go after the crown."

"That's insane!" Ilishec spluttered. "The crown might very well be on Faraçek's devious head!"

"He's not wearing it, Gardener," reminded Jess gently. She didn't like the idea of frightening Ilishec. He had enough worries. "Beazle and I spied on him, remember?"

"That doesn't make me feel any better, Jessamine." Ilishec glowered, resting his fists on his waist. "Just because he's not wearing it doesn't mean it isn't somewhere within his reach. It's a powerful relic, he'll want to have it near him at all times."

"Maybe, maybe not." Ian looked less concerned. "The Fahyli are accustomed to dangerous tasks." Ignoring the withering look the gardener shot at him, the crofter continued: "I'll ask Kite to go with you. Erasmus can keep her informed of where the enemy is, which will greatly diminish your chances of getting caught. Can Beazle and Erasmus communicate? In case you and Kite get separated?"

Jess blinked. "Uh... I don't know." She looked at Beazle wrapped around her thumb.

He looked up at her, flattening his ears with annoyance. *Erasmus is so cryptic.*

Jess looked up in triumph. "He can."

Sigh.

"Perfect," Ian nodded, pleased. "Erasmus will communicate with Ferrugin, and Ferrugin with Regalis. Regalis will—in turn—communicate with us. That's the best we can do, under the circumstances."

Jess thought that was pretty great, everything considered.

So did many of the Calyx, who whispered among themselves, sounding impressed. They'd been so quiet that Jess had almost forgotten they were there.

"This is going to be epic," said Asclepias.

"What about us?" asked Snap, getting to his feet so he could see over Aster's hair.

"What *about* you?" The gardener said in a warning tone, shooting Snap a half-lidded look of caution.

"Can I go with them?"

"Me too," said Bougain, looking even more muscly than usual.

"I'll go as well," said Rose.

"None of you are going anywhere," Ilishec growled. "This isn't a trip to the local fair."

Faces fell. Snap looked ready to spit snapdragons. "The lions chose *all* of us. We're supposed to have a part in this, otherwise why did they round up every last flora fae?"

"You've already done your part, Snap." The gardener looked around the room at the faces of his fae, looking more paternal than he ever had. "Your collective involvement gave Jess and Digit the backup they needed; witnessing the pride and relaying it to us *was* your part. It's finished. Now, all of you should be in bed."

Snap and a few others looked at Georjie. Jess knew they couldn't help it, she was an authority figure and they were hoping she might step in. But Georjayna wasn't in charge here, she was just a guest, and one that no one was quite sure served a purpose.

Ilishec looked mildly affronted. "What are you looking at her for? Go to bed."

"Georjie's one of us," Snap told Ilishec, "only far more powerful. You should see what she helped me do the other day in the hothouse. She can…"

The gardener glared at Snap, then at Georjie. "Miss, it has been a pleasure to meet you. Under other circumstances I would be interested in spending a great amount of time with you. I'm sure there is much you can share with us, but Solana is in trouble, and no one is quite sure why Elphame sent you if you're not able to solve our current problems. Perhaps it would be best if you went home. I certainly don't appreciate you putting ideas in my fae's heads."

Georjie blinked at him, nonplussed, but she wasn't cowed. "They all have capabilities that they've not accessed, Gardener. Why do you want to suppress that? Especially in the face of danger?"

Ilishec's cheeks flushed red. "That's enough from you, young lady. I'll not have my authority questioned, especially during times of risk. You can challenge me all you want when we're all safe again—I'll even welcome it, goodness knows we all have more to learn, no matter our age—but until then, I'm in charge, and I say the Calyx need to mind their own business and go to bed. Now."

Chagrined, the flora fae got up and moved toward the door of the parlor, sliding their slippered feet along the parquet. Georjie went with them.

Ilishec turned, almost walking into Ian, who was looking down at the smaller man with a bewildered expression.

"What?" Ilishec snapped. "You disagree?"

"I wouldn't dream of it," said the crofter in a low voice. "They're your fae. They answer to you. I have nothing to say on the matter."

Grumbling, the gardener stormed past the crofter and followed the last of the Calyx into the hall.

Ian looked at Jess and Digit. "Fear is a powerful thing. You just saw it in action."

That's it, thought Jess. *The crofter nailed it. Ilishec is afraid that if he lets his fae develop skills beyond what they need for life as court entertainers and perfume makers, they could be killed.*

Beazle scaled Jess's hair. *Is he wrong?*

No. He's not wrong.

"Don't judge him too harshly," Ian said, his voice softening as he looked at his twins. "I can relate to how he feels. I know I must let you do this, but... I wish it could be someone else. Please, be careful out there."

Jess swallowed hard at the fatherly affection in the crofter's gaze. She looked away, an uncomfortable silence swelling between them. She imagined she could hear the crofter's unspoken plea that the twins return safely so that they—all of them, Vivian too—could have a chance at becoming a family.

"We'll be careful. Won't we Jess?"

Jess nodded. "Promise."

"Come on, Jess." Digit broke the tension when he touched her arm. "Time is ticking. Let's find Kite. She has no clue what's happened yet and she needs to be ready to leave at dawn."

PART THREE

CHAPTER TWENTY-SIX

JESSAMINE

THEY DID MANAGE to leave at daybreak the morning after their encounter with Jezaret. After riding steadily all day, they'd spent last night at an inn where the horses were looked after by an ostler. They'd bathed, then met in the inn's cramped dining room to consume a flavorful stew. After a good night's sleep and a breakfast of greasy eggs and pastry, they'd hit the road, arriving at the unnamed forest as their stomachs were beginning to growl.

Digit swung down from his horse, patting her neck as he pulled the reins over her head. Ania hummed over to a bush covered with small white blossoms. Digit waved away a fly that buzzed in his face. Beazle swooped in and snatched it up.

"We had a lot more trouble finding this place the first time," Digit observed.

Kite hopped down, her boots squelching in the soft soil. Except when Erasmus needed a rest, they hadn't seen much of her raptor. "The horses started going in circles somewhere around here, although I have to admit, this forest looks all the same to me. We could be five miles north of where we want to be and I wouldn't know it."

"We're in the right place," said Jess as she dismounted. She took Kitabee's bridle, leading him in the direction of the river.

How are these bugs so much tastier than the ones in Solana? Beazle swooped overhead, snatching dinner out of the air and glorying in the smells of this damp place and its juicy insects.

Must be the humidity. Jess stepped over a scar of open muck as she brushed her hair back from her sticky forehead. *At least it's warmer here than back home.*

"Why aren't the horses confused this time?" Kite asked over Jess and Beazle's inner dialogue.

"Because they've been here before?" Digit offered, skirting around a copse of trees.

The river trickled cheerfully in the distance as the noonday sun sent shafts of light through the canopy, transforming into pillars of illumination thick with dancing motes.

"It's neither. Calvatia's magic is fading." Jess wondered if the flora fae's aging beetle was still alive. "She's the reason we couldn't find it the first time, but she said that she wouldn't be able to keep everyone hidden for much longer."

Keeping Kitabee as close as he would tolerate to the hindquarters of Kite's gelding, Jess followed the narrow path that Digit and Kite cut through the vegetation. They'd been jumped in this forest. Almost killed. Jess shivered at the memory, thankful that Fixnix no longer considered them his enemies. Though, he'd lost men the same night that Sy and Mae had died at Faraçek's hand. Fixnix's hoods could easily choose to blame them for that. If the Solanans hadn't turned up here looking for Isabey and Serya, Faraçek's soldiers would never have found the hidden village. She wondered if there were eyes on them right now, watching them approach.

There are, Beazle told her. *One of the hoods is up in that tree.*

Jess paused to look around before continuing. Fixnix's men knew how to be invisible; she could hardly be surprised that they'd been found already. *Does he look friendly?*

Can't tell. Hood is over his face, but there's another one behind you and he hasn't moved. They remember you.

With a sharp inhale, Jess looked over her shoulder. *Why didn't you say something earlier?*

I did. Didn't I? He snatched another plump meal from the air. *Maybe I didn't. Sorry. I guess the bugs distracted me. Fixnix is just ahead.*

"Stop," Jess barked.

Kite and Digit pulled up, reaching for their swords.

"No blades," she added.

The rustle of leaves drew their attention to the dense undergrowth ahead. The broad-shouldered figure of Fixnix emerged, congealing like a shadow transforming into flesh. He paused, surveying them from the darkness beneath his hood. Jess wished she could see his face. In the poor light, all she could make out were twin glints of light.

"Solanans," Fixnix growled. "What do you want?"

"We need to speak to Princess Isabey and Shade," Digit told him. "We know they're here. It's urgent."

"Isn't it always." Fixnix turned and headed back the way he'd come.

Digit, Kite and Jess exchanged a look.

"Do we follow?" Kite mouthed.

Jess nodded.

They followed him to the river's edge, where more hoods materialized, making Jess's heart beat faster. But the hoods just took the bridles, keeping their mounts from going any further. Fixnix told his men to look after the horses, then led Kite, Digit and Jess down to a dock. He put his fingers between his teeth and gave a shrill whistle. While they waited for a raftsman, Jess looked for the illuminated mushrooms: Calvatia's fungi.

Fixnix noticed her looking.

"There's less of them now," he told her, "but some remain. You can't see them until after nightfall. Impossible to spot at this hour."

"Calvatia's magic still protects this place?"

"For now," he grunted. "Though it seems to lose potency by the day."

His gaze was drawn upriver where a raft approached, steered by a short man whose hood lay back on his shoulders. A long stem of grass was clenched between his teeth. He pulled up to the bank without a word, held the raft steady while they got on, then pushed off gently with his pole.

Jess, Digit and Kite silently observed the shores as they floated by. It looked like a place at peace, a place unconcerned with the world beyond the swamp. The strangers were eyed with curiosity from some, hostility from others.

The scent of woodsmoke tainted the air as they pulled up to the island in the middle of the river and disembarked. Fixnix led them through the gnarled trunks of strange trees, like squat old women in rough skirts. They went under branches, over roots and between trunks until Fixnix stopped at a clearing. He gestured that they should continue ahead without him.

They stepped into a clearing with a firepit in the middle of a circle of logs, upon which were seated Isabey, Shade and Calvatia, each cradling a steaming mug. Isabey and Shade were dressed in peasant's clothing. The princess's hair was in two long braids, a milkmaid's cap on the crown of her head. When they heard people approach, all conversation ceased. Then, Isabey loosed an unladylike oath.

If she didn't want us to find her, she shouldn't have hidden in the exact same place as before, Beazle thought to Jess.

I don't think she had anywhere else to go.

She said she was going to Archelia, or Tryske.

There must be a part of her that won't let her do that, thought Jess. *That's the part we have to appeal to.*

Shade gave them an entirely different reception. He smiled broadly, looking pleasantly surprised. He wore tall boots, loose brown pants, and a worn quilted vest that was a little too small for him. He shook hands with each of them. "Well come."

"Well found," they replied in turn.

"How did you find us?" He sounded delighted that they had.

"Beazle," said Jess simply, not wanting to take the time to explain.

At the sound of his name, Isabey looked around, a warmer and more welcoming expression on her face. "Is your bat here?"

"Of course." Jessamine approached the fire and helped herself to a seat. "Where I go, Beazle goes too."

Mostly, Beazle amended, thinking of his recent scare in Rahamlar.

Jess nodded a greeting at Calvatia, who smiled, looking unsurprised to see her. If Jack was alive, as Fixnix had implied, he wasn't in sight. Calvatia handed them each an empty mug.

"Help yourselves."

Jess ladled contents of the pot into her mug then sat down again, sniffing at the steam. Broth of some kind. She took a sip and was pleased by the rich, salty flavor. It had to have been made from roasted bones.

"Well, where is he then?" Isabey inspected Jess's body and looked around in the air.

"He's upset with you," Jessamine told her, taking another sip.

Leave me out of this, Beazle fluttered around somewhere above them, spying juicy insects with regret. He was too full to eat any more.

The look on the princess's face was gratifying, though what Jess had told her wasn't remotely true. Beazle was less judgmental than fae.

"He thinks you're a coward for running away," Jess said, ignoring Beazle's squeak of indignation. Isabey heard the squeak and looked up, then back at Jess, a touch of alarm on her face.

Jess cocked an eyebrow. "See?"

Stay away for now, Beeze, Jess told him. *Remember why we're here.*

Fine.

The chagrined look that Shade gave Isabey was loaded with meaning.

Kite didn't miss it. "You agree with Beazle, don't you Shade?"

"Of course I do," said Shade, rubbing the top of his blond head. He made a kind of hopeless gesture in Isabey's direction. "She knows how I feel. I never wanted to come here. I wanted to stay and fight. I'll stand by her side, no matter what, but running grates against every part of me."

"Shade," Isabey reproached. She shook her head and sighed, like they'd been over this ground countless times before. Probably they had. "You don't know my brother."

"I beg to differ," Shade replied, speaking with more vehemence than Jess would have expected a retainer to use toward a royal.

Isabey also took note of his tone. She raised her eyebrows but he wasn't cowed.

"You can't have it both ways, Iz," he said, taking a swig of his broth.

Jess wondered if their circumstances had changed their relationship dynamic, then realized, it *had* to have. Isabey was rejecting her position and her home, and dragging Shade along against his will. What right did she have to command him or anyone else if she abdicated her responsibilities and right to rule? They seemed closer to equals now, though it was clear she wanted to hang on to her right to make the decisions for them both. Can't have it both ways indeed.

Shade punctuated his words with hand gestures, clearly aggravated. "I worked as a soldier for Rahamlar all my adult life—until I ran away with you, to protect you, because I love you. I also always believed you would return when the time was right. Rahamlar is my home, Yorin was my commander and Faraçek is his. I do know your brother."

"Not like I do." Isabey put her cup on the ground beside her. "You didn't see what he did to Serya."

Technically, it was Yorin that did it, thought Beazle.

"I know what he did to Serya," replied Shade, expression turning both angry and sorrowful. "I am sorry for that, but it's no reason to run from duty. What happened to the queen-in-waiting should have lit a fire in your veins. A fire to take back your kingdom."

"With what army, Shade?"

He looked incredulous. Jess and Digit exchanged a glance.

They came here to convince Isabey to act, but so far Shade was doing all the work.

Shade sputtered with outrage. "Solana is at your back! Or they would have been if you hadn't repaid all the kindness they've shown you by running away with not a word of your plans or where you were going. Not so much as a thank you and ta-ta."

"I told them I would leave," snapped Isabey. "I've been saying it for weeks."

Shade continued like he hadn't heard her. "Further, all of Rahamlar will be on your side, once they know you're alive. You are their rightful leader, Isabey. Their queen."

Isabey shook her head. "They'll kill me to get me out of the way."

Shade rolled his eyes. "They won't. They're loyal to the crown, not Faraçek. Many of his soldiers don't even like him. I should know. I was one of them."

"It's a bloody huge risk you want me to take, Shade." Isabey's eyes flashed. She was growing angrier by the second. "Especially for someone who supposedly loves me."

Shade softened. "You know that I love you. That doesn't mean I always have to agree with your choices. Yes, there is a risk in going back. Nothing as big as what you have waiting for you can be claimed without taking a risk. But I'll be there with you, every step of the way. I would die before I let anything happen to you."

Quiet descended over the little party. Calvatia looked up at the Solanans as she grabbed a piece of wood from the pile beside her and put it into the fire. She looked like she wanted to say something but pressed her lips shut, perhaps determined to stay out of it.

"Princess," Jess began, clearing her throat.

Isabey's big fae eyes went to Jess's face.

"There's something you have to know before you make any final decisions."

Isabey's expression turned haughty. "What makes you think my decision is not final?"

Shade hung his head in a dramatic gesture of hopelessness. It might have been comical under other circumstances.

Jess tried to keep her voice as calm and neutral as possible, a difficult task considering how much hung on Isabey's reaction. "I don't believe it will be once you know what we recently learned."

Isabey was unmoved. She feigned boredom. "And what might that be?"

"That you—and only you—as Rahamlar's rightful heir, have the ability to destroy Toryan's crown."

The quiet stretched out again as these words were absorbed.

"How do you know that?" Isabey asked quietly, pulling both of her feet up under her skirt to sit cross-legged, balancing on top of her log. She looked like a kid sitting like that.

Jess took a deep breath. Here was where she'd be called crazy. "Solana's lion told us, me and Digit."

Digit shot Jess a look of encouragement and respect. Jess supposed she could have danced around the subject, could have been vague, but why bother?

The princess was staring at Jess. "Solana's... lion?" Her nose wrinkled. "What is that, some sort of code? What does that even mean?"

Between the two of them, Digit and Jess explained what they'd experienced the night they'd followed Jezaret into the queen's lesser-used parlor. Calvatia, Isabey and Shade listened as the twins did their best to convey just how special this event was. When they were done, Jess and Digit fell quiet.

Isabey looked from one to the other as though trying to decide whether to laugh or cry. "That is quite the story. I under-estimated how far you'd go to get me to do what you want."

"You don't believe us?" Digit sounded genuinely surprised.

"*I* do," Shade told them. "That massacre was bound to have effects that echoed down the ages. All those innocent lives lost. It makes sense that their souls would live on somehow, clinging to this dimension in hopes that they'd one day be avenged…"

"In the hope that their lives weren't lost in vain," added Kite, nodding. "That one day they might find rest. I read once that those who die before their time can get stuck here, waiting for a resolution that frees them from this life before they can find peace."

"This is pathetic." Isabey's eyes blazed, and she put both her hands up, as if to ward off them and their story. "Really. You come to me with this stupid lie—that doesn't even sound remotely plausible, I might add—to try and get me to go back to the kingdom that rejected me and murdered my sister. You think you can trick me into this? Well, you're wrong. You forget that I've had that crown in my hands. I've even worn it on my head. Did anything happen to it? No. You're lying straight to my face, and you've just lost whatever sympathy I had for Solana. Deal with Faraçek yourself." She got up and marched away from the fire.

"Isabey," Shade called, but she ignored him, disappearing into the forest.

"But… it's all true," whispered Digit.

Jess closed her eyes in disappointment. It did sound too

spectacular to be believed. She was disappointed, but she couldn't say she was surprised.

There was a squeal from the forest in the direction that Isabey had gone. Shade was on his feet in a moment, going for the sword at his waist. The princess backed out of the vegetation, almost tripping over a root. She staggered and righted herself, backpedaling straight into Shade. Reflexively he wrapped his arms around her. Her gaze was glued to the vegetation as her hands clenched over Shade's.

Jezaret stalked out of the forest, tall and proud. He stopped outside their ring of logs, staring straight at Isabey. All of them scrambled to their feet but no one made a sound. The huge male stood there staring at the princess, his massive glowing paws solid on the ground, his tufted tail twitching. Jess wondered if he was communicating with her. She barely noticed when Beazle landed on her shoulder.

After a few long moments, Jezaret swung around and walked into the bush without another look.

Shade set Isabey on her feet. Out of breath, she whirled, looking from Jess to Digit and back again, her gray complexion even grayer, her pupils swimming in their whites.

Jessamine couldn't deny herself a smile of satisfaction. She crossed her arms. "You were saying, Princess?"

CHAPTER TWENTY-SEVEN

LAEC

FARAÇEK'S ARMY BEGAN to arrive three hours before sundown, darkening the horizon and filling all the low places and slopes in the pastureland south of the city. With mounting dismay, Laec stood on the ramparts near the main city gates, watching as darkness congealed not only overhead but on the land—a darkness created by the bodies, tents and horses of a horde of enemies. Enemies with big muscular frames, talons, teeth and a lack of mercy. Unseelie weren't numerous in Stavarjak because Elphame was a seelie queen. There were some who had proven themselves trustworthy, but ancient tensions still existed between the two groups, so in a seelie kingdom, unseelie were few and far between. Laec didn't know whether it was fair or not, but he'd have felt a little less anxious if the opposing forces had been made up of seelie fae. But it was the size of Faraçek's force that was the most concerning: more than eight thousand had been reported by scouts.

"You're up, Jess," Laec

said under his breath. "I hope you pull this off. Things don't look good on our end."

Regalis came to stand at Laec's side, looking remarkably calm for a soldier facing such unequal odds. "What was that?"

Laec crossed his arms and jerked his chin at the pinpricks of light flickering into existence across the hillsides: the campfires of Faraçek's forces. "Jess and Digit. Rarely has so much ridden on the shoulders of ones so young."

"Aye. It's best if we keep our expectations low," the Fahyli returned, his dark gaze on the horizon. "Sun is about to set. That's good."

"Why good?"

"They won't attack in the dark."

"No?"

Regalis shook his head, his gaze flicked upward as though receiving information from Ferrugin. "He'll want his show of force to sink in. Brutal though he is, Faraçek will want as little violence as possible. My guess is that he'll send an emissary before the sun fully disappears—one last chance at a peaceful handover."

"He won't come himself?"

"Too threatening." Regalis pointed at the hills. "Look, there."

Laec looked, and as though Regalis had conjured them with his own words, four riders approached the main gate. The leader held Rahamlar's brown flag with the orange cowbird, though it was difficult to make out in the growing darkness.

"You were right," said Laec, impressed.

Regalis flashed his teeth in a grin. "They sent a bird with a message a half-hour ago. Come, your presence is requested."

Laec shook his head at Regalis's ability to joke at such a dire time and followed the fauna fae down the steps to the crowded front gates. King Agir, the crofter, Bradburn, and four soldiers sat on horseback facing the gate and the king's road beyond it. Two saddled horses—one of them Grex—were held at the rear of the group by stablehands. Regalis mounted his and Laec mounted Grex. The gates were opened just enough for the riders to slip between them. When they were through, the gates were closed again. The sound of big beams and iron rods sliding home followed them down the doubletrack.

The evening air was cool and clammy. Laec's heart thrummed in his chest as he and Regalis brought up the rear of the company. Faraçek's riders had stopped in the road. Laec recognized Captain Yorin at the front. His face looked as craggy and scarred as the moon. He waited emotionlessly, shoulders square, gloved hands stacked on his pommel. The rider to his left held the flag. The two behind looked to be captains, with embroidery across the chests of their boiled leather, and a collection of feathers sprouting from the crests of their helmets. Yorin wore no helmet, though he was the only one with a cape—probably orange from the paleness of it—flowing over his back and across the rump of his dappled gelding.

There were no polite greetings. Yorin did not use "well come". Neither party considered this exchange to be welcome.

"What do you intend?" King Agir growled, his stallion shifting in a restless dance.

"You have until one hour after sunrise," Yorin told him flatly. "King Faraçek has graciously extended his offer until then, a concession to the Solanan people, not to you. You and the former queen may leave the city freely tonight. Provided you have crossed a border by noon, you will not be pursued. The inhabitants of the city will be required to swear allegiance tomorrow—all over the age of four—and their lives and property will be retained. Should you and your queen still be present in the city tomorrow morning, no quarter will be given to you nor any who wields a blade or bow against us. Those not armed will not be killed, though we cannot guarantee there will be no collateral deaths. Should you be found in the city, your life, those of the former queen, your daughter and any extended relations will be forfeit. Direct descendants of Prince Erasmus will not be permitted to survive. I'm sure you understand why."

"You're despicable," King Agir sneered. "If you know your history so well, you'll know that Solana has faced violence from Rahamlar before. Solana was triumphant then and we shall triumph now. Who will feed all your unseelie soldiers? How long can you sit there in my pastureland before you must go home or starve to death? We can withstand months without any movement in or out. We will simply outlast you."

"Perhaps, in another time, under another king, you could do so," allowed Captain Yorin, unaffected by Agir's rebuke. "But my sire is no ordinary king. You'll fall as easily as Stoneiron did. You commanded that all villages empty because you witnessed for yourselves that Faraçek cannot be withstood. He is a monarch of old and he will return these lands to their former heritage, an unseelie kingdom of perpetual autumn. You can feel it in the air and see it in your trees. Even the land knows that it belongs to Rahamlar. It seeks to return to autumn and there it will forever stay. The days of Solana are over. Do not be stubborn, old king. You did well while you led. Do not die foolishly in a fight you cannot win. All he need do is exhale at your gate, and you will open the doors to us."

"If it will be so easy, why have you amassed such a great army?" asked Captain Bradburn in a tone of contempt.

Yorin gave a casual shrug. "We're moving in. Solana's position is much better for our headquarters, certainly it's more beautiful than Rahamlar's fortress. Why make two trips?"

The Solanans were stunned into silence.

Captain Yorin looked at Agir. "You have until one hour after sunup."

The Rahamlarin party wheeled and cantered away, crossing off the road and into the pasture, heading toward Rahamlar's camp.

The Solanans retreated in silence; Laec and Regalis were the last to enter the gates which swung shut behind them to be bolted once more. Two beams thicker than a man's chest were lifted into the iron bracers by more than a dozen soldiers. Laec looked behind as the portcullis lowered, its prongs thumping home with a dull thud. At their highest, the stone walls were thirty-five feet of stacked stone and mortar, thick and strong, impenetrable but for siege engines, which Faraçek had not brought. The weak point was the front gates. They were twelve feet high, maybe thirteen. The portcullis extended another five feet above that, where its iron bars joined the stone arches linking the west wall to the east wall. But over the gate and beneath the arches was nothing but air. Yorin had said that all Faraçek need do is exhale and Solana would fall.

The king was talking with the crofter and Bradburn. Agir looked shaken, his face pale and beaded with perspiration as he dismounted. The crofter and Bradburn were less affected, but Laec understood why. They were there to enforce the king's wishes, obey his commands. It was Agir's decision whether to fight or not. Though he'd taken a vote, the final decision was his. He could still take his wife, their young daughter, and his closest relatives and leave Solana for good, abandoning this place to Faraçek's rule, whatever that might look like.

Agir, the crofter and Bradburn disappeared inside a squat gatehouse. The escort, including Laec and Regalis, were dismissed to return to their posts until further commands were issued.

Laec mounted the steps to the ramparts once more, looking out over the campfires stretching from one side of the horizon to the base of the Vargon where they thinned. The fires looked to have doubled since Laec had left the wall. He shook his head at the sight, the pit of his stomach feeling like it had iced over. He rested his hand on the pommel of his sword, once more wishing for his Stavarjakian magic. Then again, was there any magic in his arsenal that could combat mind-control?

He wondered if there had been pain for the soldiers who had fallen at Stoneiron. What was it like to be mind-controlled to go to your knees, allowing your own execution without any protest? Had they known what was happening? Were they trapped inside immobile, unresponsive bodies, screaming silently at themselves to take up their swords and defend themselves as doom approached? Or had they been tricked into thinking all was well? Perhaps Faraçek had whispered to their minds that there was no threat, that all they need do was kneel and everything would be fine.

Knowing what he knew of Faraçek, he doubted the experience would be peaceful. Why would the prince care about the quality of the last minutes of his enemies' lives? Laec shook off these dark musings and turned his mind to Çifta. Closing his eyes, he conjured her beautiful face.

You, he thought, as her warm smile lifted her countenance and her bright eyes looked into his. *When the blade comes for me, I'll think of you.* His heart slowed a little, some of the tension easing out of his body. *If yours is the last face I see, then dying won't be so bad.*

"Laec?"

He turned to see Graf standing at the top of the steps, looking worried. "The gardener needs you." Laec was about to protest when the boy added, "It's Hazel."

Laec arrived at Ilishec's cottage dusty and out of breath. He'd galloped up the high street on Grex, vaulting from the saddle as a stablehand caught the reins, then bolted toward the East Keep. Dashing through the gardens, his feet pounded on the paving stones as he closed the distance to Ilishec's home, where he finally stopped and bent over, sucking in air.

Not bothering to knock, Laec pushed into the cottage, heart pounding.

"In here," Ilishec called from the bedroom.

Laec approached the bedroom door, which sat open a few inches. He tented his fingers against the wood and pushed, dreading what he might find behind it.

Ilishec sat on a chair, beside the double bed where Hazel lay, holding one of her hands in his. He looked up at his nephew, his face stricken and his eyes heavy with sorrow. "I thought you might want to say goodbye."

Hazel was thin and pale and had aged to the point of being unrecognizable. Laec found it painful just looking at his aunt. Painful and confusing. What was different this time?

"I thought for sure she would get better," Laec said, voice soft. "She always did before." His feet felt rooted to the spot. He was afraid that if he got too close, his mere presence would push Hazel's fragile spirit away. He could feel her in this room, the essence of his loving, addled aunt.

"Not this time." Ilishec turned his gaze back to his wife.

"For a while, I believed that too. But, no. This is her time to go. I can feel her soul saying goodbye to mine. She's in there somewhere, trapped inside a mind that no longer works, like the ties that tether her to her body have been cut."

"Why now?"

Ilishec took a long slow inhale and exhale. "Because the seasons are going backward. She's always been extremely sensitive to nature: her moods fluctuated uncannily in sync with the weather. She can sense the ancient magic creeping over Solana. It's too much for a mind already struggling with confusion."

Ancient, unseelie magic. Faraçek's magic.

"Oh, Uncle." Laec couldn't find the words to express his sadness that Hazel, sweet innocent Hazel, was to become another casualty of this conflict. It was so unfair.

She stirred, moving her head. Her eyes opened to slits. Laec's heart redoubled its rhythm.

"Shec?" she rasped, searching for him.

"I'm here, my love." The gardener moved closer.

Laec's heart ballooned with hope. She recognized her husband, surely this had to be a good sign.

Her cloudy eyes opened further, moving a fraction until she found Ilishec. Her breathing was slow and labored. "I know you," she whispered.

The gardener smiled and dropped his head between his shoulders in relief before lifting his face to her again. "And I know you, my darling. I love you."

She looked beyond her husband to the fae standing at the foot of her bed. "Closer," she husked.

Laec moved closer, sitting on the side of the bed and putting his hand over Hazel's and Ilishec's. "Hello, Aunt Hazel."

Hazel almost smiled. "Laec, dear one. Tell your parents I love them. Look after them."

Her words washed over him like ice water. She was dying and she knew it. He had heard of those about to depart having a last moment of lucidity before they passed on. He was struck by how grateful he felt that they had this moment with her.

"I haven't time," she whispered, looking at her husband. "It comes for me. I am not afraid. We knew I would go early."

Ilishec wiped his cheeks with his free hand, but he was nodding. "These years with you have been the happiest of my life, Hazel, darling. Thank you for spending them with me. I have been blessed by you."

"And I, you." She coughed, a weak and wispy sound. "I have something to say—"

"I'm listening."

"You must free them, Shec. Your... fae."

Ilishec's face clouded with confusion. "Free them? They are not prisoners."

"They are," she argued. "You love them, but you keep them imprisoned inside your... fear. You must let them go."

"Let them go?" Ilishec echoed, looking stricken.

"Let them go... as you must... let me go," she whispered, letting her eyes drift closed. The smallest smile graced her mouth. "I love you... all."

She exhaled and Laec closed his eyes, feeling her soul depart like it was riding on the back of a butterfly, carefree. He wished her well wherever her spirit was headed, palming away tears. After a long minute of silence, Laec opened his eyes, putting his hand on Ilishec's shoulder.

The gardener bowed and leaned forward, caving in on himself as he put his forehead against the back of Hazel's hand.

Laec leaned toward his uncle, wrapping an arm around him, his head against Ilishec's side. Laec heard him whisper farewell to his wife.

They sat like that, weeping silently, for a long time.

When his uncle straightened, still holding his wife's hand, he sniffed and wiped his eyes. He sounded bewildered. "Let them go? I don't understand."

"I do," Laec said gently, looking over at him.

His uncle's brows drew down over his glistening, tear-filled eyes.

Laec squeezed his uncle's shoulder. "By let them go, she meant... let them fight."

CHAPTER TWENTY-EIGHT

JESSAMINE

"JESS WILL USE her *solidago* magic to locate Toryan's crown," Digit said, once they were seated around the fire again and Isabey had stopped hyperventilating. She was remarkably sheepish-looking now; all her disbelief and stubbornness had faded away in the wake of her meeting with Jezaret.

"It'll be locked up in the fortress," said Isabey, her teeth chattering as though she was cold. Calvatia took off her shawl and wrapped it around the princess. "I know where it's kept."

"That's good," said Digit with obvious relief. "We were worried that Faraçek might be carrying it around with him."

Isabey shook her head. "There's no chance. He would never risk losing it."

"If it's in the fortress then it should be easier for us to get to, since only a skeleton crew will be left to guard it. Right?" Jess looked at Shade for agreement.

The soldier nodded.

"Okay," Jess continued. "Let me try, just to be sure."

Kneeling, she dug her hands into the earth as Beazle flew down to the ground. Jess conjured *solidago* and watched as the stalks grew and the flowers bloomed. She pictured the ominous crown in her mind as well as she could remember it. *Where are you?*

Nothing happened.

She waited, noting that an uncomfortable pressure had begun to grow in her head. It swelled like a pufferfish in her brain, making her temples throb.

My head hurts, grumped Beazle.

Mine too.

Jess released her request and looked up at the group. "Something is blocking me. The magic isn't working."

Digit looked uneasy; Shade looked perplexed, but Isabey didn't look a bit surprised.

Kite shifted her stance. "Try again."

Jess didn't think trying a second time would work; the magic had never failed before. There was some kind of enchantment on the crown, protecting it from her. But to humor Kite, she brought up a second *solidago* stem, questing for the crown's location. The pressure in her mind returned, but worse this time. Her whole head pounded. Beazle squeaked his discomfort, shaking his head like trying to cast off the pain.

"It's not working." Jess rubbed her forehead. "It's hurting us. There's some kind of defensive magic on the crown."

Everyone looked downcast, but Isabey said; "The crown is well known to have dark magic, but it doesn't matter, I'm sure it's in the fortress. There's no other place it could be. My brother would be too afraid that something could happen to it."

Jess took a deep breath and drew herself up. "Then our best

chance is to assume that's where it is being held. In that case, Kite will escort Isabey and Shade back to Solana while Digit and I infiltrate the Rahamlar fortress and acquire the crown."

Shade looked concerned. "Just the two of you? You should have brought more... backup."

Kite, standing behind Digit, said: "These siblings have the deadliest magic Solana has ever seen. Plus, they look completely unsuspicious."

"What does that mean?" Digit craned his neck to look back at her.

"You know." Kite gestured to him then to Jess. "You look like farm kids. Pretty farm kids, but still... bumpkins."

"I don't want to go to Solana." Isabey protested, pulling Calvatia's shawl tighter around her shoulders.

"You don't?" Shade shot her a look of surprise.

Isabey shook her head, still fighting to stop her jaw from clacking. Jess realized it was fear, not cold. "Like they said, Rahamlar will be safer. Plus even if I describe to you exactly where the crown is, you'll never get it out of its box. I might as well show you the way, and destroy it right there. Why waste the extra time to give me the illusion of safety?"

Shade looked proud of her. "You sure, Iz?"

"I still don't know how I can destroy the crown. I've felt it in my hands. It's indestructible. But..." Her teeth chattered. "Lion."

Jezaret is hard to resist, thought Beazle as he flapped from Jess to Isabey's lap, as though her words meant that he was no longer angry with her.

Digit nodded. "But you weren't the heir when you last handled the crown."

Isabey made a cooing sound and cupped Beazle close

to her heart. She looked up and her jaw relaxed a fraction. "Oh, I hadn't thought of that. Yes, that's true." She seemed to straighten a little with that thought. "We can take the underground path to the fortress. I know the way. I've done it a few times now. You watch my back, and I'll get us to the crown."

"What about the well?" Jessamine asked, raising her biggest concern apart from not knowing for certain that the crown was where Isabey suspected it to be.

"We don't need to go that way," Isabey replied. "The underground network is a large web, not just that main one that was used for timbers. When Serya and I ran away, we accessed the tunnel system through an aqueduct. That's why no one saw us leave."

"Will it be guarded?" Digit asked.

Isabey shook her head. "Not unless something has changed. It is accessed through a storage cellar that's kept cool by a channel that pulls water from the Tamyrat, circulates it, then dumps it back out into the river. Those cellars are used by cooks and servants. There's no way in or out without getting wet. A soaking wet person coming up from the cellar would raise an alarm."

"Everyone thinks you're dead," said Shade to Isabey, tapping the end of his stick in the dirt where he had sketched a rough map of the fortress interior. "If you're seen, what will the servants do?"

Isabey lifted a shoulder. "I don't know, and anyway it doesn't matter. Since I agreed to do this, Rahamlar will soon know that I'm alive. I was nicer to the servants than my brother ever was. Hopefully, that will count for something." She pointed to a corner of the fortress. "Toryan's crown has always been kept here, in an enclosed turret attached to what was once my mother's room. The space hasn't been used since she died."

Digit looked up from the crude architectural plan. "Enclosed turret. What does that mean? Bricked up?"

"No. Well, yes, sort of. It was an alcove originally, it was partially bricked up and a door with a lock was installed. Inside is a kind of presentation and storage room for my mother's jewelry and other precious items—everything from gifts she was given by foreign kingdoms to important paperwork, heirlooms, that kind of thing. The crown is not on display though. It's inside a locked case in a clever hiding spot. I know where the keys are kept for both the room, and the box containing the crown, assuming that Faraçek hasn't moved them."

"And if he has?" Kite asked.

Jess felt her tummy tighten. If the keys had been moved, she might be able to use her magic to locate them at least. But it would mean losing precious time. Lives hung in the balance, and this was all so uncertain.

You can't fool yourself into thinking that we'll pull this off without anyone dying, Beazle told her as he jumped from Isabey's palm back to Jess's hair.

I want to minimize the bloodshed, Jess returned. *With Digit, we can do that. I wish I could dose someone to sleep, but nightshades don't work that way.*

Maybe you could dose someone into a bellyache, but that's about as kind as it gets.

That would be better than death, she thought.

Beazle didn't disagree, but he doubted that a bellyache was strong enough to stop an onslaught if an enemy was determined to stop or kill them.

"Then I'll have to try something else," said Isabey to Kite.

"Like what?"

"Waking up one of my former ladies' maids and asking for help."

Digit and Jess shared a long look of unease. "I wish we knew exactly where it is. It makes me nervous planning with nothing but hope that the crown is somewhere in the fortress."

Shade looked undaunted. "I'm sure Isabey is right. He's left it there."

Kite tugged on her lip, looking pensive. "Either way, it's our best option."

Shade stood. "It's getting late. We have a rough plan. Let's get some sleep, then start early. We'll have to walk all day tomorrow and well into the next night to arrive at the aqueduct."

Kite looked thoughtful. "Erasmus will stay topside and report to keep us informed of what's happening in Solana. If we keep a strong pace, we should arrive in the very early morning while it's still dark."

"That's good. The whole city will be asleep," said Shade. "Except for the night watch, of course, but they patrol the ramparts and towers, not the aqueducts."

Calvatia helped them prepare supplies: food and water-skins, weapons and lanterns. They slept by the fire wrapped in quilts. Jess felt like she'd just fallen asleep when already Digit was shaking her awake.

Crossing the swamp as the sun was a mere hint in the eastern sky, the hoods had their horses saddled and waiting. Fixing their supplies to the saddles, the group mounted and pushed the horses to keep the fastest pace that the soft earth and thick vegetation would allow. Two of Fixnix's hoods went with them, but left them at the entrance to the cave, taking all the horses back to the swamp and leaving the group to go on foot. They rested and ate a snack of dried berries and lumps of hard cheese before entering the underground through an unassuming crack in a craggy cliffside.

The network leading to the fortress was not nearly as straightforward as the underground passage—in fact it was the polar opposite. Where the passage had been broad with high ceilings, the way Isabey led them was crooked, narrow, low-ceilinged, and at times dangerous with rough footing and rock formations in the way, sharp stalactites and stalagmites interfering like errant teeth. Glowworms lit some of the way, but where there were none, they had to light their lanterns. Their exhalations echoed around them in tight spaces, and it seemed to Jessamine that the closer they got, the more the sound of liquid dripping got on her nerves. Beazle enjoyed the journey immensely, his bat's heart naturally content inside a dark cave full of defenseless worms. He couldn't stop himself from fluttering ahead, sometimes for long stretches of time, only to return to tell Jess about features the group would soon encounter.

There were many intersections, not only two paths converging, but as many as seven points coming together at once. Most of the time, Isabey and Shade knew which way to go, but at times they had to pause and think.

When they stopped to rest, they took no more than half-hour naps to refresh themselves until Isabey told them they'd reached about halfway, then they took a longer sleep. They ate the popkins that Calvatia had packed for them. Beazle snapped up glowworms, boasting to Jess that they were improving his eyesight. She was glad Beazle was so happy. She couldn't wait to get out of these caves. Digit kept nectar for Ania, who needed to eat almost constantly. Down here she couldn't forage for herself, so Digit poured little pools of sugary liquid into his palm and held it for her. The hum of her wings seemed louder than ever as the walls closed in around them.

When Kite froze and Jess nearly walked into her, Jess knew she was receiving communication from Erasmus. They waited silently until Kite told them what she'd learned.

"We need to hurry," she said, moving forward again. "Night is falling. Ferrugin told Erasmus that she heard a conversation that just occurred between Captain Yorin and King Agir; Agir and Esha have until one hour after sunup to leave the city, or Faraçek will use his mind-control powers at the gate. They'll kill anyone who resists."

Galvanized by this, they increased their pace, not talking for several hours to save their breath and focus on covering ground. They took breaks to rest their legs, drink water and eat, but the breaks were shorter now. A sense of urgency propelled them forward despite their weariness.

Just as Jessamine was about to ask how much further it was, the tunnel sloped steeply downward and the sound of running water grew loud. The air turned frosty as they picked their way down the jagged path, ducking to avoid grazing their heads.

Isabey went down first, her boots scraping along the stone until she reached the bottom. She didn't hesitate there, but hopped right into the water. Jess heard her gasp then slosh forward, out of Shade's way.

Shade's foot slipped and he gave a little cry as he slid down to the bottom, fighting to stay upright. There was a bigger splash and his lantern light was snuffed out. He surfaced, breathing hard.

Kite, Digit and Jess got a better look at the situation. Isabey hadn't stopped because the chute had no flat surface at the bottom, other than a very narrow lip—hardly the width of a big toe.

Isabey stood breast-high in the water, twisting her braids and shoving them up under the hat Calvatia had loaned her.

"Right. It keeps the cellar cold, so it's... cold." Kite set her lantern on the ground. Bracing her hands on the sides of the narrow chute, she slid down to the edge. Digit followed her, reaching the bottom just as Kite shinnied out of the way, clinging to the narrow ledge with her toes, and clutching at the edges of bricks with her fingers.

Jess skated to the bottom, fighting for balance until she bumped into Digit. He stopped her momentum and kept her out of the water by bracing his hands on each wall to make a barrier.

"Bricks!" said Digit, his exclamation echoing around them.

Except for the chute itself—which was more or less a large crack in the wall—the entire place was built of bricks stacked in an orderly and attractive herringbone pattern. The water was very clean and clear. The occasional fish flashed by, going with the flow of water.

"There's the intake that leads to the cellar." Isabey pointed at the iron grate that was more than half submerged. A round arch curved out of the water, lined with bricks. "It's deeper than it looks and the current is strong. Be careful."

"There are bars in the way." Jess eyed the thick ironwork dubiously. "And only a few inches of clearance."

"There's a way through under the water," Isabey told her. "And the clearance gets better as you go along."

Kite and Digit jumped into the water.

Digit gasped and stiffened. "It's not cold, it's freezing!"

Kite took a lantern from Jess so she could jump in. Jessamine had to stifle a cry of shock as she went up to her ribcage, her feet sliding on the sloped curve of the channel.

Isabey moved deeper, muttering, "If my sister knew I was showing this to Solanans, she'd have had me whipped."

"And what would your brother do?" Kite asked, eyeing the grate with distaste. She carried the lantern over her head, holding it so everyone could see the bars.

Isabey shot her a dirty look over her shoulder but didn't answer. Shade was now jaw-deep in the freezing water, bracing himself against the grate with what looked like a fair amount of effort as the current sought to crush him against the iron. He looked back at Isabey.

Isabey went in to her shoulders and floated toward Shade and the grate, her head tilted back. At the ironwork, she took a deep breath and went under. Her shape was a dark smudge that went down and down, to the bottom of the channel. Then she slipped forward and popped up on the other side, hooking her fingers around the grate to keep herself from being washed away. Her head bumped the ceiling as she took in a big breath.

"Watch the iron," she told Shade. "It's a little sharp. It ripped my trousers."

Shade went under, following the same path Isabey had taken. Kite handed the lantern through the grate to Shade, the flame guttering as it turned sideways.

Kite and Digit went next, leaving Jess last. When the water closed over Jessamine's head, it was so icy that she couldn't help but think of Çifta locked inside her pillar of ice. Head aching from the cold, her fingers felt stiff as they trailed down the metalwork, looking for the hole large enough for her to fit through. She found it when she sliced her finger on a barb protruding from a cut bar. The current pushed her forward and she slipped through, popping up on the other side with a gasp. With her head tilted back and her eyes focused upward, she saw Beazle clinging to the stones above her head.

It's freezing in here. Beazle ruffled his wings around himself.

You think you're freezing?!

You're right. Nothing could ever be as bad as Sylifke's winter.

Beazle dropped from the bricks and fluttered around in the small space between the water and the ceiling, then slipped away down the channel, throwing a thought back at Jess like a warning. *It's a long tunnel, Jess. Don't freeze to death.*

Jessamine growled and floated after Digit; Isabey and Shade were already out of sight. The light of the lantern was a distant glow around the curve up ahead, and rapidly receding.

It was long, but the current was fast and carried them past the joining of another aqueduct. The channel expanded as they went. Jess had enough room to lift her shoulders out of the water by the time they arrived at another grate. She bumped up against Digit and Shade just as Isabey popped up on the other side in a large yawning space with strange bulky shadows. Shade shifted the lantern to illuminate the room; it was full of crates and barrels and smelled of cheese and oak. It was so cold they could see their exhales hanging in the air. The channel went through the room and disappeared through another grate on the other side.

Jess surfaced in time to hear Digit ask Isabey: "Why has no one fixed those holes? You'd think they would check these grates for breaches."

"Keep your voice down," she whispered, though he had been far from loud. She put her hands flat on the edge of the channel and heaved herself out, streaming water. "They haven't been fixed because no one knows about them."

"You did." Digit hopped out like he had springs for legs. "Not until Shade showed me."

Jess couldn't get out of the water fast enough. The moment she saw Isabey out, she heaved herself up and out as well. Shivering, she wrung out her hair and took off her jacket, laying it over the nearest surface, a wooden crate. She rubbed at her face, trying to revive herself. Lack of proper sleep, cold, and stress were taking their toll.

Digit followed Isabey up a set of steps to a low wooden door. Jess heard them whispering as Isabey put her shoulder to the door and eased it open. Beyond the door was darkness, but Digit slipped out without hesitation. His task was to fetch dry clothing from the closets where livery was kept. All they could do until he got back was shiver and wait.

CHAPTER TWENTY-NINE

LAEC

A T TWO IN the morning, Bradburn sent Laec to the palace to rest. He rode Grex up the hill and put him into a clean stall since there were no stablehands about. Making sure the stallion had fresh hay, water and a serving of oats, Laec began the long trudge through the palace to the East Keep, and his room. The palace was eerily calm. Normally the etherlamps were amber at night but tonight they gave a dim violet glow, casting a cool illumination across the carpets and paintings. Passing a mirror, Laec's own reflection gave him a shiver; his normally pink complexion looked pale, and his red hair looked the color of dried blood. His appearance was almost unseelie. This brought a new thought into Laec's mind. Was the light chosen by some engineer? Or perhaps by Hob the steward? Or did the ether that powered Solana sense that this was a city in distress and the light was set to reflect that?

As Laec passed an intersection of hall-ways that led to rooms that the Calyx used, he heard a murmur of voices. Recognizing Georjie's voice, he turned down the hall and followed his ears. Peering through the open door of a lounge, he was surprised to see at least twenty, probably more, of the Calyx, sitting about and chatting. Georjie—in a borrowed nightdress and dressing gown—was perched on the arm of one of the sofas, listening to Marigold who was speaking intently, a serious expression on her face. There was something strange about the scene—other than that the Calyx were out of bed at this hour, which was understandable given the circumstances. But it wasn't that. Laec couldn't put his finger on what it was.

Proteas noticed Laec and his expression blossomed with hope. "What's happening at the front, Laec?"

All conversation in the room ceased and every flora fae looked to the door, waiting for his response.

"Please say the prince has come to see reason," said Peony from her place on the sofa, squeezed between Asclepias and Dahlia. Her lustrous hair was a waterfall of black silk over her shoulders, reaching below her bosom. Her villainous looking wasp was nowhere in sight. It struck Laec that that was what made the scene strange; there wasn't a single pollinator in the room. Wherever the Calyx were, insects were always present, but not tonight.

"Where're the bugs?" Laec came into the room, ignoring Peony's question. It wasn't good news and he wished he hadn't popped by.

Rose, squished into a single chair with Aster, her golden hair plaited into a thick braid over one shoulder, said: "Our familiars have been locked in the moss room off Ilishec's workshop. It's humid and warm. They should be comfortable in there."

"And safe," Aster added. Her tight corkscrew curls were in a fetching mess all over her head, making her look like a teenager.

"That's the hope," said Snap from the back of the room. He was not lounging like the others, but rather pacing behind the couches from bookcase to sideboard, while tossing what looked like a cork up and down with one hand. His eyes had a wild look in them. "From the sounds of it, that bloody crown gave the prince way more power than any lunatic of his ability should have. We might all be mind-controlled by morning."

Wisteria looked fearful. "Don't be morbid, Snap."

"You won't be mind-controlled by morning," said Laec. Because they all looked so relieved, he felt a bit guilty, but still couldn't help but add wickedly: "Maybe by noon, but not by morning."

The Calyx groaned simultaneously. Rose's complexion went positively waxen.

"You're sick," Snap told him, the only one who looked unafraid.

Georjie shot him a reproachful look. "Not funny, Laec."

"I've seen the Rahamlar army." Snap hit the length of his lap and turned back in the other direction, head swiveling. "They outnumber us but they have no siege machines. They won't get past our walls unless the prince's magic can reach us from the outside. Can it do that?"

"It's better if we assume it can," replied Peony, her back to him. "A false sense of security won't do us any good."

"The crofter, Bradburn and the king believe that as long as all inhabitants of the city stay back from the gate, which is our weakest point," Laec told them, "then we should be safe from the prince's exhalations."

"But how far back is far *enough*?" asked Marigold. "I heard he mind-controlled all of Stoneiron. I've been there. It's at least a half-mile across." She raised both her eyebrows and bobbed her head to emphasize. "That's huge!"

Proteas scratched at the back of his head. "So is a half-mile the prince's maximum, or can he reach farther than that?"

"There's no way of knowing." Laec put a hand over his stomach as it rumbled. He hadn't eaten properly since early morning. "All we can do is push back as far from the gate as we can and hope for the best."

"What if he can reach us over the walls?" Rose asked.

"Seems hopeless," mourned Wisteria, and Dahlia rubbed her back. "Maybe Agir should give himself up after all."

"Don't say that," snapped Rose. "I'd rather die than be ruled by Faraçek. Have you forgotten what he did to Greta? How he looked at us with such disdain when we performed for him? We don't have any value to the prince, and Solana will cease to be Solana if he takes over."

"I'll go back to Archelia," said Alstro quietly, his gaze on the floor. "If we survive this. You'd all be welcome there, I'm sure. Maybe we could even start our own traveling show, or something, with a perfume business on the side."

"I can't believe what I'm hearing." Snap's eyes blazed. "It's like you've all given up already."

Alstro glared at Snap. "What's your great idea?"

"Yes," sniped Peony, looking over her shoulder at Snap. "If you're so clever and brave, tell us how you expect a handful of flora fae to defeat ten thousand unseelie soldiers and a prince with the ability to control our minds? Go on, Snap. We're all ears."

Snap only looked angrier. "There must be something. The lions chose us!"

Georjie rose from her seat. "There is something—"

A skinny boy ran by the room, hooked a hand on the doorjamb to halt his momentum, then came inside, bright-eyed and huffing. "Laec!"

"Graf." Laec's heart fell. Perhaps he wouldn't get any rest after all.

"Your presence is requested on the wall," the messenger told him. The young lad looked more excited and energized about the invasion than frightened, like he'd been bored by regular life in Solana and was happy that things had sparked up a bit. "Regalis says he's sorry. He knows you're tired, but he thinks you'll want to hear the news."

"What news?" Snap said, halting mid-stride.

Graf looked at the room. "I don't know, sorry. Something to do with Miss Fontana's mission, I believe."

Expressions shifted in response to the mention of Jess.

"What about her?" barked Snap. "Why aren't we being told if something's happened?"

"Whatever it is, it's Fahyli business." Marigold shot Snap a weary look. "It's not our business."

"It is absolutely our business." Peony got to her feet, bracing her hands on her hips. Patches of pink blossomed on her cheeks as she glared at Graf, who wilted under her gaze. "She's just as important to us as she is to the Fahyli. If something's happened, we should be told."

Several flora fae grumbled their agreement and Graf looked sweaty. Laec felt sorry for the boy; he was a pleaser and there was no pleasing this lot tonight.

"Come on, Graf," he told the lad. "Best not keep him waiting. You coming with?"

"Aye, sir Laec."

"Please come back and tell us what Jess is doing, or at least send Graf back," Rose pleaded. "We're all worried for her!"

They turned toward the door. "Regalis said to tell you he has sandwiches for you, and fresh coffee." Graf looked up with an expression of hope that the food and drink might please Laec.

"What else could a weary fae possibly want?" Laec hooked an arm over the boy's skinny shoulders, steering him out of the room.

When Laec reached the top of the wall, Regalis immediately handed him food and mug of hot coffee. "Jess, Digit and Kite are inside Rahamlar."

Laec spewed his drink. He coughed, wiping his face. "What?"

Regalis nodded. "Ferrugin said they changed the objective. They meant to get Isabey and Shade and bring them back here, but it turns out that Toryan's circlet is expected to be in the fortress, and Isabey knows where it's kept. So they went to Rahamlar instead. Pickle?" He held an open jar toward Laec.

Snagging one of the briny cukes, Laec let his weight droop against the stone wall behind him. "So, they're in enemy territory."

"Focus on the positive," the Fahyli told him, spinning the jar lid back into place. "They've got Isabey, she's the true heir, therefore she can destroy the circlet. Half their objective is accomplished. Now they have to find the crown, and Erasmus says—" Regalis abruptly stopped talking. Eyes squinting, he focused on something up the high street, behind Laec and over his head. "What's that?"

Laec turned and saw a large group moving straight down the main street toward the front gate. Etherlamps cast cool circles of light along the cobbled streets. As the first of the group passed under the glow, Laec recognized Snap and Rose. Then he spotted Georjie and—with a jolt—Ilishec, at the front, and realized that it wasn't just any group, it was the Calyx, and from the looks of it… all of them.

"What the devil do they think they're doing?" asked Regalis.

Soldiers along the wall elbowed each other, directing focus to the street. The Calyx walked steadily, calm and confident in whatever it was they were doing. They wore plain leggings and tunics. They still looked painfully beautiful, even in every-day-wear. A soldier shouted for the crofter and Bradburn, who came out of the gatehouse. When they saw the Calyx approaching, they froze in place. Laec and Regalis moved along the wall, closer to the gate, for a better view.

As the flora fae passed, heads poked from windows and doors. It was a little like a parade, only different: somber and serious. A hush had fallen over the city.

Below Laec and Regalis, Bradburn and Ian were disconcerted.

"What do they think they're doing?" Laec heard Bradburn ask, echoing Regalis's query.

Regalis swore under his breath. "Are you seeing what I'm seeing?"

"What?"

"Lions," the fauna fae murmured. "A whole pride of them."

Laec frowned. "I don't see any—" but suddenly he *could* see them. There *were* lions, dozens of them, transparent and pale with a ghostly white light, walking amid the Calyx as though part of the group. Laec rubbed his eyes and stared. They were still there. A quick glance at Bradburn and the crofter, and some of the soldiers, confirmed that everyone else could see the lions too. Oddly, Laec wasn't sure that the Calyx themselves were aware that they were in the company of a pride of feline ghosts.

Ilishec and Georjie reached the gate first; the gardener was holding an etherlamp and wearing a sword. Laec was as shocked by the sight of his uncle wearing a weapon as he was by the sight of the lions.

The group came to a stop, forming a crowd of flora fae and ghostly cats, some of whom occupied the same space. Peony had a set of young cubs under her feet but appeared not to notice anything strange was going on. A huge lioness walked right through Snap then sat beside Georjie and looked up at the crofter expectantly. Laec sent a questioning look at Georjie but she was intent on those in control of the gate.

"I know you'll wish to stop us." Ilishec looked from the crofter to Bradburn. "But I must ask for your trust. Please, open the gate."

There was a long tense moment as the crofter and Bradburn exchanged a look of shock.

To Laec's surprise, Bradburn called, "Open the gate!"

"He'd never have done that if it weren't for all the lions," said Regalis.

The guardsmen jumped into action, activating the ether-powered machinery that lifted the portcullis and unbarring the smaller fae-sized door cut into the wooden gate.

Ilishec was the first to step outside.

Laec went to the outer side of the rampart over the gate and shouted down: "Uncle!"

Ilishec held the lantern aloft to illuminate the king's road as the flora fae filed out. He glanced up but didn't stop walking.

"Shall I come with you?" Laec called.

"No, nephew," the gardener called back, pausing. "Thank you, but you're better where you are."

Laec's stomach felt unsettled. "What are you doing?"

"Jessamine needs time," Ilishec said before turning away

and continuing down the road. Just before he disappeared into the darkness, his lantern a mere speck of light, Laec heard his uncle say, "And only we can give her that."

CHAPTER THIRTY

JESSAMINE

DRESSED IN RAHAMLARIN livery, Jess and her companions followed Isabey through the sleeping fortress. Torches in clawed holders fixed to the stone walls had burned down to mere dwindles of light—many gone out, leaving sections of the fortress in darkness—but Isabey never faltered. Leading with her head held high, the princess confidently swept down empty corridors, up sets of stairs and through a couple of gloomy parlors until they reached a set of double doors. Isabey paused, her hand on the doorknob, looking at the floor, appearing to brace herself. Jess was about to ask if she was alright when Shade, at Isabey's side, looked back. Something in his face told her to keep quiet. This room either meant something to Isabey, or it scared her—perhaps both—since Queen Daryli had been known as a tyrant. It was King Osvitan, Isabey's human father, who had tempered the unseelie queen's effect.

A sound like the bump of a piece of furniture against

a wall seemed to electrify the princess out of her stupor. She twisted the knob and slipped inside. Everyone followed except Shade, who would stand outside and keep watch.

It was a large bedroom with a huge, bare four-poster bed. Other furniture—chairs clustered close to a fireplace, and what must be a broad desk surrounded by bookcases—were all covered in dustsheets.

"This was my mother's room," Isabey told them in a quiet voice as she crossed to a door on the diagonal of a corner. Rounded walls curved away from the door, behind which had to be a turret. The fortress had many turrets, scattered about like pawns in a maze. On either side of the door sat cement gargoyles: one looked like a squashed dragon with a perfectly flat head, its clawed hands pressing upward and its face in a grimace; the other was a plain cowbird, with one claw curled up beneath it. A functioning clock dangled from its talons.

Isabey tried the door and found it locked, but she didn't appear surprised. Sweeping over to the sheet-swaddled desk, she lifted the fabric and half disappeared beneath it. She looked like a common servant snooping where she ought not be. There came a sound of wood sliding on wood, then she emerged, a key glinting in her hand. She opened the door and propped it with a gargoyle.

The turret was as large as a small bedroom, and its interior surprising in its elegance. There was little about Rahamlar that could be called beautiful, but this room qualified. It reminded Jess of a jewelry shop on Solana's high street, with gleaming wooden cases and drawers, each fixed with a fine brass handle in the shape of a single outstretched wing. Isabey homed in on a drawer at floor level. Tugging on the handle, she found it was also locked. She thought for a moment before crossing to another, smaller drawer. This one contained a jumble of keys in different sizes and shapes. Isabey let out a long sigh, hanging her head, then began to rifle through the pile.

Strange, thought Beazle. *Hiding important keys in a pile of other keys?*

I can't decide if it's clever or foolish, Jess returned, as she watched Isabey hold one key up to a shaft of light, then another, and another. *For someone who doesn't know what they're looking for, they'd be occupied for hours.*

Yes, until they got caught. Beazle crawled from Jess's hair, up the back of her head to the top where he could see better. *Shall I keep watch in the hall?*

Shade's doing that.

Isabey found what she was looking for, taking one key and discarding the rest.

I don't think he is.

Jess froze. *What do you mean?*

Shade isn't out there.

Where did he go?

I'll see if I can find out. Beazle winged out of the room.

Isabey bent down and tried the key. There was a satisfying click and the drawer slid open. Jess lifted her lantern to illuminate the interior. There was nothing but a lining of orange velvet.

Beazle didn't get very far before he sent Jess a message, alarm in his tone. *Someone's coming, Jess. A female.*

Isabey stared at the drawer as though not believing her eyes, then put a hand flat against her forehead. "It's been moved."

"Isabey—" Jess whispered, her pulse picking up speed.

"What's going on in here?" cried a sharp female voice.

They whirled, a guilty look on every face except Isabey's. Shade appeared in the doorway a moment later, his eyes big.

He was puffing a little. He closed the door, shutting out Beazle, who immediately began searching for a crack he could crawl through to get back in.

The female looked angry... and familiar. "Explain yourselves—"

Princess Isabey emerged from the tower, stepping in front of the group. She drew back her shoulders and stared down the intruder. "Who dares confront me in my mother's quarters?"

The female halted. A soft beam of moonlight streaming through a window illuminated her face. Recognition bloomed in Jess's memory. It was Reina, the young Prince Toryan's mother. Reina's features shifted dramatically as she recognized Isabey. Her eyes stretched wide and her cheeks took on a ghostly pallor.

"Princess?" Her voice faltered.

"Reina?" Isabey's expression warmed.

Reina dropped into a curtsy, bowing her head before looking up at Isabey again. "Can this be? Are you... real?"

Suddenly the two females were in each other's arms, hugging and weeping. Jess and Digit exchanged a look of relief, then they both shot Shade a look of chagrin.

"That was close," mouthed Digit.

Shade looked mortified. "I thought I heard something from down the hall and went to investigate," he said quietly. "I was only gone for a moment."

Kite shifted uncomfortably as Reina and Isabey wept. Jess had the feeling that Kite would be more at home aiming an arrow at an enemy than she was in the presence of two women clinging to each other like their hearts were breaking. But when they finally withdrew, there was joy in their faces too. They wiped their eyes, gazing at one another blearily.

Isabey said: "I've missed you, darling friend. I haven't seen you in so long. I hear congratulations are in order. Is it true I have a nephew?"

Reina nodded and her face crumpled, losing some of its joy. "I'm so sorry, Princess. That I couldn't tell you and had to leave without saying goodbye. He made me keep it a secret from everyone, even you, Ander and Serya. Even from your father. I never understood why. My Toryan was just the bastard child of the third-in-line. I never thought Faraçek would rule. Now I have to wonder if he planned this from the beginning."

Isabey nodded. "I have learned that my brother has been keeping many secrets from all of us. So you never moved to Tryske after all, that was a ruse?"

Reina nodded. "The moment he knew I was pregnant he moved me to Cornhollow. A nice enough place and a comfortable house, but very lonely. I was not allowed to leave the property—thankfully it was big. Toryan has led a very sheltered and safe life. Faraçek read any letters I wrote to my family, so I was never allowed to tell them either." She ran a hand over her cheek, wiping away the last of her tears. "I never knew it was going to be like this. My own parents haven't yet met their grandson."

"If we'd known. Serya and I would have helped you." Isabey enfolded Reina's hands with both of her own.

"There was nothing you could have done to help. Once I was with child, everything changed. All my goodbyes were said on paper, and he never told me when I might return to court. I became his ward."

Sounds more like a prisoner to me, thought Beazle.

Reina gazed at the princess, her eyes misting up again. "I'm so sorry, Princess. For all your losses. How does one withstand such tragedy?"

Isabey murmured her thanks and the women hugged again.

Do you think Reina knows that Faraçek killed Serya? Beazle landed on the back of Jess's tunic and scaled her back.

I doubt it. Who would have told her the truth?

"I suppose his name was Faraçek's idea," Isabey said as she withdrew, her tone flat.

"Of course." Reina lowered her voice as though afraid the stones had ears. "*I'd* never choose it, that name is evil."

"Perhaps young Toryan can give it a new reputation." Isabey squeezed Reina's upper arm in a comforting gesture, sounding optimistic, though Jess wasn't sure the princess could believe her own words. Toryan was Faraçek's boy… would he turn out like his father?

"I can only hope. He summoned us only a few months ago, making us travel half the distance in the dark. He met us in the middle of the night, like we were criminals."

We saw that, commented Beazle. *I thought the girl was an accomplice.*

An unwilling one, it sounds like. Jess shivered and drew the hood of her livery up around her neck like a shawl. This room was chilly, and they'd stopped moving. Her fingers and toes were getting cold. Worse, they were losing precious time.

"I hate to interrupt a happy reunion," Digit said—drawing the attention of both females—"but our mission is time-sensitive and we seem to have hit a snag."

Isabey reacted, squeezing Reina's hands. "Toryan's crown has been moved. Do you know where it is?"

Reina's expression clouded. She shook her head. "He would never trust me with a secret of such importance."

Isabey's shoulders slumped as she released Reina, turning

away to pace, rubbing her temples. "I haven't a clue where he might have hidden it."

Is it worth trying our solidago magic once again? Beazle asked, feeling anxious. *Maybe it will be easier here, if we're closer to the crown.*

We can only try, though I don't think it will work, and I've not seen so much as a potted plant—we'll have to go outside.

Jess sighed. "I can try again…" She trailed off, looking uncertain.

Reina didn't appear to hear Jess, but her expression suddenly cleared. "He'll have told Toryan, though."

Isabey looked surprised. "Are you sure?"

"My son and Captain Yorin are the only ones Faraçek trusts. Toryan adores his father. He may not give it up easily, but perhaps for me…" she smiled with soft eyes. "He loves his mother too."

They moved toward the door.

Kite touched Jess's elbow. "Shall I fetch some dirt for you? In case the boy won't tell?"

Jess shot the Fahyli a grateful look and it was enough. Kite swept off down the hall.

I hope we don't need it, thought Jess.

Reina led them down the corridor, passing many closed doors, until she stopped outside a room. She quietly opened the door.

"I think Shade and Digit should wait outside, but perhaps Beazle can assist," Isabey said gesturing that Jessamine could come.

Me? Beazle was mystified. *How?*

Just by being there, I guess.

Jess followed Isabey and Reina into a cozy bedroom with a

single, narrow bed. A small frame lay huddled under blankets, black hair tufting out. A tiny whistle accompanied the faeling's every exhale. Reina lit the lamp beside the bed with a match, turning the dial to stoke the largest flame. Light fell over the bed. His mother's weight on the mattress put a stop to the whistles as the boy woke.

"Mother?" Toryan rolled over, blinking sleepily as his mother stroked hair from his forehead. He yawned with his whole body, his chest pushing the covers up. "What's happening?"

He'd grown a little since Jess and Beazle had seen him last, but still looked young for an eight-year-old. Isabey sucked in a little air, seeing how like her brother Toryan looked: the obsidian eyes, the widow's peak, the angular jaw and the long, pointed ears. Jess's heart was pounding as though she'd been jogging. Seeing Toryan drew a similar reaction from her body as his father did, though the boy had a sweet expression, not yet marred by the malignancy that twisted Faraçek's mouth and drew his brows down over his cruel eyes.

"I'm sorry to wake you, my love. But there is someone important here that you need to meet," Reina told him.

With a child's ultimate trust, Toryan did not question the strange hour of this introduction, nor was he alarmed by the other stranger in the room. He pushed himself up to sitting, smiling at Isabey, then at Jessamine.

"Hello."

"This is your Auntie Isabey." Reina beckoned the princess closer.

Isabey grabbed a stool sitting near a child-sized desk and took it over to the bed. Setting it on the floor by Toryan, she reached out a hand. "It's a pleasure to meet you, nephew."

Toryan looked pleasantly mystified by Isabey's presence. He

shook her hand politely, wide-eyed and staring. "Aunt Isabey? You... you've not died then? Father said you'd died. Is Auntie Serya alive too?"

"No, little one," Isabey told him. "I'm afraid that Aunt Serya is gone."

The princess put a hand out for Jessamine to come near. Jess was surprised to have been brought into the conversation, but she obediently stepped forward.

"This is my friend, Jess," Isabey told Toryan. "She helped to save my life."

"Father will be pleased," said the boy with shining eyes, looking genuinely happy. "But he's not here and might not be back for a while. He's gone to Solana to talk with King Agir." The boy reached a hand out and Jess had no choice but to shake it.

This is beyond strange, Beazle crawled into Jess's hood. *You've just been courteously addressed by the son of your bitter enemy.*

Jess agreed, it was weird.

"Jess is flora fae," Isabey told Toryan. "Do you know what that is?"

The boy nodded, studying Jess with fresh interest. "Does that mean you're from Solana? Why are you wearing our colors?"

Jess felt like someone had just pegged her to the floor through her feet. The boy was too sharp for his age. If the lad knew that she and his father had tried to kill each other once... Did she answer the boy's question truthfully? She waited for Isabey to answer, but now all three of them were looking at her. It was Toryan's understanding that Faraçek had gone to Solana to "talk" with Agir that encouraged her to tell the truth. Faraçek was protecting his child from the much more disturbing reality.

"That's right, Toryan," Jess told him, feeling a flush creep through her body at speaking his name out loud. "I'm from Solana, and I am flora fae. I'm wearing your colors because I'm helping your Aunt Isabey."

You can come out now, Jess told Beazle, and felt him crawling to her shoulder.

When Toryan saw the bat, he reacted as most children did upon sight of such a cute and tiny creature: with naked delight.

"This is Beazle."

"Beazle is my friend too," Isabey told her nephew. "He also helped to save my life."

"It's nice to meet you, Beazle," the prince said with admirable restraint. His hands came together in a childish clasp, twisting like they were physically itching to hold Beazle.

Beazle leapt to Toryan's bed then crawled up the blankets until he was nearly at the child's knees. He looked up at Toryan with his mouse-like eyes and gave a chitter that wasn't one of Beazle's natural sounds, but he knew that others found it endearing. Reina was as enchanted by Beazle as her son, Jess was relieved to see. She'd never understand why, but some people found Beazle scary.

"Perhaps he'll let you hold him," Reina wondered.

Toryan put the back of his hand on the bed, palm open and waiting. He was old enough to have learned not to be aggressive with small animals. Obligingly, Beazle crawled on and basked in Toryan's admiration as the boy lifted him closer to his loving gaze. The boy ran a fingertip from Beazle's head down to his tail and Beazle chittered again.

The things I do for my kingdom, Beazle thought wryly, as he gave a kitten-like mewl. *He doesn't smell nearly so nice as Isabey. He had butter on his fingers when he went to sleep.*

"Is it true you can communicate with him?" Toryan looked up at Jess.

"Yes."

Toryan looked impressed. "What's he saying right now?"

My fur feels oily, Beazle grumped. *Tell him to keep his grubby fingers away from my wings.*

"He's saying that it's nice to meet you, too," Jess told the boy.

"Perhaps you can hold him again later," Isabey said gently. "Right now there is something important that we need to ask you."

Beazle took the cue and flew back to Jess's shoulder, where he started to lick the buttery remains off his fur. Toryan watched him go with the bereft expression of a child losing their favorite plaything.

Reina ran her fingers through her son's hair. "Did your father ever show you Toryan's crown, darling?"

The boy nodded. "It has our cowbird on it, but it's not very pretty."

"That's the one. Good lad," Isabey praised him. "Did he tell you where he is keeping it?"

Toryan nodded again and Reina and Isabey exchanged an excited look.

"We need you to show us," the princess said. "It's very important. Can you do that?"

But Toryan shook his head. "He made me promise not to tell anyone."

Jess had expected this. Having witnessed the adoration that Toryan had for his father, she knew that a command from Faraçek would be taken seriously. Still, he was only a child. Would his will prove stronger than his mother's and the princess's?

"I'm your mother, Toryan," Reina told him, her voice growing a fraction sterner. "And this is your aunt, your father's beloved sister. You must not keep such an important family artifact secret from us. We are all of one blood."

Toryan looked pained. "I can't tell. I'm sorry."

"If your father was here, he would tell us," Isabey lied, as though she'd been telling lies all her life. Maybe she had, certainly since she'd fallen in love with Shade. "It's important, darling. We can't wait for Faraçek to come home. We need you to show us where the crown is."

"King Faraçek," corrected the child, but without malice.

Isabey didn't miss a beat. "Yes of course, King Faraçek."

"The order of the king cannot be broken," said the child, as though reading from a rulebook.

Jess had the idea to tell Toryan that Isabey was the rightful heir, that his allegiance had to be to her, not to Faraçek. But she discarded it quickly because Toryan wouldn't understand how that could be possible without being told that his father had murdered Princess Serya. The boy probably wouldn't believe it, and it would traumatize him.

The door squeaked and Kite poked her head in, gesturing to Jess to join her in the hall.

"Excuse me a moment," said Jess, exchanging a knowing look with Isabey. The princess looked relieved that Jess was willing to try again—that there may be an alternative way to locate the crown. It would save her having to get forceful with Toryan. No one wanted to resort to that.

Jess slipped out into the hall where Kite had a wooden bucket full of soil that smelled faintly of horse manure. Crouching near the vessel, Jess put her hand over the dirt and conjured *solidago*. Beazle left her shoulder and landed on the edge of the bucket. When she saw the tender green tops emerging, she closed her eyes and pictured the crown. *Where are you?*

Nothing happened.

You asked too soon, Beazle suggested. *You always do it when the blossoms come out.*

You're right, I'm nervous because it hurt last time.

Jess waited for the *solidago* to reach maturation and once again thought of the malignant crown. *Where are you hiding?*

The pressure came more swiftly this time, an ache that sharpened immediately into something fierce. Beazle squealed and flew to the rafters, as though trying to escape the pain. Jess put her hands to either side of her throbbing head. She looked up at Kite who was watching closely, her eyes two wet orbs in the torchlight. Jess shook her head.

Kite sighed. "Then the boy is our only hope. We need to get the information out of him, and fast."

Beazle returned to Jess's shoulder as Jess and Kite went back into the bedroom. When Isabey looked up expectantly, Jess shook her head. The princess's expression grew grim.

Toryan was sitting cross-legged in bed now, looking worried. Reina had an arm around his skinny shoulders.

"My dear," Isabey turned to her nephew. "You're far too young to have to bear this burden, but I have no choice but to share something with you, something that will be upsetting."

Reina closed her eyes but didn't stop the princess, she pulled Toryan against her bosom, kissing the top of his head.

"I can handle it," said the boy. "Father says ruling is hard, and one day I'll have to be king."

Interesting phrasing, Beazle thought.

He's mature for his age. Jess moved to stand near Isabey, hugging herself.

"Your father is my elder brother and I love him dearly," Isabey said, her voice growing a little tremulous. "But he has done things... things that no one is allowed to do. Even a king. In fact, one thing he did... means he gave up his right to rule."

"What do you mean?" Toryan looked more curious than frightened by his aunt's words.

Isabey took one of her nephew's hands, holding his palm on top of hers and stroking his knuckles. "Your father... ended Princess Serya's life. I was there. I saw it with my own eyes."

Reina gasped and stared at Isabey from over her son's head, horrified.

Toryan's dark eyes didn't move from her face. He looked perplexed. "Why?"

"Well..." Isabey looked thoughtful.

At least he didn't deny it, thought Beazle. *That's surprising.*

Remember that Faraçek told him that he was "arranging" things so that Toryan could rule? Jess rubbed her arms to ward off the cold. She was starting to wonder when she'd feel warm again. The swim in the aqueduct had chilled her to the bone. *Maybe the child realizes that part of arranging things was getting competition out of the way. He's young, but he's not stupid.*

"Your father wants to rule Rahamlar," Isabey finally replied. "And Princess Serya was supposed to rule before him."

"Because she was human," Toryan said. "Father doesn't agree with that rule. He thinks the eldest should rule, no matter if they're fae or human."

"I don't necessarily disagree with your father on that. After all, I am unseelie too, like you and like him. But just because we don't agree with laws, doesn't mean we are free to break them. There are punishments for breaking rules, and not killing others is the most important rule of all. Do you understand?"

Toryan nodded, looking studious.

"When your father killed Serya he committed a crime, a crime that means he forfeited his right to rule. Which means…" She waited expectantly, hoping that Toryan would fill in the blank.

"Which means you're the queen, and Father is…"

A criminal, thought Jess.

"He is still your father, little darling," Isabey murmured, keeping her tone sweet. "He's just not allowed to be king. So you see, you were not given an order by the king after all. I, on the other hand, am your rightful queen, and I'm giving you a true order. One you must obey."

Toryan went still, his little brows pleating with the effort to wrap his mind around the situation. His breathing sped up a little under the pressure he found himself under. "But… no one has recognized you officially as the queen yet."

"You are right, but this is too important to wait until then. The sun will soon rise, my dear nephew," Isabey said. "You must tell us where the crown is. Lives depend upon it, and as your soon-to-be queen, I command you to reveal it."

Toryan was fighting tears now, his mouth working, his gaze flicking from his aunt to his mother and back again. Finally, he shook his head. "I cannot. My father made me promise."

"Do you understand what I've told you?"

Toryan nodded, one fat tear rolling down his cheek. He put his knuckles into his eyes and began to rub them. He pulled them away and looked at Isabey blearily, leaning into his mother for comfort.

Reina kissed his tousled hair again. "You can tell her, son. It's okay. You won't be in trouble. I promise."

"I understand," said Toryan, his chest hitching, "but Father asked me to keep it secret. He's still my father, even if he won't be king."

Kite let out a long, weary sigh and turned away, fighting to keep her frustration out of her movements. She walked to the window.

This is bad. Jess went to the small window overlooking the river too, shoulder to shoulder with Kite. She felt bone-tired and as cold as a corpse. She looked at the horizon where a faint glow tainted the sky. They were running out of time.

"What do we do if he won't tell?" Jess whispered, quietly enough that the words wouldn't reach the bed.

"I'm prepared to use the mother," Kite whispered. "This is too important. Our friends will die if I don't do everything possible to destroy that crown."

Beazle tunneled into Jess's hair. *Tell me she doesn't mean torture.*

Jess shot Kite a look of dread tinged with alarm, but the Fahyli looked straight ahead, her face as hard as stone.

CHAPTER THIRTY-ONE

LAEC

LAEC AWOKE WITH a crick in his neck and a pleasant smell in his nose. He had been too exhausted to return to his room, and even if he'd had the energy, he couldn't return to a warm comfy bed while his uncle and the Calyx were outside the city walls. He'd fallen asleep on the wall beside Regalis, wrapped in an itchy military-issue blanket.

The smell of flowers nudged him out of sleep, but it was the odd creaking sounds that pulled him to full wakefulness. He fought to open his eyes and found they were pasted together with sleep. Groping for his waterskin, he splashed some water into his face, rubbing at his eyes until they were able to open. The sky was just beginning to lighten, and somewhere in the distance a rooster crowed.

Laec rolled to his feet and stretched, letting his blanket fall to the stones. *What is creaking?* He looked out at the enemy encampment to find his view was blocked by a mass of shadows.

A nightwatchman

holding a torch aloft caught his eye. Laec put up a hand and the watchman returned the greeting.

Laec approached. "May I borrow your torch?"

The watchman handed it over with a grin. "Aye. It's worth a closer look."

Laec took the torch to the exterior wall. "What is worth a closer—"

His words were cut off as the torch cast a net of illumination across what looked like the long neck of a smooth-skinned dragon, green and rubbery, with short, sparse bristles of pale hair. Following the line of the neck led to a sight that shocked Laec to his soles. Rather than the head of a dragon, a marigold blossom half the size of a ship's sail lay bobbing slowly at the end of a stem as thick as a man's thigh. It creaked as it rubbed against other stems.

Laec's gaze went beyond the marigold to register the thick tangle of oversized growth that had overtaken many feet of land beyond the wall, extending in both directions as far as Laec could see. The Calyx had grown an impassable barrier between the city walls and the enemy. Laec could tell that the jungle was thick, but not precisely how far out it went. Where the torch's light pushed back the shadows, he could make out roses, irises, dahlias, prickly bougainvillea, and wisteria boughs, to name just a few. He felt breathless and tingly all over, wondering where the Calyx, Georjie and Ilishec were now.

He looked at the watchman. "Why haven't you woken everyone?"

The watchman shrugged and gave a smug smile. "Just because a miracle happened doesn't mean we break protocol."

"I'd argue a miracle is the perfect reason to break protocol," Laec said, handing the torch back. "I'll wake Regalis and the others."

The watchman flashed another grin, clearly tickled by the development. "It's been nice to have something exciting happen at night for once. Watchmen rarely get to see anything grand."

Laec returned to where Regalis slept. A pale peach was now creeping over the eastern sky. Erasmus would be wheeling over Rahamlar somewhere, watching for the results of Jessamine's mission. Laec wondered if Ferrugin knew what was happening. He touched the Fahyli's shoulder and Regalis woke with a start. Laec beckoned as the fauna fae got to his feet and stretched. He sniffed at the air and a look of confusion stole over his face. Following Laec to the outer edge of the wall, Regalis peered over. At first, he just looked even more confused, then amazement stole over his features as he registered what he was looking at.

A watchman came by to wake soldiers for their shift. Everyone stirred, then went through the same awakening Regalis had. Before long, every soldier and Fahyli stood at the outer edge of the wall, gawking at the new landscape. The sky lightened further as the first sliver of sun breached the horizon, casting the morning in a palette of pinks, yellows and oranges.

"Wish I could see their faces when they get a load of this," one soldier said, using his eyeglass to cast his gaze in one direction, then the other.

"How thick is it?" asked another. "And why didn't the night crew wake us?"

There were grumbles about not having been awakened, but the soldiers were too astonished to be resentful.

More oversized botanicals revealed themselves as dawn's light kissed the top of the jungle. Thorns the length of a horse's tail pierced through succulent stems of lily—the scent of which overpowered the other flowers and gave Laec a headache. He'd always found the smell of lilies too pungent.

"Where are the Calyx?" asked Regalis at Laec's elbow, squinting down through the tangle of vegetation as though he might be lucky enough to find the bottom. Laec wagered even sunlight would not reach the soil through this garden.

"Still out there, somewhere. They never came in last night; I asked to be woken up when they did."

"Look down there," Regalis pointed down the length of the wall right below them.

What looked like a trench of shadow between the vegetation and the city wall was actually deeper than that. It was not a trench, but a canyon that had been dug at the base of the wall. Deep enough that they couldn't see the bottom.

"Why'd they do that?" Regalis wondered. "It's like an empty moat. But what's the point of a moat if no one can get through the flowers?"

"An extra precaution?" Laec guessed. "In case someone does get through, they can't use the garden as a ladder. That would defeat the purpose. There's nothing within a person's reach to the wall, or even a leap."

"Clever."

"Clever indeed," Laec repeated, knowing that it would have been Georjie who made such a precise split in the earth. He wished he knew where she was.

Regalis looked at him with growing concern. "They've grown a barrier to keep the prince's magic at bay, but now they're stuck out there with him."

Laec and Regalis got permission to leave through the front gate to search for the Calyx. Armed and chewing the last of yesterday's popkins, they stepped outside and looked around as the door in the main gate thumped shut behind them. A narrow bridge of earth—hardly wide enough for a single soldier to cross—had been left for passage, but otherwise the moat was wide enough that no one would be able to jump it. Laec looked down into the great crack with a narrowing bottom; it was crisscrossed with sinister looking roots.

Regalis toed his way across the beam of earth ahead of Laec. Chunks of sod broke off, tumbling down into the crack. When he reached the other side, he grasped a bluebell stem as thick as a sapling for balance.

"I'm shocked." The Fahyli spoke once he'd found a safe place to stand, almost hugging the stem of the bluebell. "I had no idea the Calyx were capable of such things."

Laec made his own delicate crossing, grabbing a leathery leaf for assistance. "They aren't. Georjie did the moat, I'm sure of that, and she had a lot to do with this jungle, too."

Regalis pushed a leaf away from his face. "The Wise from Stavarjak?"

"She's actually Terran, not Stavarjakian."

Regalis stared. "I knew there was something otherworldly about her. I've never met a Terran before. I thought they didn't have fae, that they'd burned them all at stakes, or some other equally barbaric thing."

Laec tried to fill Regalis in about past treatment of fae in the Terran realm while they walked, but what began as a novel and fragrant obstacle course soon degraded into the most frustrating and painful jungle hike either of them had ever experienced. Their surroundings were a marvel one did not just get accustomed to in a day. Initially, they enjoyed identifying the plants they recognized, but eventually they quit talking unless it was to help one another navigate a dangerous thicket. Laec's neck was scraped by thorns, his hands scratched by bristly plant hairs, his clothing and fingers sticky from sap. He ached from climbing over and ducking under stems, thorny branches, and woody snake-like boughs. They both sneezed several times after encountering pollen-heavy stamens. Dense heads of oversized blossoms hung overhead, dropping colorful patches of pollen into their hair and onto their shoulders.

"Laec?"

Laec turned and a rose thorn almost poked him in the eye. "Uncle? Where are you?"

"Over here. Look up."

Laec and Regalis followed the sound of the gardener's voice and found him perched on a hibiscus leaf, his back braced against the stem—which could be more accurately described as a trunk. The gardener climbed down, achingly slowly, since he had to pick his way around a cluster of fuchsia peony buds oozing some kind of yellowish nectar.

"It wasn't my doing," he told them. "This was Georjie's idea."

"Where are they?" Regalis asked.

"Here and there. Sleeping, mostly. Last night quite exhausted them, as you can imagine. Georjie's magic boosted theirs immensely, but it still took them four hours. Do you think it's thick enough?"

"Thick enough? It's almost impenetrable. How far out does it go?"

Ilishec closed one eye, calculating. "I'd say... three hundred feet, give or take. It's thinner in some places where they were deterred by rocky ground, but the fifty of them managed to erect this barrier all the way around the city. I wish Hazel could see it. I'm so proud of them."

"I thought you were against the Calyx doing anything defensive," Regalis teased, a twinkle in his eye. He was leaning against the stem of an aster with big pink heads, and looked like a character in a fantasy painting.

"I was wrong," the gardener replied bluntly. "Come, I'll take you to those closest. You'll never find them on your own. Not in this jungle."

Laec and Regalis shadowed the gardener as Ilishec followed a thick, twisty bough of rough wood snaking along parallel to the earth. It seemed endless, and worked well as a bridge through the tangle.

Laec ducked under an arch of long, fragrant purple fronds dangling from somewhere high above, in time to see Ilishec getting down on his hands and knees to crawl through a tunnel.

"Watch it here," he said. "Plenty of things to snag your hair on."

Laec did indeed snag his hair, and had to stop and work at untangling himself without acquiring a bald patch.

Regalis made his long frame compact enough to snake through, grunting. "I haven't crawled like this since I was a baby."

"Wisteria and Bougain grew vines all the way around the city," Laec explained. "Wisteria on the south side, and bougain-villea on the north side. Follow the woody boughs and you'll find Calyx somewhere along the way."

Laec would have complimented Ilishec on this idea, but he was snagged again, and starting to get a spasm in his neck from the way he'd had to contort himself, on top of having slept on rocks last night.

"You don't say," said Regalis, sounding harassed. "Ow." A twig snapped, then another. "Good thing Jess wasn't part of this or we'd all be sick."

"We'd all be dead," corrected the gardener. "You can stand up just ahead."

They emerged in a small clearing, groaning. Laec stretched his back, his spine crackling. He opened his eyes to see Georjie looking at him from a few feet away, yawning.

"Good morning." She swung her feet over the edge of what looked like a hammock made from leaves.

The limbs of three other fae emerged from similar sleeping berths. Rose's face peered out from behind a stem, her blond hair mussed and circles of fatigue under her beautiful eyes. She tried to greet them, but a huge yawn took over instead. Bombini's fuzzy black and yellow bum could be glimpsed in her hair.

"Did you bring food?" asked a male Calyx that Laec didn't know. He was dark-skinned, bare-chested, broad-shouldered and corded with muscle. Whenever Laec had seen Calyx, they'd been fully dressed in ball regalia or walking around the palace in casual clothing. He'd never seen them in so little attire. An eyeful of this male reminded Laec that flora fae worked out for a living.

"This is Bougain," the gardener said. "You already know Rose. Peony and Dahlia are also around here somewhere."

Regalis unlatched the sack of food he'd brought and handed it to Bougain.

"What we really need are Mrs. Tierney's elixirs," said a female that had to be Dahlia—since she was the only one Laec had never met—as she emerged from her leafy hammock. "I've never worked so hard in all my life. I feel like a wrung-out dishrag."

She may have felt like one, but she didn't look like one. Laec found it difficult to avert his eyes. Dahlia wore a small white bralette and tiny white bottoms that had less coverage than most knickers. Her long limbs were elegantly muscled and her tanned skin unmarred by moles or scars of any kind. Her bare midriff was shadowed with feminine muscle. She caught him staring and looked down as though remembering that she was mostly unclothed.

"I forget that outsiders don't see us in our workout things," she said, looking up apologetically. "I took off my tunic and leggings because this was hard work and I was hot. Sorry."

"No need to apologize." Laec waved a hand, smiling.

Bougain shot her a look of exasperated amusement. "What are you apologizing for, Dahlia? Giving him an eyeful of perfection? He's probably never seen beauty like yours outside of a painting."

"Indeed." Laec grinned. "Please don't dress on our account."

Even Regalis was smiling like an idiot as Rose fully emerged in similar scant clothing, revealing a body that rivaled that of a warrior goddess. She was slightly shorter and thicker than Dahlia, powerful-looking and curvaceous. When she reached for a small pile of folded clothing, Regalis's grin faded.

"I don't know why you never let the Calyx come to balls dressed in nothing but underwear," Laec told his uncle as he propped his chin on his hand in a posture of exaggerated thoughtfulness. "I find it deeply mystifying."

"To keep lewd rogues like you at bay, of course, nephew."

"Don't know why your eyes are popping out like they're on springs," Peony sniped at Regalis as she pulled a tunic over her long glossy hair. She was narrower and paler than the other two females, possessing less outrageous curves. She reminded Laec of a sculpture of a water nymph sitting in Elphame's palace foyer. "Didn't you date Gardenia for months?"

"Aye," Regalis returned, looking a little wistful as he recalled Gardenia's otherworldly perfection. "Never saw any being to rival the beauty of a flora fae," he admitted with all seriousness.

His response punctured her grumpiness and she looked away with a blush, stepping into a pair of leggings. "How much time do we have?"

"Sun was still below the horizon when we left the gate, so maybe an hour," Laec told her. "How can we ensure that all the Calyx are behind the walls by the time Faraçek's deadline has hit?"

"Oh we're not going to hide behind any wall," Bougain said, flexing his fingers like he was warming up his magic. All the bougainvillea leaves and petals within sight trembled noisily in response. His familiar, a hawkmoth, sat on his rounded shoulder, flexing her wings.

"Excuse me?" Regalis looked electrified. "That's why we came out here. To make sure you all get back inside safely before things go bad."

"Not happening," said Rose, cinching her tunic close to her waist with a belt.

Laec and Regalis exchanged a look of dismay.

"If you want to help us, find a way to get us some of Mrs. Tierney's elixirs." Peony held her hand out to catch Sphex as he came buzzing out of the tangle of vegetation. He landed on her palm and she gave him a sad but loving look, cupping her hand over him in a protective gesture. "We need sustenance."

"Aren't you worried for him?" Laec asked. "Faraçek is not far away. Your familiars should be in the moss cave."

"Yes." Peony lifted her chin and shot him a look of defiance. "Of course I'm worried about him, but this is war. All lives are at stake here."

"Yours doesn't have to be," Regalis told her, looking concerned.

"If yours is, then mine should be too." Peony's words were

just above a whisper and she turned away, cradling Sphex against her stomach.

"I don't get it," Laec mumbled, raking his sticky hair back where it stayed put like it had clay in it. "You've already pulled off a miracle for Solana. It's time to retreat."

Rose bent over and lifted the sole of one foot, brushing it clean. It jarred Laec to see that bare sole, so vulnerable, so exposed.

"Where are your shoes?" he spluttered.

"We're more effective in bare feet," Rose told him.

"Effective at *what*?" Regalis was becoming more exasperated.

Rose noted Laec's stunned expression and came closer, kissing him on the cheek in thanks for his concern.

Ilishec tightened his belt. "War can't be won without sacrifice. You know that and we know that, so why pretend that's not the reality here?"

"You're singing a different tune, Uncle."

"Loss can do that to a person," the gardener returned.

Two more Calyx emerged from the vegetation. Laec recognized Marigold and a male he thought might be Stephanotis. A gorgeous swallowtail butterfly sat on the top of his head like a crown, fluttering her wings. Marigold's metallic green bee buzzed in lazy circles around her head.

The sound of wings beating air circulated overhead, making everyone look up.

"Ferrugin's told Ratchet you need elixirs," Regalis told the group, which expanded as three more Calyx emerged from the jungle.

"Any news on Jess?" Aster asked as she crept out from under a leafy vine; a single leaf would be large enough for her to wear as a cocktail dress.

"News from Erasmus is that Jess, Digit and Kite are inside the fortress." Regalis—neck craning to locate his familiar—paused as though to listen before continuing. "Jess's *solidago* magic hasn't been working, and the only one who knows where Faraçek has hidden the crown is his son. So far, he's not sharing."

"She'll get it," Rose said with utter confidence. "She just needs a bit more time. Right?"

Regalis nodded, then cocked his head. "The birds need you to get to a clearing. They'll have elixirs to deliver soon."

The Calyx moved away from the city walls, navigating the underbrush much more gracefully than Laec had, like they were part of it.

"Where are you going?" Laec asked, alarmed.

"To a clearing," someone called back.

"You're going the wrong way," Regalis yelled, his voice on an edge.

No one bothered to answer him; they disappeared into the foliage like ghosts. Laec and Regalis exchanged a panicked look but there was nothing they could do to stop the Calyx. Helplessly, they followed.

CHAPTER THIRTY-TWO

JESSAMINE

J ESS DIDN'T THINK she could keep Kite back much longer. Isabey kept shooting the Fahyli warning looks while she continued to reason with Toryan. Reina was looking more and more distraught; her efforts to hide her stress from her son were wearing thin.

"My dear one," Isabey said to Toryan, holding his hand. "Do you know what your father is doing? Why he has gone away from home?"

Toryan nodded. "He told me… he is going to return Solana to the way it was before, make it part of Rahamlar. He will convince King Agir to agree."

"I want you to imagine that you have a fine horse," Isabey said, her beautiful face becoming animated as she warmed to her narrative. "He's a beautiful black stallion, with white socks on his legs. Can you picture him?"

Toryan nodded. "He has a white star on his forehead."

"Perfect. What is his name?"

Toryan thought about this with all the seriousness of a life-or-death matter. "We had a cat back in Cornhollow that was like that, and we called him Shadow, but horses are shinier than cats, so I would call him Shadowlight."

That's so much more noble than Beazle. Jess's bat dangled upside down from a rafter like an acorn, trying to sleep but listening to every word instead. *He's better than you at picking names.*

"That's a wonderful name." Isabey smiled. "Now imagine that you and Shadowlight grew up together, that you've had him since you were born. He has always belonged to you, and you've always belonged to him, though somewhere in his lineage he came from a stallion in the king of Boskaya's stables."

"Okay," Toryan followed with the patience of the utterly absorbed.

Isabey's tone grew hushed with doom. "Now imagine that one day the king of Boskaya shows up at your door and tells you that because Shadowlight came from one of his stallions, he has come to claim him… take him away put him in his own stable. How would you feel?"

"I wouldn't let him. Shadowlight is mine. It wouldn't matter who his parents or grandparents were, it doesn't give the king of Boskaya the right to steal him from me."

Isabey's eyes were shining with pride at her clever nephew. "And you would be right not to let him. Now imagine that Shadowlight is Solana, and you are King Agir, and your father is the king of Boskaya. Should King Agir give Solana to your father?"

Toryan looked troubled, but Isabey let him think about the metaphor for a while.

"So… King Agir will fight Father?" Toryan asked, toying with the hem of his quilt.

"Yes, he will fight." Isabey brushed Toryan's hair back from his forehead. "And the fighting will start very soon. That's why we are here. Many people will die, from Solana—people like Jess and Beazle—and from Rahamlar. You can prevent the fighting by telling us where the crown is."

Not precisely true, but close enough, thought Jess, chewing her bottom lip and pacing near the window. She took a nervous glance at Kite, who was glowering over the scene with her eyes narrowed.

Beazle's head had appeared from beneath his wing and he looked at the scene playing out on the bed. *Just level the playing field a little, that's all we want, kid.*

"You have a chance to stop bloodshed, Toryan," Isabey told him. "But you're running out of time."

Tears ran down the boy's face, though he was not noisy in his weeping. He put his hand over his eyes and sniffed. "It's in the wall behind Father's bed. There's a stone near the floor that moves."

Yes! Beazle opened both his wings out with an excited squeak.

"Clever boy." Jess beamed at him, so relieved she wished she could sit down. "Please don't cry. You've done brilliantly."

"Good lad. Yes, you've done the right thing." Isabey shot a look at Kite and Jess. "Next door down on the left."

Jess heard Reina praising her son as they moved out of Toryan's rooms like ghosts. The boy hiccuped and sniffed.

Digit and Shade both perked up when Jess and Kite came out into the hall.

It took all four of them to move the bed away from the wall, as the wooden frame was thick and heavy. Being the smallest, Jess squeezed behind the headboard and knelt, feeling in the shadows for a stone without mortar.

Beazle landed on her shoulder as she slid the stone out of place. *Every castle in Ivryndi must have these hiding places in the walls.*

Setting the stone on the floor, Jess reached into the hole and slid out a smooth shallow box. As they shoved the bed back into place, Isabey swept into the room. She took the box from Jess, inspecting the dials on the front. They were brass and engraved with symbols.

Isabey stared at the symbols, rolling the dials to view all of them. She sat on the edge of the bed, set the dials, then tried the latch. When it didn't open, she tried again.

"You're just guessing," Kite said. "We don't have time for that. Ask Toryan."

"He doesn't know," Isabey replied, not looking up. "Shut up and let me think. I know my brother. I can do this. Let me try first."

Before what? Beazle wondered.

Before we hack into it with an axe? Jess guessed.

Isabey tried and tried, only stopping long enough between guesses to try the latch. When the latch finally popped, she looked up with a triumphant gleam in her eyes. "See?"

"What was the code?" Digit asked, curious.

"Ander, Faraçek, Serya, Isabey," the princess replied, lifting the lid.

"But they're just symbols," Jess protested. There weren't enough dials to spell out each of the siblings' names.

Each sibling has a symbol. Beazle fluttered from Jess's head to Isabey's forearm, peering into the box.

Isabey took in a breath as she gazed at the crown. "Now what?"

"Pick it up," said Kite. "See what happens."

Setting the box on the bed, Isabey reached both hands into the box and picked up the crown. She held it up for them all to see, questions in her eyes. It gleamed in the torchlight, the cowbird's onyx eyes seeming to taunt them.

"Put it on," suggested Digit.

"But... I've had it on before," Isabey said, her face full of doubt. She lifted the circlet and set it on her head, and immediately gave a cry and threw it off, like she'd been stung. It clattered on the floor. Isabey put both hands to her head, rubbing. "It hurt me! It won't allow me to wear it anymore. Something has changed."

Kite didn't hesitate to pick up the crown, though Jess thought she saw the Fahyli flinch when her hand closed over it. She brought it back to the princess and held it out. Her jaw was tight. Jess wondered what Erasmus was telling her about what was going on back home.

"Solana's lion says you have the power to destroy it," Kite seethed. "You've got to destroy it."

Isabey was tentative when she touched the crown again, but it appeared not to injure her hands. She gripped it in her fists and used her knee to exert pressure on it. She grunted, her face deepening in color. Digit handed her his dagger and Isabey tried to saw the crown, to no effect. The princess looked up at them, her eyes blazing with fury.

"You told me I could destroy it, but I can't," she hissed. "Your lion lied to you!"

"He wouldn't do that," Jess cried, feeling panic flutter

in her stomach like a cloud of moths taking flight. "Jezaret would never—"

She's not the true heir, Beazle said.

But that's impossible. There are no other siblings.

If Jezaret was right, then there must be another.

Jess's eyes widened as she recalled what Faraçek had told Toryan in the parlor, on the first night they'd ever seen the boy, about changing the law because he wanted his ascension to be legal. She snatched the crown from Isabey, who cried out in surprise. Running back to Toryan's bedroom, she burst in through the door, almost tripping when she saw Jezaret sitting on his haunches at the foot of the bed, looking at her. She sucked in a breath, but realized immediately that no others in the room were aware that Solana's lion was present, and he didn't want her to give him away.

Jezaret swung his focus to Toryan, then got up to stand on all fours. He leapt soundlessly onto the bed, mouth open, giving rapid exhales as passion built in his chest. The lion's lips peeled back from his blazing white fangs, his expression was unnerving. He was clearly snarling, though Jess heard nothing.

Jess held up the crown, looking at Toryan, now sitting on his mother's lap. "Have you ever touched this?"

Toryan stared at the crown in Jess's hands, as the others crowded in at the door.

"What are you doing?" Isabey asked.

Ignoring her, Jess strode to the bed, thrusting the crown at the boy. "Go on, lad," she insisted, "Take it from me."

Hesitantly, Toryan reached for it.

Jezaret opened his fearsome mouth wide and roared silently, his entire body flexing. Though there was no sound, the power flowing from the lion raised every hair on Jess's body and a shiver ripped through her. In her periphery, she saw that Kite was gripped by the same feeling. The Fahyli hugged herself, her eyes huge.

The moment the prince's fingers made contact, the metal turned black, then crumbled into dust, making a little pile on the floor beside the bed. Toryan cried out with shock and looked up at Jess with a look of terror.

Jezaret looked at Jess and faded away, wearing a feline smile.

"Look what you made me do!" the prince sobbed, now truly upset. He began to weep and Reina pressed his head to her bosom, shushing him.

Jess knelt by the boy and touched his back gently. "I know it feels like you betrayed your father, but what you just did saved many lives. It makes you a hero, little Toryan."

Toryan sniffed and shook his head, trying and failing to hold back his emotions.

"It's true my love," Reina whispered, kissing his hair. "You're a real, live hero."

Jess looked up at Isabey, standing at the foot of the bed, staring and wide-eyed at the pile of black dust on the floor. "I'm not the true heir," she whispered, incredulous. "He did it. He changed the law… and somehow, and the crown knew." Her hand fluttered to her forehead.

Kite moved to kneel beside Toryan. She put a fist over her heart and thumped it there, giving him a look of admiration and respect. "Thank you. I'll never forget this, young princeling."

Toryan stared in wonder at the fierce Fahyli, not seeming to comprehend the depth of her appreciation.

She touched his cheek. "If I live long enough, I will introduce you to my familiar, Erasmus. Would you like to meet him?"

"Yes." Toryan rubbed at one eye with his knuckle.

Kite patted his knee. "Then I'll do my best to make that

happen. We have to go now. We have work to do, and a long way to go."

She thumped her chest one more time and said thank you to Reina, who smiled at her and whispered, "May your pride protect you."

Kite and Jess moved toward the door where Shade and Digit were waiting, Shade's knuckles white as he gripped the torch.

Jess looked back at the princess. "Isabey? We need you to come back to Solana with us. The war is not yet won. Rahamlar's soldiers need to see with their own eyes that you are alive. They do not yet know that Toryan is the true heir, they'll think it's you. That may even be enough for them to lay down their arms."

Isabey brushed at her eyes, still dazed, but nodded. Looking at Reina, she asked: "My dear friend. Will you do something more for me?"

"Anything," Reina answered.

Isabey slid her seal off her finger, putting it in Reina's palm. "Assemble the ministers. Show them my seal to prove that I'm alive and you've seen me. Tell them everything. I go to Solana now, and I want you and them to follow as soon as you can. Will you do that for me?"

Reina looked frightened, but she nodded.

Isabey kissed Toryan and Reina, murmuring sweet nothings. Then she joined them at the door and led them through the castle. The sun was up. There was no time left.

"There should be fresh horses in the stables," Isabey told them as they jogged through the courtyard to a wide gate. Passing through that, she led them down a winding path to a barn sitting in a dip in the rocky terrain.

"Kinik! Turyn! Are you here?" Isabey barked, making Digit and Jess exchange a look of unease.

A sleepy-looking unseelie youth, dressed in brown and orange livery, came blinking out of the stable. He stared at Isabey as she came flying down the path, like he couldn't believe his eyes. He spared no glance for the rest of them.

"Princess!" He dropped to one knee and bowed his head, but he was unable to keep his eyes off her, and said in a choked voice, his eyes brimming. "Princess Isabey. You're... alive?"

Isabey was all business. "I'm alive, Turyn. We need fresh horses saddled."

"How is this possible, I don't—"

"You can be shocked later," she told him, not unkindly, as she made him get up, turned him around and pushed him toward the stables. "We need five of the fastest horses available, right now."

Turyn looked over his shoulder. "Shade," he rasped. "Am I dreaming?"

"No, you're saddling!" Isabey gave him another shove.

Poor Turyn seemed not to know where he was or what he was doing. He moved in a daze, with Isabey reassuring him that she and Shade were both fine. Turyn was too addled to get things done fast enough, so Isabey showed them where the tack room was. They assembled their own gear while she went down the stalls to see which horses looked strongest.

"Princess Isabey, Your Grace, who are these seelie fae?" Turyn finally said as the last of the buckles was tightened and the reins were adjusted. "I don't know them. Why are they here, and wearing our livery?"

The stablehand looked worried now.

"You'll be in no trouble, lad," Isabey said as she mounted. "In fact I aim to see you generously rewarded for your help this morning."

He was really more of a hindrance, thought Beazle as he fluttered around overhead, raring to go. Kite's haste had leached into all of them, and the Fahyli had already launched her mount out the door and was clattering across the courtyard.

"Wait!" Isabey called. "The gatemen! Kite!"

Isabey put heels to her mount and the gelding squealed, lurching forward. Digit and Shade were up and after her, bouncing off the ground as their horses sensed the urgency and grew frantic to join their fellows. Jess launched into her saddle, gripping the reins and a handful of mane, hanging on while her blond mare bolted after the rest, not wanting to be left behind. She could hear Isabey yelling commands to open the gate.

When Jess arrived, Isabey sat high and proud in her saddle, looking imperiously down at two young gatemen, who were both on their knees.

"Princess Isabey!" One of them stared up at her, his eyes watery and rapturous.

The other was more self-possessed, taking in Isabey's seelie cohorts, confusion in his gaze. "Princess, are these Solanans? Why are they with you, and riding our horses?"

Isabey's horse rose on his hind legs as the princess's eyes blazed with fury. She finally looked like the brave and powerful royal that the Solanans wished she'd been all along. Hooves thundered as the horse landed and danced in a circle, the princess's head turning to keep her eyes on the gateman. "Firin if you do not open this gate immediately, I'll have you reassigned to the pigpens. How dare you question my command!"

Firin and the other young fae leapt into action and the gate began inching upward, squealing as it went. Unseelie came out into the courtyard, drawn by the commotion.

"Princess Isabey!" someone yelled, running toward them, tears streaming down his face.

"The princess is alive," someone further back yelled. The cries were picked up and echoed, feet thundered on the court-yard as more came to see whether their princess had indeed been returned to them alive.

The moment the portcullis was high enough to permit them passage, Kite, Digit and Shade put heels to their horses. Jess held her mount back, just barely, waiting to make sure the princess was not stopped.

Isabey spoke to those who could hear. "Faraçek murdered Princess Serya. I saw it with my own eyes. He tried to murder me as well, and has let you, my people, believe that we ended our own lives. You can see that I am very much alive, and I am ready to testify that Serya did not end her own life either. You will know everything that happened very soon. Tell the justice, tell everyone you can the truth. Faraçek is no longer your king."

One of the gatemen fell to his knees and put a hand over his heart, as though he'd been shot. His expression was one of shock and sorrow. "Kind Princess Serya, murdered," he cried in a croak of deep loss that speared Jess's heart. "No. Oh, princess."

The self-possessed one, Firin, replied, "Fate be with you, Princess. I shall do as you ask. But where are you going?"

Isabey sounded like someone else. "To stop my brother. If I fall, I'll die knowing that you will spread the truth far and wide—my sister will be avenged. Do not fail me."

Without waiting for an answer, Isabey gave her horse his head. Jess let her mare run, hoping that her steed was sure-footed and good-sighted, because tears were streaming from Jessamine's eyes and she could see nothing but a blur.

CHAPTER THIRTY-THREE

LAEC

THE JUNGLE OF plants thinned as they reached the border of what had been grown around the city overnight. Laec and Regalis stumbled out of the tangle with the Calyx, early-morning sun warming their skin. Between the oversized garden and Rahamlar's forces lay a stretch of low, rolling terrain, spotted with shrubs and patches of wildflowers. The enemy soldiers could be seen moving about in their camp, and the sound of whinnying horses carried on the gentle breeze, bringing the tangy scent of animals. The Calyx stopped just before the open area, gazing out at dark shadows that were not shadows but soldiers. They were not close enough to see the unseelie reactions to the fresh barrier, but close enough to see some disarray and tumult.

A raptor's scream announced the arrival of Ferrugin, Ratchet and birds from the aviary, each weighed down with a small sack; the larger birds carried two. Swooping low, the sacks were dropped into the waiting hands of the flora fae. Looking left and right down the line of botanicals, Laec watched Calyx emerge from the forest, hands lifted to receive the parcels. Inside each sack was a small waterskin containing an elixir. Each had the name of a Calyx labeled on its exterior. A few of the Calyx got an elixir meant for someone else, and exchanges were made.

Ferrugin screamed and Regalis blinked up at the sun as it hoisted itself higher into the sky. His brow pleated with worry as he listened to his familiar's message. "Jess's magic still isn't working... something is blocking her from locating the crown."

Rose looked toward the enemy camp, a shadow flickering in her sky-blue eyes. Her golden hair, loose and tousled, swayed in the breeze. She put her hands on her hips and let out a long exhale of disappointment.

"There's another way she can find it," Regalis continued, "but... they need more time. She's so close."

Laec closed his eyes. *Come on, Jessamine.*

"Where's Georjie?" He asked Rose as she finished guzzling her strange-smelling brew. Shading his eyes from the morning sun, he studied the figures he could see in both directions but none of them were the Wise from Earth.

Rose pointed straight down with a finger.

Laec gave a start. "She's underground?"

Rose nodded, still swallowing. To Laec, it seemed he was able to see her fatigue vanish as the elixir gave her flora fae body what it needed. She wiped her lips with the back of her hand. "She's getting a ley line for us. She did it last night, too. That's how we were able to build this," she gestured at the incredible foliage behind them. "But she can't hold it beneath us forever. She had to let it go and rest."

Laec stared at Rose, bewildered. "Ley line?"

Rose screwed the cap back on the waterskin. "The grid of

supernatural energy that runs through the earth and fuels all earth-related magic and some other kinds too. Ley lines."

"I know what a ley line is," Laec squinted at her. "What do you mean she's *getting* one for you?"

A croak lifted their focus upward where a palace crow fluttered overhead. Rose lifted the waterskin and the bird swooped down, scooping it up then laboriously winging her way up and up until she disappeared over the top of a cluster of tubular white flowers, each blossom the size of a cathedral bell.

"She can bend them, draw them out of alignment. Last night she brought one close enough to run beneath the city. We could feel its energy pulsing beneath us." Rose eyes twinkled. "What a rush. I've never felt so powerful in all my life. I went from struggling to keep my roses in bloom, to being able to make each blossom the size of an ox!"

"So, she… what? Wants to bring it back this morning too so you can… grow more stuff? Make the jungle thicker?"

Rose shook her head but didn't answer.

"Rose…" Regalis began, his tone a warning. "I've told Ferrugin we need backup, and she's communicated that to Bradburn and the crofter, but there are challenges. They can only cross the earthen bridge at the gate one at a time, and no horses can cross over at all."

"*They* have horses," Laec jabbed his thumb toward the Rahamlar camp, reminding them of the obvious disparity between their own forces and those of the unseelie.

Regalis's gaze was on Faraçek's army, then flicked to Rose, darkening. "Then they have to make their way through that tangle, basically single file. They're coming, but not quickly, and Laec and I are not enough to protect you. You've taken your look at the enemy. Gather up the Calyx and go back to the city now. You're making me very nervous."

Rose gave Regalis a sad look, one that made Laec feel cold inside. She looked from one to the other.

"You dear fae. You don't get it." She began to walk toward the camp on the other side of the valley.

Laec was starting to get angry. "You're right about that. Retreat, Rose. Now."

"She's here." Rose looked over her shoulder, and Laec's breath caught in his throat. Her irises and pupils were gone, and in their place shone a white light. He'd only seen light like that in the eyes of one other kind of being: a Wise.

The corners of Rose's mouth tilted up. She faced the enemy again and strode toward them, her shoulders back and head high. Bombini buzzed beside her. All along the jungle border, the Calyx moved, almost as one. Snap, Aster, and all of those whom Laec could see, had the same white light beaming from their eyes. Insects and butterflies hummed through the air, trusting in their fae. It made Laec's chest feel tight. They were so small, so vulnerable, and walking straight toward deadly magic. Helpless to do anything to stop them, Laec and Regalis moved with them, keeping in stride with the flora fae as they closed the distance.

Faraçek's forces saw them coming. Commands were shouted. Horses moved to the frontline, most led by the reins, but some were mounted. Laec searched for Faraçek and found him by his big red charger. The prince stood with his hand on the bridle of his horse looking out at the opposition. Then he mounted, shifting his rapier into place at his hip as he settled in the saddle. Nudging his horse, they trotted forward a few feet then stopped, the stallion tossing his head. Faraçek issued a command and the unseelie cavalry mounted. Laec's stomach was a ball of ice, his hand resting on his blade. He flexed his fingers.

Ferrugin screamed and Regalis said with an incredulous shout, "They've done it! Toryan's crown is no more!"

Rose repeated the words softly, as did Snap and Aster, the two fae closest to her. Then Bougain, Peony and Stephanotis muttered them a second later. Those further away picked up the message. They were linked by the ley line, Laec realized, able to communicate through it.

A sound behind them drew Laec and Regalis's attention back toward the jungle, where soldiers had begun to pour out of an opening one at a time. The moment they were through, they broke into a run, spreading out and heading toward the Calyx like ants on a mission. Backup was here, but so paltry in comparison to the unseelie numbers that it did little to make Laec feel better. He and Regalis greeted soldiers as they fell in step, looking uncertainly at the flora fae.

That Jessamine had been successful was great news, but it didn't get them out of trouble, it only diminished the prince's power back to its former level—and diminished the unseelie soldiers not one bit. The army was no less vast, and Faraçek still had the power to control one person at a time.

"How much time is left?" Regalis asked one of the soldiers, speaking of Faraçek's promised charge one hour past sunrise.

"About six minutes," the soldier replied.

Kashmir burst through the jungle opening followed by Tully, then the crofter, Panther and other Fahyli. Dogs and birds, a possum, an ocelot and other animals loped across the terrain beside Fahyli wearing boiled leather and grim expressions.

Laughter drifted on the wind from the direction of the enemy.

"Jessamine destroyed the crown," Laec told the crofter—with Kashmir not far from his side—as he fell in line with him and Regalis.

"I know. Kestrel relayed it from Ratchet. Bless those faelings." The crofter's voice was strained and full of suppressed emotion. Ian put his hand on the pommel of his sword. "May it be enough to help us prevail against our enemies."

"What about them?" Laec knocked his head toward the flora fae, wondering where his uncle was.

"They showed us that they're not a liability," Ian said, full of pride. "They have more to show us yet, I hope. The gardener would not let them do this for no reason. The best we can do is protect them."

Laec's fist closed around the handle of his sword. He didn't need to remind the crofter that they were vastly outnumbered. Even though Solanan foot soldiers were still pouring out of the jungle barrier—Bradburn among them—there would never be enough to level the field.

"Where is the king? Please tell me he isn't coming out here?"

Ian pressed his lips into a thin line, then said: "We convinced him to stay behind the walls, but he's not happy. Kestrel is with him, reporting what Ratchet shows her."

The Calyx stopped and stood in a long, widely-spaced line; a flimsy barrier between the enemy and the city behind the jungle. Solanan soldiers formed a phalanx around each flora fae. Laec heard Rose telling them she needed room, and visibility.

The Rahamlar cavalry was ready to charge, just waiting for the clock to expire. They'd close the distance in a matter of twenty seconds, Laec figured. The unseelie sat arrogantly atop their horses, none more confident than Faraçek, whose face Laec could see. The prince wore a smug smile. His glittering eyes were slits as he weighed Solana's meager forces. He took a large inhale—Laec could see his chest inflate—then exhaled, slowly and for what seemed like an impossibly long time. Then he watched for the fruits of his magic.

A bolt of terror shot through Laec, thinking for a moment that the destruction of Toryan's crown hadn't given the result they'd expected. But the prince's smile faltered, then faded altogether and became an angry frown. So, only now was he realizing that his enhancement had been taken away.

A horse screamed, a sound of terror. Movement to Faraçek's right drew Laec's focus. The mare was down and struggling to get up. Her rider had tumbled over her head, rolling and springing back to his feet. As the fallen rider moved out of the way, Laec saw that the horse's body was wrapped almost completely by leafy vines, pinning her to the ground save for her head. The horse struggled and squealed, trying to get up but failing.

A wave of unease rippled through the Rahamlar cavalry.

Another horse went down, wrapped up in pink *bougainvillea* vines, held down by the strength of woody boughs with thick roots reaching deep into the ground. More frightened neighs blistered the air as horses were taken down by divergent species of flowering vines. Laec's heart became a battering ram. The juxtaposition of the colorful blossoms and glossy leaves in myriad shades of green wrapping around horses strongly enough to pull them into prone positions was breathtakingly strange.

The prince's red charger danced nervously as Faraçek bared his teeth. When he gave the signal to attack, all other thoughts fled Laec's mind. Unsheathing his sword, he moved ahead of the Calyx, shoulder to shoulder with the Solanans, determined to protect their city's most precious assets... even more precious than anyone had realized.

Chaos erupted as the unseelie horde rushed forward. Horses and soldiers fell as though sucked underwater by enormous leafy dragons. They vanished beneath snake-like vines that shot from the earth to wrap around legs and swallow them from view. But the unseelie numbers were too vast, and the oncoming rush looked like a wall of bared teeth and glinting steel.

Laec stepped in front of Rose, hefting his sword and ready to do whatever he could to defend her. Three soldiers bore down on foot as one on horseback barreled past. Laec ducked to avoid a swinging blade and brought his steel to bear against that of an enemy soldier. His heart skittered with fear—not for himself, but for Rose.

He dodged a death blow that left a slice across the upper arm of his tunic, and brought the soldier down with his own deft thrust. He wheeled, but not in time to prevent another from attacking Rose. As he dove to get between them, a wickedly sharp thorn the length of his arm shot out through the back of her attacker, spraying blood across Laec's face. Rose stepped into view and the thorn retreated. She let the soldier fall to the earth. Her expression was calm, yet fierce, her eyes like stars. Her hands flexed and her mouth opened. A hissing sound came from behind him, and Laec spun in time to see a horse and rider being ensnared by vines bristling with blood-red roses. The branches moved like tentacles, pulling their victims down. And no matter how much they struggled, Rose's vines were stronger.

He'd been trying to save her, but she had saved him. When he turned back to thank her, his pulse thready and forehead beaded with moisture, she'd already moved away, tying down another horse and rider while Regalis protected her from two unseelie swordsmen. Her arms and hands moved gracefully and her eyes were frightening to behold.

Laec saw one of the Calyx fall, swallowed from view and lost in the melee of clashing bodies. He dodged another blade and leapt a clump of Rose's vines, running from a heavyset soldier who quickly gave up the chase. Leaping over the body of a fallen Solanan soldier, Laec cast about for the Calyx he'd seen go down.

A hum filled his ears, drawing his focus to the jungle, where a cloud of bees the size of parrots swarmed over the body of an unseelie. The roar of a bear whipped his head the other way, but an incoming attack distracted him from seeing Kashmir in battle. Muscles straining and reflexes pushed to their maximum, it was all Laec could do to deflect repeated killing blows from a brute who moved faster than anyone that large had a right to. The impact of his parries reverberated through Laec's arm as the unseelie struck and struck again, fangs bared and eyes red with battle rage. When a shiny black wasp landed on the unseelie's forehead, he faltered—just enough for Laec to take advantage and claim a strike of his own. Laec recognized Sphex and was about to thank him when Sphex multiplied into dozens, maybe even hundreds, each a little bigger than the last. The unseelie screamed in pain as many stingers found soft exposed flesh. Laec looked away, feeling ill as the soldier fell to his knees, covered beneath a black swarm of legs and wings and venomous stings. Laec was disoriented now in this moving chaos, unsure of where the Calyx who had fallen had been located.

What had begun as a dense crush of horseflesh, fae, humans and vegetation was thinning as the battle shifted like angry waters. Kashmir thundered by, rreddish coat glistened under the morning sun. She was snarling in a way that made Laec's hair stand on end. Two unseelie wheeled to face the bear, one lifting his blade high and the other squatting low. Kashmir put her head down and charged, then split into two identical bears. Laec shook his head and staggered at the sight. He had no idea which duplicate was the real Kashmir and neither did the enemy, who each clashed with one. A duplicate's teeth could do as much damage as the original's, so in that sense, it didn't matter which Kashmir was real. But if they killed the real bear, both would be neutralized.

Laec didn't get to witness the bear and unseelie battle find its victor because a horse bore down on him. He dove out of the way, rolling across the ground and coming back up to his feet, his eyes finding Regalis. The Fahyli was engaged in combat, but his features were lit with glee, like this was a training exercise and he was thoroughly enjoying it. *Lunatic,* Laec thought, but not without respect.

A Solanan soldier flagging under the onslaught of his attacker drew Laec to his aid. Laec dispatched the unseelie, but it was too late. The Solanan dropped, falling to his back, clutching his chest, blood oozing between his fingers. He looked up at the sky in amazement. Laec ripped a piece of his tunic and dropped beside the soldier, staunching the wound.

"You'll be all right. Hang on." Laec set the man's bloody hand over the fabric to keep the flow under control.

"Never knew…" the soldier whispered, his green eyes finding Laec's. He was far too young to die. Not a single wrinkle pleated his face. "Never knew… after all this time."

"What?" Laec put a hand on his shoulder.

"Tell them." The soldier gasped, then coughed. Blood

appeared at the corner of his mouth. He was smiling. "Tell them it was an honor to fight beside them."

Laec nodded, understanding that he meant the Calyx. "I'll tell them."

He leapt to his feet to engage an unseelie intent on finishing him too. He parried then shoved the big fae with all his might, straight into the jaws of an enormous duplicate of Tully. The unseelie tried to twist away when Tully's teeth punctured his torso, his wrath melting into terror. Laec turned away, not feeling the need to watch the duplicate finish the soldier. He returned to the dying soldier's side. But he was gone, his eyes looking up at the sky and the smallest smile on his face.

Laec looked around. The dead—from both sides—were piling up everywhere. The unseelie were everywhere. Magic was everywhere: flowers of all types and colors, and in all kinds of unnatural sizes. Vines choked the life out of unseelie even as they decorated their dying bodies with beautiful funeral shrouds.

A flash of metallic green alerted Laec to Marigold's location as her bee duplicated and swarmed over the battleground. Some of the duplicates reached the size of small dogs, deadly and grotesque—as terrifying to look at as they were impossible to fight.

Butterflies and birds flew overhead, seeming at times to fill the sky. More than once Laec witnessed duplicates of Ratchet divebomb the enemy. Ratchet was supposed to be the king's eyes, but perhaps he simply couldn't be kept from the action. Some familiars were less obedient than others. A huge duplicate of Ferrugin picked up an enemy soldier by the shoulders, wings beating slowly and powerfully. She carried him, swinging and kicking, then dropped him into the thickest part of the jungle.

Laec combed the bizarre battleground, looking for any fallen Calyx, and for the prince. It was by turns terrifying, inspiring, and shocking. The unseelie had adjusted to the surprises, but fared much better against both fae and human soldiers than they did against flora fae and duplicates, whose magic was unpredictable and easy to underestimate. Laec could hardly imagine anything more frustrating than fighting with copies: copies with teeth or stingers or talons or fangs. To strike down a duplicate and have it disintegrate in a puff of fog enraged the unseelie.

When a pink dragon that looked like it was made of flower petals reared its head from the melee, giving away Snap's position, Laec's jaw dropped. It surged upward, opening its mouth in a soundless roar. It was the size of a horse and disappeared as quickly as it had appeared, vanishing in a puff of pink smoke.

A dark-skinned arm, willowy and feminine, drew Laec's gaze to the earth. He ran toward it, sliding on his knees to reach her, and pushed the body of a Solanan soldier off the fallen fae. The exquisite face of Lotus came into view, her eyes closed and her face peaceful.

"No," Laec whisper-screamed, searching for a pulse in her neck. A stunning brown and tawny butterfly, with markings on his wings that looked uncannily like yellow owl eyes, moved from Lotus's armpit.

"Caligo," he said. "If you're alive, then she is too."

Caligo waved his antennae, crawling up Lotus's breast to her neck. With a glance around to make sure there were no impending attacks, Laec got one arm under Lotus's knees and another under her back. Lifting her waifish form, he headed toward the main gate. A growl to his left made Laec turn, but as the soldier bore down on him, Tully—or a duplicate of Tully, Laec couldn't tell—barreled into the soldier, knocking him off course. Laec picked up speed, thighs and biceps burning.

It was a long way to the city but he couldn't leave Lotus out here to die.

Light congealed before Laec's eyes, blinding him as it took the shape of a pillar. Squinting, he staggered back, fighting to keep his footing. The light coalesced into a feminine form with long pale hair. Georjayna—yet she was magnificent, angelic and so illuminated with ley line energy that he hardly recognized her. She came close and lay a hand over Lotus's forehead. Lotus stirred, her face curling toward his neck.

He cradled her protectively. "Will she live?"

Light-Georjie nodded, then slipped into the ground like a sheet of sparkling rain. Thundering feet heralded three soldiers, bloody and battle-enraged, bearing down.

He almost dropped Lotus to free his arms to defend her, but a deep groan from beneath their feet preceded a split opening in the earth between them and the approaching soldiers. Running too fast to stop, and taken by surprise, two of them tumbled straight into the crevice. The other slid in while attempting to brake. Rolling over the edge, he grabbed at the rim with both fists, his sword plummeting into the trench as his feet dangled over darkness.

When the earth clamped shut over all three of them, Laec almost fell again as the ground shuddered and jerked. Turning toward the city, he did his best to run with Lotus in his arms. As he passed by those engaged in combat, Georjie ran interference. She made unseelie disappear, then crushed them, the ground knitting itself closed over them. It was like they'd never existed.

Laec reached the narrow path leading to the front gate. Solanan soldiers were a continuous stream, rushing out as Laec went in. Taking a last look over his shoulder, his heart sank. Solana's fae were putting up an incredible fight, but the unseelie numbers were vast. The Calyx and Fahyli had become their prime targets, the flora and fauna fae their most deadly threats.

The battleground was littered with bodies, and clumps of plants beneath which bodies were hidden. He needed to get Lotus to safety then return. Solana's fae had to be protected. They had become the city's brightest hope.

CHAPTER THIRTY-FOUR

JESSAMINE

RAHAMLAR'S HORSES WERE strong, bred for the terrain—
but no mount could gallop full-out the entire distance
from Rahamlar to Solana. They pushed the horses to
maintain a fast trot, but had to slow on the steep switchbacks.

Jess calculated and recalculated. The first time she'd traveled
to Rahamlar, it had taken the better part of a day, but their horses
had been laden with supplies for Prince Ander's requiem, and
had been kept to a walk. Presently, there were five decent riders
without any heavy load, and five strong and fresh horses. Could
they cut the time in half? Could they do better than half?

"Kite," she called, urging her horse to catch up to the
Fahyli. "What's happening?"

"Jess, you wouldn't believe it if I told you."

"Why? What's Ferrugin telling Erasmus?"

Kite's mouth flattened into a line, but there was
a glimmer in her eye. "The Calyx grew a barrier
around the entire city. Overnight. I have
no idea how. Divine intervention,
surely."

Jess gripped the reins. "A barrier... what do you mean?"

Kite's mouth quirked. "A garden surrounds the city. It'll keep the unseelie forces back from the city walls. For a while at least."

A garden? She's almost as cryptic as Erasmus, Beazle interjected.

Jess was having a difficult time picturing the kind of garden that could keep Faraçek out of where he was determined to go. "And where are the Calyx now?"

"They're on the frontline, Jess." She shook her head. "Ferrugin is involved in the battle, so we're not getting any more updates. I only pray that whatever magic helped them grow that jungle also protected them when the enemy charged."

Jess's breath felt caught in her chest.

Beeze?

Jess could feel his curiosity bubbling up to match her own. *I can reach Solana before you. Shall I go?*

If you have the energy, little love. I don't understand what Kite is telling us.

It was a long way for Beazle to go on his own, but they needed Erasmus to stay and keep watch over the riders.

Please be careful.

Don't worry, Beazle said with all the confidence of a pirate. *I'm invisible, remember?*

Jess fought against the paralyzing fear that wanted to take ahold of her whenever she and Beazle were separated by great distance. She pressed her knees against her mount, asking for more, and her horse surged forward, seeming to enjoy the challenging climb.

What would her kingdom look like when she arrived? Who might have been lost? Jess shoved the dark thoughts aside and leaned into the journey. There was nothing they could do but ride.

Jess's thighs, hips and buttocks were numb. Part of her wondered if she'd be able to unclench her legs from around her horse's ribcage when it came time to dismount. As the trees thinned, and the valley around the city came into view, they drew their horses to a halt on a crest. Jess could make out pools of shadow around the city walls, but those walls were obscured by a very strange forest of trees with brightly colored branches and tops: the Calyx garden. Beazle had shown her, but until she saw it… What the Calyx had done was unheard of. Impossible.

It was clear that the conflict was in full force. They could hear the evidence of it even from this distance, although it was difficult to tell the unseelie side from the Solanans.

"You need to stay back," Kite told Isabey. "We can't take any chances with your life."

"I'm not the true heir," Isabey said. Her hair had come loose during the ride. It flowed around her shoulders, thick and wavy and rich brown, the color of freshly turned earth. Her eyes were dark with worry and anger, her cheeks pink. Jess thought she'd never looked more beautiful than in this moment, despite her obvious trepidation.

"That doesn't matter." Digit paused to take a swig from his waterskin, which he'd filled at a stream. "They believe you to be dead. Your very presence will unsettle them, which can only help us."

Shade brought his horse alongside Isabey's, reaching across the space to take her hand. "I'm proud of you, Iz."

Isabey cast her eyes down. "I don't know why. I did all the wrong things."

"You can reflect on regrets later." Jess flexed her fingers in anticipation. They were so close, a little further and she would be able to help her friends.

Isabey nodded at Jess like this was a reasonable proposition. "I'll keep out of the fray."

"I'll stay with you," Shade added. "Always."

Nudging their mounts forward, they galloped down the road, losing sight of the battle as it disappeared behind the terrain. Knowing they were so close fed Jess with a burst of energy. Her weariness fell away as adrenaline pumped through her body. Her mind sharpened. The most important thing was to bring this battle to an end, ideally by bringing down Faraçek.

The horses sensed the urgency. Digit came along Jess's left, and Kite along her right as the road widened, letting them thunder along shoulder to shoulder. Shade and Isabey fell back.

Strange sights peppered the landscape. Clouds of insect duplicates surged in and out of existence. Cracks opened in the earth, swallowing Rahamlar soldiers before snapping shut. Vines—tightly knotted and covered in flowers—had wrapped themselves over the forms of soldiers and horses. Pinned horses, eyes rolling, were apparently unhurt beneath all the greenery, which couldn't be said about the fae-like shapes. Rahamlar soldiers were swarming the jungle in front of the gates, trying to hack and slash their way through the growth. An iris blossom the size of a horse trough swayed then tilted with a crack, felled by a sword.

Jess combed the chaos for Faraçek but there were too many bodies and too much action. She spied Aster being carried by Panther just as they disappeared into the jungle. Her heart climbed into her throat and she prayed that Aster had not been killed. She worked to steady herself as she noted more Calyx—easily recognized by their pale clothing—being either carried or helped to safety by Solanans.

Kite yelled over the thunder of hoofbeats: "Erasmus says the Calyx are tired. The command from the crofter is to get all the flora fae off the battlefield."

"And the gardener?" Jess called. "Is he out here too?"

Kite nodded. "The crofter knows where we are. His orders are to help the Calyx. Don't worry about Ilishec. He's not a target the way the flora fae are. Half of them are still out here."

I'll look for Calyx, Beazle told her, winging high overhead. *Keep an eye out for the prince, too.*

Beazle acknowledged her request and she felt him redirect with intent.

The battlefield was spread over a large area, with space between clashes that ebbed and flowed, emptied and filled, like flotsam in a stormy sea. They barreled into the fray, dodging and careering around soldiers, trying to keep their speed up and get through the thickest of the Rahamlarin forces.

So many bodies. So many dead, on both sides, and the fighting continued. Jess's heart went into her mouth when she recognized Nympha's pale form lying on the ground, blood pooling beneath her body. Drawing up, Jess sprang from the saddle and skidded to her knees. Digit was beside her in a moment, helping to pull Nympha from beneath a fallen unseelie. The smell of vomit was thick in the air. A wound across Nympha's neck looked angry, oozing blood and a pale green fluid. Jess looked away, not wanting to study it. Together they got Nympha over the front of Jess's saddle.

An unseelie soldier came pounding after them, longsword flashing in the sun.

"Digit!" Jess panted, halfway into the saddle.

He whirled, bringing his hands up with a hiss. The air wavered and the unseelie clutched his heart, made a choking sound, then crashed to the earth facedown. He skidded almost up to Digit's boots.

Bracing Nympha as well as she could with one hand, Jess nudged the horse toward the break in the jungle where she'd seen Panther disappear with Aster. Behind her, Digit mounted and followed. It was like riding through the eye of a storm.

When they reached the jungle, Digit leapt off and lifted Nympha down, settling her in his arms. Jess got down and unsheathed her short sword, covering him as he ducked to enter the break in the vegetation. When she was confident no one was coming after them, Jess ducked inside, going backward until she needed to watch her footing.

A narrow way had been cut through the thick growth. The scent of plant juices, nectar, perfume and blood mingled in the air, making Jess feel dizzy. Digit followed the path and Jess followed him, almost screaming when Alstroemeria loomed out of the shadows in front of them.

"Jess!" His eyes were big in his dark face. "You did it!"

It took Jess a second to figure out why he looked so happy, then she remembered Toryan's crown. It seemed so long ago, and like it had done so little to help.

Alstro opened his muscular arms to take Nympha. "Give her to me."

Jess and Digit handed her off and returned to the battle-field. Ania hummed up to them, orbited at high speed, then disappeared again.

"She's found Dahlia!" Digit broke into a run.

Jess kept pace, following her twin as he leapt bodies and ducked enemies. He dropped five unseelie soldiers with simple flicks of his hands, a process that frightened Jess because of how close he had to get to deliver the killing doses. All the while he was able to follow Ania.

They found Dahlia, her back braced against the side of a vine-wrapped horse. She looked pale and was cradling her left wrist against her stomach. Not far away an unseelie soldier was on his knees and staring at her with so much hatred it made Jess's breath catch. He had a dagger in his fist but remained just out of reach. Jess was wondering why he hadn't simply finished Dahlia off when he flipped his blade so the steel was pinched in his fingers. He hefted it as though to throw it when a swarm of fuzzy digger bees burst into existence before his face. It was only the threat of her bee that had been keeping him from killing her. He screamed and fell back, thrashing at the air as Antho's duplicates swarmed over him.

Jess and Digit got Dahlia to her feet, her good arm braced over Digit's shoulders. He half-carried her for several feet, then decided it would be better to just pick her up. She mewled with pain but clung tightly, her head against his shoulder. Jess covered them as they returned to the relative safety of the jungle. This time they deposited their charge into the arms of Proteas, who had dark circles under his eyes and a glazed grin for Jess and Digit.

As they returned to the battlefield once more, they were confronted by two unseelie who had spied what they were up to. Jess dodged the slash of a sword and rolled over the ground before a burst of *belladonna* chromatypes swirled from her hands. Her magic was not instant; she had to scramble to keep out of reach until the *atropa* brought the unseelie to his knees, gagging.

Together, the poison twins—with the help of Ania—recovered six more wounded Calyx from the field, passing them to Fahyli and Solanan soldiers working in teams to get the exhausted flora fae to safety.

Beazle's thought was a glimmer in the buzz of Jess's mind. *I found him.*

Jess pulled Digit into the jungle, forcing him to duck down behind oversized *bougainvillea* leaves.

"Beazle found the prince," she told Digit. "Wait."

He's about one hundred and fifty feet from you, away from the main gate, where the jungle meets the pasture. It's mayhem. Do you want me to show you?

Too dangerous. I have to keep my own vision. We're coming.

After relaying Beazle's information, Digit and Jess moved out of the jungle, then ran, skirting the edge. The sound of conflict was loud, making it difficult to hear Beazle's warning inside her mind: *Prepare yourself.*

Jess knew they were getting close when she saw spindly orange fungus cresting through the long grasses. *Cordyceps.* Evidence of Faraçek's presence. The fungi grew denser as the twins closed in on a circle of unseelie. They weren't engaged in combat, though their swords were unsheathed. They craned their necks to look upward while shading their eyes from the sunlight. Jess's blood froze in her veins.

In the center of the circle of unseelie, several Solanan soldiers, as well as Anthurium and Columbine, clung to overgrown stalks and trunks. All of them were making attempts to get higher, shuffling upward like monkeys, using thorns or the stems of leaves to climb. The unseelie were so preoccupied with the spectacle that they didn't notice Jess and Digit slip among them. When one of the Solanan soldiers reached the tallest bough he could reach, he jumped without hesitation, his body plummeting to the ground. The unseelie laughed and cheered.

One of them tugged a ring from his taloned finger, handing it grudgingly to another.

They're making bets on who jumps first, Jess thought with horror.

I told you to brace yourself, Beazle whispered.

I thought you meant for battle!

Pushing their way through the crowd, Jess and Digit reached the inner circle of unseelie, where Faraçek held Amaryllis cruelly by the back of the neck.

"No!" Jess screamed, but she was drowned out by a victory cheer as another Solanan fell from great heights.

Faraçek exhaled into Amaryllis's pale face then let her go. She swayed drunkenly for a moment, her expression vacant. Then she looked around, dazed but searching. When she saw the jungle, she went toward it, moving stiffly.

Jess tried to surge forward but found herself held back against a chest. Her skin tingled and she squirmed, expecting at any moment her throat would be sliced open, but Digit got there first. Her captor stiffened, then collapsed forward on top of her, crushing her down to the ground with him. She landed hard, bruising her ribs and knees as all the air expressed harshly from her lungs. She tried and failed to inhale. She tried and failed to move her body, to shift the dead weight to stop it from crushing her. His body felt like a sack filled with hot, wet cement.

She heard more laughter, and the thud of another body hitting the earth. She felt the weight of the unseelie shifting as Digit tried to push the body off her, then felt Beazle's rage as he exploded into a cauldron of bats, screeching, clawing, and biting at the unseelie pressing in around them. She tried to look up, twisting her head to the side. An orange *cordyceps* fungus loomed next to her face. Instinctively, she recoiled. Black spots popped in her vision. Panic crept over her foggy mind. She was going to pass out.

Beazle's duplicates pressed the soldiers back, giving Digit enough room to shove the soldier off. Jess rolled over, finally able to fill her lungs. Sucking in air, she looked up at the swarm of Beazles, her vision clearing. Some were as large as Ferrugin and terrifying, with sharp white teeth, black rolling eyes, and enormous jaws that seemed to open so wide they looked unhinged. The unseelie thrashed blades in the air, trying to drive the bats off. Puffs of black smoke burst where duplicates were destroyed.

Digit pulled Jess to her feet. "Anything broken? I'm so sorry. I didn't know he'd fall on you."

She shook her head, still trying to catch her breath. She was grateful for Digit's magic.

I can't hold them back much longer, Beazle sent her.

It's okay, you helped plenty. Thank you.

The duplicates thinned, dissipating into black fog. As the last of them vanished and the mist disintegrated, Jess saw that they were surrounded by unseelie soldiers. They stood at a distance, cautious of the twins' magic, leaving a vacant ring of grass and clusters of *cordyceps* fungi. Faraçek joined his soldiers at the inner edge of the circle, dark eyes gleaming with a mania that made Jess feel cold all over. His hair had come loose and his talons and fangs has distended, enhancing his vampiric appearance.

"We meet again." He performed a mocking bow, his rapier sheathed at his hip, the blade rising as he bent at the waist. He straightened, his gaze flicking to Digit. "Who is this?"

Jess glared at the prince, one hand over her chest where her lungs still burned.

Faraçek raised a pointed brow. "Come, you were not so tongue-tied before, Miss Jessamine Fontana of the Kingdom of Solana."

Beyond the circle Jess could hear the sounds of battle. It was like she and Digit had been partitioned away from the action, corralled into a private audience. She wondered vaguely if this had been a set up, but pushed the notion away. There was no way the prince could have known that she would make a beeline for him, or even known where he was.

Yes there is, Beazle told her. *He knows we're spies, Jess. He knows we have ways of finding him.*

"I'm her brother," Digit told the prince, since Jess hadn't answered.

Faraçek lifted his chin in a tilt of acknowledgment. "The brother. You're what? Seventeen? Eighteen? You're just faelings, but you're far deadlier than you look." It was a statement, made as the prince gestured to the body of the unseelie that had almost crushed Jess. "I see no wounds on him. I see no signs of poison either. What is this magic that you have?"

Digit smiled without humor. "Come closer and I'll show you."

Unease rippled through the crowd, but some of them chuckled or outright laughed, finding the threats of a teenage faeling humorous, especially toward their prince—a controller of minds.

Faraçek sent a subtle signal to someone behind the twins. Digit whirled, putting his back to Jess's, his shoulder blades pressing up against hers. She lifted her hands, palms out, skin tingling. Several unseelie pressed in. Chromatypes burst into the air like a cloud of soap bubbles, spinning from her fingers and spreading outward like slow-moving shrapnel.

The unseelie recoiled, teeth bared as they watched her mystic blooms drift, picked up on the breeze. But Jess's satisfaction was short-lived. Digit's head cracked hard against the back of hers. Stars of light and pain burst in her vision. Beazle tried to tell her something but his words were muddled. She fought for consciousness as she felt Digit's body sag, shoving her forward. She turned but was too late to catch him. Collapsing in a tangle of limbs, Jess fought for sight. The pain in her head was immense. Her vision returned, and she rolled Digit's limp body so she could see his face. His eyes were closed, his face white. The skin at his temple was split and bleeding, a goose-egg forming. Blood ran over one eye and down one cheek, back into his hair, turning it black.

It was a rock... ock... ock..., Beazle's words came through like an echo in a canyon. *He dropped three unseelie, then someone threw a rock...*

"Digit," she wheezed, searching for a pulse.

Feet stormed around her. Rough hands grabbed her, lifting her off the ground like she was a puppy. Poison swept into her mouth as the air around her exploded into a swarm of angry bats. She pursed her lips, preparing to spit... then Faraçek's face loomed in her fuzzy vision and a warm, mulchy wind swept over her face.

CHAPTER THIRTY-FIVE

LAEC

EIGHT OF THE forty-nine Calyx had yet to be found, and it had grown increasingly difficult to save them. Unseelie had broken through the Solanan lines in many places now in an attempt to thwart those carrying injured fae to safety. However, the unseelie attempting to get through the maze of botanicals had found themselves moving so laboriously that they became easy targets for the raptors and other familiars. Working together, the familiars and their duplicates—who had no fear and did not care about pain—could pick them off. The battlefield was dominated by the unseelie, but the jungle was dominated by the Fahyli—and as long as that held, no unseelie could get anywhere near the gates.

Looking for Ilishec, whom he hadn't seen since dawn, Laec spied Captain Yorin engaged in battle with two Solanan soldiers. The soldiers were holding their own but flagging, and would not last much longer against the brutal Rahamlar captain, who'd always struck Laec as being made more of granite than of flesh and bone.

Spying a short spear

on the ground—identical to the kind Yorin had used to kill Serya—Laec tossed his sword from his right hand to his left as he jogged to it. Scooping up the spear, he hefted it back to throw, watching as Yorin hammered back one Solanan soldier until he fell, then turned to pierce the other. Yanking his sword free, Yorin spun to finish the fallen soldier and Laec saw his opening. Chest and bicep burning, he fired with everything he had, his overused muscles crying out. Throwing had never been Laec's strongest skill and he missed his target—Yorin's chest— but nevertheless the spear found a mark, piercing the captain in the left armpit. With a yowl of pain, Yorin yanked the projectile free, and used it to finish the soldier, before homing in on Laec.

Laec tossed his sword back to his right hand, baring his teeth in a feral grin and beckoning for the captain to come. Yorin closed the distance, blood flowing over the boiled leather protecting his left ribs.

"If it isn't the princess-murdering whelp of Rahamlar," Laec taunted. "The stab-an-unarmed-woman-in-the-back-in-front-of-her-sister, stinking unseelie coward." Laec eyed the position of the noonday sun and danced in a semi-circle, drawing the captain to where he wanted him. "You're nothing but a stooge for the whims of a tyrant, worth less than a heap of dung on the side of the road."

Apparently not the bantering type, Yorin came on silently, blade ready and wrath burning in his face. Smaller, and with a lighter sword, Laec would have to be faster, cleverer to win this, but Stavarjakians were nothing if not fast and clever. As the captain moved in, Laec angled his blade, reflecting a beam of sunlight into Yorin's eyes. The captain blinked and faltered, but only long enough for Laec to land a glancing blow on Yorin's forearm as he lifted it in defense. Dropping out of the path of

Yorin's attack, Laec moved low and in, sliding to the side like water, below Yorin's elbow, then bringing a fist up into his belly. The captain grunted and brought his elbow down on the back of Laec's shoulder, driving him to the ground. Going with it, Laec rolled away, narrowly escaping a jugular-opening slice as Yorin brought his sword around.

Getting his feet under him, Laec strode forward into a storm of thrusts and feints, parries and jabs. Each offensive hit was deflected, the repeated blows vibrating up Laec's arm. His muscles were throbbing, reminding him of how much fighting he'd already done today. Ignoring the pain, Laec fought on, noting that Yorin still appeared strong, unaffected by loss of blood. A strike on the bracer of his right wrist caused Laec's hand to go numb. He could not feel the handle of his sword pressing into his palm for what seemed like forever, and had to rely on muscle memory to keep him alive.

"Where is your prince, eh?" Laec deflected another blow before making a feint, tricking Yorin into a poorly aimed waste of energy. "Where is the usurping princeling? The murdering, lying, thieving, whoring—" Laec had to stop, save his breath as Yorin launched a fresh attack, movements furious. That was good. If he was angry, he would make a fatal mistake. It was only a matter of time.

Laec felt the sting when Yorin's blade bit his upper thigh. The pain was a red light flashing behind his eyes, burning into his brain that this threat had to be dealt with. Now. Laec let his body slip into its memory of hours of training with a blade in his hand. Against this hardened unseelie, Laec didn't know whether his training would be enough, but it was all he had.

When the tip of his blade found the soft meat under Yorin's chin, Laec tasted victory as deeply as he could feel the blood gushing from his leg, soaking the thigh of his leggings, and thrust deeper. He then limped back and the captain fell, dead before he hit the ground.

Panting, Laec wiped his blade on the grass, grinning in spite of his pain, then froze as three unseelie soldiers who'd witnessed their captain's death moved to surround him.

The sound of hoofbeats reached Laec's ears but he couldn't look for the rider without risking death. Hefting his sword and moving away from Yorin's prone form, Laec doubted his Stavarjakian combinations would be much good against all three brutes.

If I never see you again, he thought as Çifta's face surfaced in his mind, *know that I loved you as I've never loved anyone. I found myself again thanks to you. If I die today, I die as Laec Fairijak, and not a drunken shadow of him.*

The unseelie lifted their blades, two of them fat and curved, like Kazery's favored steel, the other a longsword. Laec's shorter blade was lighter and faster, but to get to these soldiers' vital parts he would need the reach of a giant.

Yelping and howling from the direction of the king's road was not a sound any of them could ignore; it was immense and painful to the ears. The unseelie froze, obsidian eyes widening. They turned, facing the new threat and giving Laec a chance to look.

Three enormous white dire wolves launched themselves, snarling and snapping, leaping at the throats of the unseelie. Two went down, grappling with their attackers. One managed to drive his blade into the chest of the wolf who'd leapt upon him, and she dissipated into a white fog that obscured everything like a cloud of flour. Laec took the opportunity to dance in. Finding the looming shadow of his enemy, he shoved his blade between ribs. It was an inelegant but effective blow, and the final soldier collapsed.

Rialta and her duplicates streaked into the fray, filling the air with the sound of furious canine predators and terrified soldiers. Searching the hilltops, Laec spied Swanmoor and Sasha. His heart doubled its rhythm and his body rushed with adrenaline as he witnessed Sasha aim one frost-white palm at the nearest unseelie, encasing his head in a block of ice. The enemy fell fast and hard, crushed to the earth by the weight of frozen water. A red splash burst inside the ice, then leaked through a spiderweb of cracks.

Solanan soldiers raised a rallying cry, but Sasha seemed not to hear, intent on bringing down any enemy within reach of his magic. Behind Sasha, another rider appeared. On a bay mount and riding bareback, she clung to her horse like a tick while unleashing arrows. Behind her mount was a white streak too small to be a wolf, running in a zigzag fashion. As the hare zagged, duplicates zigged in a spray, bounding through the battlefield, getting under unseelie feet, tripping and distracting—generally unleashing chaos for the enemy. Laec whooped, finding the sight marvelous.

Sasha's companion was a Silverfae female, with fierce warrior-like hair and a fiercer expression. As deft as Kite with her bow, she rained death on any enemy she took aim at. The arrows in her quiver grew few, and when she leapt from the horse to retrieve one from a fallen body, she used it to slaughter a second time.

The impact of these newcomers rippled through the unseelie, uncertainty and fear leeching confidence like a bleeding wound. Their captain had fallen, their prince was not to be found in this vicinity—no leaders were around to bolster their courage.

When the unseelie began to fall back—at a run—getting out of Sasha and Swanmoor's path, Laec whooped again, but a fresh wave of pain pulled him back to his body. He took a moment to rip a piece of cloth from his tunic and wrap it around his thigh, then limped toward the safety of the jungle, still scanning for signs of Ilishec and the missing Calyx.

CHAPTER THIRTY-SIX

JESSAMINE

THE WOODY BOUGHS were rough under her hands, her palms scraped and bleeding, but it didn't matter. The only thing that mattered was getting to the top. She would reach the sky and release herself to the ultimate liberty. It was so close she could almost taste it. Hand over hand, foot over foot, she navigated thorn-like protrusions sturdy enough to hold her weight and take her higher. Fuchsia pink leaves rustled around her as the wind touched them, brushing them into her face. She wished it were quieter. The din was unbearable: yelling, screaming, clashing steel, howls, growls, yips. The noise made her want to scream, tell them all to shut up. She almost did, then she heard laughter and it was so out of place that it startled her.

Jess.

She ignored the voice—just another sound in the uproar—and found the next hold. The foliage was thick but she thought she could see the top.

Something plopped

onto her shoulder, light but noticeable. She ignored it too. But then it screamed into her ear, making her flinch. She reached for it, feeling something small and furry under her palm. Grabbing it, she flung it off. It came back immediately, landing on her head this time. She reached up to rip it away, but when her hand arrived it had taken off, only to land on her other shoulder. It screeched again in her other ear, and there were words inside the scream.

Wake up!

She *was* awake. She didn't know what this bothersome creature wanted, and wished it would leave her alone. It continued taunting her, landing and taking off, landing and taking off, screaming at her, invading her mind. She uttered her own scream of frustration, but reaching the top was more important than freeing herself from this pest. She ignored it and continued her race to freedom. The branches beneath her were willowy now, and swayed under her weight. All her attention was needed to reach the highest heights.

A vibration shook her tree, followed by the sound of something heavy climbing up after her. Forcing herself to look down—something she was loath to do because it felt like going backward—fear gripped her throat. A huge black cat, rippling with muscle, was climbing up the bark. She was its target, there was no doubt about that. Its green gaze was intense, bright with intention. Its ears lay flat against its skull as it pierced the wood with frighteningly long talons. Its muscles bunched as it leapt upward, catching the trunk with those fearsome claws and gaining upon her. It saw her looking down and bared its teeth, uttering a strange chirping bark.

Below the midnight-colored cat, a large white streak shot by on the ground. It barreled into a group of soldiers, ripping and tearing before someone flashed a sword. Another joined, bringing their blade to bear against the white thing. A puff of pale smoke filled the air, like the explosion of a fog-filled party balloon.

But the cat was still coming so Jess redoubled her efforts. Her breath came ragged in her throat, her muscles burned. Likewise, the annoying little pest still would not leave her alone, landing on her forehead, then her back, then her leg, screaming into her mind. She did her best to ignore it, but then it landed in the crook of her neck and scrambled toward her ear with sharp little claws. Pain shot through her earlobe as it sank its teeth into her flesh. She screamed in pain and reached for it, to rip it from her ear and crush it in her fist. But her hand closed on air. She whimpered, feeling like someone had lit fire to the side of her head.

A snort made her look down, and her heart clawed back up her throat. The black cat was directly below her, making the branch sway. Something cracked. Jess kicked at the cat's face. Its head recoiled into its shoulders, but it was not deterred.

Jess. Wake up! The little thing that had bit her was back. *It's me! Beazle!*

Something about the name made her pause, and the cat took the advantage to climb between her legs. It chirruped, not an unfriendly sound, and surged upward, shoving its head between her body and the trunk. She kicked and the cat grunted as her boot connected with its ribcage. In the next moment she lost her footing as the cat pushed her away from the tree, wanting her to let go. Jess's legs flailed as she dangled, slithering against the body of the cat as it pushed up further. Its head was at her neck now, her arms forced to stretch and stretch as the cat nosed its way fully between her and the tree. Her fingers burned and clung, but finally had to let go. The cat was much stronger than her. With a cry, she clung to the animal, wrapping her arms around its neck. She looked longingly up at the top of the foliage, no longer in control of her mission.

Hold on, came the voice in her mind. *Hold on tight!*

Blood poured down her neck, wet and sticky. Her ear throbbed. She clung to the cat, wishing it to take her higher. But the cat left the trunk with a powerful leap, twisting as it dropped. Its paws raked wood as they landed and slid, scrabbling for something solid. It could not stay where it landed, and leapt again. Jess clenched her eyes shut and held on with her whole body, wanting to cry as she felt their downward motion.

Opening her eyes a slit, Jess found herself looking straight into the eyes of a transparent lion cub, sitting in the crook of a branch. It gazed at her, licking it's lips. A child's voice echoed through her mind, completely different from the pest's voice.

What is your name?

The cat moved again, dropping and dropping. She lost sight of the cub as she was jarred and almost fell off. The cat paused, letting her get a better grip.

The lion cub reappeared on a branch by her face. *Your name?*

She wanted to give the cub what it wanted, and opened her mouth to answer, but no answer came. She thought back to the name she'd been told earlier. It was the only name aside from the pest's that was available to her mind.

"Jess," she croaked.

Her identity came rushing back, filling the empty places in her brain like a wave rushing into an inlet. Knowledge and memory saturated her. She gasped, sucking in air. Moisture coated her cheek and her earlobe ached.

"Tully," she said, clinging to the back of Panther's cat.

Tully chirruped, a relieved sound. She paused on a thick branch, swinging her head back to try to look at Jess.

Beazle? Jess quested tentatively, understanding now that the pest had been him trying to reach her, and she'd almost killed him.

I'm here. He landed on her shoulder. His relief was tangible. *I'm sorry I bit you. I didn't know what else to do.*

I know. I'm sorry I tried to hurt you. Jess found herself stable enough to wipe tears from her cheeks. Faraçek's spell had been broken a second time, but she had no time to delay. Something was going on below, a ruckus that was different than before.

Jess looked down, searching for Digit, her heart sinking at the number of bodies lying on the ground. Faraçek and his legion of unseelie had moved on. High-pitched yaps and deep-chested growls—like that of big fighting dogs—drew her attention beyond the bodies.

Writhing white streaks clashed with unseelie soldiers in random places all over the battlefield. Her vision was whirling, and she shook her head trying to clear it. Rialta, many Rialtas, fighting the way wolves fought: with fang and claw and speed, ripping and shredding, spinning and snarling. Unseelie fought back with sword and dagger, their victims vanishing under lethal blows and bursting into puffs of white fog that temporarily blinded anyone within it.

"Sasha," Jess whispered, her heart a drum in her chest. "Sasha's back."

Tully let Jess off and she climbed down the rest of the way. Her head ached and her throat burned, her hands felt scraped raw. Tully stayed protectively close, as though she wasn't altogether convinced that Jess wouldn't lapse back into a suicidal state.

"I'm okay, Tully." On the ground, Jess hugged the cat. "You saved my life... again. Thank you."

The cat butted Jess in the forehead, chirruping sweetly before bounding off and splitting into four more Tullys, identical except for a slight variation in size.

Jess searched the ground for her fallen twin. She couldn't remember anything that had happened after Faraçek breathed into her face. Sasha was here somewhere, and the thought made her heart burst with the desire to see him, but she had to find Digit first.

Thankful that the action had moved away from here, Jess combed the bodies. She held back tears as she saw how many Solanan soldiers in blue and green livery Faraçek had mind-controlled into killing themselves. Amaryllis was beautiful even in death, her long limbs splayed like she was floating in a pool of water, her gray-green eyes open, staring at the sky. Someone moved, and Jess realized Anthurium was alive. He pushed himself up to sitting, blood crusted on his forehead and his left arm. His face crumpled when he saw Amaryllis, dead beside him. Jess ran over as Anthurium drew Amaryllis into his arms, cradling her.

Jess came to her knees beside him. Touching him, amazed that he looked mostly unhurt, with only a shallow wound at his hairline and a clean slice across the meat of his shoulder. He lifted dark brown eyes to hers, pain-filled but clear with understanding.

"A lion saved me." He hugged Amaryllis closer to his chest. "Why couldn't he have saved her instead?"

Jess's throat closed up. She wanted to tell him she was sorry, but it was also a miracle that he'd been saved at all. She understood his guilt.

"Digit is over there." Anthurium jutted his chin behind Jess. "I'm so sorry, Jessamine."

Cold overcame her and she scrambled to her feet and ran, finding her twin lying in the grass, his eyes closed and blood crusted on his forehead and face. A glimmer of Ania's teal feathers could just be seen inside Digit's armpit, where his familiar had burrowed. Jess fell to his side, groping at his neck for a pulse. Her eyes welled with tears, but widened with hope when she felt a pulse, weak and slow beneath her fingers. He was not yet departed.

"Digit." She put a hand beneath his neck, gently turning him to face her, whispering: "Julian? Come back to me, brother. Please."

When his eyes cracked open to slits, she burst into tears of relief.

"Ow," he croaked.

Ania peeped and her head popped out of his armpit. She opened and closed her beak, her ink-drop eyes seeing Jess then darting around at the vicinity.

Jess felt Digit's hand pat her arm lightly. Dropping her face into his chest, she exhaled her gratitude that he'd been spared, moisture pouring from her eyes.

"My head is splitting." He reached toward his temple. She helped him up to sitting as he touched his scalp, wincing. He drew his fingers away, red with blood. Ania hummed onto his leg, where she stretched her wings out. "I'm so thirsty, and I can't remember anything. All I remember is standing back-to-back with you, fighting, then… what?"

"Someone threw a rock. It knocked you out," she explained. "Sasha is here somewhere. Rialta, she… she's fighting the unseelie."

Her twin stared at her without comprehension. Understanding slowly sank in, but Ania peeped and his eyes fastened on something beyond Jess.

"Hello," he said in a friendly tone. "Who're you?"

Jess turned to see who he was talking to, thinking she'd see nothing, that his brains had been addled as much as hers had been. A tall white hare with pink eyes and a sharp, fierce face was sitting nearby. He went back on his haunches, standing up to sniff at the air, and Jess realized the creature was wearing a harness. He studied them cautiously before deciding they weren't going to hurt him. He hopped forward, displaying an immense restrained power in his hind legs. Landing beside them, he began to nibble at the grass. Jess reached for the harness which held a pack strapped to his side. Undoing the buckle at the hare's chest, it fell away, heavy in her hand. The animal blinked at them, chewing, then bounded away in a zigzag pattern.

Jess opened the pack and found a small waterskin, bandages, some kind of salve and a few other medical items. Hands shaking, Jess gave the water to Digit, who forced it back at her, refusing to drink until she did. The cool water was fresh and clean and cleared the last of the *cordyceps* magic from her mind. She drank half and handed the rest to her twin. He finished it while she cleaned and treated his forehead.

"Who was that?" Digit screwed the cap back onto the waterskin. "There aren't any Fahyli with a hare familiar."

"That was Walloon," Jess told him, hardly able to process what the hare's presence meant. "Halyn's familiar."

"Halyn?" Digit looked lost.

"Sasha's mother." Jess got to her feet and helped Digit to his, aware that the din of battle had lessened.

They looked over the pastureland, trying to understand what they were seeing. The unseelie were retreating, leaving great swathes of open land littered with bodies. Scattered throughout the valley there were a few skirmishes with Rialta's duplicates and other duplicates as well. Raptors swirled overhead, diving and multiplying in bursts of action before climbing into the sky—a single entity once more. Tully was a frightening cluster of four panthers circling a group of unseelie. One of them threw down his blade, going to his knees. The panthers stilled, watching as the other unseelie joined the first.

"There are still so many." Digit was disbelieving of the sincerity of the surrender they'd just witnessed. "More than enough to keep fighting. Why do they withdraw?"

As the bulk of soldiers removed themselves from the center of battle, clearing the way, Jess saw Swanmoor, and Sasha sitting atop her, his long white hair thrashing in the wind.

"Can you walk?" she asked Digit, unable to tear her eyes away from her beloved.

"Of course. I got my head knocked, not my legs broken."

They followed the jungle toward the front gate, then angled across the emptying battleground, passing unseelie with frozen limbs—an arm or a leg encased in ice, not enough to kill them but enough to put them out of commission. The pain of the frozen limbs twisted their faces into something so dreadful that Jess could hardly look at them. Some had died from other wounds, lying in wet grasses darkened by blood. So many bodies.

Near Sasha, Faraçek lay face down on the ground, all four limbs encased in ice. He lay still, but Jess could tell he was alive.

Sasha leapt from Swanmoor when he saw Jess, running toward her. She ran to meet him, crashing into him, tears of relief running from her eyes.

"You're here," she whispered. "How are you here? Did you know what was happening?"

He kissed the top of her head, holding her close, tucking her head under his chin. "No. I didn't expect to come back to… this." He released her, studying her top to bottom and back again. "Are you hurt? What's this?" He gestured to the blood on her neck.

"Beazle bit me to save me. It's nothing. It doesn't hurt."

Liar, whispered Beazle.

Jess found a smile for Sasha. "You caught the prince. The unseelie are retreating."

The approach of Halyn put Jess in silence as she studied Sasha's mother. She was almost as tall as Sasha, with icy green eyes and hair in a style Jess had never seen before; short at the back but long at the front, braided close to the scalp down one side of her face to her jaw. She held a rough-made bow, and a quiver for arrows could be seen over one shoulder. Her clothing reminded Jess of the traveling minstrels that came through Dagevli: skins and furs, leather thongs crisscrossed over the body, holding it all together. The white hare stood at Halyn's feet, up on his hind legs, white paws dangling together at his chest. Fine lines bracketed Halyn's eyes and an uncertain expression filled those eyes as she observed Jess and Sasha.

"Your mother," Jess said.

Sasha smiled. "I went to find her, but instead she found me, on the road just past Kittrell. She received a bird from Elphame informing her that I was looking for her. Çifta told Elphame that I was returning to Solana, but that I had hoped to find my mother in Silverfall."

Halyn approached, Walloon hopping along at her side.

"It's a pleasure to meet you," Jess said. "Well come. I'm

Jessamine, and this is Beazle." She gestured to where her bat sat on her shoulder.

Halyn nodded, and Walloon bobbed his head in what might have been a greeting. Her voice was rough and pleasant, low for a female. "A pleasure to meet you also. Well found. My son tells me this is the traditional response in Solana. I remembered it right?"

"You did. I only *wish* we were well found," Jess told her. "Thank you for your help."

"I'm glad we arrived in time to be of service." Halyn's pale green gaze softened. "Especially for one so important to my son."

Jess looked up at Sasha, eyes shining and heart full of both sorrow and love.

CHAPTER THIRTY-SEVEN

JESSAMINE

WHEN GEORJIE WITHDREW the overgrown garden blocking the gates, everyone—unseelie, seelie and human, and every animal too—became captured by the sight. Lit from within, each stem, leaf and petal cast a dim colored glow as it shrank, fading into the earth. The sound of deep thunder beneath the earth's crust, and a vibration that could be felt through the soles of Jessamine's boots, accompanied the botanicals decline, like a tide going out.

Once the plants were gone, Jess saw that the gates were fully open, and a crowd of soldiers on horseback waited to exit. The first horses stepped tentatively forward, sniffing at the raw, churned earth near the gate, testing it with their weight. Deciding it was safe, they moved forward at a trot, followed by not just soldiers but civilians carrying backpacks. Horses dragged stacks of stretchers laden with tools. In the midst of the disorganized rush of assistance pouring from the gates rode King Agir and

Queen Esha, their faces pale and drawn, having aged a decade in the last few weeks.

Help spread to every corner of the battlefield. It was noisy and chaotic once more. Jess found herself seated on a rock and under the ministrations of a servant from the palace. Jess's protests that she was fine were ignored as her ear was cleaned. Jess saw Georjayna emerge from the earth like a beautiful wraith, formed first of light, then darkening into solid form. Like an angel, she moved to the nearest injured soldier and knelt at his side.

As soon as Jess was released, she arrowed for the crofter, who was organizing piles of supplies as they arrived. Several temporary canvas shelters had been erected. With a pang, she noted crusted blood across his left shoulder blade, and a bandage-wrapped arm held in a sling.

"Orders, Crofter?"

He turned, his eyes darkening with relief. He moved forward, lifting his good arm as though to hug her. Jess hesitated and he stopped himself. "I'm glad to find you well, Jess. Your brother?"

"Digit is also mostly unharmed," she told him.

"Mostly?"

"He took a nasty hit to the head. He is working with Kestrel to free the horses."

"Why don't you help him?"

She dipped her head and jogged toward places where vine-wrapped equines dotted the land like fresh-cut heaps of hay. Wary unseelie soldiers were working at freeing the horses near the Rahamlar camp, while Solanans cut away the vines pinning the animals nearer the city. The parties mostly ignored each other, except for occasional bitter glances.

Scattered throughout the field were clusters of dying mushrooms. Subdued unseelie soldiers collected weapons and supplies, humiliation evident in their every movement. Jess watched them with little satisfaction. It all seemed so pointless, their victory echoed hollowly in the wake of so much death and suffering.

Daylight dwindled, and etherlamps were erected by Solanan engineers. The cleanup would continue through the night and into the next day, probably longer.

Princess Isabey rode through the camp, stopping to exchange words with Rahamlarin soldiers. Each of them bowed, tugging their forelocks in deference. One kissed her booted foot. Behind the princess followed another group of riders, including Reina, with Toryan on the saddle before her. The young unseelie looked around with a somber expression that made him appear much older than his years. Isabey, Reina and Toryan were accompanied by three mature-looking humans: two males and a female, gray-haired and well-dressed. Rings flashed on their fingers, and each wore a gold badge in the shape of the cowbird pinned to their breast. Behind them came younger soldiers, two of whom Jess recognized as the Rahamlar fortress gatekeepers.

Princess Isabey made a slow and steady beeline toward a Solanan tent where King Agir and Queen Esha waited with the crofter and Captain Bradburn.

Want me to follow them? Beazle asked. His curiosity matched her own in its intensity.

You mean spy on our own sovereigns?

I won't hide. If they tell me to scram, I'll scram. If they let me stay, that's as good as permission.

Go on, then, Jess bent to cut the vines pinning a black gelding. Lush white roses speckled the equine's body. Jess marveled that Rose had had the presence of mind to ensure it manifested no thorns to jab the animal. The boughs of the rose were as thick as Jess's forearm, crisscrossing the body tightly enough to prevent him from rising, but not so tightly that they stopped his circulation. Each trapped horse had been found in a similar situation. The kindness of the Calyx responsible—Rose, Wisteria, Bougain, Clematis and others—brought a mist into Jess's eyes. She hoped with her entire being that they were all unharmed. She'd seen none of the Calyx, other than the dead, since the fighting had ceased. Nor had any of the Calyx reappeared for the cleanup. Jess had been told they were exhausted and dehydrated, but still had to be forced to rest by Mrs. Tierney, Olinya and Queen Esha, who had taken charge in Ilishec's absence.

Jess cut the last of the vines and stroked the gelding, who lifted his head to look at her, uncertain as to whether he was actually free or not.

"Go on. Get up. Get some blood flowing into those legs," she told him.

The horse took his time getting to his feet, then shook himself as all the others had. Jess stroked his shoulder and he nosed at her tunic in gratitude. The tack was all still in place, though Jess was sure he would want to get it off as soon as possible. He lifted his head when someone from the Rahamlar camp whistled high and loud, then trotted away.

Jess moved to the next animal, chewing her lip. The gardener was another worry. No one had seen him since the conflict began. The longer he was missing, the more concerned Jess grew.

Princess Isabey drew her mount to a stop as Beazle zipped within hearing distance, landing on a wooden post holding the canvas tent erect.

Do you want to see? Beazle asked.

Just hear. I need to see what I'm doing, otherwise I might accidentally hurt an animal.

Princess Isabey's voice penetrated Jess's ears as though she was standing by her side.

"Where is he?" Her words were hard, vibrating with rage. She lowered her voice for the next words. "My brother will die for this, and other crimes. I promise you."

"He is caged," King Agir replied. "I will not release him to you, though. He will be moved to a cell to await trial."

"He has offended me as much as you, King Agir. May I remind you that he murdered my sister in front of me? And attempted to murder me."

Queen Esha asked gently: "Is this the son?"

"Jess?" The crofter's voice, loud and unexpected, made Jess jump. "I know you're listening. You can come. You have earned the right to be here if you want."

Releasing the horse, Jess sheathed her dagger and walked to the tent, moths fluttering in her stomach. She put a hand up to catch Digit's attention, letting him know where she was going. He returned her signal then bent to another pinned animal, slicing away boughs of bright orange bougainvillea vines.

By the time Jess arrived, the group was moving toward the ice cage that Sasha had manufactured for Faraçek. Sasha and Halyn were a short distance away, talking with two Solanan captains. When they saw who was coming, they fell silent. Jess skirted the sovereigns to join Sasha, getting a better view of the prince.

Faraçek's cage was a hollow but barred cube of ice, large enough only for the prince to stand up or sit cross-legged. The bars were misshapen but thick, impossible to break by hand and painful to touch with bare skin. The prince sat in the middle of the floor of the cell, staying away from the frigid walls. His hands were bound behind his back, locked in irons, his ankles too, and—most importantly—a covering had been tied over his mouth to prevent his exhalations from reaching anyone. The prince had not been gagged beneath the covering.

"He's said nothing since he was caught," Sasha told her.

The gloves and boots of ice had kept Faraçek pinned down until the Solanans could subdue him, then had been melted by Sasha.

"You didn't kill him," Jess whispered.

"It was unnecessary in order to restrain him," Sasha replied. "Besides, I'd rather see him stand trial. Wouldn't you?"

Jess nodded, remembering that Solanan law dictated those about to stand trial were not to be harmed.

As though he knew they were discussing him, Faraçek's gaze darted toward Sasha, then dropped to Jess.

Jess couldn't stop herself from giving the prince a smile of victory and a little wave that said, *you failed to kill me yet again.*

The prince glared at her, and Sasha wrapped an arm around Jess's shoulders, squeezing her into his side. She was pleasantly reminded that—in spite of the phenomenal things they could do with ice—Silverfae were not, in fact, cold themselves. His warmth soaked into her, steadying and grounding her.

The prince looked toward Agir and Esha as they approached. They parted to allow Princess Isabey through to the front. When Faraçek saw his sister, his eyes expressed a frozen shock that seemed to echo out from his very soul. He stared—pale and astounded—for a long time, and she stared back, saying nothing.

Isabey broke the silence. "Wondering how I survived, brother?"

Faraçek now looked at her with a strange expression, one Jess couldn't place.

"I won't give you the satisfaction of an explanation." She threaded her fingers together in front of her hips. "Let's just say that fate decided that you were not meant to be the first unseelie ruler of Rahamlar in over five hundred years. I know that was always your ambition."

"It should have been everyone's ambition," Faraçek replied, his words muffled by the covering over his mouth. "The laws are prejudiced and deeply offensive."

"I know it."

"Then why are you working against me?"

"I'm not, at least not on that issue. I would like to see an unseelie on our throne, too. Just not you." Her eyes were filled with rage, the skin around her mouth was white. "You are the worst of us. You give unseelie a bad name, dismantling efforts to level the field for our kind."

"I never wanted to hurt you, sister. It was nothing personal," Faraçek said, his voice soft and warm.

The princess gave a sarcastic laugh. "Nothing *personal*?!"

"I am better for the kingdom, better for the unseelie, a stronger ruler. Ruling requires making difficult decisions, decisions that I'm prepared to make."

"In case you have forgotten, I am unseelie too. And you made it as personal as it could possibly get when you had your thug stab Serya in the back... in front of me, no less, then you tried to kill me too!" The princess's voice broke, her eyes glazed with pain and moisture. Her voice dropped to just above a whisper. "How *could* you, Faraçek? We loved you! You were our brother."

"I'm unseelie before I am anything, and a descendant of Toryan." His voice had a pleading edge that sounded strange coming from under the prince's face covering. He sincerely wished for her to understand his motivation.

"No," she snapped, brushing away an angry tear. "You don't get to plead 'it's in my nature.' I would never... *never* do what you have done. None of it. I've met your *unseelie* son, by the way. The nephew you've been keeping from us since his birth."

Faraçek recoiled, as though struck by a physical blow.

"And *he* would never do this either." She let this hit home, studying her brother as he absorbed what she had said. "In spite of you, he is a remarkable faeling." She narrowed her eyes and shook her head. "He looks like you, but he is nothing like you, and for that I'll be eternally grateful."

Reina sidled through the crowd, coming to the front with Toryan, standing where Faraçek could see them. She kept the boy in front of her, hands resting on his little collarbones.

Faraçek's voice was a torn cry as he peered at his son through the bars: "Toryan, my boy. Come to me."

The boy lifted a foot to step forward but Reina held him back, gently saying: "Remember what we talked about, my love."

Faraçek's voice was full of ghastly malice, a wounded sound mingled with betrayal. "You've turned him against me?"

"No." Reina looked at the prince, brows drawn. "We have done no such thing. Toryan loves you. He always has and he always will, whether you deserve it or not. But we have made a very clever lad, you and I, one who was born with the gift of wisdom. He knows right from wrong and good from evil better than any of us, especially you."

"Toryan, lad." Faraçek's voice was soft again. "I explained all of this to you. You agreed that it made sense, that it was all for the best. I did this for you, my prince, my son. I did not do this for myself. I wished to hand you a kingdom rich with the old magic, the way it once was. I wished to restore Rahamlar, and present you with it, whole and one."

Toryan's eyes were huge and watery. To the boy's credit though, he did not cry. Jess's heart felt slashed by the heartbreak and disappointment on the child's face. Sasha must have felt for the boy too, for he squeezed her harder to his side.

"You didn't explain this." The boy made a small gesture at the battlefield. "You said they would see it your way. You said…" He took a shuddering breath. "You never said you would do this part. The… killing part. If having Solana means killing, then I don't want it. Why do we even need it? We have enough, don't we? And once you fix the problem with your magic, make all those mushrooms go away, we can go back to normal. Make it like it was before, and we can be together." He was increasingly upset now, his face cramping with grief. He started to shake, Jess could see it from where she stood. It was traumatizing for Toryan to see his father like this. Jessamine closed her eyes, wishing the faeling had been spared this, but though he deserved to be protected, he also had a right to know. He was the true heir. Whatever Reina had told the boy, she had not explained that Faraçek would stand trial and be executed for what he had done. There would be no going back to anything for the prince.

"That's enough," said Reina, pulling Toryan away.

"No. Wait! Toryan!" Faraçek pressed his face against the

cage, unmindful of the ice. "I love you! Toryan!" He struck the bars with his forehead. "Bring him back! Damn you. He is my son! My boy! Let me reason with him!"

Isabey turned her back on Faraçek, saying to Agir: "Thank you. I am finished with him. Your men can take him away."

King Agir signaled Bradburn, who in turn signaled soldiers to move in. Sasha dealt with the ice cage, melting it down. Soldiers put a second bag over the prince's head before leading him away toward the gates of the city.

Jess was holding the head of a wounded soldier—helping him to drink from a waterskin while he waited for Georjie's healing attentions—when someone yelled her name. It took her a moment to spot the tiny figure of Laec, waving both his arms overhead, trying to get her to see him. Setting the soldier's head back gently, she got up and brushed off her knees. Looking around for Beazle, she began to jog toward Laec.

I'm already with him, Beazle whispered into her mind. *He's found Ilishec.*

Jess almost tripped as worry closed her throat. *Do I need to bring anything? Do we need a stretcher?*

Just come.

Once Laec saw she was coming, he disappeared behind a knoll. Jess sprinted, leaping tussocks and dodging bodies. Cresting the rise, she saw Laec's red hair as he knelt behind a boulder. She reached him, panting, and found Ilishec lying on his back in the long grass, Laec beside him, a waterskin in his hand. The gardener's eyes were open, and Jess felt a rush of relief as she saw life in them. But she also saw the stab wound in his chest. *So close to his heart.* Her mind balked and her heart fell.

"We need help." Jess looked at Laec, and his look hit her like a punch. He shook his head, his eyes shining, his mouth downturned.

"No," Ilishec whispered on an exhale. He lifted his right hand and Jess took it. Laec picked up his uncle's left hand, cradling it.

"Why no? Georjie can save you." Jess squeezed his hand, putting her other palm on his temple, brushing his gray hair back.

"Let her save others," Ilishec said, blood appearing at the corner of his mouth. His eyes tracked to hers. The slightest smile lifted his mouth. "I go to be with my Hazel."

Hot tears filled Jess's eyes, running down her cheeks. "No," she choked. "Hazel too?" A glance at Laec confirmed it.

"Don't cry, my Jessamine. My beautiful faeling." Ilishec's chest hitched and his face momentarily cramped with agony. He took a few shallow breaths, and the pain on his face eased. He squeezed her hand. "I love you both. My nephew..." He looked at Laec, who palmed away the moisture on one cheek. Ilishec's gaze swung back to Jess again. "My daughter."

Jess began to sob in earnest, feeling Beazle burrow into her hair at her neck and come out the other side, not wanting to witness this, but not wanting to hide from it either. If she could not escape this moment, Beazle wouldn't abandon her to experience it alone.

"No," she whispered. "Please don't leave me. I love you. You're the closest to a father I've ever had. I can't lose you."

He spoke slowly and with effort. "Do not forget that you have gained another father. He wants to love you, if you will let him." He squeezed her hand. "Let him, Jess. Love is the greatest gift."

His pupils dilated, and his breathing grew shallow.

Jess lowered her cheek to the back of his hand, pressing his cold skin against her warmth. Tears and sorrow ravaged her face. She could hear Laec sniffing but couldn't look at him. If she did, the final tether on her control would snap. Leaning forward, she kissed the gardener's cheeks, then his forehead.

"I love you, my Ilishec," she whispered.

He smiled, his inhales turning into short sips of air. His eyes drifted closed and his final exhale was long and slow. She felt him slip away slowly, like a long, satisfied sigh of relief after the world's longest, hardest day.

Jess was wracked by sobs. She felt Laec touch her shoulder and squeeze it in an attempt to comfort her. Laec was Ilishec's blood family, Jess should be comforting him, but she felt broken, utterly empty. She lay her forehead on Ilishec's shoulder and wept, her head throbbing. She was a hollow cave, with nothing to offer but tears and bitter sorrow. Laec put his arm around her and pulled her into his lap, enfolding her. Tucking her head under his chin, he held her like a child as she cried. She felt his own tears dropping into her hair as she clutched at his tunic, grieving in a way she had never grieved, even for Marion. Grieving for her surrogate father, and for all of the losses she had yet to fully process.

Ilishec had gone into the fray knowing it would mean sacrifice. He'd made his peace with that, but Jess couldn't make peace with it. It was too unjust, too unfair. Maybe it made her selfish, to want Ilishec to stay when he was ready to leave, but she couldn't find the will to care.

Laec held her until she'd cried herself out. Then he held her while she sat in stillness, feeling numb and shocked and so, so tired. She let her eyes close, feeling safe in Laec's embrace. He kissed the top of her head and whispered her name.

"Something is happening."

He released her, and they knelt side by side next to Ilishec's body. Jess's eyes felt so puffy and swollen from crying that it took her a long time to focus. There *was* something happening. A pale mist rose from the gardener's body, drifting into the air, softly illuminated. They shuffled back, gripping one another. The mist congealed and brightened.

The broad, muscular body of a lion with a magnificent mane came together, his sturdy legs and paws disappearing into Ilishec's form. He swung his head to look at them, and in this lion's white-lit eyes, Jessamine could see Ilishec's spirit looking back at them. The lion licked his lips and his mouth opened in a feline smile.

"Uncle?" Laec said, his voice hoarse.

The lion lifted his head abruptly, his rounded ears perking as though hearing something in the distance. Jess heard nothing, but followed the lion's gaze toward the eastern horizon. Where the hilltop met the sky, illumination simmered into life. Moving like a sea of light, the pride stood on the hilltop, waiting.

A lioness emerged, petite and perfect, stalking away from the pride. Ilishec's lion jogged forward, then sprinted, loping over the gentle dip and up the hill toward the female. He slowed as he approached her. Their foreheads pressed together, their heads and necks rubbing in affectionate greeting. Together they walked, ribs pressing to ribs, shoulder pressing to shoulder, toward the pride. Their light was absorbed as they joined the family and disappeared.

Jess and Laec stared at the vacant hillside. She rubbed a hand across her nose, sniffing.

"He didn't even look back."

"No." Laec squeezed her hand. "That was the best way to go out that I've ever seen. May my own death be so noble and beautiful."

Jess found that the crushing sorrow had lifted, and she wondered who had decided to let them witness Ilishec and Hazel's reunion. It had been a gift for them, a balm to their distress. She decided that it had to have been Jezaret, the alpha male, the wreathed lion of Solana. She closed her eyes and bowed her head in thanks.

It was the single greatest act of kindness that she had ever received.

CHAPTER THIRTY-EIGHT

LAEC

L AEC ROLLED OVER under the heavy goose-down blanket as the sound of an unfamiliar bird trilled at the window. Opening his eyes, a smile crept across his face as he realized Çifta was gazing at him lovingly with those extraordinary eyes.

"How long have you been awake?" He touched her cheek, moving a lock of black hair back from her jawline.

"You must be joking," she said with a smile. "I haven't slept yet. I'm too excited. I keep worrying that if I fall asleep, I'll wake up to learn that this is all a dream. Did Elphame's permission really arrive the day after the battle?"

"It really did. I didn't even have to ask a second time." Laec shifted toward her, wrapping his arms around her. Çifta turned, snugging her backside into his lap and pulling his arm around her waist. Warmth blossomed between them.

"You arrived so tired and so exhausted that we've had no chance to talk... or... anything," Çifta murmured. "I've been dying of curiosity, among other things."

He chuckled, nosing into her hair. She smelled like amber and vanilla. "We have the rest of our lives to talk."

"We had news of the battle and Solana's victory, but no details have been forthcoming. What of our friends? What of Sasha and Halyn? Did you meet her? How is Jessamine? What of your uncle? And Auvo, and the Calyx and all your Fahyli friends? I've been so worried for everyone. How are Agir and Esha? Should I send something? I was so torn when I learned of the invasion, I wanted to help, but my advisers explained that it would destabilize Silverfall. I had only just arrived, I couldn't just up and leave again, abandon my kingdom for another. It would send a damaging message, one that I might never be able to reverse. I understood that, but I—" She pushed out a harsh breath. "It's been very challenging."

"Well…" He inhaled, allowing himself to gather waking thoughts. He could easily sleep for another three hours. The journey he and Grex had made up from Solana had been grueling, making the eight-day ride in six. "First of all, your advisers were correct. Your kingdom is coming out of its own dark period; they've been waiting for you a long time. You can't show up for every foreign conflict. Did you ever receive a request from Agir or Esha to assist them?"

"No," she said, doubtfully.

"Then they didn't want you there, otherwise they would have invited you. Kingdoms don't rush to the aid of other kingdoms unless asked. Besides, you sent Sasha, and I suspect he single-handedly brought down five-hundred soldiers. Silverfall was well represented. Halyn and her hare were likewise indispensable. Rialta saved my life."

She made a noncommittal sound, but listened as Laec gave her an idea of what had gone on. She expressed amazement when he told her of the Calyx's plan, their sacrifice. She wept when she learned that nearly all the insect pollinators had shown signs of *cordyceps* infestation shortly after the battle. The majority of them would die, but she managed to smile through her tears when he told her that new familiars could be expected for some, and they would comfort the grieving fae. She was rendered silent in amazement when he told her of the Wise that Elphame had sent to help, and how she enhanced the lion-hearted flora fae so they could fight. She clenched the sheet with her fists when Laec told her of Hazel's illness and subsequent death, then Ilishec's change of heart, and his passing. She sobbed when he described how his uncle had gone to join the ranks of Solana's lions.

He took a break when a servant delivered breakfast—eggs, steamed fish, and buttered toast with thick cream and dollops of jam—to their room, but while they ate, he told her about Jessamine's discovery about who her father was, and her twin. He sipped hot tea while patiently answering every question Çifta lobbed at him, as the bright sun moved across the sparkling white cityscape of Silverfall City.

"Do you think she'll forgive Ian, one day?" Çifta asked, blowing on her cup of coffee.

"I know she will," Laec replied, stroking her cheek with the back of his knuckles. "One day. Ilishec told her that love is the greatest gift, and he's right. No one can resist genuine love, not forever."

"And he really loves her... like his daughter, I mean?"

Laec put down his cup and gently took Çifta's from her, setting it on the table. He moved forward to kiss her. She responded with enthusiasm and he pulled her onto his lap. He kissed her deeply, then nuzzled her neck before looking into her eyes. "Enough about everyone else? What about us?"

"Us," she echoed dreamily. "I love that word. Do you think... one day, that 'us' might include more than two?"

Laec gave a start, then laughed, his body quickening to her implication. She felt it and gave him a lazy cat smile of satisfaction.

"I'll take that as a yes." She pressed her lips to his.

Epilogue

T HE LEAVES WERE tinged with fall colors, but the weather was still hot. A noonday sun beat down upon Solana's gardens, illuminating the late summer blooms as they gave the last of their beauty and fragrance.

Running ahead of Sasha, Jess, and Digit as they carried baskets to a large fig tree near a rear wall, Rialta lifted her nose to sniff at the air. Beazle fluttered down to settle in the fur on the back of the wolf's neck, burrowing in until he was cozy and invisible, the way he did in Jessamine's hair.

Vivian, Ian and Halyn were already beneath the fig tree, spreading a large blanket for their picnic. Kashmir lay in the dirt beneath a tall oleander, sleeping with her nose half buried in soil. Waloon hopped slowly along the edges of the rose garden, nibbling at clover, while Ania zipped around the late-blooming *lobelia* and *salvia* growing between the rose shrubs.

A small group of Calyx emerged from around the side of a hothouse, drawing Jess's ear. She glanced over her shoulder, seeing Rose, Aster and Snap among the group. They were in conversation with the new Royal Gardener: a flora fae, also from Stavarjak but younger than Ilishec, and female. Portia was connected to *echinacea*, and—though he was aged—she still had her familiar—a brown and yellow finch named Siksin that sang beautifully from the eavestrough on the workshop's roof.

Snap waved. Jess could just make out his new familiar fluttering among the hydrangea. A few days after Jalla had died, a beautiful black and blue butterfly had bonded with Snap. He was the first to get a new familiar, and Astya's arrival sent a wave of hope through the ranks of the Calyx. Aster received hers three days later: a leafcutter bee she named Chile. After that, new familiars arrived daily; Proteas bonded with a spectacular green metallic bee that reminded everyone of Marigold's departed familiar, Nympha imprinted with a crested hummingbird she named Rufous, Bougain received a petite indigo carpenter bee he called Ceratina, and on it went, until the only one still left without a pollinator was Rose.

The Calyx waited impatiently, nervous on Rose's behalf, worried that the most prolific and important flora fae in the retinue might not get a new familiar, that her career at the palace was over. Ironically, Rose herself seemed unbothered, and waited with all the patience of a Solanan lion, having faith that her magic had not departed for good. Jess, Aster and Digit worried that she might be fooling herself. How long would she wait? For her part, Queen Esha had made it clear that Rose could wait as long as she had a will to, that her place among the Calyx was locked until Rose herself decided otherwise.

Jess waved back at Snap, and the Calyx and the new gardener disappeared between the hothouses.

Halyn and Sasha knelt on the blanket and began pulling wrapped popkins out of the basket the kitchen had prepared.

Digit laid out plates and cutlery while Vivian tossed and dressed the salad. Ian distributed napkins while Jess poured glasses of sweet iced-tea. They chatted as they ate, enjoying the birdsong and watching pollinators buzz and flutter around the garden.

"How was your visit to Rahamlar?" Ian asked the twins, pouring Vivian another glass of tea.

Digit and Jess exchanged a look. Along with Kite and Sasha, they'd gone to Rahamlar last week. Kite had made a promise to the young king-in-waiting that he would get to meet Erasmus, and she was a Fahyli of her word, so that was the pretense they'd used, but really, they'd gone to attend a secret ceremony. Ian, Halyn and Vivian were still unaware of the real reason.

Rialta lay on her side in the grass, eyes closed but ears twitching. Jess could feel Beazle dozing in and out, catching bits of the conversation.

Digit wiped his hands on a napkin. "They seem well and the kingdom is recovering under the regent's guidance. The fungus infestation has mostly died off. Isabey, Toryan and Reina are sad, of course, and the people are still in shock over the manner of Serya's death. You can see it in Isabey's eyes; she will mourn for her family—including Faraçek—for a very long time."

Jess nodded. "He really broke her heart. But she makes a wonderful regent, young Toryan couldn't ask for a better mentor. She adores her nephew."

"Somewhere along the way," Digit said, "she found the courage to be a leader."

Jess casually slipped in the news: "She and Shade were married in a private ceremony."

Ian's brows shot up, but he looked pleased. "You never said."

Digit dimpled. "We weren't free to say until now."

"And the little lad?" Vivian asked, uncrossing her legs to

447

stretch them out behind Halyn. "How was he? I'm sure it was not easy to deliver the news of his father's execution."

"We left that to Isabey and Reina," said Digit, "but he seems to have taken it better than many of the adults. He spends a lot of time with horses, and he really loved seeing Beazle again."

"And meeting Erasmus," Jess added, tilting the last of her tea into her mouth.

Sasha drew his knees up, wrapping his arms around them. "Probably he feels safe and at peace when he's with animals. They don't talk about royal responsibility or Faraçek's folly."

Sasha would know, thought Beazle, sleepily. *He must have heard a lot about Elvio's folly when he was little.*

Jess thought about all the hardship Sasha had endured when he was a young Silverfae. He had known such suffering as a youngster, and his wolf had been his only real friend for many years. The look of love that Halyn gave Sasha made Jess wonder if Halyn was thinking something similar.

"Faelings are more resilient than we give them credit for." Halyn's voice was soft. Sasha smiled at her.

Jess felt Ian's eyes on her. She smiled at him, then pulled the basket near her hip onto her lap, pulling out a bottle of pearlescent purple liquid while Digit produced a small stack of glasses.

"What's that?" Halyn peered at the label. "I'm not sure I've ever seen a drink that color before."

"It's called Caludia. It's from Archelia." Jess turned the corkscrew into the cork but struggled to get it out of the bottle. "This was Ilishec and Hazel's favorite drink. I thought we might toast them, and the rest of our departed."

"Need some help with that, Jess?" Ian asked.

She handed the bottle to him, the corkscrew stuck in the stopper. "Thank you, Papa."

The group was quiet as the crofter took the bottle and worked the cork out of the neck. Everyone present knew the moment was historic, but the only sign Ian gave that Jess had acknowledged him as her father for the first time was a tiny smile and a flush in the apples of his cheeks.

Beazle emerged from Rialta's ruff to fly to Jessamine's shoulder, while Ania zipped back to land on Digit's hair. Rialta got to her feet and came to sit on her haunches beside Sasha. Kashmir lifted her head, then got up with a grunt and lumbered over to lay on her belly in the grass beside Ian, sitting up on her elbows.

The cork came out with a pop, and Ian poured a small amount of the liquor into each glass. Jess and Digit distributed them.

"To Ilishec and Hazel," said Jess, watching the liquid swirl.

Digit lifted his glass. "To Heath, Columbine, Amaryllis, Dianthus, Asclepias, Nasturtium, and all the lost familiars."

"To Georjayna Sutherland, who is gone from Ivryndi, but will always be a Solanan flora fae," said Jess.

Sasha held his glass out. "To all the soldiers, fae and human, who fell protecting Solana."

Ian looked at Jess soberly. "To Tansy Littlehale, Andrew Littlehale, the twin faelings Elwin and Elsie, and Papilio."

Jess nodded, lips trembling, hoping he could see what it meant to her that he included Marion and her first family.

"To Elphame, for sending Laec and Georjie to help us," said Vivian.

"To all those we loved, who've gone before us," said Sasha, his voice full of emotion.

"To those who've gone before," the group murmured.

Jess closed her eyes and touched the glass to her lips, thinking of how full the graveyard beyond the palace had grown in the past year. When the liquid slipped down her throat to warm her belly, she pulled in a long breath and held it. She let it go out slowly, through her nose, seeing Ilishec, Marion and Hazel's faces in her mind's eye. *You'll all be missed.*

After a minute's silence, Digit and Jess gathered the glasses and put them into the basket. Ian put the stopper back in the bottle and slipped the rest of the Caludia into the basket as they cleaned up after their picnic.

"Jessamine?"

Turning at the sound of her name, Jess saw Rose standing a short distance away, her hands behind her back. She wore a simple pale pink shift dress, her blond hair piled up in a messy bun on top of her head.

"I don't mean to interrupt—"

"Come join us, Rose," invited Vivian. "We have popkins left. Are you hungry?"

Rose smiled. "Thank you, but no. I just wondered if I might steal Jessamine away for a second?"

Jess got up, brushing off her leggings. She approached her friend and Rose fell in step beside her as they walked away from the picnic.

"What is it, Rose?"

"I was just wondering," Rose began, the color high in her cheeks, her eyes glistening, "if you might help me name him?"

Rose brought her hands from behind her back, and there— perched on the curve of her left thumb, flexing his wings and waving his antennae—sat a beautiful monarch butterfly.

Afterword & Acknowledgments

Finishing a series is always a bittersweet experience. I'll miss these characters, but I'm happy to be able to put the final book into the hands of those who have been patiently waiting for it. *The Scented Court* represents the most complex plot, the largest cast, the longest manuscripts, and the most in-depth world-building I have ever done. It stretched me as an author and a creator, and while at times it was extremely difficult (ordering the *A Daughter of Winter* chapters was a mind-bender) it has been so rewarding to read the reviews and see the joy and escape that it has brought into reader's lives.

I wanted to create a world you could feel wrapped up in, part of, and amazed by. I hope I've achieved some level of that. One of the questions I never fail to get asked when finishing a series, is whether I'll write more for the characters of Ivryndi. If you've been reading my work for very long, you'll already know how much I love doing spin-offs, so I can think I can safely say; that's a likely story.

Thank you to Nicola Aquino, my editor and PA. You've been with me almost since the beginning, and your feedback and ideas always make my stories so much better. Thank you to S.D. Petersen, specifically for your sensitivity to terminology, word choice, and character behavior. Thank you to Markus Jager for your care and incredible attention to detail when translating these works for German readers. The reviews say it all. Thank you to the members of my VIP Reader Lounge for your cheerleading, your enthusiasm, and your amazing reviews. Without you, this work would be very lonely. Thank you to my husband, Deniz, and to my family who have been so supportive and encouraging. Last but never least, thank you, dear reader. Without you, I'd be... well, it's hard to say now... probably peddling plush toys or biodegradable toothbrushes. I certainly wouldn't be living in a villa along the Mediterranean, pruning lemon trees and watching my cantaloupe grow so fast that I'm actually a little afraid of it. Thank you. Your support means I get to keep writing, and I'll never take that for granted.

Love always,
Abby, 2023

ABOUT THE AUTHOR

A.L. Knorr is a Canadian fantasy writer who won the Readers' Favorite Gold Medal for YA Fantasy in 2018 with her mermaid fantasy; Born of Water. Abby has authored more than 35 titles since then and continues to enchant readers with stories of elemental magic, transformation, friendship, adventure, international travel, and of course, love. Though Abby's stories are clean young adult fantasy, readers of every age enjoy them. Abby lives on the Mediterranean coast with her floofy cat Pamuk and her talented chef husband. Visit www.alknorr-books.com for more information.